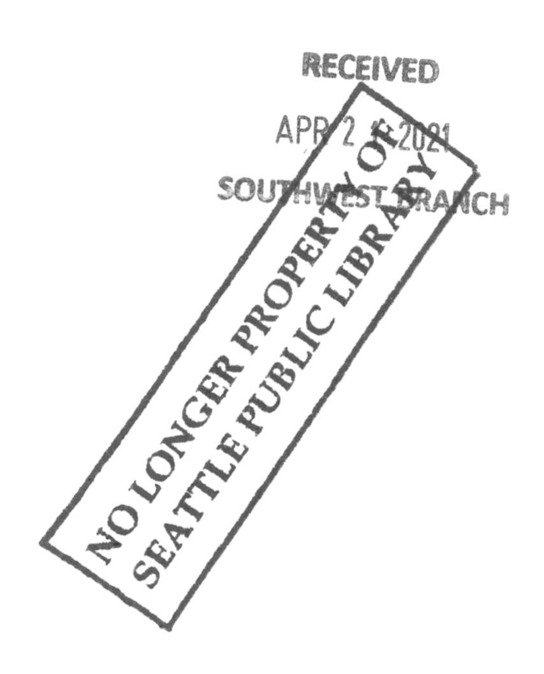

The Prince of Spies

Books by Elizabeth Camden

HOPE AND GLORY SERIES

The Spice King

A Gilded Lady

The Prince of Spies

The Lady of Bolton Hill

The Rose of Winslow Street

Against the Tide

Into the Whirlwind

With Every Breath

Beyond All Dreams

Toward the Sunrise: An Until the Dawn *Novella*

Until the Dawn

Summer of Dreams: A From This Moment *Novella*

From This Moment

To the Farthest Shores

A Dangerous Legacy

A Daring Venture

A Desperate Hope

HOPE AND GLORY

BOOK THREE

The Prince of Spies

ELIZABETH CAMDEN

BETHANYHOUSE
a division of Baker Publishing Group
Minneapolis, Minnesota

Published by Bethany House Publishers
11400 Hampshire Avenue South
Bloomington, Minnesota 55438
www.bethanyhouse.com

Bethany House Publishers is a division of
Baker Publishing Group, Grand Rapids, Michigan

Library of Congress Cataloging-in-Publication Data
Names: Camden, Elizabeth, author.
Title: The prince of spies / Elizabeth Camden.
Description: Minneapolis, Minnesota : Bethany House, [2021] | Series: Hope and glory ; 3
Identifiers: LCCN 2020046123 | ISBN 9780764232138 (trade paperback) | ISBN 9780764238093 (casebound) | ISBN 9781493429974 (ebook)

Subjects: GSAFD: Romantic suspense fiction.
Classification: LCC PS3553.A429 P75 2021 | DDC 813/.54—dc23
LC record available at https://lccn.loc.gov/2020046123
This is a work of historical reconstruction; the appearances of certain historical figures are therefore inevitable. All other characters, however, are products of the author's imagination, and any resemblance to actual persons, living or dead, is coincidental.

Cover design by Jennifer Parker
Cover photography by Mike Habermann Photography, LLC

Author is represented by the Steve Laube Agency.

21 22 23 24 25 26 27 7 6 5 4 3 2 1

One

January 1902

Marianne ventured farther onto the frozen river despite the people warning her against it. "Don't do it, ma'am!" someone shouted. "You're going to fall through the ice!"

Several other bystanders urged her back to safety, but she couldn't ignore the pitiful howls of Bandit, who had fallen through the ice. The dog wasn't going to be able to get out on his own. Marianne had already spent an agonizing five minutes encouraging the border collie to clamber out. Bandit tried, but each time it looked as if he'd succeed, another section of ice broke, and he plunged back into the freezing water.

Marianne crawled on all fours across the ice, the cold quickly penetrating her thin leather gloves.

"If the ice can't hold a dog, it can't hold you!" someone on the shore shouted.

Maybe, but she knew the Boundary Channel better than most of the city dwellers who walked alongside this oddly shaped tail of the Potomac River in the heart of Washington, DC. She had photographed it last spring, wearing hip-high galoshes and wading into the shallows to take pictures for the Department of the Interior. Most of the lagoon was shallow and only got deep out in the middle where Bandit had fallen through. The ice beneath her was probably frozen solid.

Probably. If she thought about it any longer, she'd be too scared to continue, so she lowered herself to lie flat on the ice, using her feet to nudge closer to Bandit.

"Get him, Aunt Marianne, please!" Sam was the only person among the dozens on shore who urged her forward. What nine-year-old boy didn't love his dog? She had to at least try to save Bandit. The only tool she had was a fishermen's net that had been abandoned on the riverbank. She'd throw it toward Bandit and hope she could pull him out.

Her teeth chattered. Was it from cold or fear? Probably both. A layer of crusty snow atop the ice gave her enough traction to creep farther ahead.

Then a man's voice, louder than the others, sounded over the crowd. "Luke, don't be a fool!"

"Please, mister," Sam begged. "Please help Aunt Marianne save my dog!"

She risked a glance over her shoulder, grateful to see another man crawling out onto the ice. She hadn't wanted to do this alone, but no one else volunteered.

"I don't think the ice can hold both of us," she called back to him, her voice shaking from the cold.

"It can where you are," he said, then lowered himself to his stomach. He gave a healthy push against a post sticking through the ice and propelled quickly across the frozen channel toward her.

What a handsome man. Black hair, dark eyes, and a face animated with both fear and exhilaration. He was soon alongside her, his breath coming in white wisps.

"Hello, Aunt Marianne," he said. They both lay flat on the ice, side by side. An odd way to meet a perfect stranger.

"Careful," she cautioned. "The water gets deeper only a couple of feet ahead. I don't think it will hold us both."

"I *know* it won't," he said. "Hand me the net."

"Are you sure? I'm lighter. It might be better if I go."

His gaze flicked down her length. They both wore long wool coats, gloves, and boots, but he was a lot taller than she was.

"One of us is probably going to end up in the water," he said. "Your skirts will be a big problem if it's you. I'll be okay."

"I don't think it's safe." Her teeth started to chatter again.

"Of course it's not safe." He grinned. "Hand me the net."

"Luke, get back to shore this instant!" an angry voice commanded, but Luke didn't even glance back.

"Don't worry about that guy," Luke said. "It's only my brother, Gray. Being a worrywart is what older brothers are supposed to do."

She laughed a little. "I know all about big brothers. I've got one too. Here's the net. If you can make it a few more feet, you can toss it to the dog."

He nodded, but instead of taking the net, he grabbed her hand and squeezed. "This is sort of fun, don't you think?"

"Actually, I'm a little terrified," she admitted.

"Me too."

How odd. He was afraid but still seemed elated. Her eyes felt captured by his, and even through their gloves, it felt like a spark of electricity hummed between them.

"Luke!" Gray shouted again from the shore. "The ice can't hold you. Both of you need to come back. Someone has sent for a boat."

Bandit wasn't whining anymore. He was barely even moving, just wiggling enough to keep his snout above water. Marianne met Luke's eyes. Going back would be the prudent thing to do, but she'd come too far to turn back now.

"Bandit can't last until the boat gets here," she said.

"I know. Give me the net, and I'll go get him. Wish me luck, Aunt Marianne."

With that, he began sliding forward. The stern man on shore

continued to holler warnings, but others cheered him on. Luke was moving over the deeper part of the lagoon now, where the ice wasn't solid. It let out a *crack*, and Luke stopped, still a few yards from the dog. The net would extend his reach a few feet, but not much. After a moment Luke began inching forward again. Bandit sensed help was near and started struggling, reaching a paw onto the ice and trying to climb out.

More cracks sounded, like whips slicing through the air. The ledge of ice tilted, and water sloshed up, soaking Luke with a wave of icy water in his face, but he calmly tossed the net toward Bandit, whose scrabbling paws got caught in its mesh. Luke began tugging, but the ice broke, and he plunged into the water.

A cry tore from Marianne's throat. Luke was completely submerged, but within seconds, his head rose above the surface, and with a mighty push, he shoved Bandit up onto the ice. Cheers rose from the crowd as Bandit staggered toward land.

Luke was still in the water and needed help. He flung the net toward her, still hanging on to one end. She reached for it but screamed in frustration when it proved a few inches beyond her reach. She held her breath and moved forward, terrified the ice would break, but Luke's stricken face was white with pain. She moved another inch, stretched her hand farther, and managed to wrap her fingers around a loop in the net.

"I've got it!" she yelled. She tugged but couldn't pull Luke out.

"Hang on, ma'am. We're coming."

The grim voice came from behind her. Luke's brother was traversing the solid portion of ice, lying flat as he reached out toward her. He grabbed her ankle and pulled on it, but she slid only a few inches before the slack in the net went taut with Luke's weight, and she stopped.

Another set of hands grabbed her other ankle and pulled. The bystanders on the shore formed a human chain as the men pulled with all they had. The net between her and Luke squeaked from the tension, but it gave Luke enough momentum to climb out onto the ice. Now that he was out of the water, the men were able to pull a lot harder, and Marianne zoomed backwards toward the shoreline, Luke following. She scrambled safely up onto solid land.

Luke arrived right behind her. His teeth chattered, and trembling racked his entire body. A pair of men hauled him upright to yank his sopping coat off, then his shirt. His skin was blanched white as his brother bundled him into a dry coat, then used a scarf to dry his hair.

Luke was laughing. He still quaked with cold, but she'd never seen such a good-natured smile as people reached out to shake his hand and slap him on the back. He looked around for Bandit, who was getting a rubdown from Sam. Luke went to meet the dog.

It was the perfect photograph.

She raced to the juniper tree where she'd abandoned her government-issued Brownie camera. It didn't take long to fling the lanyard around her neck and return to the bank. By now Luke had picked up Bandit, holding the shivering dog against his bare chest, still laughing.

"Can I take your photograph?" she asked.

His smile deepened in a combination of pride and happiness. It was all the permission she needed. She steadied the boxy camera against her diaphragm as she looked down through the viewfinder, slid the aperture open, and pressed the lever to take the photograph. The sun reflecting on snow made plenty of ambient light, so it only took a few seconds to capture the image.

"Thanks," she said.

Luke bent over to set Bandit on the ground. "Thank *you*, Aunt Marianne."

He looked like he wanted to say more, but his brother, a tall dark-haired man who looked similar to Luke except a lot more serious, was dragging him toward a carriage.

"Let's get you home and in front of a warm fire," Gray said. "We'll be lucky if you don't catch your death of cold."

"Always a ray of sunshine," Luke chided, but he didn't resist as his brother nudged him toward the carriage. Luke climbed inside, but before he closed the carriage door, he met her gaze across the frozen landscape and flashed her a wink.

The carriage rolled away, and just like that, the most amazing man she'd ever met was gone.

Luke Delacroix wrapped his hands around the mug of hot cocoa, leaning so close to the fireplace that the heat from the flames baked the side of his face. He savored the sensation, for he was still chilled to the bone. A weird sense of elation lingered as he thought of that moment on the ice, lying flat with his hand clinging to a woman who had more courage than all the bystanders on the shore put together. She was a complete stranger who didn't feel like a stranger at all. She had dark hair and pretty blue eyes filled with trepidation, but she was out there. He'd been in her presence for only a few minutes but already admired her. Sometimes people revealed their true character very quickly.

He didn't know who she was, but he'd have it figured out before the end of the day. It would be easy. Number one: he was a spy and good at ferreting out information. Number two: the Brownie camera she used had a government stamp on the case, meaning she probably worked for the Department of the Interior. How many female photographers named Marianne worked for the Department of the Interior?

Gray stomped into the parlor and set a bowl of steaming chowder on the table along with a wedge of cheese.

"Eat all of it," he ordered, still annoyed over what had happened at the Boundary Channel. They had been on their way to move in to Luke's new office when snarled traffic slowed their carriage and Luke noticed the bystanders watching a lone woman venture onto the ice to save a floundering dog. He'd ordered the carriage to stop so he could help.

Luke exchanged the mug of cocoa for the soup and began eating even though he wasn't hungry. The chowder was hot, filling, and the doctor said he still needed to gain another ten pounds to replace the thirty he'd lost in Cuba.

"Should I send a wire to the landlord, telling him we can't take possession of the office today?" Gray asked. "I don't want you leaving the house if your hair is still wet. You could get pneumonia."

Luke was thirty years old, but Gray still smothered him like a mother hen since he got back from Cuba, sick and emaciated. Luke didn't mind. He'd put his family through a lot over the past year, and he owed them. So he tolerated Gray's fussing, ate even when he was no longer hungry, and tried to behave himself.

Tried but didn't always succeed. What sort of man would he be if he ignored that woman attempting to rescue a dog all on her own?

He leaned his head toward the fire, rubbing his hair to make it dry faster. "We can still move in today. I need to get the Washington bureau of the magazine up and running. The November elections might seem a long way off, but I've got an interview with Dickie Shuster at the end of the week. I need to be moved in before that."

"We have to be careful," Gray said, and this time Luke knew the warning had nothing to do with wet hair or proper nutrition. It had everything to do with the fact that Dickie Shuster was slick, underhanded, and probably the cleverest reporter in all of Washington. "Dickie is still an ally of the Magruders. He will be quietly working to undermine you in hopes of promoting Clyde and the Magruder cause."

"Wrong," Luke replied. "Dickie will do whatever is necessary to promote *himself*."

The Delacroixs and the Magruders had been bitter rivals for generations. They'd never liked each other, but their animosity boiled over shortly after the Civil War. The Delacroix family, long one of the wealthiest merchant families in Virginia, had lost everything in the war. Their home was burned to the ground, and all four of their merchant vessels were seized by the federal government and never returned. Following the war, their ships were put up for auction. Luke's father attended the auction to bid on *The Sparrow*, the smallest of the ships, in a desperate attempt to start rebuilding their fortune.

Gloating at the auction was Jedidiah Magruder, the patriarch of the Magruder clan, who drove the price higher and higher. Luke's father couldn't compete, and the Magruders bought *The Sparrow* for a fraction of its worth. The Magruders didn't even export their goods, so they had no need for a merchant ship. They simply bought it to rub his father's nose in the fact that they could. If there was any doubt about the Magruders' motives, that was put to rest when Jedidiah stripped the ship of its valuables, then burned it in the harbor. "We had a great Confederate bonfire!" he had bragged to the press.

That incident elevated the bitter family feud into one of seething hatred, and it grew worse over the years. The Magruders weren't above bribing journalists to throw mud at the Delacroixs, and they'd used Dickie Shuster in the past.

"Dickie can be flipped, and I intend to flip him," Luke said.

It wouldn't be easy, but Luke had plenty of connections in this city. He was also smarter than the Magruders. He didn't mind cozying up to Dickie Shuster in order to get an upper hand in the local press. Now that his health was on the mend, it was time to resume his life as a journalist, and that meant moving into his new office.

Freezing air shocked his system the moment he stepped outside again. He ignored it and climbed into the carriage, Gray following. If all went well, they could still get him settled into his new office by the end of the day. He tried to beat back his shivers as the carriage set off toward downtown Washington.

"Have the Magruders made any progress stealing revenue from our spice business?" Luke asked, desperate to get his mind off the chill seeping into his core again.

The corners of Gray's mouth turned down. "They're trying. Their bottled spices went nowhere, but they're stealing a ton of my business in vanilla extract."

The Delacroix family had built their fortune on expensive spices and seasonings, while the Magruders became even richer by selling canned foods. The families had always been rivals, but now the gloves were off and the stakes were higher. Clyde Magruder, the leader of the family, had been elected to Congress and would surely try to wield that power to grind the Delacroixs into the dirt.

"The Magruders are using chemicals to imitate vanilla," Gray continued. "It's a concoction cooked up in a laboratory, made of wood-tar creosote and chemical flavorings. It costs pennies to produce by the vat, so I'll never be able to compete on price. Yes, they're hurting our business."

And Delacroix Global Spice was a very lucrative business. They imported the finest spices from around the world and were the most prestigious brand on the market. The Delacroix name was synonymous with quality and prestige, but the Magruders were the opposite. They made their fortune mass producing consumer staples like canned beans and potted ham. They adulterated their products with fillers and preservatives, but they kept their prices low. Now they were encroaching into the spice business, and it was a threat.

Luke pulled the edges of his coat tighter as he stared out at the gloomy January cityscape. He wore his warmest winter coat, thick gloves, and a wool scarf, but the chill was still getting to him. Even the air in his lungs felt cold, and he began shivering again.

"Luke, this isn't a good idea," Gray said.

If they could just get to the new office building, he wouldn't be so cold. It had a coal-fired heater, and he'd be able to warm up eventually.

"I'll be okay," he said, wishing his teeth did not chatter as he spoke. "And I really hate the Magruders. Or *Congressman* Magruder, I now must say. Can you believe it? I heard he's renting the fanciest town house on Franklin Square. Now that I'm back in Washington, I'll make sure his chances for reelection evaporate."

Gray leaned forward and opened the panel behind the driver's bench. "Please turn the carriage around," he instructed the driver. "We're heading home." He settled back into his bench, concern darkening his face. "Don't let impatience lead you into doing something foolish. You'll be out of the action for weeks if you come down with a case of pneumonia."

Luke sighed. Gray was probably right, but this was about so much more than the enmity between two families or the price of spices. This was about the niggling, insatiable need to take Clyde Magruder down a peg. The man didn't belong in Congress, and Luke could get him out.

His gaze strayed out the carriage window to where the Capitol Building loomed in the distance, its iconic white dome a symbol of the power wielded by the men of this city. Somehow he was going to figure out a way to influence what went on beneath that dome. It would probably take decades, but he'd get there in the end. Gray was right. He couldn't afford to get sick just because he was impatient.

The carriage turned around, and he noticed a flower cart brimming with roses and carnations. The rest of the city was dreary, overcast, and covered in snow, but the splash of red caught his eye.

"I wonder how they get roses to bloom in January."

Gray followed his gaze to the flower cart. "The Department

of Agriculture has acres of greenhouses. They can force anything to bloom."

"Stop the carriage," Luke said impulsively. In a world blanketed by ice and snow, it was suddenly vitally important to admire those flowers. Once the carriage stopped, he bounded outside and reached for the largest bundle of roses on the man's cart. "Can you have these delivered?" he asked.

A young boy helping at the cart eagerly accepted the task in exchange for a few coins.

"Do you want to send a message with it?" the vendor asked.

He did. The vendor handed him a card. Luke's hand shook from the cold, but he quickly jotted a message.

Thank you for a memorable morning. Luke.

"Send them to the Department of the Interior, addressed to Miss Marianne," he said.

He beamed with elation as he returned to the carriage.

Two

Marianne Magruder arranged her photographs on the dining room table, wishing she had more room to spread them out. She had moved into this town house when her father was elected to Congress last year. It was one of the most spacious town houses in all of Washington, but it was cramped compared to the dining room in their Baltimore mansion. Here, there was barely room for the mahogany table and sideboard. There was no natural light, but the room had electricity that provided a flood of brightness no matter the time of day, and her father wouldn't be home until late.

This review of her photographs was a special weekly ritual. She picked the best of her work and laid them out for her father's insight, because he understood the needs of Washington bureaucrats better than she did, and his advice was priceless. This week she selected photographs of the Washington Monument, the Baltimore and Potomac Railroad Station, and children playing in the snow outside the Library of Congress.

"Why don't you add the one of that man with Sam's dog?" her mother asked. Vera had been alternately horrified and impressed by Marianne's adventure on the ice, and the photograph of the soaked man holding Bandit in triumph was the best picture she'd taken all week. She had been dazzled as she watched the photograph develop in the dark room. The man she knew only as Luke must have been freezing, but it didn't dim the exuberance in his laughing gaze as he stared straight at her with Bandit hugged against his bare chest. The photograph captured a raw, heroic man only seconds after emerging from the ice, his impulsive act the embodiment of masculine courage and strength.

"It's not the sort of picture the government hired me to take," she said as she set out more mundane photographs.

She hadn't been able to stop thinking about Luke, especially after the arrival of a dozen red roses. They had been waiting for her when she arrived at work the day after the incident. She wished he had signed his complete name to the card so she could send a note of thanks, but just like his quick arrival and departure at the ice, he seemed to dip into her life like a whirlwind and leave just as quickly.

"The picture of the man with the dog is better than these boring shots of buildings," Vera said as she scanned the photographs. She let out a delicate yawn and fought to keep her eyes open.

"Why don't you head up to bed?" Marianne asked.

Vera waved her question away with a perfumed handkerchief. "Nonsense. I want to be here when your father returns."

That probably wouldn't be for at least another hour. Clyde Magruder had spent most of his first year in Congress at meetings, business dinners, and in smoke-filled rooms. Tonight he was dining with the chairman of the Committee on Manufactures, which was Clyde's only committee appointment, and he was eager to impress the young chairman.

Life in Congress had been a difficult adjustment for her father. He was used to helming one of the richest companies in America, but now he was a freshman congressman who answered to a man half his age. It was rare for him to return home before nine o'clock. And sometimes he didn't return home at all.

As much as Marianne idolized her father, she wished he could be a better husband.

Still, she wouldn't change this past year in Washington for anything in the world. She and Vera had grown extraordinarily close ever since moving here. Her mother had been nervous about leaving Baltimore, where she was the reigning queen of high society. Now she had to start over in a new city as a mere freshman congressman's wife, and suddenly she had grown very dependent on Marianne. They did everything together. They shopped together, planned Vera's tea parties together, and even gossiped together. For the first time in Marianne's life, it felt like they had a normal mother-daughter relationship, and she savored every hour of it.

Vera wandered over to the sideboard where the week's rejected photographs were in a stack. She pulled out the one of Luke and wiggled it suggestively. "This is the best of the lot. Go ahead and add it into the stack to show your father."

Marianne considered the suggestion. Although the Department of the Interior primarily wanted photographs documenting specific government initiatives, they liked occasional artistic shots taken in the city.

"I don't think that's a good idea," Marianne said. Yesterday she'd told Papa about the incident with the dog, but not about the photograph. Something about it seemed too personal. It was a shared moment of communion between herself and a complete stranger as they embarked on a daring venture together. It had been one of the most exciting moments of her life, and she wasn't ready to share it yet. Normally she let her father witness her entire life through her photographs. She showed him everything. But she didn't want him seeing that man with the dog. Something warned her against it.

It was almost ten o'clock before her father arrived home, and masculine voices outside the door indicated Clyde had brought company. Vera immediately fled upstairs in horror. Her mother had already taken her hair down and wore nothing but a casual lounging dress without the painfully tight corset. Appearances were everything to Vera, and she would never let herself be seen so casually attired.

Marianne had no such qualms and did nothing aside from straightening the collar of her blouse before heading to the entryway to greet her father, who was already hanging up his jacket. His guest was a redheaded man with an enormous walrus mustache. She suspected he was Congressman Roland Dern, because Clyde had told her how much he disapproved of that mustache. Congressman Dern was in his mid-thirties and the chairman of her father's only committee assignment. That meant Congressman Dern was her father's boss.

"Roland, I'd like to introduce my daughter, Marianne. She's the one I brag incessantly about."

Congressman Dern gave a polite nod. "I've come to see your photographs," he said. "I didn't realize when we began our dinner that you have a standing appointment with your father every Thursday night. I'm sorry to have delayed the ritual, so let's not beat around the bush. Show me your pictures."

She looked to Clyde for permission. Normally the weekly ritual was an event she and her parents enjoyed together. Clyde seemed uneasy as he gave a stiff nod of consent. How awkward it must be for her father to be beholden to a man young enough to be his son, but Marianne pretended not to notice the tension as she led the way into the dining room, where the best of her photographs were on display.

The scent of cigar smoke lingered on both men as they circled the table. Her father paused before the photograph she'd taken of children playing in the snow outside the Library of Congress. The picture captured the spirit of unabashed joy as the children romped and played.

"This belongs in a museum," Clyde said, chuckling at the snow-encrusted children. "The lighting, the expressions, the composition . . . all of it is sheer poetry captured on celluloid. It makes me want to pick those boys up and take them home with me."

She smiled but didn't miss the hint of regret in his voice. Clyde had always wanted lots of children, but her mother's fragile health precluded more.

"The government pays you to take photographs like this?" Congressman Dern asked, disapproval plain in his voice.

Her father heard it and jumped to her defense. "They need as many photographs as possible in preparation for the McMillan Plan."

The McMillan Plan was an optimistic vision to tear down old government buildings and clear the way for a huge national park around which new cultural and administrative buildings would be erected. Everyone she knew, including most of the people at the Department of the Interior, thought the McMillan Plan was an extravagant waste of money. That was why she'd been assigned to photograph the existing architecture and how people used the public spaces.

"The entire McMillan Plan is a misuse of taxpayer funds," Congressman Dern said. "It's all so that Washington can compete with the great capital cities of Europe. I say the business of our country is *business*. Not lavish green spaces."

"I agree," Clyde said as he wandered over to her collection of images of the Baltimore and Potomac Railroad Station. "This one is okay," he said after a pause.

It was faint praise. Her father was no artist, but he had keen instincts, and she trusted his judgment.

"What's wrong with it?" she asked.

He continued frowning at the picture as he studied it. "Do you have any others of the train station?"

"I haven't enlarged them, but I've got a dozen or so other shots."

"I'd like to see them."

The other pictures were only three-by-five inches in size, the standard format of the Brownie camera. After she developed the film, she selected only the best photographs to enlarge. The eight-by-ten-inch pictures would be added to the government repositories that would document the city for future generations. Even without the McMillan Plan, Washington was undergoing a state of regeneration as the red brick buildings of the colonial era were torn down and replaced by monumental buildings in the neoclassical style. She'd been hired to document the process as old buildings were torn down, the land graded and levelled, and the skeletal frameworks of new buildings were erected.

She brought over the other pictures of the Baltimore and Potomac and handed them to her father, who flipped through them quickly, identifying three and setting them on the dining table.

"These might make your case better," he said.

"Why?" she asked. The three close-up photographs seemed boring and didn't capture the gothic beauty of the station. The B&P was only thirty years old and a masterful example of Victorian gothic architecture. It was made of red brick and featured three towers with slate roofs and ornamental ironwork. Its beauty made it one of the most popular images on the postcards bought by tourists. It was only three blocks from the Capitol and was the primary railroad station used by everyone serving in Congress.

"If the McMillan Plan passes, the B&P is slated for demolition," Clyde said. "Congressmen see it every day, but your close-ups highlight the expense that went into creating the hand-carved entablatures and the ornamental ironwork. There's value in that. Roland? What do you think?"

The younger man nodded. "If the government tears down a perfectly good railroad station for the benefit of a public park, I think the nation should know what we stand to lose."

Clyde walked over to the sideboard to return the smaller pictures, then paused. "What's this?"

She stiffened. Her father held Luke's photograph in his hands, and his face was a mask of disapproval. True, Luke wore no shirt in the picture, but it wasn't a lewd photograph. A coat was draped over his shoulders, and Bandit covered most of his torso.

"That's the man who got Bandit out of the ice," she said. "I couldn't resist taking a picture."

"*This* is the man who rescued Bandit?" he asked in a surprised tone.

"Yes. He was very heroic." She was about to say that he had even sent her roses afterward, but the grim look on Clyde's face made her reconsider.

After a moment he set the picture back on the stack. "It's probably best you don't see that man again," he said stiffly.

He gestured for Congressman Dern to follow him into his private office, leaving Marianne to stare after him in bewildered confusion.

Luke's jaunt beneath the ice turned out to be more troublesome than expected. He didn't catch pneumonia or anything drastic like Gray had feared. It simply sapped his strength beyond all reason. He spent the next few days buried underneath a mound of blankets in his bedroom, as it seemed each time he emerged from beneath the covers, he got the shivers again.

What an irony. For fifteen months he'd been locked up in a Cuban jail cell, sweltering in the relentless heat and tormented by fantasies of a tall, ice-cold glass of water. God must have a strange sense of humor, for now Luke never wanted to experience ice water again.

By Monday he was ready to take possession of the new office. The faster he could get the Washington bureau for *Modern Century* magazine established, the quicker he could launch his bid to knock a handful of congressmen out of office. The November elections seemed a long way off, but researching these men's weaknesses and beginning the subtle campaign to take them down would need careful planning.

His desk, the meeting table, and the shelving had already been delivered to the new office, but the books, typewriter, telephone, and office equipment all needed to be lugged in. The most difficult item to navigate up the twisting stairwell was the six-foot bulletin board. Luke banged his shin three times on the journey to the third floor.

"Where do you want it?" Gray asked when they finally got the bulletin board inside the office.

"On the wall behind the desk."

It was a large room with two windows overlooking a working-class part of town. The desk was on one side of the office, the table in the middle, and the hip-high bookshelves lined the walls beneath the windows. There was a separate table for a telephone and typewriter. For now Luke was the only reporter, but if the Washington bureau proved fruitful, there might someday be more.

The board was soon hung, and the first thing Luke tacked onto it was a list of five congressmen's names. Beside it he pinned a postcard of the Philadelphia skyline.

Gray cocked a brow as he studied the list of congressmen. "I already know why you want Clyde Magruder out of office, but what's wrong with the guy from Michigan?"

"He's in Clyde's back pocket," Luke replied. "All these men are following Magruder's lead in blocking reform of the food and drug industry. If any congressman looks the other way while manufacturers dump chemicals into the nation's food supply, I'm going to ensure he loses the next election." He gave an angelic smile and placed a hand over his heart. "My civic duty."

Gray stared at the postcard of Philadelphia, his face suddenly sad. "Luke . . . I think you need to ease up. What happened to those people in Philadelphia wasn't your fault."

Philadelphia would forever represent Luke's greatest shame. Five years ago, their family had briefly tried to forge a truce with Clyde Magruder. Luke had been chosen to lead the charge because there was too much bad blood among the other members of their family. The Delacroixs and the Magruders would never be friends, but the hope was to ease the tension with a modest joint venture. The plan would combine the Delacroix reputation for quality with the Magruders' ability to mass produce food. Clyde Magruder proposed a line of pricey coffee, using the Magruder packaging facilities but branded with the Delacroix name. Both companies stood to gain.

Luke held his nose and worked with Clyde on a distribution plan. Gray imported the finest coffee beans from Kenya, and the Magruders did everything else. They rolled out the new line of coffee in Philadelphia, a city famous for its fine coffeehouses.

Luke should have known better than to trust Clyde Magruder, who adulterated their top-notch coffee with cheap ground chicory and artificial flavorings to mask the chicory aftertaste. The resulting coffee tasted fine, with a smooth flavor and enticing aroma, but the cannisters bore no indication that there was anything but coffee inside. The chemical combination proved fatal to three people within a week of the coffee going on sale. While most people could easily digest the cheap concoction cooked up in the Magruder factory, some people had sensitivities to chicory root that proved fatal.

Three people died because of that coffee. All of them had family, friends, and children. The devastation left in the wake of the tainted coffee would ripple through those people's lives for decades, and no, Luke couldn't blithely forget about it.

"Could you help me with this box of books?" Luke asked. He didn't really need help with it, but he'd do anything to divert the conversation from Philadelphia.

Gray moved the box over to the bookshelves. "You've been taking risks and pressing your luck ever since Philadelphia. You practically killed yourself in Cuba. When are you going to move past it?"

"Maybe when those five congressmen have been booted out of office. Maybe when there are finally laws to stop the Magruders from polluting their food with fillers and adulterants. That would be a start."

"Luke, what happened in Philadelphia wasn't your fault. You couldn't have known. You tried your best."

"And my best resulted in three dead people." He wandered to the window, staring out over the bleak view of wet concrete and melting slush. "Whenever I start to laugh, I think about them," he whispered. "When I hear beautiful music, I am reminded that they can't hear it too. They are three ghosts who sit on my shoulder wherever I go."

"And are they good ghosts or bad ghosts?" Gray asked.

"Oh, for pity's sake, they're *ghosts*, Gray! The kind who wake you up at night and steal your joy and make you pray to God for forgiveness. That kind of ghost."

Slow footsteps indicated Gray was coming up behind him, but Luke kept staring out the window, even when his brother laid a hand on his shoulder. "Then you're going to have to defeat them. Or turn them into something that inspires you to be a better man."

Luke pushed away from the window and began unpacking the books. For years Gray had been trying to nudge him toward a life of safe, law-abiding good sense. Obey the rules, stay within the lines, don't rock the boat. It wasn't in his nature.

"I really hate the Magruders," Luke said. "They never paid a dime to those people in Philadelphia."

"But we did," Gray said. "Those families were all compensated and signed off on the legal settlements."

"*You* paid them. The Magruders got off scot-free. They'll do anything for money, so I intend to strike where it will hurt. First I'll knock Clyde out of Congress, then I'll go after their company. I'll burn it down and force them to start over."

"Absolutely not!" Gray lashed out.

Luke let out a snort of laughter. "Don't be so literal," he teased. "Of course I won't actually burn down their factory. I bet it's fully insured, so where's the advantage in that? I'll expose the Magruders for who they really are, ruin their business, and change the laws so that they can never exploit those loopholes again."

Across the room, Gray still looked at him with that mournful, somber expression. While Luke used to tease Gray about his overly protective ways, Gray had been a hero over the past year. Luke wouldn't have survived the crucible of imprisonment in Cuba if Gray hadn't made repeated visits to keep his flagging spirits alive. They were complete opposites, but over the past year Luke had learned to love and admire his older brother.

"Gray, I'm sorry," he said. "When I was in Cuba, I thought I was going to die. My biggest regret was that I was going to leave this world without making so much as a scratch on it. That wasn't how I wanted to leave. I told myself that if I made it out of there, I would do something to make the world a better place. I had fifteen months with nothing to do but read the Bible and pray to God. In the end, the only sense I could make of what happened in Philadelphia was that it was a clarion wake-up call. A blast from a trumpet shaking me out of complacency and setting me on a course to do something important. And getting Congress cleaned up will be a good starting point."

Gray sighed. "Luke, you've already accomplished great things. You single-handedly broke up a spy ring in Cuba and stamped out corruption in the War Department. The articles you write for *Modern Century* go out all over the nation to sway opinion. I spend my time figuring out a better way to sell pepper or paprika, but your stories move the world. I'm proud of you. Dad never said it, but I will."

Luke paused. Gray was twelve years older than he was, so he'd always been more like a father than a brother, and his opinion meant the world to Luke.

"Thanks for that," he said, a little embarrassed at the emotion in his voice.

Gray turned away and lifted a thick package wrapped in butcher's paper from the box he was unpacking. "What's this?"

The breath in Luke's lungs froze. "Nothing! Let me have it." He crossed the office in two steps and snatched the package, then shoved it into the bottom drawer of his desk. He was tempted to lock the drawer except it would be a dead giveaway that these papers were precious to him.

"Good heavens," Gray said. "Love letters? International intrigue? I can't imagine what's got your protective hackles so raised."

Luke scratched behind his ear and looked out the window. "Like I said, it's nothing."

"When you were a little kid, do you know how I could always tell when you were lying?"

Luke quit scratching behind his ear. It was an old tell he'd forgotten about. He folded his hands across his chest and grinned. "Fine, it's something," he admitted. "I'm not ready to tell anyone about it yet."

"Whatever it is, it's making you blush."

He was blushing because he was nervous and embarrassed. He wasn't ready to peel back the layers of his soul and expose this wildly romantic, overblown experiment to his fusty older brother.

"Maybe someday I'll be brave enough to show it to the world, but for now?" He leaned over and locked the drawer. "For now, I'm keeping it to myself."

Once Luke's office was operational, he set about tracking down the lovely Marianne. He knew almost nothing about her except that she was pretty and valiant and that he hadn't been able to stop thinking about her in the two weeks since they met on the ice.

The Department of the Interior was housed in a massive building on F Street with two marble wings built atop a granite foundation. The department was a hodgepodge of government agencies that didn't neatly fit anywhere else. It oversaw the US Geological Survey, the Census Bureau, the Patent and Trademark Office, the Bureau of Indian Affairs, the Bureau of Pensions, and a dozen smaller agencies.

Luke had an old friend who worked in the department's accounting office. Oscar might have access to payroll records that could lead to Marianne's identity.

Luke got straight to the point after entering Oscar's crowded office. "I know the department has a team of photographers documenting the state of the city," he said. "Do you know one named Marianne?"

Sadly, Oscar had no access to employee records. Over six hundred people worked for the Department of the Interior, and Oscar didn't know of anyone named Marianne, but he managed payments for the department's external vendors.

"I pay a weekly bill for our photographers to use a darkroom on Twelfth Street every Friday morning," Oscar said. "You could probably track her down there. Better hurry, though. There's a rumor that the government photographers will be getting the axe soon."

"What do you mean?"

Oscar rolled his eyes. "Penny pinchers are always looking for ways to trim the budget. They're saying that the government has plenty of blueprints to document all our buildings and bridges, so they don't think the photographs add anything."

Luke frowned. It was hard for a woman to make her way in this city, and he didn't like the thought of Marianne losing her job because of tightfisted government bureaucrats.

"Thanks," he said to Oscar, casually strolling from the office.

Where did this clawing sense of urgency to protect Marianne come from? He didn't even know her, but he felt an instinctive need to look after her. He had connections throughout the city, and if Marianne needed help, he would be there to provide it.

Three

Marianne trudged down the sidewalk on Friday morning, cradling the satchel of photographic negatives for the pictures she'd taken this week. Ice and a crusty film of snow covered most of the sidewalk, but she aimed for the few patches of bare concrete as she made her way to the Gunderson Photography Studio. It was the largest studio in the city, with a gallery in the lobby, a studio for making portraits, and darkroom space that could be rented by the hour.

It was mercifully warm inside. She flashed a smile toward old Mrs. Gunderson at the front counter. "Is the government darkroom available?"

"Abel Zakowski is still using it, but he should be out soon." Abel also worked for the Department of the Interior, although they performed drastically different tasks. While she took photographs of people and buildings all over the city, Abel took photographs at government speeches and events.

Marianne took a seat in the waiting area. It was crowded today, with a number of families lined up to have their portraits made. Photography was becoming more affordable, with some people coming every few years for new family pictures. Marianne's gaze ran across the photographs mounted on the wall. None of them were to her liking. They were formal poses taken before props of Grecian columns or painted backdrops, whereas Marianne preferred capturing people out in the real world. Sometimes it was pictures of workday routines that were the most moving. Last year she had photographed girls working in a fish cannery down by the wharves, and those pictures had been submitted to the Bureau of Labor to argue for better enforcement of child labor laws. Three of those girls were only fourteen years old, and seeing their young faces drawn with exhaustion was more persuasive than any dry government report.

She still had a few minutes before Abel left the darkroom, so she took a well-thumbed novel from her handbag. Opening the book, she was soon transported to the arid landscapes of seventeenth-century Spain and the adventures of long-ago people.

"Hello, Aunt Marianne."

She caught her breath as her gaze flew up to the man standing beside her chair.

"Hello, Luke," she said, trying to block the thrill from her voice but probably failing. He'd come looking for her. This couldn't be a coincidence. Not after the roses, and especially not after the way he was currently gazing down at her with roguish delight. "Thank you for the roses."

"You're welcome. May I join you?"

There was an empty chair beside her, and he filled it the moment she nodded.

"Have you recovered from the ice?" she asked.

"Fully. How's the dog?"

"Bandit is doing well, and my nephew thinks you are the bravest man in the city. How did you know I would be here?" Her heart still pounded at Luke's unexpected arrival, for he was as attractive as she remembered.

"Rumor has it that the photographers who work at Interior get their photographs developed here on Friday mornings, and

I couldn't resist the temptation to seek you out." There wasn't much room in the crowded lobby, so he was pressed close to her side, and energy and excitement immediately hummed between them.

"I'm glad you did," she said, seeing no reason to be coy.

His gaze dropped to the book on her lap, and he tilted to read the spine. "*Don Quixote*?"

"It's my favorite novel," she said.

Luke slanted her a disapproving glance. "But you're reading a terrible translation."

"I am? I didn't know there was more than one."

"*Don Quixote* has been translated into English eleven times in the last two hundred years," Luke said. "The twelfth will be out later this year, and it's the best."

"How do you know?"

"Because I'm the translator."

She burst into laughter. "No!"

He grinned. "Yes!"

"Why are you bothering to translate a book that's already been translated so often?"

"Because the other translations are lousy. I've read them all, and know I can do better."

It was such an arrogant thing to say, but it was impossible not to smile at his unabashed boasting, and if he had read eleven different translations of *Don Quixote*, he must love the novel as much as she did.

"Please don't tell anyone," he continued. "This translation is shamefully close to my heart, and aside from my editor at the publishing company, no one knows about it."

The fact that he shared the secret with her triggered a tiny thrill. "Why haven't you told anyone about it?"

"It's embarrassing." He blushed madly as he spoke, so apparently he was genuinely sensitive about it. This was a man who risked his life to save a stranger's dog but was embarrassed about his secret translation project. "It's not a traditional translation. I've modernized it. I'm not as long-winded as Cervantes, and English is a very different language than Spanish. I'm afraid I took some literary license. A lot, actually."

Marianne's brows rose. "Are you allowed to do that?"

He shrugged. "I'm doing it. The other translations are so literal. A word-for-word translation sounds unnatural in English. I want the text to heave with emotion. I don't want Don Quixote to be sad, I want him to rend his garments and howl in despair. I want blood and tears on the page. It's going to be a controversial translation. A lot of people will hate it."

"Blood and tears on the page? My, we *are* extravagant today."

He preened at her comment. "We are extravagant every day," he admitted. "Passion is what sets the world ablaze and drives men to strike out for the horizon and discover new worlds. It makes me get up in the morning looking for a new dragon to slay or an antiquated text begging for the breath of new life."

She couldn't wait for his *Don Quixote* translation. If he wrote with the same fervor with which he spoke, the book would probably burst into flame while she read it.

"The darkroom is all yours, Marianne."

It was Abel Zakowski, her fellow photographer from the department, nodding to her on his way out the front door. Never had she been less eager to head into the darkroom.

She sent an apologetic glance to Luke. "I only get an hour, so I can't loiter."

"I've never been in a darkroom," Luke said. "Can I join you?"

She longed to spend more time with him, but a darkroom wasn't the ideal place. "It can be a little stinky."

"I don't mind stinky," he said with a good-humored wink.

She had a lot of work to squeeze into the next hour, so she tucked *Don Quixote* into her satchel and stood. "Then let's go," she said, and he rose to follow her.

Was this really happening? Was the world's most charming

and exciting man only steps behind her as they headed down a narrow hallway toward the darkroom?

She led the way inside, where the sharp scent of silver nitrate was ever-present in the air. She pulled the heavy drape away from the only window to let daylight into the room.

"This is where all the magic happens," she said. The room wasn't much bigger than a closet, with a worktable mounted against a wall and shelves laden with jugs of chemicals. She watched him scan the room, noting the bathing trays, the glass plates, the wooden frames, and stacks of mounting paper. Taking pictures was easy. It was developing them that was the challenge.

"I was planning to enlarge pictures today," she said. "My camera only takes small photographs, but the government needs them to be at least eight-by-eleven inches, so we use an enlarging box to make them bigger."

"Don't let me interfere," Luke said. "Do exactly what you would do on any other day. Pretend I'm not here."

"As if that would be possible," she quipped as she took a stack of small photographs from her satchel. She kept the negatives in a tin box but would only enlarge the best of them because paper and developing solution were expensive. "Here," she said, handing Luke the stack. "Have a look and tell me which you think I should enlarge."

"I'd rather sit here and watch you work. You're more interesting than"—he glanced at the top picture—"a photograph of the US Capitol. I see it every day. *You*, on the other hand, are a living piece of art. A Gibson Girl. A Fragonard milkmaid. A Botticelli nymph."

"I'm not a Botticelli."

"No? Botticelli's women are beautiful."

"They're naked."

His smile was pure mischief. "Not *all* of them."

"Most are. Look at those photographs of the Capitol and tell me which you think I should enlarge."

She watched his expression as he studied them. He moved through the photographs quickly, but the narrowing of his eyes indicated complete concentration.

Then he froze, his expression shocked. "You took this?" he said, his voice aghast as he showed her a photograph of the Capitol dome.

"I did."

"You had to be crawling on the dome to get this shot!"

"I was."

"Are you insane?"

She fought not to laugh. "No. And I'm proud of that photograph. I had to work hard for it."

"You had to risk your *neck* for it. How did you get up there?"

In truth, it had been rather daunting, but her father had pulled strings to get her access, and he was with her the whole way. The dome was eighteen stories high, and she climbed a series of interior spiral and zigzag staircases to get most of the way up. Things didn't get truly frightening until she climbed higher, where interior metal trusses supported the weight of the dome. It gave her a claustrophobic feeling, and the windowless space made her feel like she was in the hull of a ship, completely surrounded by trusses peppered with bolts the size of her forearm to hold up the concrete dome.

She and her father crawled outside onto the narrow exterior workmen's ledge so she could photograph the city from two hundred feet in the air. Stepping out into the bright sunlight had been awe-inspiring, but the wind tearing at her hair and clothing had been the biggest surprise. She'd gotten spectacular panoramic photographs of the city, as well as some close-ups of the embellishments on the Capitol dome.

She described the process of getting onto the dome, and Luke seemed both fascinated and appalled that she had done such a thing.

"My father was with me the whole time," she said.

"He actually permitted you to do such a foolhardy thing?"

"My father has never stopped me from doing anything I truly wanted," she replied. "Just the opposite. From the time I was a child, he taught me to dream big, and that if I wanted something badly enough, he'd let me fight for it. It didn't matter that I was a girl. I've always known that he would be behind me the whole way."

"Your father sounds like a wise man."

She nodded. "I'm very lucky. Now, tell me which of the dome photos you think I should enlarge. I can only do four close-ups and five cityscapes."

Luke handed the stack back to her. "I'm not an artist. You pick."

She quickly selected the shots that showed the dome at its worst. An appropriations bill for restoring government buildings would be voted on soon, and the top of the dome wasn't something officials could examine themselves.

She attached a large piece of bromide paper to a frame on one end of the enlarging box, then slid the original negative into a smaller frame on the other side.

"Now we need to darken the room, but I'm going to use the arc lamp to send a bright beam of light through the lens and then wait two minutes. The image will be imprinted on the larger piece of paper."

She pulled the drapes closed, plunging the room into darkness, then switched on the tungsten bulb to provide a dim amber glow in the room. The arc lamp at the small end of the enlarging box beamed through the negative, casting the image onto the bromide paper.

"I feel like I should whisper," Luke murmured in the darkness.

"You don't have to," she whispered back. "All we have to do is hold still and not jostle the box. The chemicals are doing all the work."

She repeated the process to enlarge twelve additional pictures, then began the process of developing the photographs.

"This is the stinky part," she warned as she poured solution into the developing trays. She set the first page into the chemical bath, and Luke stood by her shoulder, watching as she gently tipped the tray to keep the liquid gently washing the paper. The images developed quickly, but if she didn't lift them from the solution in time, they darkened to an unacceptable degree. After a minute, she lifted the paper out with tongs and set it in the stop bath to neutralize the chemicals. Ten seconds later, she set it in the final tray to fix the image. Then she clipped the photograph onto a clothesline to dry.

After Luke watched the process a few times, he wanted to try. He caught on quickly, and soon she happily turned the task over to him. He was fun to watch as he went through the steps she'd taught him.

"Do you like being a government photographer?" he asked as he clipped another photograph to the clothesline.

"I love it. Developing the pictures is the most tedious part, but now that I've got you on the job, my life is just about perfect."

He smiled, but it vanished quickly. "I've heard some rumors about the photographers who work at your department."

She wondered about the note of concern in his voice. "That they're going to give us the axe?"

"That's the one."

"Maybe. All the photographers are compiling portfolios of our best work. The hope is that we can convince the department that a picture can tell an important story, but I'll be fine no matter what happens. My father won't let me starve."

Luke continued clipping up her photographs, and even in the dim light she could see the affection on his face. "If your father lets you down, let me know," he said. "I like rescuing damsels in distress."

"I'm not a damsel in distress."

"Could you pretend? I'm actually just searching for an excuse to see you again. Do you think that's something we can arrange?"

"I hope so." She'd never in her life been so attracted to a man, and she scrambled for an opportunity for them to be together. "My father has tickets to a performance at the Lafayette Square Opera House. He'll let us use them if I ask nicely."

Luke let out a low whistle. "He must be well-connected. I tried and failed to get tickets."

"He's a congressman. People tend to offer him things like that."

Luke swiveled to look at her. "Oh? Who is he?"

"Clyde Magruder, representative from the fourth district in Maryland."

Luke blanched and swallowed hard. She smiled, because despite her father's lofty title, he wasn't an intimidating person.

"Your father is Clyde Magruder?" he asked in an awful whisper.

"Yes. Do you know him?" It could be the only reason for his strange behavior.

"Did you know my last name is Delacroix?"

It felt like her heart stopped beating. She blinked, hoping she had misunderstood. "As in Delacroix Global Spice?" she finally stammered. "Are you joking?"

"I wish I was."

She felt like a sleepwalker as she wandered to the window. The Delacroixs were terrible people. They were arrogant, privileged snobs who looked down on hardworking people like her father and grandfather.

"Your brother has said horrible things about my family," she managed to say. "Unforgivable things."

"That was a long time ago," Luke said.

Not long enough for her to forget. She still remembered

coming home from school one blustery autumn day, delighted that she'd finally passed her math class, only to see her mother's tear-stained face as she held a magazine on her lap. Gray Delacroix thought nothing of slandering them in the press, and that interview in which he attacked their entire family caused her parents no end of pain. Her grandfather won a libel suit against him, and the Delacroixs had to pay a shocking settlement fee, but money couldn't restore a tainted reputation.

Her mother wasn't the sort of person who could absorb a punch. Words could leave scars, and that was one her mother still carried.

"Your brother said my grandfather had dirt beneath his fingernails," she said in a pained voice. "That he wasn't fit to be in the food industry."

"That was my brother, not me."

She placed a hand over her heart, willing it to stop racing. She couldn't blame Luke for something his brother had said. After all, it was years ago, and Luke was too young to have been involved in that nasty lawsuit. He was a good man. He risked his life to save Bandit. They held hands and laughed on the ice, even though they'd both been afraid. The Delacroixs had been trying to drive her family out of business for decades, but surely that was other people in his family, not Luke.

She risked a glance at him. "You don't believe all those terrible things your brother said about us, do you?"

She wanted an immediate denial, but the sadness and regret on his face was all the answer she needed. He *did* believe those things. They *were* enemies.

"Marianne, I'm so sorry," he said. "You seem like a great person, but there's too much bad blood here. We probably shouldn't see each other again."

"You're probably right," she admitted. Any sort of liaison between them would be too difficult, but that didn't stop the wanting. "I only wish we could have had another day or two before we found out."

"Maybe a week," Luke agreed.

"A month?"

"How about a year?"

She had to laugh at how easily he bantered with her. He was fun, but seeing him would be like throwing a bomb into her family's home. It wasn't worth it. At least now she understood why her father got so annoyed when he saw her picture of Luke with the dog. He'd known who Luke was and suggested she have nothing more to do with him. Blood was thicker than water. *Even ice water*, she thought inanely.

At the door, Luke turned to her with an impish smile and wagged his finger in her face. "No more crawling on the Capitol dome, young lady."

"Too dangerous?"

"Too dangerous," he affirmed.

"It probably was," she admitted. "Good luck with the *Don Quixote* translation. I'll look forward to it."

He winked at her. "It will be the best."

Then the amusement in his face turned into reluctant admiration as he glanced back at the photographs hanging on the clothesline. "No matter what else happens, I think your pictures are wonderful. And so are you."

He closed the door behind him, and Marianne felt like she'd just lost a good friend.

Luke was still mulling over his bad luck as he rode the streetcar back to the Alexandria neighborhood where he'd been born and raised.

Marianne Magruder. *Magruder*. Luke had plenty of friends, thousands of acquaintances, a handful of rivals, but only one real enemy in the world, and his name was Clyde Magruder.

Luke wouldn't let an inconvenient attraction stand in the way of a lifelong grudge. No matter how much he admired Marianne, he intended to get Clyde kicked out of Congress.

He walked the last few blocks to the three-story colonial town house he shared with Gray and his wife. He was inexplicably tired as he mounted the steps and prepared to unlock the front door, but then paused.

Arguing voices could be heard inside. He cocked his ear closer to listen, for it was clearly Gray's voice berating Annabelle over something, and that was odd. Gray worshipped the ground Annabelle walked on, and they were still newlyweds. Luke didn't want to walk into an embarrassing quarrel, but he still couldn't tell the nature of their disagreement.

It sounded like they were arguing about Annabelle's job. She'd been working as a lab assistant at the Department of Agriculture for over a year, and she loved the work, but they were clearly squabbling about it. Annabelle said she liked her supervisor and didn't want to quit.

Then Gray said something too low to hear, and they both started laughing. It was freezing out here, and since it didn't sound like a horrible lovers' quarrel, Luke inserted his key in the lock and let himself inside. Gray and Annabelle were in the kitchen down the hall, and he stamped the snow from his feet to let them know he was there.

"Luke!" Annabelle said warmly. "Come into the kitchen. I've made lamb stew for lunch. You're the perfect person to help me talk sense into Gray."

Luke loved the sound of her voice. Everything about Annabelle was cheerful and optimistic, but as usual, Gray looked brooding and annoyed. The scent of simmering meat was too tempting to resist, and he helped himself to a bowl before joining them at the small kitchen table.

"There's a new initiative in the chemistry division at the Department of Agriculture," Annabelle said. "They're finally getting serious about proving the detrimental effect of chemical preservatives on human health and are launching a controlled scientific study to document the consequences."

"Excellent!" Luke said, wolfing another mouthful of stew. "Long past due, if you ask me."

Annabelle worked in the cereal grass laboratory, but lately she had been spending a few hours per week at the lab that tested some of the worst of the preservatives being pumped into the nation's milk and meat supply. Borax, benzoate, and formaldehyde were supposed to extend the shelf life of dairy and meat, but none of them had ever been proven safe. There were no laws against the sale of adulterated food, and cost-cutting methods were shockingly creative. Butter was often only beef tallow steeped in yellow food dye. Chalk powder was used to disguise milk diluted with water. Children's candy was colored with lead dyes.

And sometimes coffee was adulterated with chicory and chemical flavorings, leading to three dead people in Philadelphia.

He looked at Gray. "What's your problem with the study? We ought to be dancing in the streets now that someone is finally doing something about this."

Gray's face was somber. "They're planning to use human test subjects," he said quietly.

Luke glanced at Annabelle. "True?"

"True," she confirmed. "But Dr. Wiley will be overseeing the experiment, and surely he wouldn't do anything to harm the volunteers. He's a medical doctor, after all."

"He'll be feeding people borax!" Gray said. "Formaldehyde. How does one safely consume formaldehyde?"

It looked like he wanted to say more, but Luke interrupted him. "Who will the test subjects be?"

"We'll be looking for twelve healthy young men," Annabelle said. "They'll get free room and board in exchange for participation."

Luke sagged back in his chair, a world of possibility opening up. For five years he'd been tormented by his role in the death of those people in Philadelphia. This could be his chance to repay his debt. His chance to strike a blow at the Magruders and any other food producer who pumped chemicals into their food. If he served as a test subject, he could cover the story as a journalist from the inside, and it would make news around the world.

"Where do I sign up?" he asked. He was suddenly on his feet.

"Oh, for pity's sake!" Gray roared. "Sit back down. You're not going anywhere."

"I'm going to sign up," he repeated, looking at Annabelle, who seemed as stunned as Gray. "Tell me where I go to volunteer."

"Luke, I don't think you're healthy enough to volunteer," she said.

"You're sick and underweight and not thinking with a clear head," Gray said.

Luke took his bowl to the stove, adding two more heaping scoops of meaty stew. "I won't be underweight for long."

A new field of combat in his war against the Magruders had just opened, and he was going to be on the front lines.

Four

Vera Magruder was sobbing as she dragged a trunk out of the storage closet and toward her bedroom.

"Mama, please," Marianne urged. "Please put the trunk back. Papa will be home soon and will be able to explain everything."

At least she hoped he would. Clyde had been in Baltimore to meet with his constituents and was supposed to have returned last night, and Vera suspected the worst.

Her mother opened the lid of the trunk to throw a handful of Clyde's shirts inside. "He's with that woman," she wept. "I called home twice last night and the butler had no explanation for where he was. He's with her! Her and that child."

"Shh," Marianne said. "Sam might overhear." Her nephew was visiting them again, and he was too young to learn about Clyde's infidelities.

It was impossible to know why Clyde had overstayed his visit to Baltimore, but it might well have been to see his young son, who was now eighteen months old. Clyde refused to cut ties with the boy's mother because of the child they shared. He swore the affair was over, but he set Lottie O'Grady up in her own house and paid monthly support for her and the baby.

Vera normally insisted on accompanying Clyde whenever business called him to Baltimore, but she had been feeling poorly last Friday, and Clyde swore on a stack of Bibles that he would behave himself. His failure to return last night awakened all of Vera's fears.

Vera threw some trousers atop the shirts, then dumped Clyde's shoes into the trunk. "I won't raise another illegitimate child. I won't! I shouldn't have agreed to it the first time."

Marianne looked away. She loved her mother, but sometimes Vera could be so thoughtless, and it hurt. Vera noticed and immediately switched tones.

"Not that I regret it, darling! Come, give Mama a nice big hug." She dragged Marianne into her arms. "You know I don't mean anything by it. I love you like one of my own."

Marianne had always known Vera adopted her. As a child she had been told that her real mother died, but that wasn't true. Her real mother had an affair with Clyde and had been paid handsomely to surrender the baby to the Magruders. Clyde wanted more children, but the doctor warned that Vera could never carry another baby after the trauma of her only son's birth. Clyde never asked Vera if she would accept another child, he simply presented his wife with the three-month-old baby from his short-lived affair with an opera singer. Although Clyde doted on her, there was always a hint of tension where Vera was concerned. They could go months in loving harmony, but then something could trigger Vera's insecurities, and the coldness returned.

And that "something" had reared its head eighteen months ago when Clyde was caught in another affair. This time there was a little boy named Tommy as a result. At first Clyde tried to hide Tommy's existence from Vera, but she found out, and their entire family had been walking on eggshells ever since.

"Don't frown, Marianne, it will make those grooves on your face permanent," Vera coaxed. "Smile! There's my pretty girl.

A lady must always pay careful attention to her complexion." As if taking her own advice, Vera blotted away her tears and reached for a box of powder to begin repairing her face.

"Shall I hang Papa's clothes back in the wardrobe?" Marianne asked. The bedroom looked like a bomb had exploded, with drawers hanging open and clothing mounded atop the open trunk.

Vera's fingers stilled, but only for a moment. "Leave everything right there. If he returns today, he can see evidence of what he's put me through. And if he doesn't return today, I shall finish packing the trunk."

The sight of the chaotic bedroom was a painful window into what Vera must have gone through twenty-six years ago when Marianne arrived as an infant in the Magruder household. Why couldn't she have come from a normal family? It seemed there was always drama. A lawsuit, an affair, a scandal. The family patriarch, Jedidiah Magruder, had been born in a cabin with a dirt floor. He had a third-grade education, scars on his body from childhood labor, and a bottomless well of ambition leading to an aggressive style of business that always skirted the edges of legality. Everyone respected Jedidiah, even though he was too old to run the company anymore. Clyde had been in charge for a decade but had to step down when he was elected to Congress. Her older brother, Andrew, now led the company.

The clopping of hooves signaled the arrival of a carriage, and Marianne darted to the window to peek outside. She sagged in relief as her father stepped down from the carriage. "He's here!"

She raced downstairs and outside, even though the damp chill of the morning was biting. She didn't want to waste time grabbing her coat. They wouldn't have long to speak, and Vera shouldn't overhear.

"Welcome home!" she said as she embraced Clyde on the front stoop. "How was Baltimore?"

"Fine. Andrew has a good command of the business. He's doing well."

"Good. And little Tommy?"

A grin flashed across his face. "Cute as a button. Teething. The boy's got a set of lungs in him, but already smart as a whip."

She'd seen her half-brother from a distance a few times. He had sandy auburn hair like Clyde. As much as she wanted to meet the boy, loyalty to Vera prevented her.

"Mama dragged out one of the trunks and filled it with your clothes," she warned. "We expected you home last night, and she tried placing a telephone call to the house twice. She suspects the worst."

Clyde led the way inside and sent a critical eye toward the upstairs balcony. "I told her I broke things off with Lottie. It was a perfectly innocent visit with my son."

"You overstayed the visit," she whispered, hoping she didn't sound like a nag and a scold. But didn't he have any idea of what this did to Vera?

Clyde rummaged through his jacket, dragging out a slim velvet box. "Have a look at that," he whispered as he opened the box to show her the diamond and pearl drop earrings inside. "Do you think she'll like them?"

"Of course she will, but maybe you should wait before giving them to her." The pearls would make Vera happy for about five minutes, but then she would be angry again. "Right now you should go upstairs and apologize for being late. Tell her she looks pretty. Make her feel like you missed her."

It was horrible to be cast into the role of mediator between her parents. She loved them both, but ever since Tommy's arrival, they fought incessantly, and Vera held all the cards. If she made good on her threat to leave Clyde, he would be destroyed, for he truly did love her. He also liked being a congressman, and a scandal could cost him his reelection in November.

"These earrings cost more than most men earn in a year," he defended in a fierce whisper.

"They cost what you earn in a day. They won't mean nearly as much as a genuine apology and saying whatever Mama needs to make her feel adored."

Clyde snapped the lid of the box shut. "That was what these pearls were supposed to do."

Her mother's voice called out from upstairs. "Marianne, if that man is still in the house, tell him he's not welcome home."

Marianne took the velvet box. "Go upstairs and talk to her," she urged. "Be nice. That's what she wants."

She watched Clyde trudge up the stairs like a man walking to his own execution. Even after he disappeared inside the bedroom, his pleading voice could be overheard downstairs.

"I didn't lay a finger on her," he said. "You know you're the only woman I love. Vera, darling—"

His pleas were cut off when something crashed against the wall.

"That was an eighteenth-century vase," Clyde shouted.

Vera shouted back, but Marianne didn't want to hear it. She didn't want her nephew hearing it either, because Sam had enough family turmoil at his home in Baltimore. He was in the dining room, his dog snuggled beside him as he lined up toy soldiers to recreate the Battle of Bull Run. She snapped her fingers to get his attention.

"Let's take Bandit out for a walk, shall we?"

Marianne took Sam to the Franklin Square park, where the dog would have plenty of space to run in the five-acre lawn. Marianne sat on a bench while Sam hurled a stick for Bandit to retrieve. The damp February morning was uncomfortably chilly, and she hoped her parents would finish their argument soon. Apparently the family trait for combat had been inherited by her brother. Andrew often locked horns with his son, which was why Sam was sometimes sent to Washington for a reprieve.

Sam was talkative as he threw the stick for Bandit. "I like coming here because I can play with Bandit whenever I want and Mama doesn't get mad. She doesn't like Bandit."

Which came as no surprise to Marianne. Delia Magruder disliked most things that took attention away from her, and the fact that Bandit was a normal dog that barked and shed was a constant annoyance to her.

Sam continued prattling about life in Baltimore until an odd question came out of the blue. "Aunt Marianne, what's a dynasty?"

It took a while for her to find the words to describe the concept. "It means a very powerful family. Like the Bourbon kings or the rulers of China. Those would be dynasties."

"Oh." Sam didn't seem satisfied as he waited for Bandit to come racing back. After he hurled the stick again, he continued talking. "Grandpa says our family is a dynasty. And that I have to be a part of the dynasty."

She quirked her brow. She'd never heard her father use that term, but it made sense. Clyde had a rather grandiose view of their family, but she tried to put it in positive terms for Sam. "Your grandfather is very proud of what the Magruders have accomplished. You've heard how your great-grandfather had to quit school when he was only ten years old. He still became very rich because he worked so hard."

"And then Grandpa worked hard and got elected to Congress."

"Yes, and now your father runs the company. All three of them worked to make Magruder Food a successful company, so that's a kind of dynasty, I suppose."

This time Sam didn't smile when Bandit dropped the stick at his feet. "Does that mean I have to work for Magruder Food too?"

She had no doubt that everyone expected Sam to join the company someday, but maybe three generations was enough.

"You can do whatever you want when you grow up," she said. "What would you like to do?"

"I think I'd like to be a mailman."

She bit back a gulp of laughter, for he said it with the utmost seriousness. "Why a mailman?"

"They get to walk all over the city. See things. My father has to sit in an office all day, and I don't think I'd like that."

"Then I think you would make a very good mailman," she said warmly. Sam would probably change his mind a dozen times before he came of age, and that was how life was supposed to be. He had the freedom to become anything he chose.

That wasn't quite the case for women. Lately, her parents had been pressuring her to marry, and her father had already handpicked a candidate for her. She'd met Colonel Henry Phelps twice. He was a handsome and eligible bachelor, but he didn't set her imagination on fire.

Not like Luke Delacroix.

Thinking about Luke made her heart squeeze, but she would forget him eventually. Someday she would have the sort of perfect family she'd seen depicted on sentimental postcards and in storybooks. She would have to choose her husband wisely. She wanted no raging fights or vases hurled through the air. No generational family feuds or lawsuits or people who schemed behind one another's backs.

And that meant no Luke Delacroix. He would blast her chaotic family's drama to new and terrible heights, so it was best to forget about him.

But she couldn't help wishing it were otherwise.

Five

To call Luke's one-man office the "Washington bureau" of *Modern Century* was a stretch, but he believed in putting a good face on things. The magazine was based in Boston, but they needed someone stationed in Washington to advance legislative reform. Someday Luke might be able to hire a secretary and additional reporters, but for now he was a one-man operation.

He'd been writing for *Modern Century* for six years, covering gritty subjects like graft and child labor. Last month he'd written an eight-page article exposing corruption in the War Department, in which an officer was caught diverting funds and stoking the rebellion in Cuba. Luke uncovered the source of the corruption by enduring a fifteen-month stint in a Cuban prison and spying on imprisoned members of the rebellion. Luke had been privately awarded a medal by President Roosevelt upon his return to the States, but his undercover work for the government would forever remain a secret.

He sat at his desk and continued scanning government reports about the need for better testing for food preservatives. Current safety standards required a rabbit to be fed a dose of the preservative. If the rabbit was still alive the next day, the substance was deemed safe for use.

Luke took a long drink of milk and continued munching on a wedge of apple strudel. Anything to get his weight up. The Department of Agriculture would begin interviewing volunteers for their "hygienic table trials" tomorrow. What an awful name for such a daring experiment. Nevertheless, he needed to prove himself fit and healthy enough to qualify for the trials. According to the Surgeon General, a man of Luke's height should weigh between 161 and 183 pounds to be considered healthy. He currently weighed 153. He finished the milk, then started on the second slice of the apple strudel. He was going to qualify for that experiment if it killed him.

He bit back a smile, because it truly *might* kill him, but he never shied away from a challenge. Besides, it shouldn't be too hideous. According to the advertisement, only half the men would be subjected to the chemically tainted meals while the other half would be in the control group eating wholesome food.

Luke secretly hoped he'd be in the group with the tainted meals. He *wanted* to tough it out. It would be a privilege to volunteer his own body in a quest to prove the danger of chemical preservatives.

A knock sounded on the door. "Come in!" he said through a mouthful of strudel. The man from the telephone company must be early to set up the service, but all to the good.

It wasn't the man from the telephone company. It was Clyde Magruder, looking like a black cloud.

Luke masked his surprise, wiped his mouth, and stood. "Hello, Clyde," he said casually.

It had been almost two years since they'd seen each other. Aside from a few more strands of silver in Clyde's sandy hair, there had been little change. He still looked big, imposing, and had the mean-eyed charm of a python.

Clyde's nose wrinkled in distaste as he surveyed the office. "Such a shame that your two-bit magazine can't afford decent office space."

A flash of blue sparkled on Clyde's hand. Clyde excelled in all the pretentions of the newly rich, so a pinky ring shouldn't be a surprise, but Luke couldn't resist a little mockery.

"Nice ring," he said. "Very classy. Then again, I've always said you can spot a Magruder a mile away by their vulgar jewelry and the gilt paint they slap on everything."

"Would you care to make more insults about my family?" Clyde said. "I'm not due in Congress for another hour, so please. Let it all out, Luke. Perhaps it would do you good to get rid of some of that bile."

"And as a Magruder, you know all about bile." Luke opened his top desk drawer and tossed a can of Magruder's potted ham at Clyde. "My brother had a chemist dissect this. It's eighty percent ham and ten percent beef tallow. We couldn't figure out what the rest of it was. Mind helping us out?"

Clyde tossed the can back to him. "It's a moneymaker that bought me a summer house in Maine. Do you mind telling me about this?"

Clyde set a slip of paper on his desk. It was the card that accompanied the roses Luke had sent to Marianne. He hadn't known who she was when he sent them, or he wouldn't have done it. He hoped it hadn't landed her in trouble.

He used a single finger to slide the card back toward Clyde. "It's nothing."

"Any time you tamper with my daughter, it's something," Clyde said, his voice lethally calm. "I saw the photograph of you with my grandson's dog. I'm giving you only one warning. Stay away from my family. If you want to lob your nasty assaults at me, have at it, but if you *ever* touch my daughter, there won't be enough of you left to mop off the ground."

He grabbed the can of potted ham and threw it at the window, shattering the glass as the can arced outside. Clyde left the office without another word, slamming the door so hard that the glass in the door's window broke too.

Luke's hands clenched. He really hoped Marianne hadn't caught grief for those roses. He hadn't known who she was! He wouldn't have gone within ten yards of her if he'd known she was Clyde's daughter.

He fought to rein in his breathing as he strolled to the window, the glass shards crunching beneath his boots. The can of ham had fallen harmlessly to the street below, which was a blessing, since they were on the fourth floor and there could have been people beneath the window. Clyde's act was a typical low-class Magruder tantrum.

Cold wind blew into the office. Luke would have to hire a glazier to repair both the window and the door, but in the meantime, he had work to do.

Clyde's visit was like waving a red flag before a bull. Every instinct cried out for Luke to go find Marianne and start courting her in earnest. He could shower her with gifts and compliments and charm her until she was breathless. Two years ago that was exactly what he would have done in response to Clyde's threat.

But his time locked in a Cuban jail cell had taught him a great deal. He had been taught patience and wisdom. He would do nothing to hurt Marianne, but he would double his fire at Clyde. The man had to be removed from Congress.

Luke swallowed back his anger and thought strategically. He cut another slice of strudel and made himself eat. There were so many reasons he wanted a front-row seat in the government's study of poisonous food additives, but at the top of the list was a chance to personally strike a body blow against Clyde Magruder.

The advertisement calling for medical volunteers instructed men to apply at the Department of Agriculture beginning at nine o'clock. Applicants would be required to pass a physical exam and fall within the acceptable weight range for their height. Luke was still seven pounds underweight, but a gallon of water weighed eight pounds. He could fake it. He'd already drunk a quart of water but felt so bloated he didn't know if he could get the rest of it down. Hopefully he wouldn't have to, because there probably wouldn't be many volunteers.

Slinging the jug of water over his shoulder, he meandered toward the Department of Agriculture, enjoying the warmth of the sun on his face. Winter was such a dicey time in Washington. Sometimes it was a frosty misery, but today he barely needed a coat.

As he rounded the corner, he was stunned to see dozens of men lined up outside the Department of Agriculture. Who were all these people? The line snaked down the steps and around the front of the building. Luke approached the last man in the line. "What's everyone waiting for?"

"Free room and board!" the man said. He held out a copy of the advertisement for the experiment. "All we need to do is pass a physical and agree to eat all our meals here. The doors open at nine o'clock."

Luke scanned the crowd of young healthy men. There had to be over a hundred people in this line, and the department was only taking a dozen volunteers.

Luke uncorked the jug of water and began drinking. He was going to have to get the whole gallon down, and fast. It was going to take some quick thinking to convince the test administrators that he was as healthy as the other men in this line, but Luke had always been good at quick thinking.

By ten o'clock all the men had filled out basic forms to apply for the research study, then were ushered into the room where a doctor would make the first round of cuts. Luke reluctantly followed instructions to shuck off his heavy winter coat and boots before stepping on the scale. Nature was calling, but he couldn't use the restroom until after he'd been weighed. A doctor and a nurse were doing the preliminary screen, weighing the men, shining a light into their eyes, a tongue depressor down their throats, and banging a hammer on their knees.

"We're all insane for being here," a tall volunteer with curly blond hair said. "They should probably use that hammer on our heads."

"My head is harder," a man beside him said. They looked so much alike that they had to be brothers.

"But mine is bigger," the other replied.

"Yeah, but Mom still loves me the most."

The two brothers kept up a nonstop stream of competitive banter all morning. When the doctor complimented the taller brother for how fast his eyes dilated, the other begged to be tested so he could dilate faster. They gave their names as Ted and Bradley Rollins, two brothers currently attending Georgetown University who rowed crew for the college. Luke simply thought of them as Big Rollins and Little Rollins. They were eager to flex their muscles for the fresh-faced nurse who seemed charmed as they argued about who had better grades, who had more muscle, and who could hold their breath longer. Big Rollins began boasting about the five-minute mile he'd run last weekend.

"Five minutes? That's nothing," the man next to Luke said. He had a lanky, athletic build and floppy dark hair. "I can run a five-minute mile with hurdles in the mix."

"I don't believe it," Little Rollins said.

The lanky man offered a hand. "I'm Wesley Sparks, fourth place finisher in the Paris Olympics hurdle race in 1900."

"Ouch, fourth place," Little Rollins said.

"I know!" Wesley replied. "Do you know what coming in fourth place in the Olympics does to a man? Do you?"

"Let me guess," Nurse Hollister said. "It makes you want to enroll in risky tests of human endurance."

The nurse's dry humor didn't make a dent in the skinny man's earnest demeanor. "No, it makes me wake up at two o'clock in the morning, reliving that race over and over. I remember it like it was yesterday. The eyes of the nation were on me after years of training and sacrifice. Two thousand years of history and sportsmanship awaited my performance, but as I took my position at the starting line, I started worrying my left shoe wasn't tied properly. I lost out to Belgium because that shoelace distracted me. *Belgium!* So now I'm here for the free room and board so I can train for the St. Louis Olympics in two years. There will be no fourth-place finish in St. Louis, and I *will* qualify for this study."

"Step up on the scale, St. Louis," Nurse Hollister said. "You're on the scrawny side for this."

Luke held his breath, hoping St. Louis would qualify. Anyone tormented by old regrets, even if it was only missing out on a medal, deserved his sympathy.

"You pass to the next round," the nurse said. "Next."

This was it. Luke stepped forward, praying he weighed enough to qualify for the next round.

"Take off your belt," the nurse intoned when he tried to step on the scale.

Blast! He'd worn his heaviest belt buckle to gain a few ounces. He yanked it off and stepped onto the scale, resisting the urge to shift with the need to relieve himself.

"One hundred and sixty-one pounds," the nurse announced as she marked it on his chart.

Thank the good Lord! He dared not ask to use the bathroom, lest she realize what he'd done. "Can I step outside?" he asked. "I saw a water fountain in the hallway."

"Don't be long," Nurse Hollister said with a nod.

He didn't even bother to tug his shoes back on, just ran down the hall toward the men's lavatory in stocking feet. On his way back, he took a sip from the water fountain just to keep himself honest, but he was now ready to compete against the other men in earnest.

By the time he got back, most of the volunteers had been dismissed for failing to meet the basic physical requirements, but Luke, the two brothers, St. Louis, and twenty other men were still in the running. The brothers were arguing about who was a better sailor when Luke approached the taller of the two brothers and offered his hand.

"Luke Delacroix," he introduced himself. "I won the two-man sculling contest three years in a row in college, and according to Nurse Hollister's chart, my eyes dilated a second faster than both of you loafers."

They were fighting words. Big Rollins challenged him to a rowing race after the trials, and Little Rollins said he had the advantage over all the volunteers because of his cast-iron stomach.

"That will be useful against the poison you people are going to feed us, right, Nurse Hollister?" Little Rollins asked.

"I'm not at liberty to say exactly what will be in the meals," the nurse replied.

"Acid?" St. Louis asked. "Formaldehyde? Paint thinner?"

"Let's not dwell on it," Luke said. "It's all poison."

"Then we shall be your poison eaters," Little Rollins said to the nurse.

"That doesn't sound quite right," the other brother commented. "Poison crew? Poison team?"

"Poison squad," St. Louis offered, and Luke had to admit that name had a certain flair.

They were soon all ushered into a new room for the physical tests.

"In this room we will test for basic physical coordination," a young doctor in a white lab coat said. "Nothing exotic and no hurdles, but we need to see if you can toss a beanbag from hand to hand for a full sixty seconds."

Big Rollins snorted. "Let's see if we can juggle for two minutes."

"Deal!" Little Rollins said.

Luke was curious to see if they could actually do it, but these men were both young, healthy, and had obviously spent too much time in foolish competitions. They both juggled quite well, and the nurse tried to get them to stop after a minute, but they insisted on continuing to see who could outlast the other. Given their health and vigor, it was obvious these two would be selected for the study. If Luke could keep pace with them, surely he'd be among the men chosen too.

The brothers continued their frantic juggling, laughing as they tossed the beanbags in ever-faster motions to impress the nurse. Big Rollins won by twenty seconds and surrendered his two beanbags.

"That's nothing," Luke said. "I can do it with *my feet*."

That got everyone's attention, earning catcalls and howls of disbelief, but these people didn't know him. When a man spent fifteen months trapped in a prison cell with little to do . . . yes, he had learned to juggle with his feet.

He was out of practice, so he only took one beanbag. He still had his shoes off, and he lay on the floor, propping himself up on his elbows and holding his knees in the air. After balancing the beanbag on top of a foot, he tossed it in the air, then caught it on top of his other foot. The nurse started the timer, and Luke continued batting the beanbag from foot to foot. The other men began applauding as he crossed the sixty-second mark. He could have gone the full two minutes if he hadn't been laughing so hard, but eventually the beanbag went glancing off his foot too far for him to capture, and he sprang back to his feet, accepting congratulations from some of the men and even the doctor.

But not the brothers. "We're going to have to kill him," Little Rollins said.

Luke grinned and offered his hand. "You can't kill me. After today we're all teammates on the Poison Squad."

Ten minutes later his assertion was proven correct as he, the two brothers, St. Louis, and eight other men were given the paperwork to become the inaugural members of the Poison Squad.

When Luke joined the experiment, he hadn't realized the strain it would put on both Gray and his wife. After all, it was his body and his mission, but if he put himself in danger's way, it affected others. Annabelle was tormenting herself for telling him about the study, and it was obvious Gray wanted him to have nothing to do with it. Today they were both helping him move into the boardinghouse where he'd live for the next four months. It was a slim three-story building only blocks from the Department of Agriculture.

Gray did his best to talk Luke out of going inside. "You haven't signed any contract committing you to this study. You are free to walk away at any time. I say you walk away now. Before it even begins."

Luke headed up the steps to the front porch. "I have to do it."

"No, you don't. You've already given enough of yourself."

It hurt to see the expression on Gray's face as he stood on the sidewalk with Luke's trunk slung over his shoulder. Gray had been his lifeline over the past year, visiting him repeatedly in that Cuban jail and then tending him while he recovered his health. He didn't want to repay that generosity by thumbing his nose at Gray's concerns, but he felt called to this assignment.

"Here, I'll take the trunk. You don't need to stay."

When he reached for the strap, Gray twisted past him and headed into the boardinghouse. A clerk in the foyer directed Luke to a third-floor bedroom he would be sharing with three other men.

It was going to be a tight fit. There were two bunk beds, a single desk, a single chest of drawers, and a slim window overlooking an alley. Luke was the first of the test subjects to arrive and chose the lower bunk closest to the window. Gray hoisted his trunk onto the mattress.

"Oh, Luke." Annabelle sighed as she scanned the room with worried eyes. "Are you sure? No one will think badly of you if you back out."

"I would," he said instinctively.

Annabelle and Gray didn't understand. He was *elated* by this chance to prove himself. Adventure and danger had always been carved onto his heart. In his younger years it ran wild, leading him into foolhardy exploits and trouble with the law, but he was learning to funnel it toward the good. He needed to test his physical strength against a challenge. He needed to match wits with a worthy opponent and win. Five days out of the week he sat at a desk and did paperwork, but his soul craved more. There was a wildness inside that needed a mission to both challenge and frighten him.

This need was so deeply embedded that he had no doubt God instilled it in him. Luke had never done his finest praying in a church pew. He did it out in the real world. He had proven himself in the sweltering battlefields of Cuba and in exposing corruption on the pages of *Modern Century*.

Now it was time to test his mettle with the Poison Squad.

Six

Marianne headed toward her supervisor's office, her footsteps echoing in the marble hallway of the Interior building. Willard Schmidt oversaw the photographers, and each week he provided her with a list of the buildings and subjects he wanted photographed. He was a thickset middle-aged man with a shiny bald head.

"Here you go, Miss Magruder," he said as he pushed her assignment toward her. Most of the subjects were familiar to her, but two were odd.

"The District of Columbia Jail?" she asked.

Mr. Schmidt nodded. "It falls under our purview. Lately there have been complaints that the facility is inadequate. It was built in 1872 but has never been photographed. We need to prove it is a safe and well-maintained facility. I trust you can make sure that happens," he said with a critical look over the top of his spectacles.

One of the nice things about coming from a wealthy family was that the roof over Marianne's head was not dependent upon Mr. Schmidt. If the prison was dreadful, her photographs would capture its true condition. She wouldn't use her camera to lie and show it in a positive light.

"I'll do a good job," she said, still studying her list of assignments. "What are the hygienic table trials?"

"A new initiative at the Department of Agriculture. They're taking volunteers who agree to be test subjects for food preservatives. The doctor wants every man photographed before the testing begins. Poor fools. Lord only knows what they'll look like in a few months."

"What do you mean by 'food preservatives'?" she asked. Most of the food sold in markets today had preservatives in it. It was safer than eating meat that had been sweltering in hot railway cars without preservatives. Her father was an expert at ensuring that meat, milk, and canned food were safe, and chemical preservatives were a blessing of modern science.

"It's a controlled experiment with a dozen men living in a boardinghouse, eating food heavily laced with chemicals, and having their health monitored. You couldn't pay me enough to be a part of it, but it looks like the folks over at Ag found a dozen fellows willing to do it. They need to be photographed this morning because they start eating the poisoned stuff at lunch."

She pocketed the list. It seemed like a fool's errand, but she would do it.

Marianne arrived at the boardinghouse on Grove Street promptly at eleven o'clock, which would give her plenty of time to take photographs of the men participating in the research study before they were served lunch. She'd been told to take individual portraits of each man staring straight at the camera. This sort of documentation was important for the scientific aspects of the study, but she'd also take some group poses of the men who had volunteered to be human test subjects.

She knocked on the door of the boardinghouse, but no one answered, and she doubted anyone heard. It sounded like quite a rumpus was going on inside. There was stomping feet, banging, and shouting. She knocked a second time and waited, but it was obvious she couldn't be heard over the commotion. When no one answered, she gave up and stepped inside.

Then ducked to avoid the tennis ball flying straight at her.

A man with a racket threw himself after the ball, bumping into her but managing to return the ball into a room on the other side of the entryway. Good heavens! She clutched the satchel containing her camera against her chest, aghast at the tumult. It looked like there were three simultaneous games of tennis happening, as the entire ground floor swarmed with men, all armed with rackets and batting tennis balls between the parlor on her left and the dining room on the other side. A curly-headed man stood on the second-floor balcony, volleying a ball with the man in the entryway who had just slammed into her.

These weren't men, they were a pack of animals! She gaped at the free-for-all as men scrambled after the balls flying every direction, smacking into walls and furniture. One man ran straight toward a sofa, then launched into the air in an amazing leap to vault right over it. She darted a few steps up the staircase, possibly the only place where she could avoid the men's bodies hurtling through space.

A loud whistle split the air, and the men began to settle down, but a few stray tennis balls continued to bounce.

"Pardon us, ma'am," a tall blond man said, still panting. "You must be the photographer?"

"I am."

"You'll want to get a picture of me first, because I'm much better looking than my brother."

"Yeah, but I'm the better tennis player," the man beside him challenged.

A tennis ball came flying out of nowhere and smacked the self-proclaimed better-looking brother on the back of the shoulder. He chased after it and hurled it back, almost clipping her with it.

There were a few ways she could handle this. She could simply leave. She could scold them all and warn them to behave. Or she could go along with them and get some truly amazing photographs. They were rumpled, laughing, and out of breath. The choice was obvious.

"Line up exactly as you are," she said. "Keep your rackets. No, no—don't straighten your hair. Don't tuck in your shirts. I want to catch you exactly as you are. Disheveled and irreverent." *And dazzling*, she silently added.

She pointed to where she wanted them to stand so the backlighting from the window wouldn't interfere with the photograph. "Taller men in the back, shorter men on one knee in the front."

It was the wrong thing to say, as a couple of men started arguing over who was taller, but they did as she asked, nudging and bickering as they sorted themselves into two rows. They were a handsome lot, all of them vibrant and lively as they joked. She scanned the group, mentally forming the composition, but one man stood a little off to the side, watching her.

Luke!

A smile broke across her face at the sight of him, for he was beaming at her in a wonderfully irreverent way that lit his whole face.

"What are you doing here?" she asked.

"I'm on the Poison Squad."

Poison Squad? It seemed a suitable nickname, but this was quite possibly the last place she ever expected to see a Delacroix. They seemed so wealthy and refined, not the sort to delve into an experiment like this. And yet here he was, his darkly handsome face flushed with excitement as he watched her.

"Go ahead and hunker down in front of Mr. Princeton," she said.

"How did you know I went to Princeton?" a gangly man with a trim mustache asked.

"Who else would wear a black jacket with orange piping?" she asked.

Her guess caused another round of ribbing. She handed Princeton a tennis racket, then tossed a ball to Luke. He snatched it out of the air with one hand and flashed a wink at her. She wished that wink didn't send a thrill through her, but oh, he was handsome. He radiated charisma, even amidst this loud, boisterous crew.

She moved quickly to prepare her camera, desperate to capture this image before the men settled down. Already a few were straightening their collars, and she didn't want that. She grabbed another tennis ball and tossed it toward the center of the group.

"Catch!" she said, and it injected an immediate spark of energy back into the men. She held the camera against her waist, cranked the roll of new film into place, and looked down through the viewfinder. "Don't move or say anything, but I want each of you to think about which of you is the best tennis player in the group."

The challenge worked like a charm, inserting a jolt of competitive spirit even as they held still, and she got two good photographs. Then she had the rows trade places, moved the tennis rackets among the men, and took four more.

These would surely be her best pictures of the day, but she needed to take the boring individual pictures that would be used to document each man's appearance before they began eating tainted food.

She counted out a number for each man, leaving Luke for last. Her reasoning wouldn't bear much scrutiny, but if she finished quickly, perhaps they could have a few minutes to talk before he headed into lunch to begin this disagreeable experiment.

The man she had dubbed Princeton was first. She asked him to stand against a portion of the wall devoid of any decoration so she could take the plainest of all possible pictures.

"No smiling," she said. "Just look straight ahead with a blank stare."

He did as she asked, and then the next man in line took his place. All the while she felt Luke quietly watching her as he lounged against the arched doorway that led into the foyer. Why on earth was he here?

The portraits were so routine that in less than ten minutes she had processed eleven men. Then it was Luke's turn. Having watched all the men before him, he knew the procedure as he took his position against the blank wall and straightened his shoulders to face her.

"No smiling," she said.

"I'm not smiling."

And strangely, he wasn't. It only seemed like he was smiling because the keen animation in his face conveyed energy and excitement. She took the picture.

"Thank you," she said, replacing the cover over the lens.

She'd done everything on her assignment card, and there was still fifteen minutes before lunch would be served. When Luke would start eating poison. At least so he believed.

"Why are you here?" she asked. "This test is a pointless abomination. I'm sure you don't need the free room and board."

"Most of us don't," Luke said. "We're here for the challenge."

"The challenge of seeing how sick you can get?"

"The challenge of seeing if we can do something great."

She turned away to avoid the accusatory look that suddenly appeared on Luke's face. In fifteen minutes these men were going to sit down to a meal tainted with massive doses of preservatives. It was a meaningless endeavor. The food industry had been using preservatives for decades, and they had already been proven safe.

"Can I see the kitchen?" she impulsively asked.

"*You* can. None of the volunteers are allowed to see what's going on in there."

"But you'll eat whatever they bring out?"

"Yes, but I'm not too worried. There won't be any Magruder foods on the menu."

The direct attack took her by surprise, but maybe it shouldn't have. For years the Delacroix family had been accusing the Magruders of adulterating their food. Last year Gray Delacroix had launched an infamous campaign against her father over applesauce that almost cost him the election. It was a petty and spiteful act that still smarted.

"Chemical preservatives have saved countless lives over the years," she said. "Just because your family is leery of science—"

"Anyone with a functioning brain ought to be leery of what your father dumps into his food. It's science run amok."

She wasn't going to stand here and listen to her family be slandered like this. She set down her satchel, undid the buttons on her collar, then yanked her blouse down to expose a small round scar on her shoulder.

"That is a smallpox vaccination," she snapped. "I'll bet you have one exactly like it. People were once terrified of getting vaccinated, but they've been doing it for more than fifty years, and I thank God for it!" She jerked her blouse back into place and tried to calm her breathing, but he made her so angry. "It's normal for people to be cautious of scientific progress, but the Delacroixs aren't normal. You people are highbrow snobs who will do anything to ruin us."

Her fingers shook as she rebuttoned her blouse, and she couldn't even look at him because if she did, she might start crying, and that would be horrible.

She grabbed her satchel and stormed out the door.

"Wait!" Luke called, but she wasn't interested in anything else he had to say.

Luke picked up the piece of paper that fluttered to the ground after Marianne stormed out the door. He already regretted shooting his mouth off. He glanced at the paper, which listed assignments throughout the city. It was her work schedule for the week.

He didn't even bother to reach for a coat before following her outside. The winter chill cut straight through his thin cotton shirt, but he couldn't let her leave without apologizing.

"Marianne, wait," he called after her as she hustled down the sidewalk toward the streetcar stop. He had to sprint to draw up alongside her. "I'm sorry. You didn't deserve that."

"That's right, I didn't," she said. "Neither did my family or my grandfather, and what your brother said about—"

"Stop," he said. He didn't want to hear her litany of accusations. He could answer every one of them, but that didn't mean he harbored a grudge against her. He admired her too much. It took a lot for a woman to walk into a group of rowdy men and handle them as masterfully as she just had. All except him, and that was entirely his fault. "Let's not talk about our families. They're never going to get along, but I like you too much to be mean to you. Here. You dropped this."

She sucked in a quick breath when she saw the list and snatched it from him. "Thank you! I'd be in trouble without this."

"The assignments look interesting, except the one at the DC Jail."

"I think it will be the most interesting on the list," she replied. "Not particularly fun, but interesting."

"Have you ever been in a jail before?"

She laughed a little. "Never."

"They are neither interesting nor fun."

The thought of stepping back into a jail was enough to make

his entire body break out into a sweat even though he was freezing as he hugged himself on the sidewalk. He probably shouldn't have darted outside without a coat, but he needed to catch her.

"Let me go with you," he said impulsively.

"To the jail?" He nodded, and she asked why on earth he would want to go.

Luke was ready with an answer. "Because the people at the jail aren't going to be rowdy men playing tennis, they'll be rowdy criminals who haven't seen a woman in ages."

"Luke, you'll catch your death of cold out here. Don't worry about me, I'll be fine."

He shook his head. "Promise me you'll let me take you to the jail. You shouldn't go alone." He blew into his cupped hands and hopped in place, anything to keep his blood moving.

"Yes."

He grinned. Even with the chill, he wished he could linger more, but a three-course lunch was about to be set out, and he needed to be there.

"Until Wednesday, then," he said, loving the sparkle in her eyes. "I'll meet you at the Michigan Avenue streetcar stop at one o'clock."

He darted back to the boardinghouse and sprang up the steps, already counting down the hours until he could see Marianne again. She was like an itch he couldn't scratch, and he just wanted to be with her, even if it meant he had to walk back into a jail.

But first he had to survive lunch with the Poison Squad.

Lunch.

That innocuous word had never sounded so ominous before, but Luke sensed the tension the moment he entered the dining room. It was a spacious room with plain walls, two windows facing the street, and two large tables. Such a mundane room for an extraordinary experiment. The overturned chairs from the impromptu tennis match had been put to rights by the time Luke entered.

Dr. Wiley assigned each man to a seat. Everyone already knew that one table would be the control group, which would be served untainted food. The other table would get a meal laced with a hefty dose of preservatives, but no one knew which table would get the adulterated food. The first round of the experiment would last for two weeks, then the control group would get the toxic hash and the first group would earn a reprieve.

Luke was seated between Big Rollins and a loud-mouthed Italian named Nicolo. That was good, because he liked the tall blond giant, and they were going to be stuck together for months to come.

"Here we are," Nurse Hollister said cheerfully as she rolled a stainless-steel cart into the room. The nurse would be on hand for every meal, helping serve the food and wait on the tables, but also to keep an eye out in case anyone fell ill.

Dr. Wiley stood in the corner, a balding man with widely spaced eyes who peered at them intently, almost like an owl. "It's important that you eat everything on your plate," he said. "Each serving has been weighed and measured. I certainly hope you find it tasty."

Was it possible for poison to be tasty? Luke might be about to find out. The tomato soup looked perfectly ordinary in the plain white bowl that was set before him. The first course came with a slice of bread and a pat of butter.

Luke bowed his head and silently prayed. *Lord, thank you for this food. I know what it is to be hungry, so I'm grateful for whatever is before me, even if it's tainted. I pray that this experiment will be successful and make the world a better place. I pray it will help make me worthy in your eyes.*

He straightened, picked up his spoon, and dove in. The first spoonful of soup tasted fine. So did the second. He glanced around the room. No one else was eating. They were all just watching him, waiting for his reaction.

"What are you namby-pamby weaklings waiting for?" he taunted.

The challenge jolted the men into action, and most of them immediately picked up their spoons and began to work on the soup. Little Rollins hesitated until heckling from his brother goaded him into eating.

Luke analyzed the taste of his next bite carefully. There was a tang. But all tomato soup tasted tangy, didn't it? He didn't mind taking a hit of poison, but today would be a bad time to be ill, because he had a meeting with his sister, Caroline, after lunch. She was already worrying herself into a tizzy over him, and he didn't want to get sick right off the bat. His stomach felt a little queasy as he finished the soup and pushed the bowl away, but maybe it was just his imagination.

A quick glance around the table showed other looks of uncertainty, but the men at the other table looked the same. They were all ill at ease, and surely the chemical preservatives wouldn't affect anyone so quickly. It was probably just nerves getting to him.

The main course was a slice of roasted turkey breast, green beans, and rice in some sort of sauce.

"I'll bet the chemicals are in the sauce on the rice," Big Rollins whispered to him, and Luke had to agree. It would be too hard to infuse it into the turkey or the green beans.

"Please finish your meal," Dr. Wiley stated from his stool in the corner. "The study can only be valid if each man consumes the exact same meals each day."

"I don't like rice," Nicolo said in his thickly accented voice. "Americans don't know how to make rice."

"I'm not a big fan of rice either," Princeton said.

"All of you have already stated you have no food allergies, so please finish everything on the plate," Dr. Wiley admonished.

Everyone reluctantly dove in.

Luke finished quickly because his appointment with Caroline loomed. She wanted his insight on the latest proposal from the McMillan Commission, an ambitious plan to transform the heart of Washington with a huge open park. A group of congressmen, city planners, and opinion makers had been formed to advance the plan, and Caroline was serving on the commission. Few people were as well versed in Washington society as Caroline Delacroix, and she had been selected to help sway public opinion to support the plan. Lunch concluded without incident, and he headed out to meet her.

It was a bleak winter day with barren trees and a leaden gray sky, but Caroline looked splendid as Luke joined her near the proposed park. Her sapphire velvet cloak matched the blue of her eyes, and her blond hair was perfectly styled beneath the cloak's wide hood. She held on to his arm as they carefully stepped across the mushy land surrounding the tidal basin.

"This is where the proposed memorial to President Lincoln will be built," she said, gesturing to acres of swampy ground. "We'll need to install a drainage system and build up the land. Someday we'll clear these trees away, and you'll have a clear view all the way from Lincoln's memorial to the Capitol."

"It's going to be a tough sell to Congress," he said. Half a dozen buildings would need to be torn down, and they would have to reroute the B&P Railroad tracks. There was also a thickly wooded arboretum with meandering trails and ponds that were popular with residents. The McMillan Plan would clear it all away. Two miles of land would be planted with grass, rivalling the great parks in the capitals of Europe.

"We are envisioning a huge, open park," Caroline said. "It can be used in inaugural ceremonies or big festivals. We'll build a national archive and museums all along the mall. We'll plant an alleyway of American elm trees on both sides of the park. Someday those trees will form a shaded avenue as people walk all the way from the Capitol to the Lincoln Memorial."

The excitement in her voice was contagious. The vision she painted would be a celebration of American culture and history. Monuments would pay homage to their greatest heroes, and Caroline could help sell the idea to a skeptical public.

Although Caroline had once been his partner in mischief when they were growing up, she had become a sophisticated woman and had spent almost two years as the social secretary for the first lady of the United States. That came to an abrupt end with President McKinley's assassination last September, but during those two years, Caroline became one of the most well-connected people in the city. She knew where the bad blood lay, how to flatter intransigent congressmen, and whose door to knock on for a favor. In the coming years, her insight would be priceless in helping the McMillan Commission navigate a political minefield and orchestrate a new plan for the city.

"How are you going to pay for it?" he asked.

"That's still in the works. But the new mall will be—"

"Not good enough," Luke interrupted. "The first thing you need to do is come up with a better answer to that question because it will be your biggest stumbling block. The other problem is that Washington has plenty of calcified elected officials who don't like change. Take the B&P Railroad Station. They like it because it's only three blocks from the Capitol, but your proposed new station is twice as far."

"Six blocks isn't that far," she said defensively.

Sleet started falling, and they hurried to a nearby gazebo for shelter. Looking at the expanse of barren trees and waterlogged soil made it hard to imagine the future. The McMillan Plan, even if it passed Congress, would take decades to transform this mishmash of old buildings and chopped-up parkland.

The sleet turned into rain, and neither of them had brought an umbrella, so they were trapped in the gazebo because Caroline refused to put her new cloak in danger. Luke joined her on the bench and encouraged her to talk about her upcoming wedding, even though he'd rather have a tooth pulled than contemplate his dazzling sister's marriage to the fastidiously sober Nathaniel Trask. She'd fallen in love with the Secret Service officer when they were both working in the White House. Gray was thrilled that Caroline had found such a responsible man to marry, but Luke dreaded losing his best friend and chief confidant.

It was a perfect example of his selfishness. He loved Caroline more than anyone on earth, but he dreaded the prospect of her marriage. What kind of howling void lurked in his soul to make him resent Caroline's happiness? He didn't like anything about the man she was going to marry. Nathaniel seemed completely wrong for her, but was it any odder than a Delacroix falling for a Magruder?

He turned to Caroline in curiosity. "Was Nathaniel off-limits when the two of you were working in the White House?"

"There were never any rules keeping us apart," she said with a cheerful shrug. "His natural fustiness kept him at arm's distance from me."

He nudged her with his elbow. "You're doing a terrible job of convincing me he's the right man for you."

"Was that what I was supposed to do?"

"It would help. I have no idea why you're marrying such a stick-in-the-mud."

Her laughter rippled out over the gloomy landscape like a ray of gilded sunshine. "Oh, darling, don't you understand that there is something deep inside every woman that longs for a courageous, steady man she can't intimidate? Nathaniel has my back. He is my foundation. We seem like complete opposites, but we fly together in tandem."

We fly together in tandem. It was how he felt about Marianne. He barely knew her, but their spontaneous attraction was dangerous.

Then again, Luke had always loved flirting with danger.

Marianne struggled with a niggling sense of guilt for agreeing to let Luke accompany her to the DC Jail. Her father had suggested it would be best if she didn't see Luke again, but he hadn't actually forbidden it. She and Luke would visit the prison, take some photographs, then go their separate ways. She would forever remember him fondly. Someday this friendly interlude might even serve as a stepping-stone to lowering tensions between their families.

She arrived at the streetcar stop and leaned her tripod against the bench. The lighting inside the jail would be poor, requiring a longer exposure time and the use of a tripod. She adjusted the sit of her hat, wishing the weather would have let her wear something prettier than this plain knitted cap for warmth.

The streetcar was headed her way, and Luke still wasn't there. She bit her lip. Should she proceed to the jail without him? Perhaps he had reconsidered the risk in seeing her and decided not to come. The streetcar began to slow and she stood, glancing down the avenue in hope of seeing Luke madly running this way, but she couldn't afford to wait another twenty minutes for the next streetcar. She gathered up her camera case and tripod, ready to board.

The streetcar door opened, and Luke was standing in the entrance. "Hello, Marianne."

She smiled in relief, kicking herself for doubting him. "Good afternoon, Luke," she said as she boarded.

She liked saying his name. She liked the gentlemanly way he carried her tripod and found them both a seat near the rear of the streetcar. She especially liked the smile he sent her the moment they were seated. The streetcar set off toward the next stop while she gazed into his eyes. He looked vibrant and lively even though he was three days into the poison experiment.

"How are you feeling?" she asked.

He didn't need any clarification as to what she was driving at. "Okay," he said without much conviction. "I still don't know if I'm in the control group or not."

"Good," she said, because it seemed the polite thing to say. Both groups would surely be fine, but she didn't want to argue about chemical preservatives. "Thank you for taking time away from your work to accompany me today."

"The good thing about my job is that I get to set my own hours," he said, and she realized she had no idea what he did for a living. "I'm a journalist," he explained in response to her question. "I'm in the process of creating a Washington bureau for *Modern Century* magazine."

She wrinkled her nose. "My father hates that magazine." She immediately bit her tongue, regretting bringing Clyde into the conversation, but Luke merely laughed.

"That does not surprise me," he said good-naturedly.

"What kind of magazine is it? *Modern Century* is forbidden reading in our house."

He described the magazine, and she could understand why her father disapproved. It sounded like the kind of rabble-rousing Clyde hated, but she liked the way Luke spoke about Cornelius Newman, the magazine's editor. It almost sounded like he had a hero-worship for the elderly man who had been tackling unpopular causes for decades.

"Cornelius and I both think we need someone in Washington to keep an eye on legislation. That's why I'm opening a Washington bureau." Luke paused, then turned a hesitant glance to her. "Maybe you could take some photographs of the office. We could publish them in the magazine to announce the new bureau."

She shouldn't. Only thirty minutes ago she had vowed that today would be their last meeting, and already she was losing her resolve.

"My father would be annoyed if he found out," she said. "There isn't a lot of forgiveness in the Magruder household. When we were growing up, if my brother or I ran amok, my mother warned us about what happened to poor Aunt Stella."

"And what happened to poor Aunt Stella?"

"She fell in love with the wrong sort of man. It happened before I was born, so I never met her, but she was my father's sister. After she eloped, her name was stricken from the family Bible and she was disinherited."

She told Luke what little she knew from family lore, which claimed Stella moved out west with her unsuitable husband. However, Stella's mother had kept up a secret correspondence with her banished daughter. Marianne only learned of it when she was visiting her grandparents for a week and saw a letter from Stella arrive before her grandmother panicked and hid it away. It had been an ordinary envelope, but it was addressed with purple ink. That purple ink made Marianne's secret admiration for her daring aunt shoot even higher.

"After my grandmother died, no one kept in touch with Stella. I always wondered what happened to her. I know I shouldn't, but a part of me admires her. Leaving everything behind couldn't have been easy, but she was brave. A risk-taker."

The streetcar rounded the bend into a blighted neighborhood

and finally to the grounds of the District of Columbia Jail, built in 1872 and suffering from a bad reputation ever since.

A large, bleak building of red brick sat isolated in a muddy field. During epidemics the field was filled with temporary wooden shanties to house the sick who were too destitute to afford a hospital, but for now it was empty. The entire area seemed like a vast wasteland of despair.

"Here we are," she said in an artificially bright voice.

"So we are," Luke said, holding her hand to help her descend from the streetcar. He carried the tripod as they walked through the slushy field still covered with patches of melting snow. There was nothing pleasant about the assignment before her, and despite her earlier bravado, she was glad for his company.

"Why were you so determined to come with me?" she asked him.

"It could be dangerous," he instantly said.

"All the really dangerous people will be locked up behind bars."

He looked at her with a hint of amusement. "They might get out. Or say something rude to you. I feel compelled to defend your honor."

"And yet you poke fun at your older brother for being overprotective," she answered. "Maybe you take after him."

He briefly considered the statement. "While it would be a compliment, I'm afraid Gray and I are complete opposites. He's the good brother, I'm the bad. It's the roles we were cast in from our first moments on earth."

She didn't know anything good about Gray Delacroix and shouldn't have brought him up. Any discussion of their families was simply too volatile.

Luke held the door for her at the jailhouse entrance. She had no idea what to expect, but the front lobby seemed perfectly normal. There was a sitting area with benches, some potted plants in the corner, and a desk with a male clerk filing some cards. She approached the clerk.

"I'm Marianne Magruder from the Department of the Interior," she said. "I was told to meet Superintendent Castor to take some photographs."

"Yes, we've been expecting you." The clerk disappeared into an office.

Superintendent Castor soon emerged, a small, balding man with thick glasses and a dapper suit. He shook her hand with vigor. "For the past ten years we've had a growing prisoner population and a shrinking budget. The roof is leaking, and the building is falling into disrepair. I've been trying to sound the alarm for years, so maybe some photographs will be more persuasive. This jail is a perfectly horrible place. I would appreciate it if you could document the mold blooms, the leaking roof, and the overcrowded conditions."

He gestured for her to follow him down a hallway. The first sign she was in a jail was when the superintendent needed to unlock the door leading to a hallway. His keys jangled as he twisted the lock open. She and Luke followed the superintendent, and the door clanged shut behind them.

Echoes of male voices bounced off concrete block walls. The dank air in the hallway smelled of wet metal and unwashed bodies. She covered her nose. She'd been prepared for some ugly sights but foolishly hadn't braced herself for the smells or noise.

"One moment while I lock the door to the lobby," Mr. Castor said, turning to secure the door. "This hallway leads to the prisoners on the first floor. The other hall leads to the laundry, the kitchens, and the detention hall, where prisoners are allowed an hour of exercise each day. Follow me, please."

Marianne followed the small man who moved at a startlingly brisk pace. The concrete hallway was painted pale blue. The superintendent told her it was to imitate the sky, but it still looked bleak and unnatural to her.

"There will be prisoners in here taking a walk," Mr. Castor told her as he arrived at the door, preparing to unlock it. "You may photograph the prisoners if you wish, but the most important thing to capture is the corrosion running down the east wall. This is where the damage from the leaking roof is the worst."

She nodded and glanced around for Luke, surprised that he hung several yards back, an unsettled look on his face.

"You go on ahead," Luke said. "I'll wait here."

"Are you okay?" The way he had a hand braced on the wall and was bent over a little made him look sick.

"I'm fine, but I'd rather wait here."

"I'd prefer you come with us," the superintendent said. "I can't have unattended visitors in the building, and I don't have the staff to escort you."

Luke nodded and adjusted his coat as he joined them, but he didn't look happy.

Mr. Castor unlocked the door and waited for them to step inside the cavernous detention hall, where the noise was even worse. Loud and echoey. She jumped a little as the door clanged shut behind her and the bolt shot into place.

These prisoners weren't behind bars. She was actually locked in with them as they walked in circles around the perimeter of the otherwise empty room. Two guards stood in the corner of the room, and they had both batons and pistols on their belts, so she shouldn't be frightened. She glanced at Luke for reassurance, but he looked unnerved too.

"You can see the damaged wall I mentioned," Mr. Castor said, gesturing to the far side of the room. It had a high ceiling, which probably accounted for all the echoey noise. There were no windows on the ground level, but a few near the ceiling let in enough light to take pictures. Barely. The superintendent steered the prisoners to one side of the room so she could have a clear shot of the corrosion.

Everything looked and smelled awful in here. She took shallow breaths while setting up her tripod and screwing the camera into place. She centered the viewfinder on the blooms of white scale and the rust stains trailing down the wall. What a horrible room, and this was where the men came for recreation? Even if she wanted to obey her supervisor's instructions to make the jail look good, it would be impossible. This place was an abomination.

"I keep painting, but it doesn't do much good," the superintendent said. He continued talking about how he wanted a decent security fence so he could let the prisoners outdoors for an hour each day, but the funding never materialized.

She took half a dozen photographs and was about to move the tripod to get a different angle when Luke grabbed her arm.

"Marianne, I've got to get out of here." It was cold, but his face was covered with perspiration. He looked like he was about to throw up.

"Yes, let's go," she said immediately.

She picked up the camera and tripod in one swoop. There would be time to take the photographs later, but something was wrong with Luke, and she urged the superintendent to unlock the door quickly.

As soon as they were out, Luke strode into the hallway, sucking in great gulps of air.

"Is there a washroom he can use?" she asked the superintendent.

Luke shook his head. "I just need to get outside into the fresh air. Please hurry," he urged Superintendent Castor as the older man unlocked the final door to the lobby.

The moment the door was open, Luke bounded through and headed outside. She sent an apologetic look to the superintendent and followed Luke.

He paced in a tight little square on the prison's front stoop, still breathing heavily. Every time she'd seen Luke before, he had been charming and irreverent, but now he looked nervous and sick.

"I'm sorry," he finally said on a shaky breath. "I'm not a big fan of jails."

"Any particular reason?" It was a terribly intrusive question, but he was so agitated, and she desperately wanted to know why.

"Your father didn't tell you?"

"No, he hasn't told me anything about you."

Luke wiped the perspiration from his face and kept pacing—three steps forward, half-pivot, then three steps that way. He did the same pattern several times before speaking.

"I did a stint in jail," he said. "Most of it was in a Cuban jail, but some of it was the American military prison in Havana. I'm surprised your father didn't tell you that I was a traitor and a spy for the Cuban rebels."

It took a while to find her breath, she was so appalled. "Were you?"

He shook his head. "I was spying for the Americans, not the Cubans. The mission took a bad turn, and I ended up in jail, accused of treason."

He pulled her down to sit beside him on the top step and recounted the whole story. He had been sent down to infiltrate a group of Cuban rebels who were being helped by a traitor inside the American military. Luke pretended to be sympathetic to the rebels in order to learn the identity of the turncoat. When he was imprisoned, he couldn't confess the truth without endangering the entire mission. He was put in jail alongside a dozen of the Cuban rebels and eventually managed to win their trust and learn the name of the American traitor.

"How long were you in jail?"

"Fifteen months, in a six-by-ten-foot cell. I got out in September. This is the first time I've been back in any sort of locked facility, and it caught me off guard. The looks and smells are different, but the *clang* of the locks slamming shut is the same. It was unsettling. I wasn't prepared for it."

His hands shook as he spoke. The fact that he had been willing to accompany her into a jail made him even more impressive in her eyes. It was easy to be fearless when a person was ignorant of the danger, but Luke walked back into his personal nightmare to be at her side.

"Look, can you forget everything you just saw?" he asked. "Having an attack of the vapors over a few jarring noises isn't something I'm proud of. Pretend it never happened. I'll be myself again shortly. I'm not a coward."

"I knew that the moment you stepped onto the ice to save Bandit," she said. "Why do you keep pushing yourself into reckless things? The ice. The Poison Squad. Now walking back into a jail."

Luke gazed into the bleak landscape while considering his answer. "I don't know. I've got this churning desire to venture out and conquer. I need to accomplish things. It's what a man does."

I need to accomplish things. His words resonated, because she felt the same way. Her hands tightened around her camera, and she glanced back toward the jail. She found it unpleasant but not truly frightening, and she needed to get those photographs.

Luke must have noticed her glance toward the door. "You go ahead," he said. "I'll wait for you out here."

"Are you sure?"

He sent her a semi-scolding look. "Please don't emasculate me any more than I already have been. Go do your job. I'll be fine."

He managed a smile, so she went, but what had just happened lingered the entire time she moved throughout the jail. The superintendent brought her to see the cells, where men were caged like animals and had an exhausted, hopeless look in their eyes. She asked two men permission to take their photographs, and both agreed. Throughout the afternoon she wondered about Luke's time in jail. Had he looked like these men? Used the same foul facilities and suffered the same sense of helplessness?

Marianne breathed a sigh of relief as she concluded the assignment. Her supervisor wasn't going to be pleased with these pictures, but there was no way she could sugarcoat what she'd just seen. Not after knowing that Luke had been locked up in a similar situation.

He was in a better frame of mind when she rejoined him to ride the streetcar back into the center of town.

"You'll still come to photograph my office?" he asked, a hint of unease back in his face. Maybe he feared she would think less of him for his fit of nerves in the jail, when nothing could be further from the truth.

"Of course," she said lightly, but inside was the growing fear she was stepping into dangerous territory.

Eight

Luke had to sprint the last few blocks to make it to the boardinghouse in time for dinner. The trip to the jail had taken longer than expected due to his humiliating collapse in the detention hall. He'd known visiting a jail might prove difficult and had braced himself for what he might see, but it was the sounds that caught him by surprise. An overwhelming sense of claustrophobia roared to life the moment he heard that dead bolt clang into place. Even now the memory of that noise made him feel ill.

Well. It was best not to think about it.

"What's on the menu, today?" he asked Nurse Hollister as he took his seat between Big Rollins and Nicolo.

"Meatloaf, buttered peas, and mashed potatoes," the nurse said, setting a plate with the measured portions before him. Days of suffering from a slight but persistent headache made him almost certain he was in the test group. The chemicals were either in the meatloaf or the mashed potatoes.

Nicolo must have been thinking the same thing. "Want my potatoes?"

Dr. Wiley's head jerked up. "Everyone is to eat their own meals," he said, even though Nicolo had only been teasing. As far as Luke could tell, no one had been shirking their duties, and in truth, the food didn't taste bad. He tried not to think about it as he lowered his head and said a quick, silent prayer. The men of the Poison Squad were a rowdy bunch, and prayer had never been a part of their routine, but Luke vowed not to take a single meal for granted.

"Who's up for a snowball fight after dinner?" St. Louis asked from the neighboring table.

Half the men in the room raised their hands. They shouted insults at the others for declining. Dr. Wiley insisted they wait half an hour after the meal, lest the roughhousing cause someone to lose their dinner, which provoked another round of boasting about whose stomach was tougher.

This was typical of the evenings Luke had spent in the boardinghouse. Some of the men indulged in sport, others a game of cards, and Nicolo usually challenged people to arm wrestling. For a man of such small stature, he was pure muscle and usually won.

"What about you?" Princeton asked Luke as men began picking sides for the snowball fight. "I could use you on my team."

Normally Luke would have loved to join in, but he had an important meeting in a few hours. "I'll take a pass tonight," he said.

That earned him a cuff on the head from Princeton, but Luke didn't care. The battle he was fighting was far more important than a romp in the snow, and he needed to be in top form for his meeting tonight.

Luke met Dickie Shuster at a crowded tavern near the Marine Hospital. The lighting was dim and the air smoky, but it had booths with high backs so he and Dickie could speak privately. Gray thought he was insane for meeting with Dickie, but Luke knew how the wily journalist for *The Washington Post* operated and intended to use it to his advantage.

"Good heavens, you look ghastly," Dickie said as he arrived at the booth and slid onto the opposite bench. "Almost like you've been moldering in a Cuban prison cell for the past two years."

"What a colorful imagination you have," Luke replied.

Dickie wore a floppy yellow tie embroidered with tiny blue and red hummingbirds. It clashed with his cheerful green vest, but it was all part of the disguise Dickie wore to make him appear to be a harmless gadfly. Friendly, fun, and not to be taken too seriously.

The first two qualities were true; the last was a mistake most people made when dealing with Dickie Shuster, who had tentacles that reached throughout Washington society. Although Dickie had a history of pandering to the Magruders, Luke was confident that the only thing Dickie truly cared about was himself.

"I'm wondering if maybe we should cooperate," Luke said. "No one covers Washington politics the way you can, but I've got better access to the national magazines. I've had three cover stories for *Modern Century*."

"Not lately you haven't," Dickie pointed out.

"I've been otherwise occupied." Those fifteen months in a Cuban prison again. "You and I haven't gotten along in the past," Luke continued. "I'd be willing to give you the inside scoop on an interesting project going on in the Department of Agriculture in exchange for your help with a little research."

Dickie looked intrigued, so Luke slid a piece of paper across the table with five names written on it.

"Tell me what you know about the chances of these congressmen keeping their seats in the November election."

Dickie skimmed the list. If anyone would be able to identify the weaknesses of these congressmen, it was him.

"There are some powerful men here," Dickie said. "Roper and Garza are totally safe in the next election. Magruder and Westheimer are likely to win, but vulnerable. I've heard rumors that the fifth man is about to retire. Somehow I think the only man you really care about on this list is Clyde Magruder."

"I care about them all," Luke said. To see a particular bill passed, he needed all five of these men to lose their next election. But Dickie was right. He cared mostly about Clyde. "What is Magruder's greatest vulnerability?"

"What's the scoop you've promised me over at Ag?" Dickie replied.

"They're conducting a study using human test subjects to identify toxic food additives."

Dickie rolled his eyes. "Old news. It was already blanketed all over the newspapers when they called for volunteers. Dr. Wiley has been closemouthed, so I doubt anything will leak out until the study is over."

"I'm one of the volunteers," Luke said.

Dickie immediately dropped his nonchalant attitude. He straightened his spine, whipped out a pad of paper, and leaned forward. "Tell me more," he purred.

"I can tell you everything. What's on the menu, how people are feeling, how they collect data. For now they line us up each night to take our temperatures and record our symptoms, but soon they'll start drawing blood and taking other samples. You'll be the only man in Washington with that sort of insight. Things will get more interesting as the test progresses."

Already Luke was suffering persistent headaches and achy joints. Maybe it was all in his mind, but he'd know more in a few days. He wouldn't pass the information along for free, though, and nodded to the list of congressmen still on the table.

"In exchange for exclusive insight, you tell me everything you know about Clyde Magruder and anything that makes him vulnerable in the next election."

"My friend, we have a deal," Dickie said. "Now lean in close while I tell you about Clyde's newest addition to the family, an adorable little child named Tommy."

Luke was pensive as he walked back to the boardinghouse, flipping up the collar of his overcoat to ward off the chill. It was hard to know what to do with the troubling gossip Dickie had passed along.

He already knew about the child Clyde had fathered almost two years ago. The mother had been Sam Magruder's nanny, and there had been plenty of nasty rumors at the time. Apparently Clyde himself spread the rumor that the nanny had been fired for theft in hope of his wife never discovering the child. It hadn't worked, and now he was secretly funneling money to support the nanny and her child in their own household.

Luke drew his coat tighter and walked faster, trying to avoid the truth. Marianne adored her father. It was obvious from the way she praised and defended him. It would be difficult to strike at Clyde without hurting her.

There would be time to worry about Clyde and his illegitimate child later. For now, Luke just wanted to get into bed, grab a hot water bottle, and huddle under a mound of warm blankets. It might make his achy body feel better. It was after eleven o'clock by the time he let himself into the boardinghouse.

A pair of oil lamps cast amber illumination in the parlor. Princeton was still awake, lounging on the parlor sofa with his nose in a dime novel. Luke shrugged out of his coat, shook off the snow, and hung it on a hook.

"How are you feeling?" he asked Princeton.

"Lousy. My joints ache."

"Mine too," he replied. "Is the book any good?"

Princeton glanced at the cover. "It's about the adventures of Davy Crockett. I found a whole cache of them in the back room. Want to borrow one? The landlady loans them out for free."

Luke shook his head. He could squeeze in another hour of

working on the *Don Quixote* translation. When it was published, maybe he would screw up the courage to send a copy to Marianne. He started trudging up the stairs, his limbs suddenly unbearably heavy.

"Delacroix?" Princeton called out.

He turned around. "Yeah?"

"Hang in there."

Nine

Marianne brought two entire rolls of film to photograph Luke's office. She had no idea what she'd find, but she planned to take a few more pictures of him. He photographed well. No matter the angle, the planes of his face seemed to reveal sharp intelligence and engagement with the world around him.

She looked about in curiosity as she stepped off the streetcar at the appointed stop, a neighborhood she'd never been to before. Most journalists worked closer to the Capitol, and this street seemed a lot shabbier. Luke worked in a four-story building of old red brick located between a tanning operation and a cigar factory. A board in the office building's cramped entryway showed various rooms for a bookkeeper, several insurance companies, and a cabinetmaker. Luke's nameplate looked brand new, proudly stating *Modern Century, Washington Bureau.*

Well, he should be proud! Maybe it was only a one-man operation now, but she liked that he had the ambition to start something important.

She hurried up the stairs, eager to see him. The building was solidly built, but cracked tiles and faded paint betrayed its age. The rattling of typewriter keys led her to the open doorway of Luke's office.

He was bent over a typewriter, pecking at the keys with

amazing speed. She took a moment simply to admire him. A lock of dark hair spilled across his forehead, and his open collar exposed the strong column of his neck. His face was tight with concentration as his fingers flew over the keys.

"You can type?"

He pulled away from the typewriter and stood, his smile wide. "Welcome to *Modern Century*." He skirted the typewriter table, banging into a wastebasket in his eagerness to close the space between them. He clasped both her hands in his. The warmth was heaven on her icy fingers, and she let herself savor the fleeting intimacy before pulling away. They shouldn't be so familiar with each other.

"What a nice office," she said, admiring the spacious room and the two windows that flooded the area with light.

"I hope to expand soon," he said. "Government business is too big for one man to cover, so I picked an office with plenty of room to grow. Come, sit." He tugged a chair out from the conference table for her.

"I shouldn't. I just came to take a few photographs." Though she desperately wanted to know if he'd recovered from his queasiness in the jail, it was time to start stepping away from this magnetic attraction that flared to life every time they were within sight of each other. She set the camera case on the table and began unbuckling the straps. "Give me a tour so I can photograph the important things. I've already seen that you type your own stories. Very impressive, by the way. What else should I know?"

He nodded to the bookshelves beneath the windows. "These reference manuals cover all the committees in Congress," he said. "Did you know Congress publishes a list of all the bills moving through the legislative process? It's a literal blizzard of paperwork, and only a fraction of the proposals survive the winnowing process, but that's what I'm tracking in each of these binders."

He opened one so she could see. The form inside was about compensation for the government inspection of railways. She turned the page, and then another. Altogether there were five pages on that single topic. "You actually read all this?"

He sat on the table and propped his feet on a chair, looking ridiculously comfortable in his one-man office. "I have to. It's the only way to track what's going on in Congress."

It was hard to imagine a dynamo like Luke paging through these mind-numbing binders. She wandered the perimeter of the office, noting the schedule of upcoming congressional votes tacked to a bulletin board.

Then her heart seized. Her father's name leapt out from a list tacked on the board. "What's this?"

He followed her gaze, but his expression didn't change. "It's nothing."

"Nonsense. You have this list of men tacked up here for a reason. Who are they?"

"They're men who are blocking a bill I am interested in," he said. He remained sitting on the worktable, his arms casually balanced on his knees, but his mood had gone serious. He watched her like a cat stalking its prey.

"What sort of bill?" she asked.

"Let's not talk about politics," he said. "The reason I have those names up there is only about a bill. It's not a personal vendetta."

She prepared her camera and took a few photographs, but that list nagged at the edges of her mind the entire time. It was surely no coincidence that Luke had taken interest in something her father was involved in, and it probably didn't bode well. What a shame that when she finally met a man who captured her imagination, he turned out to be a Delacroix.

"I wish you weren't a Delacroix and I wasn't a Magruder," she finally said. "I wonder what things could be like between us if our names were Smith and Jones."

A poignant smile flashed across his face. "I think it would mean afternoons basking in the sunlight together. Maybe a few moonlit strolls along the Potomac."

"Having someone to help me in the darkroom."

"Having a best friend," Luke said. "A port in a storm. A person to laugh and flirt with. To hold and kiss and comfort."

He'd said exactly what she was feeling. She wanted those things so badly it ached.

She wandered over to stand beside him at the table, laying a hand on his arm. "But our names are not Smith and Jones."

"They could be." He shifted to clasp both her hands. "We could run away to San Francisco and start our lives over. No past, no future, only the present."

Now he was being silly, but it was a fun sort of silliness, and she wasn't ready to return to reality yet. She balanced her hip on the table beside him. "What would we do in San Francisco?"

"We could start our own newspaper, and you could take the photographs. We could watch the sun set over the Pacific, eat the fish we caught ourselves, dance in the moonlight. We could live in a little garret apartment."

"A garret?"

He grinned. "That's where all the starving artists and love-struck poets live. It's an essential part of the fantasy."

"All right, we've found ourselves the perfect garret," she said. "What then?"

"We would have complete freedom to live life as we choose."

How she would love to step into his fantasy, but it could never be. "We could live that way until you started feeling guilty about abandoning *Modern Century*. And I would torture myself, worrying about my mother and if she was holding her own against my father."

He cupped the side of her face with his hand, and she leaned into it. She ought to be offended by the intimacy, but she savored it for a moment longer, since this was likely as close as they would ever be.

"Come to church with me tomorrow morning," he said.

She pulled away from his hand in surprise. "You're a churchgoer?" If he'd told her he was a polka dancer, she could not have been more surprised.

"Every Sunday, plus prayers on my knees each evening before bed." His eyes danced as he said it, but she sensed he was telling the truth.

"Have you always been this devout?" she asked curiously.

He shook his head. "I didn't see the light until I was locked up in a Cuban jail. There was a Bible in my cell, and I read it cover to cover half a dozen times. There wasn't much else to do. That time was brutal, but I thank God for it now. It forced me to take a good look at my life, and I didn't like what I saw. I wanted to become a better man."

"All from reading the Bible?" She didn't want to be disrespectful, but the Bible had always seemed a weighty, convoluted book. She couldn't imagine a daredevil like Luke becoming sucked in to it.

The humor drained from him, replaced by a serious, inscrutable look. "The Bible helped, but it was more than that," he finally said. "It took a while for the words to sink in, but when they did, I felt the enveloping love of God, even in that stinking jail cell. I accepted that even a miserable rat like me was unconditionally forgiven if only I would open my heart to salvation. For the first time in my life, I experienced the love of God, but I also felt the fist of God, the crushing sense that I had squandered so much of my life. I needed to tame the wildness inside and turn it toward the good. And then there was a third feeling, a powerful mystic force surrounding me even in the darkest nights when I felt alone and abandoned. I knew there was a God, and I wanted to escape back out into the world where I could shout the good news from the mountaintops.

So how about it, Marianne? Would you like to come to church with me tomorrow?"

She pulled away. With each new facet of his personality, Luke grew in complexity and fascination. He was like a lodestone drawing her into dangerous territory, and this was moving too fast. For one thing, she couldn't trust him.

"Tell me the reason you have those five men pinned to your bulletin board, and I'll consider it."

The gleam in Luke's eyes faded. He sighed and looked away before he spoke. "It's just politics, Marianne. Don't go making it bigger than it needs to be."

"My father's name is on that list. I can't help it." She buckled her camera back into its case. Coming here was a mistake. No matter how much fun it was toying with the idea of running off to San Francisco to live like bohemian artists, she endangered her relationship with her father each time she saw Luke.

Clyde had taken her in as an infant even though it rocked the boat with her mother. He had loved and supported her for all these years, but she wasn't so naive as to think his love was unconditional. He had banished his own sister from the family after Aunt Stella fell in love with an unsuitable man, and Marianne couldn't be certain it wouldn't happen to her as well. She owed her father everything, including her loyalty.

She walked to the list on the bulletin board and unpinned it, holding it up to Luke's face. "Why is my father's name on this list?"

He kept his eyes locked on her and said only a single word. "Politics."

It was time for her to leave. If she had to choose between her father and Luke, her father won every time, but her heart still felt heavy as she set the list down and retrieved the camera.

"I'll send you copies of the photographs and the negatives within a week," she said. "Feel free to use them as you like."

She left the office without a backward glance.

It was Friday, which meant Luke would be able to find Marianne at the darkroom. He needed to apologize for being so curt when she visited his office. Their families didn't get along, but that didn't mean they couldn't.

He shared the washroom sink with Princeton while they shaved, carefully drawing the razor along his jaw. It didn't matter that he felt crummy from food tainted with chemicals. He was going to see Marianne and wanted to look sharp.

He arrived an hour ahead of her regular appointment at the photography studio, and the moment the darkroom was vacant, he slipped inside to wait and surprise her.

Trouble started the moment he closed the door. It was suffocating in here. Small, cramped, and tight. He stepped to the window to yank the heavy drape aside. Light filled the room, and he breathed a sigh of relief as the panic began to fade. He turned the lever on the window to crank it open and let cold air pour into the room. He held on to the lever, willing the last of the panic to drain away.

Strange. This crawling sensation of dread hadn't happened the first time he'd been in this room; it only started after his visit to the jail.

He wouldn't let it get the better of him. He needed to see Marianne but couldn't knock on Clyde Magruder's front door and ask permission. A darkroom was the ideal place to sneak a visit, and he wouldn't let these perplexing anxieties stand in his way.

It took several minutes for his heart to resume its normal rate, but he got there. He was still standing beside the open window when the door opened and Marianne entered. She was bundled up, and her cheeks were flushed with the winter's chill, and in her arms she carried a large satchel with her supplies.

"What are you doing here?" She looked surprised and pleased

and impossibly pretty. Had he ever seen eyes that blue? They reminded him of the violet shade of forget-me-nots, which had always been his favorite flower.

"I was short-tempered in my office the other day and needed to see you again and apologize. I was in a lousy mood, but that wasn't your fault. Here, let me help you with those." He took the bulky satchel from her arms.

"Not to worry," she said. "It's freezing in here. Why is the window open?"

He set the satchel down, then cranked the window shut. "The stink of silver nitrate was pretty strong when I got here."

He was glad she didn't continue to push, and even happier when she invited him to stay and help develop pictures. It was as if their momentary tiff in his office never happened as he set out the bathing trays in the same pattern she used last time. He watched as she poured the chemicals and began developing the first roll of film. He braced himself for the moment she pulled the drapes closed and plunged the room into darkness, but the panic only tugged at his nerves without overwhelming him. She turned on the arc lamp, and if she noticed his unease, she made no comment.

"How is the *Don Quixote* translation coming?" she asked.

"It still needs work. I'm not sure how long it will take." His headaches in the evenings led to eye strain, but someday he'd be off the Poison Squad and would be able to make more progress.

"Can I read it?"

He straightened. "I don't know. I already warned you it's turning into an overblown torrent of emotionalism."

She turned around and propped a hand on her hip. Even in the dim orange-hued light, she looked amused. "Are you afraid to let me read it?"

"Terrified." How easily she could see through him. He'd rather risk his neck out on the ice than show her that manuscript and lay bare his overly emotional heart. What the college professors thought of his translation couldn't hurt him. What Marianne thought could. "I've put a lot of heart into it, but it's not a traditional translation and will probably ruffle some feathers."

"Then why are you doing it?" Her back was to him as she worked. How delicate her fingers looked as she lifted, tipped, and rinsed the developing photograph, but at the same time she had her ear turned to let him know she was listening to every word.

He chose them carefully. "It's as if I don't feel worthy if I'm not aiming for something big."

"Have you ever failed?"

He had to stifle a laugh at the question. "Over and over," he admitted.

He was a failure in his father's eyes before he was even out of short pants. Gray was a hard act to follow, and his father constantly pointed out his shortcomings compared to his older brother's brilliance. Luke didn't want to rehash his many shortcomings to her. And yet . . . why not? He wanted her to truly know him, so he told her.

"I got expelled from college a semester shy of graduation," he said. "All over a silly prank. Then I helped a friend out by poking around in Cuba, looking for traitors. You know how that one ended."

"But they caught the bad guys in the end."

"Not before I put my family through fifteen months of misery." To top it off, he couldn't even walk into an enclosed space without getting the vapors, another failure to add to his list.

"And now the Poison Squad," Marianne added.

"Yes, now the Poison Squad." Even saying the name made his joints ache worse.

Marianne clipped another photograph to the clothesline and turned to face him. "When will it be enough? Why do you keep tilting at windmills?"

Since she didn't seem inclined to develop the next picture, he would do it. He carefully lifted one of her freshly prepared enlargements and lowered it into the tray of chemical solution. Somehow it was easier to talk about painful things while part of his mind was occupied elsewhere.

"My father lost everything in the Civil War," he said. "His home was burned down to its foundations, his wife died, his fleet of merchant ships was seized, and his savings were rendered worthless through inflation. Gray was five at the end of the war, so he lived through those years restoring our business from scratch. By the time my father remarried and I came along, I was born into the lap of luxury. Success in business was the only thing my father admired, and I was never good at it."

Luke had tried a few times to join his father and Gray in business meetings, but none of it made much sense to him. How could he concentrate on international tariffs or production schedules when there was a sailboat race calling his name? Or a curfew to break? A pretty girl to court?

All those amusements had been fun, but the problem with amusement was that the moment it was over, it no longer sustained him. A few years ago, he learned that it was in doing the hard things that he found the most sustenance. The countless hours spent translating a three-hundred-year-old manuscript weren't particularly fun, but he was proud of it. Nothing about those months sweltering in a Cuban jail had been fun, but he would forever be proud of enduring the deprivation that led to rooting out corruption in the military.

Marianne took pride in hard work too. Born into one of the richest families in America, she didn't have to work, and yet she did. For the hundredth time he wished her last name was not Magruder. He moved to stand behind her. She was facing away from him, but he set his hands on her shoulders.

"I wish we were in San Francisco right now . . . Miss Jones."

She leaned back against him, laying her head on his shoulder. "What would we do in San Francisco, Mr. Smith?"

He held his breath, wanting her so badly he ached. "I would build you a house with my own two hands," he whispered against the side of her cheek. "I'd carry you across the threshold, and we could be Mr. and Mrs. Smith, two people who risked everything to be together."

He couldn't resist the temptation and pressed a kiss to the side of her neck.

"Turn around," he said quietly, and she did. The amber light from the lamp was almost like candlelight, softly illuminating the side of her face in the dim room. He lowered his head and kissed her properly.

Then he kissed her improperly, and she twined her arms around his neck. He might regret this, but everything about cradling Marianne Magruder in his arms and kissing her as if there was no tomorrow felt completely right.

Ten

The scorching kiss in the darkroom stayed with Marianne the rest of the day and all through the night. Was this what it felt like to fall in love? The most amazing thing was that Luke seemed to be falling right alongside her with no fear, only that joyous sense of excitement.

But Marianne was afraid. She wasn't a risk-taker. She only wanted a normal peaceful family with no bellowing voices or vases hurled through the air. If she threw her lot in with Luke, she would probably have to become like Aunt Stella, and that wasn't a possibility. Her dream of a perfect family included her parents, and that would never change.

By breakfast the forbidden joy of Luke's kiss still lingered with her. Even the fact that her brother was visiting couldn't dampen her mood.

"Andrew, would you like another slice of strudel?" Vera asked from the head of the breakfast table. "I know it's your favorite, and I brought home two from the bakery especially for you and Sam."

But mainly for Andrew, Marianne thought as she sprinkled salt on her scrambled eggs. Her brother and nephew visited Washington at least once a month. Andrew's wife rarely came, because everyone knew that Delia didn't get along with Vera.

The way Vera hovered over Andrew annoyed her sister-in-law, and Marianne was glad not to put up with Delia's disapproving presence.

From the opposite end of the table, her father was lording over the gathering. "There will be a vote on shipping tariffs this afternoon. Would you like to see your grandfather vote on that?" he asked Sam, and Marianne held her breath, hoping the nine-year-old would eagerly agree. Clyde was justifiably proud of his position in Congress and wanted his grandson to witness him in action.

"What's a shipping tariff?" Sam asked.

"It's when the government makes other countries pay a fee to sell their goods in the United States," Clyde explained. "Tariffs are good. They protect our business, so you can come and watch me fight for the good of Magruder Food. Won't that be fun?"

Sam looked to his father for how to respond. "Um, yes?" he said uncertainly.

The lack of enthusiasm didn't sit well with Clyde, who grabbed a copy of *The Washington Post* and snapped it open. "You need to start educating your boy about the world around him," he said to Andrew.

"That's not fair," Vera rushed to say. "Andrew is a wonderful father. Just look at how often he brings Sam to Washington to teach him about the ways of the nation."

It was more likely that Andrew visited because he was still struggling at managing the company. Andrew had taken over Magruder Food when Clyde began serving in Congress, and he still needed plenty of advice.

Vera listed all of Andrew's wonderful achievements, but her father was completely absorbed in the newspaper. His entire body went stiff, and his eyes narrowed in an expression that always frightened her as a child. Something in the newspaper had made him angry, and she was glad it wasn't her.

Then he lowered the paper and skewered her with a piercing

glare across the breakfast table. "Marianne," he said carefully, "didn't you tell me that you took the official photographs of the men volunteering for that pointless study at the Department of Agriculture?"

Her fingers froze. "I did."

Without a word, Clyde folded the newspaper into quarters, then flung it across the table at her. It landed on top of her scrambled eggs with a *splat*. She carefully lifted the newspaper and saw the photograph of the Poison Squad lined up in the parlor of their boardinghouse.

Her mouth went dry, for there in the front row was Luke Delacroix, crouching on one knee. He wasn't smiling, but his eyes were still laughing as he looked directly into the camera. The headline jumped out at her:

Daring Team of Men Taunt Fate as They Join the Poison Squad

She set down the newspaper. "Yes, I took that photograph," she admitted, then casually took a bite of eggs even though they tasted like sawdust.

"I forbid you to see that man again," her father warned.

"I didn't know he would be there," she said truthfully. "I couldn't have turned around and walked out."

"Have you seen him on any other occasions?" Clyde demanded, his face pure flint.

Marianne glanced away, fearful her father would see too much on her face. She'd seen Luke often enough to start falling in love, and she was terrible at disguising her feelings.

"A few times," she admitted.

"What man?" Vera demanded. "Is Marianne seeing a man and didn't tell me?"

Andrew grabbed the newspaper, shaking off a few bits of egg and reading the article. His eyes quickly skimmed the text, and he began reading aloud from the story.

"'A sign printed by the men hangs over the dining room entrance, reading "Only the Brave Dare Eat the Fare." The men joke and tease during the meals, speculating about where the poison is hidden.'" Andrew glanced at her over the rim of the paper. "And you have something to do with this nonsense?"

"I only took a photograph for documentation," she said. "I have nothing at all to do with that experiment."

"Good, because it's pointless," Andrew snapped. "Food preservatives are perfectly safe, and these men are stirring up paranoia for no good reason. Listen to this nonsense." He picked up the newspaper and began reading again. "'*The men jest about whose stomach is stronger. They claim the coffee cake was dusted with brown sugar, cinnamon, and a heaping spoonful of Rough on Rats.*'"

Sam giggled at the name of the popular household rodent killer. "They eat rat poison?" he asked in excited wonder.

"Don't be silly," Marianne rushed to say. "The food is preserved with a bit of borax and formaldehyde, just like your daddy uses in our factory."

"I want to try it," Sam said.

"Marianne, who is this man your father is annoyed about?" Vera asked.

She risked a glance at Clyde, who clenched his fork as he smoldered at her from across the table. He nodded for her to answer.

"His name is Luke Delacroix," she said. "He's a—"

"I know who he is!" Vera cut her off. "Why on earth are you consorting with him?"

"I haven't consorted with him! I was asked by my supervisor to take a photograph of the group, and he happened to be on the team." This was exactly what she had feared. Why couldn't she come from a normal family where she didn't have to walk on eggshells or worry about lifelong feuds? She dared not mention the passionate kiss she had shared with Luke in the darkroom, but it might slip out that she'd also taken photographs of his office, and it would be best if she confessed that now. "I also took a few pictures of his office as a courtesy," she said without meeting anyone's eyes.

"I trust there will be no more such photographs," Clyde stated.

"I'm supposed to take another set of the Poison Squad one month into the experiment. That will be next week at the beginning of March."

"You will tell your supervisor that you are unable to take those photographs." Clyde's voice was implacable. "I want you to look me in the eye and promise me that you will do so."

Her mouth went dry. Aunt Stella had been banished from the family for consorting with an unsuitable man. She didn't *think* it could happen to her, but she couldn't risk her entire world over a flirtation, no matter how charming the man.

"Yes, of course," she said.

"I've been very lenient with you," Clyde continued. "You traipse around town at all hours, and I've permitted it because I have faith that you are a sensible young lady. If my trust falters, you could be on the next train to Baltimore to live with Andrew and Delia."

"Come live with us!" Sam said, still completely oblivious to the tension crackling in the air. Marianne would rather live in the North Pole before subjecting herself to life in Andrew and Delia's household.

In the end, it turned out Marianne didn't need to ask her supervisor to be taken off the Poison Squad assignment. That night as she brushed her hair, preparing to braid it before going to bed, a soft tapping came at her door.

"Come in."

Her father opened the door, his face ice cold. "I've called Mr. Schmidt and told him you will be unable to take any more photographs of the Poison Squad."

"Yes, sir." She wasn't usually so formal, but Clyde was still fuming.

"And if you ever see that man again, you are to report it to me."

The door closed behind him with a gentle click, which somehow frightened her more than if he'd slammed it.

Eleven

A sense of elation still lingered as Luke awoke the following morning. The blazing kiss he'd shared with Marianne was probably enough to keep him fueled for weeks, and he set off for the office the moment he finished breakfast.

He hadn't gotten two steps out the front door when he noticed a cluster of onlookers gathered outside the boardinghouse.

"Are you one of the volunteers?" a young man in a postal uniform asked. He looked barely old enough to shave and had a hopeful, eager expression.

"I am," Luke acknowledged.

The young man thrust a section of the newspaper toward him. "Will you sign the photograph? I already got the autographs of the two brothers and a little Italian guy. I want to get all twelve autographs."

Luke glanced at the newspaper folded to the article about the Poison Squad. He took the pencil and signed his name beside his picture, and then two more people rose off a nearby bench to approach him. One lady also wanted his autograph on her newspaper, while a man with a thick mustache had a Brownie camera and wanted to take his picture.

Princeton and St. Louis must have heard the commotion, because they were soon on the landing too, signing autographs and posing for pictures.

"What's it like?" the postal worker asked. "Are you sick all the time? Or only when you eat?"

"Say, can I sign up?" the mustached man asked. "I think it sounds like a cracking-good adventure."

A man with a notebook pushed through the crowd. "Brian Musgrove from the *New York Times,*" he introduced himself. "Can we arrange an interview?"

Luke glanced around the crowd of people in amazement. This sort of publicity hadn't been his intention when he spoke with Dickie. The story was supposed to influence legislation, not make celebrities of the volunteers, but it looked like that was happening. Princeton smiled broadly as he posed for a picture before the front door of the boardinghouse, and St. Louis was setting up a meeting with the journalist for an interview.

Luke shrugged and slipped away. It couldn't do any harm, and if it drew the public's attention to adulterated food, so much the better. He saw no need to linger and indulge the public's curiosity. He was due to meet Dickie this morning to make headway on getting those five men knocked out of Congress.

He walked faster, but it made his knees and ankles hurt. All his joints hurt these days, but he wouldn't let it slow him down. Clyde Magruder was cementing his power in Washington by the day, and Luke couldn't afford the luxury of waiting until the illness passed before beginning his campaign to undermine Clyde's reelection.

His office building was old, but it had excellent gas heating, and the warmth felt good on his achy joints as he stepped inside and climbed the three flights to his top-floor office.

Something was wrong. The door was ajar, and he was certain he had locked it last night. He approached cautiously. Could the janitor have forgotten to close the door?

He pushed the door open and gasped.

The bookshelves had been tipped over and the binders strewn across the floor. His desk had been overturned and every drawer from the file cabinet pulled out and its contents dumped. Scattered papers littered the floor, and it looked like someone had taken a hammer to the typewriter. The cover plate had been pried off and the keys bashed to pieces.

He laid his hand over the mangled keyboard and closed his eyes against the pain blooming in his chest. This hurt more than anything else. Over the years he had typed a lot of good work on this trusty old typewriter. Seeing it abused like this hurt. It was silly to get sentimental over a piece of metal, but this typewriter was almost like a partner. It had been with him from the beginning of his career and whenever he poured out his heart onto a piece of paper.

The *Don Quixote* manuscript!

Dread filled him as he darted to his overturned desk and tugged on the bottom drawer. He almost fainted with relief when the steel lock held, meaning they hadn't gotten to his manuscript. It looked like they tried to smash the lock but failed, so his only copy of the translation was safe.

He glanced up at the bulletin board, still anchored to the wall. His list of five men was missing. Little surprise. Clyde Magruder was surely behind this.

Luke's shoulders ached as he peeled off his overcoat and hung it on the hook beside the door. It didn't take long to get the bookshelves upright and stack the manuals in order, but he wouldn't be able to get the desk up without help. He began putting his files back together, but it was going to take hours to restore this place to order.

"It looks like a tornado came through here." Dickie Shuster stood in the open doorway, staring at the mess in appalled wonder. "Who did it?"

"Who do you think?"

"I think there's still no love lost between the Delacroixs and the Magruders."

Luke stacked another batch of files together. He didn't want

Dickie's roving eye looking at the various projects he had in progress, but he wanted to get down to business immediately.

"What have you learned about the five congressmen?" he asked.

Dickie tossed a small packet of pages onto the table. "That's all I've got and all you're going to get. My editor has pulled the plug on any future stories about the Poison Squad."

Luke looked up in surprise. "Why? It's generating a huge amount of publicity. People were lined up outside the boardinghouse for more autographs only this morning."

"It also generated threat of a lawsuit from the Food and Spice Association. They claim there's no proof the chemicals are unsafe, and by branding the experiment as the Poison Squad, you are slandering the entire packaged food industry. They want a moratorium on any future articles until the results of the study are in."

"That will take years."

Dickie shrugged. "Then it takes years. I'm not going to risk my job over this, and the *Post* won't publish anything more for fear of a lawsuit."

"I don't like private organizations dictating what journalists are allowed to print." Nevertheless, he began skimming the pages Dickie had brought him. One was a newspaper article suggesting financial irregularities regarding Congressman Roper. Another was news of a promising young challenger in Congressman Westheimer's district.

It was the last item that was the most confusing. It was an old handbill from a traveling opera company. Luke looked at Dickie in confusion, but it must mean something, for Dickie had the scheming, delighted look of a man sitting on a big secret.

"That opera featured Miss Roxanne Armond. She was briefly Clyde Magruder's mistress."

Luke quirked a brow, but the date on the handbill was more than twenty years old, and although it could be damaging, it wasn't likely to knock him out of Congress. "Yesterday's news," he said dismissively.

"Not really," Dickie said smugly. "Miss Armond bore Mr. Magruder a child twenty-six years ago. And that illegitimate child still lives with him to this day, having been successfully passed off as Vera Magruder's only daughter."

Luke's mind reeled. This sort of gossip would be a broadside that could tarnish Clyde forever. "Does she know?"

"Who?"

"The illegitimate child." He didn't like referring to Marianne like that, but he couldn't let Dickie know of his friendship with her. It was too dangerous. Dickie was the sort who could use it as ammunition against him someday.

"I have no idea. All I know is that I have more than delivered on the deal we struck." He stood and took another glance around his catastrophe of an office. "Such a shame about the mess. Clyde certainly has a flair for drama."

Luke sighed as Dickie left, and then got back to work repairing the space. He could speak with the landlord about putting an additional lock on the door, but there wasn't much to stop Clyde from launching more attacks against him.

His day got worse with the delivery of the afternoon mail. There was only a single large envelope with no return address. He opened it with curiosity, and his heart began to pound as he pulled out a photograph of himself holding that dog only moments after getting out of the ice.

There was a note from Marianne.

Luke,

You won't be hearing from me again, as things have gotten difficult at home. I will forever treasure the time we had together and wish you only the best.

Marianne

The note was more than just a blow, it flat-out clobbered him. He studied the photograph. His hair was sopping wet and his skin was still damp, but his face was alive with exuberance. His happiness at that moment wasn't from saving a dog, it was because he'd been gazing at Marianne, a woman he was already half in love with when she snapped this picture of him.

Worry penetrated his fog of disappointment. Clyde had obviously discovered their clandestine meetings, and this explained the ransacking of his office. It probably hadn't been any easier on Marianne.

"Oh, Marianne," he whispered into the quiet of the office. She had made her choice, and Clyde Magruder had won. Luke would honor her request to keep his distance, but this hurt.

His head sagged. He'd lived through worse. He could probably put this behind him someday.

Probably.

He prayed Marianne could repair whatever damage she was facing with her father, or else she was destined to follow in her Aunt Stella's footsteps, and that would wound her forever.

Luke was still dispirited when he sat down to dinner. The plate before him contained baked chicken, au gratin potatoes, and green beans. It smelled good, but he wished he could throw the potatoes out the window, because that was surely the only logical place to infuse a tablespoon of chemicals.

"*Bon appétit*," Nurse Hollister said with good cheer as she delivered their meals, but Dr. Wiley looked darkly ominous as he followed her into the dining room.

"I've heard there have been a number of visitors prowling around the house, asking for information and even autographs," he said. "I want it understood that this sort of publicity is not welcome, and I want it stopped immediately."

"We can't help it," Nicolo said. "They love us."

"It is going to stop immediately," Dr. Wiley said. "None of you joined this assignment for the glory. It is a controlled experiment for the good of science. The editor of the newspaper in question has agreed he won't publish any additional reports until the study is concluded. I want this to be the last time I have to issue this warning."

There was plenty of grumbling, but even though no one actually agreed to anything, Dr. Wiley must have assumed he'd made his point, as he retreated behind the swinging door leading to the kitchen.

"It seems wrong to deny my adoring public access to my autograph," St. Louis said.

"Your adoring public is nothing compared to mine," Nicolo said in his florid Italian accent. "Half of the female clerks at the Census Bureau wanted my autograph. They all marveled at my bravery. I got cramps in my hand signing all those newspapers."

Luke felt too ill to participate in the conversation as he cut into his chicken. Besides, the less attention he drew to himself, the better, because he wasn't going to let press attention fade away.

Clyde Magruder might have frightened off the editor of *The Washington Post*, but from now on *Modern Century* would be getting exclusive stories with all the details. His editor had never been afraid of a lawsuit, and Luke would keep publishing those articles for as long as he was a part of this study. He'd never told Dr. Wiley the name of the journal he worked for, which meant he could get away with publishing his articles anonymously.

Before the ransacking of his office, Luke had been motivated by science. Now he was motivated by the need to take Clyde Magruder down.

It was time for Andrew and Sam to return to Baltimore, and Marianne accompanied them to the train station. She'd been trying all week to have a private conversation with her brother, but it seemed her mother or Sam was always hovering nearby. There was no privacy in the bustling Baltimore and Potomac Railroad Station, but it would have to do. They still had twenty minutes before their train boarded, and she steered Andrew toward a bench on the far side of the waiting area.

"Why don't you take Bandit for a walk?" she suggested to Sam. The last thing she wanted was a nine-year-old to overhear this conversation. "You'll be cooped up on the train for a while, so let him walk off some energy now."

"Don't go too far," Andrew warned as Sam headed toward the row of newsstands and vendors selling treats to the passengers.

Marianne pinched the tips of her fingers to wiggle off the tight gloves as she searched for the most delicate way to phrase her question, but there was no dignified way to ask if their father was still being unfaithful with Lottie O'Grady.

"Do you think Papa's visits to see Tommy are entirely innocent?"

Andrew's expression grew stormy. "They'd better be."

"Do you have any reason to suspect otherwise?"

Andrew shifted on the bench and folded his arms. "I don't go with him on the visits. I have no desire to see that woman or the child."

His bitterness was blatant. Lottie O'Grady had been Sam's nanny. It was impossible to know when her affair with Clyde began, but Sam was six when it became obvious the nanny was carrying a child. Clyde did some fancy footwork to move Lottie into her own town house before the baby was born. Vera found out anyway and left Clyde for six months. She lived with Andrew and Delia before Clyde succeeded in winning her back with lavish apologies and vows of eternal fidelity.

But Clyde's visits to Lottie still rankled both Andrew and her mother. Marianne could understand Andrew's disdain for Lottie, but the child was innocent.

"Aren't you at least curious about Tommy?" she asked.

"No. I witnessed six months of Mother's agony when she lived with us after it happened. I wish Dad would wash his hands of both Lottie and the child. It's the least he could do for Mother. There's no reason a lawyer can't simply write the woman a monthly check and be done with it."

It was impossible to share his sentiments. Marianne was grateful down to the marrow of her bones that Clyde hadn't abandoned her. She had been given the gift of two loving parents and a stable household. That wouldn't have happened had she been raised by the opera singer who was paid to turn her over to Clyde, then made no attempt to contact her again.

"I wouldn't mind meeting him," she said quietly.

It was the wrong thing to say. Andrew whirled on the bench and shook his finger in her face. "Don't you dare," he said vehemently. "It would kill Mother. She's been through enough, and you can't repay her generosity by extending an olive branch to the O'Gradys. Mother did more than enough when she took you in twenty-six years ago."

"Shh!" she warned. "Sam might overhear."

The boy was loping toward them with Bandit at his heels. "Can I have a nickel for a pretzel?" he asked Andrew. "Bandit wants one too, so that means two nickels."

Andrew scrounged in his vest pocket and produced the coins, then waved Sam away. His voice was calmer when he turned back to her. "I'm sorry for speaking bluntly of things better left in the past, but my loyalty will always be to Mother. I've told Dad that if I catch him being unfaithful again, I'll quit working for the company."

"You would really do that?" she asked in surprise.

"I would." His face was somber as he watched Sam buy two enormous pretzels. "Managing the company is harder than I expected. It seems like every day new problems crop up."

"But you enjoy the work, don't you?"

He shrugged. "It's not like I get to spend my days taking pretty pictures. It's one headache after another."

She ignored the swipe. Andrew had never approved of her job, and surely his work was more stressful than hers.

"Do you remember that article in the newspaper a few days ago?" she asked. "The one that Papa got so angry about?"

"I remember."

"Is there any truth to the notion that the chemicals we use are unsafe?"

"It would be worse if we didn't use them," he replied. "We put a tiny bit of preservatives into canned foods that could sit on store shelves for months. Just this year I spent a fortune commissioning tests that *prove* our preservatives are safe."

"You did?" she asked hopefully. "I thought you said tests like that were too expensive."

Andrew gave an embarrassed laugh. "Let me clarify. The committee Dad works on paid for the tests. They hired a bunch of college laboratories to buy hundreds of rabbits and run the experiments."

"And what did the tests show?"

He shrugged. "They won't be finished for a few months. Look, our food is perfectly safe, and you need to keep away from that Poison Squad nonsense that uses human test subjects. I've never seen Dad so annoyed as when he spotted that article in the newspaper."

Andrew consulted his watch and called for Sam to return. Their train had just pulled into the station, but before boarding, Andrew turned to her.

"Don't make Dad angry," he said. "I may be in charge of the company, but he's still in charge of the family. You don't want to end up like Aunt Stella."

Andrew snapped his fingers to summon Sam, then boarded the train without even saying good-bye.

The strangest thing happened when Luke went shopping for a new typewriter. He went to a department store to try out all three models on display. He fed a piece of paper beneath the roller of the first typewriter and twisted the knob to position it, then began banging out text until he heard the satisfying *ding* at the end of the line. He pushed the carriage return lever and commenced another line.

He tried all three machines. Price was no object. A typewriter was going to be the single most important tool he'd use to start changing the world. All three machines were perfectly fine, and he could buy one, walk out of the shop, and be back in business within an hour.

Except he couldn't do it.

It was irrational to mourn a broken piece of equipment, but he did. He'd had that machine for more than a decade. He took it to college with him and wrote his first published article on it. He wrote his translation of *Don Quixote* on it. That old, mangled typewriter was an inanimate object beyond repair, and he shouldn't feel disloyal for buying a replacement.

The salesman came over to check on him. "Well, sir? Will one of these suffice?"

This embarrassing surge of sentimentality for his old typewriter was ridiculous, and he needed to get over it.

But not quite yet. Gray had a typewriter he could borrow for a while.

He pulled the paper-release bar and lifted the practice page from the machine. "I'll be back in a few days," he told the salesman. Maybe then he'd have his head screwed on firmly enough to quit worrying about the feelings of a broken typewriter.

And a cheerful, high-spirited girl who took a picture of him with a dog.

He wallowed in the memories the entire journey to the Delacroix Global Spice factory. He might fall for another woman someday, but it would be impossible to forget Marianne. She crawled out onto the ice! Onto the Capitol dome! She was brave enough to walk into a jail but tenderly compassionate when he hightailed it out of there like a weakling. Normally he considered his overblown emotionalism an asset, but today it just made him ache.

A heady wall of aroma hit Luke the moment he stepped inside the noisy spice factory and looked for Joseph, the factory foreman since Luke was a child. The spice factory covered an entire city block, a large cavernous space filled with twelve-foot-tall tanks that used hammer mills to grind the spices.

Luke soon found Joseph, who was recalibrating a machine. "Is my brother here?" Luke called out over the din. The hammer mills made it loud.

Joseph nodded and pointed back to the office hallway.

Luke breathed a sigh of relief when he left the noisy factory floor. All he was looking for today was permission to use the typewriter Gray kept for correspondence. The top of his brother's office door was glass, and Gray was hunched over a page full of columns. Luke would go stark raving mad if he had to sit at a desk all day analyzing numbers, but Gray appeared fascinated as he rubbed his jaw and turned another page.

Luke tapped on the glass, and Gray stood. Surprise was evident as he yanked the door open.

"Luke! How are you feeling?"

"Better," he said as he wandered inside the office. "I'm getting decent food this week."

"How can you tell?" Gray asked.

"Do you *really* need to ask that?"

"Well, now that you've sacrificed yourself on the altar of science, why don't you get off that assignment?"

Luke dropped into the chair opposite Gray's desk and propped his feet on a shipping crate from Indonesia. "There are several more rounds to go, and before you ask, yes, I will be staying on board for as long as I am physically capable. But I didn't come here to argue about food. I need a favor."

"Name it."

Luke glanced at the typewriter sitting on a corner table. Gray couldn't type, but his secretary could. With the exception of a few business letters, that thing gathered dust most of the time.

"Can I borrow your typewriter for a few days? Mine had a mishap."

Gray's brow furrowed. "What sort of mishap?"

There was no point in lying. Gray and Caroline planned to visit his office this weekend, and there was no way he could get everything repaired in time.

"Somebody ransacked my office. I'm pretty certain it was Clyde Magruder."

Gray's face hardened. Several seconds elapsed as he paced in the tight confines of his office. "Have you reported it to the police?"

"It won't do any good."

"Think," Gray pointed out. "If a sitting US congressman is ransacking the offices of journalists, you don't think that could hurt his chances for reelection?"

It was embarrassing Luke hadn't thought of that himself. He'd been too busy getting mopey and sentimental about an old typewriter, but Gray was right. There might be some way to make political capital out of this.

"We all know the Magruders hate the idea of the Poison Squad," Gray said. "By hitting at you, they can strike two birds with one stone. They would do anything to shut down that experiment."

Except in his soul Luke knew this wasn't about the experiment. Bringing his older brother into his confidence was a risk, but Luke would trust Gray with his life.

"I don't think it's about the Poison Squad," he said, then affected a deliberately casual tone. "Did you know Clyde Magruder has a daughter? We met her that day on the ice. Aunt Marianne."

Gray turned to face him from the far side of the office. He must have noticed something about the way Luke said *Marianne.* Or maybe it was the overly casual tone. Either way, Gray's expression morphed from annoyance into caution. "The one you sent flowers to?"

"The very one. She's amazing."

Gray's shoulders sagged. "Luke . . . no," he finally said.

Luke hunkered down farther in his chair, steepling his hands to partially cover his face. Anything to shield himself from the thundercloud of disapproval coming from Gray. "I can't help it. I care about her."

"You care because she's forbidden fruit," Gray said, and Luke shook his head.

"It's more than that." He put his feet flat on the floor and scrambled for the right words. "There's a feeling I get when I'm with her, a mix of peace and exhilaration at the same time.

When I'm with her I want to slay a dragon or grab her hand and run away to the West Coast where we can live like gypsies."

"And Clyde knows about this?"

Luke shrugged. "He knows we've seen each other a few times. He doesn't like it."

"I don't either."

"Oh, snap out of it, Gray. Don't blame Marianne because her family is a swarming vat of pestilent lice. Can I use your typewriter or not?"

"Not here."

Luke was dumbfounded. "You're being stingy with a typewriter because I like a Magruder?"

"I'm being stingy because I have three hundred thousand dollars' worth of equipment in this factory. I can't afford to have it vandalized if Magruder's henchmen decide to come after you here. Take the typewriter, but use it somewhere else."

It was the best he was going to get. Luke packed up the typewriter to take to his boardinghouse, but thoughts of Marianne still tormented him. He had a sinking sensation that Marianne Magruder would forever be his huge, once-in-a-lifetime regret.

He would let her go, but not without sending her a token of remembrance. He visited a jeweler's shop and found an enamel pendant shaped like a small spray of forget-me-nots. The pale blue petals were the exact shade of Marianne's eyes. He paid for the jeweler to wrap the pin and have it delivered to the Department of the Interior with no note or return address.

His interlude with Marianne was over, but echoes of their brief, magical time together would live with him forever.

Thirteen

Winter eventually released its grip on Washington, DC, and soon the ice was gone and tiny, bright green buds appeared on the branches as March warmed into April and then May.

Luke whistled as he strode back to the boardinghouse, the current issue of *The Washington Post* folded beneath his arm. On the bottom of the front page was the announcement that Oscar Garza was resigning from Congress. Luke tried not to preen, but he'd been working for months on exposing the bribery scandal leading to Congressman Garza's resignation. It was his second triumph, for last month he'd succeeded in pressuring Alfred Westheimer into declining a bid for reelection. Two congressmen down, three more to go.

Luke had a spring in his stride as he vaulted up the boardinghouse steps. Partly it was his good mood from making progress on removing undesirable characters from Congress, but partly it was from almost two weeks of not ingesting any poison.

There had been turnover on the Poison Squad. Four men had left because they'd had enough of Dr. Wiley's tainted meals, but most of the original crew was still here. By now they'd become almost like a family. A loud, brash family hailing from different walks of life, but Luke was grateful for them. Something about enduring hard times together turned strangers into brothers-in-arms very quickly.

Dinner smelled good as he stepped through the front door. Princeton was reading a novel in the parlor while the Rollins brothers played a game of chess. It looked like Little Rollins was losing, but perhaps his loss could be chalked up to sketchy concentration from whatever poison he was being fed this week. Over time Luke was beginning to recognize different batches of symptoms depending on whichever preservative was being tested that month. Sometimes he suffered nausea and stomach problems. Sometimes it was headaches and painful joints. This week the people ingesting the preservatives had poor concentration and difficulty sleeping. Perhaps one of these days he'd learn which preservatives they were being subjected to, but for now he honored Dr. Wiley's rules about staying out of the kitchen. They all submitted to weekly draws of blood and fluid samples, a questionnaire, and a brief physical exam.

Nurse Hollister entered. "Dinner is served," she said, looking unusually nervous. "Go ahead and start eating, but please stay at your places. Dr. Wiley is expected to join us soon, and he asked that everyone remain in the dining room until he gets here."

"What's up?" Princeton asked.

"I don't know, but he's been in a bad mood all day."

Little Rollins snorted. "Maybe he's been eating what we've been getting all week. That would put anyone in a bad mood."

Luke wandered into the dining room and took his assigned seat. The plates had already been set on the table. Tonight it was chipped ham with a cherry glaze, corn bread, and green bean casserole. The poison could be anywhere, but his plate was almost certainly chemical-free. He'd simply been feeling too good this week to believe he was among the test subjects.

"I love ham," Princeton said as he sat down.

"Want some of mine?" Little Rollins called from the other

table. There was no need to answer. Everyone knew the rules and had been abiding by them.

Luke bowed his head in prayer. He used to endure a good bit of ribbing from some of the others who thought it hysterical that he prayed before a meal likely infused with poison. Luke had cheerfully pointed out that was all the more reason to pray.

Dr. Wiley's heavy footsteps thumped into the room. Luke knew what was wrong the moment he spotted the issue of *Modern Century* in the doctor's hand.

"Who here has been speaking to the press?" he demanded, holding the magazine up for everyone to see. "This is the second time in the past three months that an article about the hygienic table trials has appeared in this magazine. There is too much insight in this article for the reporter to have gleaned it from external observation. Someone on the inside is speaking with him."

"What's the name of the journalist?" Nicolo asked. "I'll go pry the truth out of him."

"It's an anonymous article," Dr. Wiley replied.

Luke broke off a section of corn bread and casually slathered it with butter. Looking back on events, it was a good thing Clyde Magruder had vandalized *Modern Century's* Washington office. Luke had figured Clyde might strike again and decided to close the office rather than tolerate additional attacks. Now he quietly typed his articles at his family's town house in Alexandria. He published occasional articles in journals all over the East Coast and kept his special affiliation with *Modern Century* quiet from the men in this house.

"Well?" Dr. Wiley pressed. "Are any of you going to own up to being responsible for this breach of confidentiality?"

Luke set down his butter knife. "What's the problem with sharing news of the study with the public? The taxpayers are paying for the study. Don't they have a right to know about it?"

"Too much ruckus," Dr. Wiley pronounced. "Everyone remembers what happened the first week, with people lining up outside our door and clamoring for details. They were making celebrities out of you."

"That's the best part of the whole study," Nicolo said. "The ladies at the Census Bureau still look at me with respect. For once in my life! Do you know how hard it is for a man as short as me to get that kind of admiration?"

There was plenty of laughter at Nicolo's comment, and a little wind went out of Dr. Wiley. "I know it's flattering, but this is a controlled scientific study. The men of the hygienic table trials are—"

"We're the Poison Squad," Princeton interrupted. "At least get our name right."

Dr. Wiley bowed his head in concession. "I suppose you all have earned the right to name yourselves whatever you want. But you don't have the right to tattle to the press. I intend to send a firmly worded letter to the editor of *Modern Century* and demand the name of his source. I will be sorely disappointed if it turns out to be one of you."

Luke went back to his ham. The magazine's editor wouldn't give him away. Cornelius Newman was a living legend who had been fighting for causes since before the Civil War. He'd stood up to anarchist threats, rowdy labor unions, and the Ku Klux Klan. A firmly worded letter from Dr. Wiley wasn't going to frighten him.

After dinner a bunch of the men planned to head out to a vaudeville show, but Luke had translation work to complete. His final revision of the *Don Quixote* manuscript was due to his editor at the end of the week. The project had taken longer than expected because during the long nights of February, he started losing heart. Anxiety about the book's reception plagued him. Literary critics were going to savage him for it, and he didn't want to see his translation ripped to shreds in the press.

Wasn't that odd? He didn't mind subjecting his own body to

these risky trials or undergoing extreme deprivation in Cuba, but he'd been overly protective of that translation to the point that he set it aside rather than see it blasted apart by the critics.

And then he received a letter from Marianne.

It wasn't even a letter. It was simply an article clipped from a magazine about the growing acceptance of non-literal translations for foreign works of fiction. There was no note and no return address, but he knew in the marrow of his bones that she had sent it to him.

After that day, she became his muse. He stopped caring what college professors and critics would think, and he wrote the translation for Marianne. She fired his imagination to capture the spirit behind the prose and translate it for modern sensibilities.

Luke had the bedroom to himself after dinner. He flung himself on his bunk and reached for the small passel of letters Marianne had sent him over the past few months. None of them contained a single word from her, but he knew she had sent them. One was a photograph of her young nephew playing with the dog he'd rescued from the ice. It must be a recent photograph, since the boy was squatting beside some crocuses. It was good to see the dog was none the worse for his dip in the frozen river. Another was an announcement from the Surgeon General about some recent laboratory studies of food preservatives.

He had been sending Marianne things too. He sent everything to the Department of the Interior, and like her, he used no words. After the forget-me-not pendant necklace, he sent her an etching of Don Quixote kneeling down to offer a flower to Dulcinea, the object of his unrequited love.

Then Marianne sent him a postcard depicting the harbor of San Francisco. She wrote three words on the back: *The Promised Land.*

He carried that postcard everywhere. Would he and Marianne ever run off to San Francisco? He didn't know if he could go the rest of his life without seeing her again. She was a jeweled memory that flashed and glinted in the darkness, keeping him awake at night and fueling his days. He would probably never see her again, but the fire she inspired drove him to keep dreaming, keep trying, keep enduring.

She made him want to become a better man, and for now, that was enough.

Marianne sat beside her mother in the dressmaker's shop, poring over a design book in search of the perfect gown for an upcoming charity gala. The theme of the gala was the Golden Age of Art, and guests were invited to come costumed like any character from seventeenth-century masterpieces.

"What about this one?" Marianne asked as she pushed an open book toward Vera.

Vera clasped a hand to her throat. "My, that would be lovely! So much nicer than all those frumpy Dutch puritan ladies dressed in black."

Vera marked the page and continued looking. It was Marianne's goal today to keep her mother calm. These high-society events always set Vera on edge, and the selection of a costume only added to the stress.

"Why did they have to choose such a silly theme?" Vera asked for the tenth time. "I have a dozen ball gowns designed by Charles Worth himself, but they are useless at a costume party."

"I understand these costume parties are well-known in Washington," Marianne replied, and the Stepanovic gala promised to be the social event of the season. In theory it was a charity gala to raise money for a girls' school, but in reality it was an excuse for the cream of Washington society to dress up in extravagant costumes, mingle beneath the stars, laugh, dine, and enjoy moonlit boat rides on the river.

Marianne had already selected her own gown. She showed

the dressmaker a painting by Rembrandt of a simple milkmaid dressed in a robin's-egg-blue skirt with a white peasant's blouse and a lace-up vest.

She couldn't help wondering if Luke would be there, but she doubted it. He was still a member of the Poison Squad, and it would be cruel to attend a banquet and not be allowed a crumb to eat. Still, she missed him and wondered what he was doing at that very moment. It had been four months since she'd seen him, but he was never far from her thoughts.

Vera finally chose a dress based on a painting of Nell Gwynn, the lovely mistress of King Charles II who had been immortalized in dozens of portraits. After their labors at the dressmaker Vera insisted they treat themselves to lunch at an elegant café.

It was warm enough to sit outside, and Vera wanted to show off her smart new hat artfully perched on the side of her head. It featured an enormous brim with a spray of silk roses nestled on one side. She positioned herself at a table that was easily seen by people strolling by. Whenever Vera nodded a greeting to someone, the entire hat dipped at a fetching angle and demanded attention. She looked like a work of art and was loving the admiring glances.

Among the passersby came an oddly dressed man sporting a blue-and-yellow-striped suit with a daffodil pinned to the lapel. He casually swung a gold-tipped walking cane as he ambled toward them. Like every other man with a pulse, he was admiring Vera, but instead of strolling by, he initiated a conversation.

"Mrs. Magruder, am I correct?" he asked.

Vera managed a thin smile but no warmth. "You are indeed."

"Dickie Shuster of *The Washington Post*," the man introduced himself, and Vera's reaction immediately morphed into delighted enthusiasm.

"Why, of course! We met last year at my husband's swearing-in ceremony. Won't you join us?"

"Delighted."

Vera performed the introductions, and Marianne gathered that Dickie had published several favorable stories about her father in the past. While Marianne was proud of her father, she rarely paid much attention to what was written about him in the press.

Not so her mother. The first thing Vera did every morning was scan both of Washington's daily newspapers in search of any mention of herself or Clyde. No doubt she was hoping her amazing hat might garner some commentary in the social pages. Perhaps she was hoping Dickie Shuster might mention it, because in addition to politics, he wrote a weekly column covering Washington gossip and scandal.

Dickie proceeded to compliment Vera on her hat, and she regaled him with the trauma of spending an entire morning searching for an appropriate costume for the Stepanovic gala.

"The theme is seventeenth-century masterpieces." Vera pouted. "That leaves me only two choices. I can look like a sober Dutch puritan with an itchy ruff around my neck, or go as a half-naked strumpet."

Dickie's laugh sounded like a purr. "My dear, count yourself fortunate you weren't here for the costume party Senator Redford threw to celebrate American agriculture. It looked like a barnyard. Women actually pinned feathers and shafts of wheat to their gowns. It was the talk of the town for ages, and not in a good way."

The reporter continued regaling them with stories of Mrs. Redford's catastrophic costume party. Marianne laughed so much that she dared not risk tasting her soup, lest she embarrass herself.

"And what costume will Congressman Magruder wear?" Dickie asked.

Vera's lips thinned. "I'm afraid my husband will be unable to attend. He supposedly has committee obligations that evening."

"Supposedly?" Dickie's eyes gleamed, and he leaned forward like a bloodhound sensing fresh meat. Airing family squabbles in public was never a good idea, but it was especially dangerous in front of a reporter.

Vera breezily explained herself with a wave of her silk handkerchief. "Some sort of dinner meeting with military officers to discuss munitions, whatever that is. It sounds terribly dull to me, especially since he won't be able to escort me to the gala. Luckily, I have my lovely daughter, who will attend in his place."

Dickie's smile remained plastered in place. "Yes, how lucky you are to have such a charming . . . daughter."

Marianne stiffened. That note of hesitation in his voice awakened all her deepest insecurities about her birth. Could this journalist know something about her awkward arrival in the Magruder household twenty-six years ago?

Then Dickie cracked a joke about the vice-president's impersonation of Lady Macbeth, and she nearly split her sides in laughter. She was being ridiculous. It was only her own insecurity that made her imagine such a threat, for Dickie Shuster seemed completely harmless.

Fourteen

Marianne cinched Vera's waist down to nineteen inches to fit into her Nell Gwynn costume gown of shimmering gold silk. The shoulder and underarm seams were so closely sewn that Vera couldn't lift her arms more than a few inches. Although Marianne would never be able to compete with her mother's hourglass waist, her milkmaid outfit was still surprisingly attractive, with a full skirt of French blue, an ivory blouse, and a lace-up vest. The flouncy sleeves and loose skirt allowed far more freedom than Vera's gown.

Which was a good thing when Bandit came bounding into the room, entranced by the swaths of iridescent fabric on Vera's gown. Vera squealed in dismay as the dog drew near, but Marianne sprang forward to grab his collar.

"Down, boy," she urged, even though Bandit didn't mean any harm. He had been sent to live with them as a punishment for Sam. According to Andrew, her nephew was starting to indulge in "disrespectful back talk" to his parents. Separating the boy from his dog was the greatest punishment Andrew could imagine, so Marianne had agreed to look after Bandit for a month.

Vera clasped her hands over her heart. "Thank heavens that creature didn't ruin my gown!"

"Mama, it's all right. You're going to be the most beautiful congressman's wife in attendance tonight." Vera always looked spectacular but still wasn't comfortable in Washington society and needed constant reassurance.

"Please leave your camera at home," Vera said. "It's not ladylike to carry it about, and this isn't the sort of gathering where people will expect to be photographed, hmm, darling?"

"Of course, Mama." Although Marianne secretly disagreed. When people were enjoying themselves was precisely when they most welcomed a photograph, but this was Vera's evening. Her mother lived for these glamorous events, and Marianne would do her best to make it perfect for her.

Twilight had just begun to darken the sky as their carriage arrived at the riverside park. Torches lined a garden path leading to the gala, and Marianne craned her neck to admire the lavish display. A vine-covered trellis lined both sides of the pathway, but every few yards there was an alcove nestled amidst the plants where actors had been hired to pose in tableaux of famous paintings. There was *The Return of the Prodigal Son* by Rembrandt, *Girl with a Pearl Earring* by Vermeer, and the *Arnolfini Portrait* depicting a wealthy merchant and his wife by Jan van Eyck. The actors were exquisitely dressed down to the last detail and valiantly held their poses despite the high-society guests gaping at the display. She wished she had her camera, because everywhere she looked was a feast for the eyes.

At the end of the avenue of tableaux was a flower-draped awning where guests were greeted by the two women hosting the charity gala. The older woman wore a silk turban with a stone as large as a robin's egg in the center. The younger blond woman was even more shocking, for she was dressed like a man in the exquisitely tailored uniform of a seventeenth-century musketeer. The outfit was complete with trousers, flaring white sleeves, a scarlet cape flung over one shoulder, and a hat tilted at a jaunty angle. She even wore knee-high leather boots. Both women laughed as they greeted each guest.

"Isn't this fun?" Vera asked as they funneled closer to their hostesses, and Marianne had to agree. This was going to be an evening to cherish.

"Welcome, Mr. Trent," the hostess wearing the musketeer outfit said to the couple in front of her. "We are so grateful that you, your wife, and your wallet could attend our little soiree. Have you met Mrs. Stepanovic?" she asked as she introduced the turban-wearing woman.

"Indeed," Mr. Trent boomed. "And this is my wife, Martha Trent. Martha, this is Caroline Delacroix, hostess extraordinaire."

Marianne sucked in a breath. She hadn't realized this charity gala was being hosted by Luke's twin sister. She'd heard of Caroline Delacroix, of course. Who hadn't? But Marianne had never seen the daring socialite, and it appeared all the rumors were true. She was beautiful, bold, and confident.

Vera leaned in close. "Delacroix?" she whispered harshly. "Is she one of *those* Delacroixs?"

"Yes, Mama, she is, but this isn't the place for dramatics." Thank heavens her father wasn't here, because he was far less likely to play by the rules of polite society. Could Caroline? With so many people crowded behind them, there was no way to escape the meeting.

"Welcome!" Caroline Delacroix said warmly as Marianne and Vera stepped beneath the flower-draped arch. "I don't believe I've had the pleasure."

Marianne met her eyes. "I'm Marianne Magruder, and this is my mother, Mrs. Vera Magruder."

Caroline's eyes widened briefly in recognition, but she quickly masked whatever else she was feeling. "Well! Aren't you brave," she said with a coy wink. "Tonight, we are all friends! Especially if you are willing to open your purses to fund a worthy cause. The vocational school for women is going to sponsor an additional fifty students for next year's classes, and I'm sure the Magruders would love a chance to show their generosity."

Caroline turned her attention to the couple behind them, and another thought hit Marianne. Would Luke be here?

There must be two hundred people already gathered. A dance floor had been set up on the lawn, and senators dressed as Dutch burghers mingled with women wearing elaborate collars. Tapestries covered tables weighed down with bowls of fruit, mimicking the still life paintings so popular during the high golden age of Dutch art. Hundreds of votive candles were scattered around the garden amidst the baronial splendor. On the far side of the park, guests lined up for rides on the river barge. A cluster of men smoking cigars gathered near a bar serving drinks, but she didn't see Luke anywhere.

Disappointment tugged at her as she and Vera headed farther into the park. She both feared and longed for a chance to see Luke again. They'd only had a few weeks together, but knowing him had left a mark. He had changed her for the better. He inspired her to be less complacent and braver about taking risks.

Vera had insisted that they eat nothing before the gala. Her mother's nineteen-inch waist didn't allow room for anything so inconsequential as food, but Marianne was hungry, and the gala's refreshments smelled divine. A table filled with miniature quiches was tempting, and she helped herself to a plate. She stood on the edge of the dance floor to eat, wondering if she knew anyone here. The clerical people she worked with at Interior weren't the sort to attend a charity gala, and her parents' friends weren't her friends. She probably had more in common with the waiters and the musicians than the guests.

Her gaze trailed to the string quartet, and her heart nearly stopped.

There he was.

Luke sat with the musicians and plucked a lute held loosely in his arms. His face was gripped with concentration as he studied the sheet music on the stand before him. How intent he looked! She hadn't known he played an instrument, and somehow that made him even more appealing. The longing for him she'd been trying to suppress for months came roaring back to life.

Then she noticed his costume and smiled so wide it made her face hurt. He was dressed exactly like his sister in a musketeer uniform, complete with a tunic, white puffy sleeves, and a hat at a rakish angle.

As if sensing her presence, Luke glanced up and caught her gaze. His fingers froze as he gaped at her. The other musicians kept playing, but Luke had stopped. It felt like electricity flared between them, filling her with light and buoyancy. After a moment he simply set the lute on the ground, stood, and crossed over to her.

"I can't believe you're here," he said, his face suffused with happiness.

"Me either," she said, barely able to draw a full breath. "Aren't you needed with the musicians?"

He shook his head. "I was just filling in for a guy who got hungry. They're probably better off without me."

"I doubt that." He made everything better just by being there. His optimism, his excitement.

They stood in the middle of the dance floor. The evening was young, and no one had started dancing yet, but plenty of people carried platters of food and glasses brimming with punch.

"Do you still have your job? The poison job?" she asked.

He nodded. "Do you still have yours?"

"Yes. They decided not to fire us after all. They said they need our pictures."

"Good!" Then he stilled, his eyes taking on a hint of caution. "Is your father here?"

"No, he had a committee meeting he couldn't miss."

"Even better!" He took the plate of quiche from her and

set it aside. "Let's get out of here. There's a place behind the service tent where we can be alone."

"Yes."

She ought to resist the temptation, but she couldn't. Luke was already headed that way, and she followed. Why had they forced themselves to stay apart all this time? Everything about this felt right, and the grudge between their families was antiquated and foolish.

A few torches lit the way to the tent, where waiters hastily refilled trays of hors d'oeuvres. A tall hedge bordered the back, and Luke led her behind it, then turned to face her, grabbing her hands. He was trembling.

"I thought about you every day," he said quietly.

"I thought of you too." There was no point in denying it. No matter how hard she'd tried to corral her wayward thoughts, they inevitably drifted to Luke and what he was doing.

"I wanted to pound down the door at the Department of the Interior and ask where you were."

That sounded familiar. "I sometimes walked past the boardinghouse, looking for you," she admitted.

Luke preened. "Did you ever see me?"

"Twice. I hid behind the wall at the end of the street because I'm a coward."

"Nonsense," Luke teased. "You are probably the bravest girl I've ever met. I'm the coward. I didn't have the guts to publish the *Don Quixote* translation until your article came to me. Thanks for sending it."

Her spirit lit. "Is it published?"

"It went to the printers on Monday."

Her heart swelled with pride at his accomplishment. "Congratulations. I can't wait to read it."

"You might hate it," he cautioned. "It's different. Even my editor suggested it was a little overblown."

"And Don Quixote isn't? He might be the most overblown

character in the history of literature. No matter what the critics say, good or bad, you would have regretted it for the rest of your life if you didn't publish it. I'm so glad you did."

He touched the side of her face, affection and a hint of gratitude in his eyes. The idea that she could inspire this bold, audacious man to finish his book filled her with pride. She wasn't nearly as brave as Luke, but in this one area he was painfully vulnerable.

This was moving too fast. It felt as if they'd never been apart, and she wanted to reach out to him with both hands. She took a breath and stepped back to admire his musketeer outfit.

"I saw your sister at the entrance wearing a similar costume. She seems very daring. Is your brother dressed as the third musketeer?"

Luke grinned. "We tried, but Gray refused to wear anything other than a formal black suit. But that's Gray for you. Come, let me introduce you to him."

She tensed. "I think this is the part where I remind you I'm not very brave. I don't think that's a good idea."

"Why not?"

"We don't need to revisit how much he hates my family, do we? Please say no."

It was dark now, and the crickets were chirping. Flickering torchlight illuminated the planes of Luke's face, and once again she wished his name were anything besides Delacroix.

"All right," Luke conceded. "Let's revisit how morally wrong it is to waste even a moment of the sheer perfection of this night. There's a bench overlooking the river. We can spy on the barges and poke fun at the costumes."

"Let's!" she readily agreed.

In the end they barely gave the partygoers on the barge a second thought as they held hands and recounted the past four months. He spoke about his work traveling all over the city to help his sister gather support for the McMillan Plan. She told him about Bandit and the new camera she'd bought. Never had time flown so quickly, but it couldn't last forever.

"I need to check on my mother," she said reluctantly. "She's wearing the world's most impractical gown and needs help if she's going to do anything more strenuous than blink."

Luke grabbed her arm before she could rise from the bench. "When can I see you again?"

She ought to say never. She ought to wish him a fond farewell. The memory of her father's scorching anger back in February had diminished, but it would be awful if he caught her out a second time.

A few yards behind them, a pair of waiters left the service tent carrying platters of crab cakes and roasted lamb. It all smelled divine, but Luke looked away. He couldn't eat a single morsel that wasn't prepared in a boardinghouse kitchen where scientists adulterated his food with overdoses of chemical preservatives.

No matter what her father said, Luke Delacroix was a man of selfless valor. What other man in his position would endure months of restrictive food trials in the name of science?

She bit the side of her lip as indecision clawed at her. Never had she felt so accepted by another human being as she did when she was with Luke, and she couldn't walk away from that feeling quite yet.

"I still go to the Gunderson studio every Friday morning to develop my photographs," she whispered.

"I can't wait until Friday. Where are you taking pictures next?"

On Monday she was slated to photograph the navy's shipyard at low tide, which meant six o'clock in the evening. She would be alone. There would be no fear of discovery if they met at the isolated dry dock.

"I'll be at the Navy Yard at six o'clock on Monday evening," she said. "Can you meet me then?"

He shook his head. "I eat with the Poison Squad at six o'clock sharp, and there's no escaping it. Can you wait? I'll eat fast and can be there by seven."

"I'll wait for you," she said, her heart already speeding up at the prospect. "Now I need to go find my mother."

She didn't look back as she hastened toward the torchlit gathering under the awnings, but she felt Luke watching her the entire way.

Vera was incensed by the time Marianne found her. "Where have you been?" she whispered fiercely. "I need to use the ladies' room and can hardly do so without assistance."

"Yes, Mama."

Vera took little mincing steps, which was all the gown allowed, as they headed toward the building with the facilities. Even after emerging from the stall, Vera continued pointing out the problems caused by Marianne's absence, including the fact that Marianne had the compact of rice powder, and Vera's nose had grown unacceptably shiny.

"I've looked like an oil slick for the last half hour," she said reproachfully as she dabbed the powder puff across the slight sheen on her face. "Where on earth did you disappear to?"

"I was admiring the sights," Marianne said, which was certainly the truth.

"Well, don't disappear again," Vera castigated, but the moment they emerged from the building, her face assumed the beatific look of an angel as she glided toward the party. For the next hour Vera exchanged air kisses with other Washington socialites, flirted with a Supreme Court justice, playfully tapped her fan against the shoulder of a Russian diplomat, and generally appeared to be walking on air.

All the while Marianne watched Luke from the corner of her eye. He mingled with ease, bantering with men and flirting with women. He didn't touch a morsel of food or drink. She took care not to let Vera notice where her attention strayed, but she savored every forbidden glance at him.

Then Luke stepped onto the dance floor with his sister, and he became impossible to ignore. He and Caroline created quite a stir in their identical musketeer uniforms as they effortlessly launched into a waltz. How dazzling they looked!

"Altogether appalling," Vera whispered into her ear, but Marianne disagreed, as did most of Washington society, who seemed delighted to admire the two master dancers execute a flamboyant waltz. Other dancers pulled aside as Luke and Caroline cut a swath across the floor. Caroline's trousers and high leather boots made it easy to watch their footwork as they swooped, slid, and twirled in tandem. They were both laughing, as were the people lining the dance floor who started applauding even while the duo continued to waltz.

Even Gray Delacroix was smiling, watching his younger siblings. He glanced up and caught Marianne watching him.

Did he know who she was? He must, for his smile faded as he locked eyes with her across the dance floor. Luke's older brother was a stranger to her except for the one time he grabbed her ankle and dragged her off the ice on a bitterly cold day in January. After she scrambled back onto shore, he had been entirely focused on tending Luke and hadn't spared her a second glance.

How different things were this warm summer evening beneath the stars. Gray nodded to her. It was a stiff nod, full of formality and brooding concern, but it was polite. Barely.

The dancing came to an end shortly after that terse nod, and then it was time for speeches, always to be expected during a charity event. Caroline still seemed a little breathless as she took command of the evening by speaking about the importance of the school to train women for skilled jobs in the workforce. Then she began auctioning off donated items, raising thousands of dollars in the space of twenty minutes.

They auctioned items large and small. An emerald bracelet, a painting by Edgar Degas, and box seats at the opera commanded steep prices. Other items were more fun, like the baseball signed by the entire Washington Senators team and a set of model train cars donated by President Roosevelt.

Then a pair of attendants carried out ten individual garlands of flowering blossoms that had been used to decorate the venue this evening. The garlands perfectly complemented Botticelli's *Primavera,* and now that the evening was drawing to a close, they would be awarded to the first ten people who promised to donate fifty dollars to the girls' school.

Luke's hand shot up, along with a handful of other men's. The garlands were soon gone, and Luke stepped forward to claim his prize. He poked and prodded among the garlands, and it looked like he selected the one primarily featuring rich blue forget-me-nots.

Marianne's eyes widened as she realized his intent. No sooner had Luke claimed his garland than he began heading straight toward her. Didn't he realize her mother was standing right beside her? His smile was wide as he looped the garland around her neck.

"For the prettiest lady at the gala," he said, his eyes twinkling.

"You shouldn't have," she stammered.

"Why not? The flowers are the exact shade of your eyes." It looked like he wanted to add more, but he must have noticed the alarm on her face, and his eyes flicked to Vera. Luke proffered her mother a little bow and stepped back a pace. "Have a good evening, ladies."

Vera's hand tightened around Marianne's arm like a claw. "Your father is to know nothing about this, but don't you dare put me in a position like that ever again."

Fifteen

At breakfast the next morning, Vera chattered nonstop about the gala, the costumes, and the assorted delicacies served throughout the evening. Clyde listened politely as Vera rambled in exhaustive detail about the items auctioned and who wore what.

The one thing Vera didn't mention was the presence of the Delacroixs, for which Marianne was grateful. If her father knew the gala had been hosted and attended by all three Delacroix siblings, it would cause trouble. When Vera laughed at her own joke about how odd a waltz played on a harpsichord sounded, Clyde managed to interject a comment about his own evening.

"I had a productive meeting with the Committee on Military Affairs," he said. "It was mostly congressmen, but a few men from the army were there, including Colonel Phelps." Clyde met Marianne's eyes across the table. "I think he would be a good match for you."

She tried not to choke on her bite of cranberry muffin. Her father's efforts to encourage a match between her and the young colonel had been simmering for months, but he'd never been so blatant before.

Clyde continued cutting into his ham while he sang Colonel Phelps's praises. "He's likely to become a general before he turns forty," he said to Vera. "What do you think, my dear? Would it be good to have a general in the family?"

"He would be an excellent choice," Vera responded.

Marianne set down her fork. "I'd rather find a man of my own choosing."

"Then you'd best get on with it," Clyde said. "You're twenty-six and not getting any younger. I doubt you'll meet anyone of quality at the Department of the Interior. What about last night's gala? Did you meet anyone with prospects there?"

She was halfway in love with Luke Delacroix but could hardly say so, leaving her at a loss for words. Her mother came to the rescue.

"She saw no one all night," Vera said, her voice tight. "Isn't that right, Marianne?"

"That's right, Mama," she said, avoiding everyone's eyes. She didn't want an army colonel, she wanted Luke Delacroix.

"Let's plan a dinner and invite Colonel Phelps," Clyde said. "I would very much like to see an alliance of that sort, but it will have to be after we get back from Baltimore."

On Tuesday they were all going to Baltimore, where they would celebrate Andrew's thirtieth birthday. They would return Bandit and spend the entire week back home, but all Marianne could think about was Monday night, when she'd have a chance to see Luke again.

Luke ran out of the boardinghouse the instant he'd finished scraping his dinner plate clean on Monday evening. Good-natured hoots from the others followed him out of the house. Everyone suspected he had an assignation tonight, and they were right.

He took a carriage straight to the navy shipyard southeast of town. It was one of the navy's older shipyards and still had its original ceremonial entrance. Latrobe Gate displayed classical grandeur, but behind it was the gritty world of a shipyard. There were plenty of men in uniform wandering about, so it was presumably safe, but he didn't like the idea of Marianne alone here.

She was on the far end of an empty dry dock, walking alongside it as she studied the massive chains used to cable a ship in place. She spotted him from a block away and sent him a cheerful wave.

He waved back, quickening his steps while she hiked her skirts to run toward him. He held his arms wide, and she squealed with delight as he scooped her up and twirled her about.

He kissed her before setting her down. He hadn't dared last night, with her mother only yards away, but they were anonymous here, just a man and a woman who adored each other, and he kissed her deeply.

"Thanks for waiting," he said when he finally released her.

"Thanks for coming." Her face was flushed and beautiful, and light glinted on the forget-me-not pendant he'd given her.

"I like your necklace. Thanks for wearing it."

"I love it. Thanks for giving it to me."

"Marianne, if we thank each other one more time, we're both candidates for the insane asylum. Come on. Let's go take your pictures, and you can tell me why the government wants photographs of the world's ugliest dry dock."

He loved watching as she took the photographs. She explained that the pictures were to support upcoming renovations to the shipyard. The algae-stained concrete walls of the dry dock were an unappealing subject, but her face was still so intent while she worked, and he loved that about her. Anyone who was so passionate about their job was appealing, and he was fascinated by her fingers as she manipulated the dials and levers of the camera.

"How long can you stay?" he asked once she had completed the assignment.

"My parents are both at the opera. They won't return until midnight."

He cocked out his elbow, and she smiled as she wrapped her hand around his bicep. They walked toward the Latrobe Gate in the cool of the evening.

"I adore this time of day," Marianne said. "It's called the blue hour. It's right after the sun slips below the horizon, but there's still ambient light. It's the very best time for photographs. There are no shadows, no glares, just a soft, magical light everywhere."

A glance above the trees proved the truth of her words. The twilight was enchanting, and in a few moments it would be gone.

"Give me your camera," he said, suddenly desperate to capture this moment and preserve it for all time. "You already have a photograph of me, but I don't have one of you."

She gamely looped the lanyard over his neck and agreed. He'd used a Brownie camera before, but this light would be tricky.

"How long do I need to hold the exposure?" he asked.

"At least five seconds, and you'll need to set the camera on a table to keep it motionless."

There was one beside a park bench, but she had to kneel to get in the shot. The boxwood hedge behind her was a perfect backdrop, and he loved what he saw through the viewfinder. Her face brimmed with character and simple, feminine beauty. He pressed the exposure lever and held it, counting to five.

"You'll send me a copy?" he asked as she stood and brushed the grit from her knees.

"I will. It won't be for a while, as I'll be in Baltimore for the rest of the week. It's my brother's birthday, and my mother always makes a big fuss over it."

They walked along the harbor wall, listening to the gentle slosh of waves against the pilings. Where was this forbidden romance going to lead? There was no good ending he could think of, but that didn't mean he couldn't enjoy these few stolen hours.

Unfortunately, it seemed her mind was traveling along the same lines, and she brought up the topic he least wanted to discuss.

"During your sister's gala, I saw you talking with Congressman Roper."

He stiffened. "That's right."

"He's one of the five congressmen you had on that list in your office. Two of those men will already be gone by the next election. Is Congressman Roper your next target?"

No, her father was his next target. "Marianne, let's not talk about this."

"I think it's a fair question. My father is on that list, and I know you hope he loses in November. I have a feeling you're going to do everything in your power to ensure he isn't reelected."

He kept walking but stared straight ahead rather than risk looking at her. "It's just politics."

"It's not politics; it's my family. I want to know if you intend to tamper with my father's career."

"There are forty-two thousand voters in your father's district. They will decide his fate, not me. Marianne, please, let's not talk about this. Tell me more about the blue hour."

She drew a huge breath and blew it out, struggling for control. He could practically hear the wheels turning in her mind, but there was no way she could ever dissuade him from this path.

Finally, she spoke again. "Explain the politics to me. If there is a reason besides the family feud, I'd like to know."

He owed her at least that much. It meant telling her about the ill-fated coffee fiasco he embarked on with her father in Philadelphia, but maybe it would help her understand why he distrusted the reckless use of food additives and preservatives.

He gestured to the old stone wall bordering the river and braced his elbows atop it. She joined him as he laid out the story of how he and Gray worked hard to produce a gourmet blend of coffee, only to see it adulterated with cheap fillers and chemical flavorings. Three people died, and their ghosts were still with him.

Marianne swallowed hard. "How do you know it was the additives? Surely thousands of people drank that coffee."

"True, but we spoke with physicians. The chemical flavorings are known to cause an allergic reaction in a tiny fraction of the population, and there was no indication on the canister that there was anything other than ground coffee beans inside."

Marianne was ready with more arguments to dismiss his position, but he wasn't going to debate with her. Their time together was too scarce to spend it bickering over a topic on which neither of them would ever budge, but he needed her to understand why he fought.

"God has set eternity in the human heart," he said, looking out over the river at the tiny bit of fading light on the edge of the horizon. What a huge and wonderful world God built for them, and the wildness inside him began to swell in the face of its immensity. "There is a longing to do something great in all of us, and I've always had a yearning to be tested. I need a mission and a purpose to fight for. Ever since the coffee debacle, I've known I had to make things right somehow."

He turned to face her, hoping she could understand this wildness inside, but he hadn't made a dent on her.

"Luke, what if you're wrong? What if those five congressmen on your list are the good guys, and instead of making the world safer, you end up hurting it instead?"

He folded her hand between his and squeezed. "That's why I eat three meals a day with the Poison Squad. We'll know soon."

Marianne closed her eyes in resignation and touched her

forehead to his. "No one can accuse you of taking the easy way out."

He enclosed her in his arms, loving the way she fit perfectly against him. "No matter what happens, please know that I adore everything about you. Your intelligence and curiosity. Your loyalty. Someday that loyalty is likely to drive us apart, but for tonight, we have each other."

Visiting her sister-in-law's house was always a challenge for Marianne. Delia and Andrew lived only two doors down from her parents' home in Baltimore's wealthiest neighborhood. Andrew's house was like a museum. Most of the furniture was antique, and the fabric for the draperies was imported from Europe. Delia's pride was the mantelpiece surrounding the fireplace in the front hall, which had once been owned by the Earl of Rutledge before he had to sell his estate. Somehow Delia managed to make sure each guest to her home learned of the mantelpiece's exalted lineage within moments of arrival.

Marianne's task today was to help plan Andrew's birthday party on Friday without letting a war break out. Vera and Delia had a massive dislike for each other, which Marianne thought was probably because the two women were so alike. Neither ever openly acknowledged their antipathy, but it simmered beneath the surface as each subtly vied for supremacy at every encounter. Marianne's loyalty would always be to Vera, but Delia was Sam's mother and doing a good job raising the boy, so she maintained cordial relations with her difficult sister-in-law.

"I'd like a cake sculpted to look like the America's Cup

trophy," Delia said. With her tiny frame and carefully styled honey-blond hair, Delia had always been one of the prettiest people Marianne knew. "I heard that Mrs. Astor had one like it, so I think it will be perfect for Andrew."

"I can't see your cook being able to pull that off," Vera said. "The Neapolitan cake she made for lunch today was on the lackluster side."

Delia's mouth thinned. "I plan to get the cake from the bakery on Carleton Street. They do exceptional work. I've also arranged for a magician to surprise everyone with a release of doves during the party. Won't that be nice? Oh, and Marianne, you can take photographs of the guests. That job of yours ought to come in useful for something. After you develop the pictures, I shall send them to the guests along with a thank-you note."

"I'd be happy to." Marianne had heard the sideways swipe at her profession but didn't bother defending it. In Delia's eyes there was no higher calling than being a mother, and she often managed to craftily point out Marianne's failure to marry and continue building the Magruder family dynasty.

Marianne wandered to a chair and sat, fiddling with the pendant at her throat and wishing she could be with Luke. He was always so fun. He never indulged in underhanded gamesmanship. When they disagreed, he came straight out and told her his issue.

"Marianne, please don't sit on that chair," Delia said. "It's an antique, not really a piece of furniture."

Marianne immediately stood, but Vera's tone turned icy. "And which piece of furniture is acceptable for my daughter to sit on?"

"Mama, it's all right," Marianne said, eager to smooth her ruffled feathers.

"Of course it's all right," Delia rushed to say. "Please sit anywhere except the chairs that have the curved gilt legs. They're from the Regency era and very fragile."

Before Marianne could sit again, there was a disturbance in the front hall. It sounded like a child was crying, followed by Andrew's voice as he stomped inside. It was a Wednesday, so Andrew was supposed to be at Magruder Food and Sam ought to be in school, but something must be wrong.

"Now, stop that sniveling and go apologize to your mother," Andrew ordered, his tone furious.

Sam came down the front hall, shoulders cringing and his hands fisted in front of his chest as he sobbed uncontrollably. "I'm sorry, Mama," he managed to stammer through his tears.

Delia looked horrified as she rushed to kneel before the boy, pulling him into her embrace. "My goodness, what's happened?" she asked, looking to her husband for an explanation.

Andrew stood in the doorway of the parlor like a thundercloud, two bright spots of anger on his cheekbones. "Tell her, Sam."

Sam flung himself deeper into Delia's arms and shook his head against her neck, too distraught to speak.

"Andrew, what's going on?" Delia demanded, her voice losing patience.

"Our son was caught cheating on a mathematics test. Isn't that right, boy?"

Sam only cried harder. Marianne's heart ached for him, but there was little she could say to heal the wound. He was obviously guilty or he wouldn't be so distraught. Andrew continued to fulminate, recounting how he'd been notified at the office of Sam's transgression and how he immediately went to the private school to yank the boy out of class for a good dressing down.

Marianne gestured to Vera. "Come, Mama. Maybe we should leave for a while."

"No, no," Andrew said. "This sort of humiliation is what happens to boys who get caught cheating. It is a stain on the family name and will require a public show of remorse."

"I'm sorry," Sam said again, still not lifting his head from Delia's neck. "I said I'm sorry, and I don't know what else to do."

From deep in the house came Bandit's yelps. Delia insisted the dog be kept confined to the servants' workroom, but he'd obviously heard Sam and was trying to get out. What a terrible mess! These visits to Andrew and Delia's house were always difficult, but this was simply awful.

Andrew stomped down the hallway, slamming doors and yelling orders at the servants. Soon he came back to the parlor, leading Bandit by the leash.

"Say good-bye to your dog, boy. If you can't be trusted to handle a school test, you can't be responsible for a dog."

"No!" Sam said as he sprang away from Delia. His crying stopped, replaced with a white look of fear. "Please don't take Bandit away again."

"You should have thought of that before you cheated. You won't be seeing Bandit again."

Andrew led the dog down the front hall, but Marianne couldn't believe he truly meant to give the dog away. He was probably just taking him down to their parents' house, which was fine. She wouldn't mind looking after Bandit until Sam's punishment was over.

"Calm down, calm down," Delia shushed Sam. She used a lacy handkerchief to blot his tears, then held it to his nose. "Blow," she coaxed. With Andrew gone, Delia proceeded to mother Sam the way she usually did when her husband wasn't there. "Now, tell me what happened and why you had to cheat on that test."

Marianne met Vera's eyes. She fully expected Delia to find some way to blame Sam's transgression on the teacher or perhaps even the school itself. Sam tearfully admitted he didn't understand how to add fractions because the teacher didn't teach it very well, and lots of students in his class cheated. By the time Andrew returned a few minutes later, Delia was fully armed to defend her son.

"Apparently the whole class was cheating, but Sam was the only one singled out for punishment," she told Andrew, who was in no mood to hear it. He demanded Delia follow him to his study to discuss it in private, which was a good thing, because Sam shouldn't hear his mother defend the indefensible.

It was hard to continue planning Andrew's birthday party after the blowup, especially since Delia remained sequestered in the study while a muffled argument could be overheard. Marianne and Vera didn't have enough insight to discuss the guest list, but they walked through the main floor of the house and considered ideas for decorating. Everything in the mansion was already so lavishly ornamented, it was hard to think of ways to make it look even more festive.

Dinner was a somber affair. They dined at Andrew's house, and her father carried the bulk of the conversation because Andrew was still silently fuming. Sam wouldn't meet anyone's eyes and barely touched his food. After dinner, the grown-ups went to the parlor to enjoy a late-night cordial, but Sam retreated upstairs.

Marianne gave in to temptation and followed, softly tapping on his closed bedroom door.

Sam tore it open a moment later, hope on his face, but it vanished when he saw her. "Oh," he said, his shoulders drooping. "I thought Papa was back with Bandit."

She followed him inside and sat on the edge of his bed. "I think Bandit will be staying at our house for a while."

"Can you get him back?" he pleaded. "Please, Aunt Marianne. I promise I won't ever cheat again. I won't be a mailman. I'll study hard and work in Papa's office and be part of the family dynasty. Just please help me get Bandit back."

She ruffled his hair and gave him a reassuring smile. She couldn't make any promises, nor was she going to undermine

Andrew's decisions in this matter. She just wished she came from a normal family where harsh punishments and raging tantrums were not standard fare.

Maybe someday she would have such a family, but she was learning that constantly seeking appeasement carried its own set of problems.

Marianne was surprised not to see Bandit when she returned home that evening. Her father merely shrugged off her questions about the dog, and all Vera could do was complain about how Delia had mishandled the situation.

"No wonder that boy is growing up weak-willed," she said. "I certainly hope Andrew puts his foot down."

"No fear of that," Clyde said as he continued smoking a cheroot, perusing the evening newspaper.

Her grandfather sat in the corner of the parlor, whittling a block of wood. At eighty years of age, Jedidiah had turned over management of the food company to his son and grandson. He now lived with Clyde in a mansion that was a far cry from the cabin with a dirt floor where he'd been born, but her grandfather had never lost the backwoods twang in his accent.

"Andrew's too hard and Delia's too soft," Jedidiah said. "No wonder the boy is a little screwy."

That triggered another round of discussion about Delia's shortcomings, since no one was allowed to say a critical word about Andrew. Soon responsibility for Sam's cheating had been entirely ascribed to Delia's failings as a mother, and Marianne would rather do anything than continue this discussion.

"How was your day at Magruder Food?" she asked Clyde, eager to divert the topic.

Clyde folded up the newspaper and flashed her a delighted grin. "Fabulous! Andrew is learning quickly and rolling out a new process for pickling cucumbers. It should cut production time in half and earn a pretty penny once it's implemented."

It wouldn't have happened without Clyde's mentorship. Andrew followed in lockstep behind her father, and maybe that was for the best. There certainly hadn't been any changes in their position on artificial fillers or chemical preservatives under Andrew's leadership. What if Luke was right? Could Andrew ever develop the fortitude to change the direction of the company?

Her attention began to wander. If Luke had his way, her father's political career would come to an end in November, and that would be terrible. She could never forgive Luke if he wantonly destroyed her father's career, for she owed Clyde Magruder the world. What other man would take an illegitimate child into his home and lavish her with as much affection as Clyde had done?

Vera turned in early. Spending time with Delia always wore her out, but particularly so today, considering the uproar over Sam. Her father retreated into his study to deal with paperwork, and Marianne pounced on the opportunity to coax her grandfather into a late evening stroll.

The crickets chirped as they set out down the slate pathway toward the street. She loved this walk beneath the spreading oak trees. The homes on this street were so stately, with their manicured lawns and the lights glowing inside the windows. It made it look like happy families lived inside.

"Fine night for a stroll," Jedidiah said. "Anything to escape the catawampus at Andrew's house. And we ain't heard the end of it."

"What makes you say that?"

"I done told you," Jedidiah said. "Andrew is too hard with the boy, and Delia is too soft. It ain't going to end well."

Something about his ominous tone made her suspect he knew something. Jedidiah had been home all day and might have more insight into what went on this afternoon. Many of the homes had their windows open, so she waited until they passed Andrew and Delia's house to broach her question.

"Where is Bandit?" she asked, watching her grandfather carefully.

Jedidiah scowled. "Bandit is gone."

Obviously he wasn't at their house, but how long did Andrew intend to keep the dog away as punishment this time? She'd be happy to take Bandit to Washington again. Dogs bonded with people, so he shouldn't be left with strangers.

"Gone where?" she pressed.

Jedidiah sighed. "I'm sorry to say that he's gone for good. Andrew had one of the boys down at the stable shoot him dead."

"No!" She stopped walking, too light-headed to keep moving. "No, I can't believe it. Even Andrew wouldn't do such a thing."

"Believe it," Jedidiah said. "Delia never liked that dog. Bandit sometimes brings fleas into the house, and you know how she is about that house. Andrew got to please his wife and punish his son, all with one bullet."

Andrew had always been hard, but this went beyond the pale. Her gaze trailed down the street, where Andrew and Delia's palatial house sat on a two-acre lot, the lights softly burning inside. How could someone who lived in such a picturesque home do something so foul?

"How did you learn this?" she asked.

"Andrew told me. He was proud of it."

Marianne swallowed hard. Her grandfather's memory was sometimes sketchy. Could he have misheard? Or misunderstood? In the past year, both Andrew and her father had grown increasingly insistent that Jedidiah no longer be allowed to play any role in the company. They mistrusted his judgment and accused him of forgetting details. Maybe this was more of the same.

Even as she stared at Andrew's house, a few of the lights switched off. It was too late to call on her brother tonight to demand the truth, but she would find out in the morning.

Marianne decided to visit Andrew at his office to hear from his own mouth what happened to Bandit. She didn't want to confront him at home where Delia could interfere, and Jedidiah insisted on accompanying her to the factory.

Magruder Food was located on the industrial side of town. A squat brick building housed the canning and bottling operations, while a separate warehouse stored their inventory. A small building for the business offices was built off to the side. The only ornamentation on the property was a pair of boxwood shrubs framing the door to the offices.

Andrew loathed the location of the business offices, but Jedidiah always insisted on thrift. It was significantly cheaper to keep the entire company located in this industrial area, even though it annoyed her father and brother to no end. They were eager to leave this gritty part of town, but since Jedidiah was still the majority shareholder in the company, there was nothing they could do. Andrew once told her that as soon as Jedidiah died, he planned to move business operations to the other side of town, where rents were sky-high but the location would add prestige to the family's reputation.

Jedidiah held the door open for her to enter, his smile worried. "I don't think confronting Andrew is a good idea. That boy has got a temper."

"I need to look him in the eyes and demand the truth," she replied, and Jedidiah gave a brief nod. He respected her decision even if he disapproved of it.

The hallway to Andrew's office was shabby but clean, and the door to his office was open. He sat at a massive oak desk that had been Jedidiah's first and only luxury once Magruder Food started earning a fortune decades earlier. Andrew had covered the floor with a fine oriental rug, but the rest of the office was filled with workaday filing cabinets, a few chairs, and a single window with the same moss-green draperies she remembered from visiting her father here as a child.

"This is a surprise," Andrew said as he rose to his feet. "Come in. Have a seat."

Jedidiah sat, but she felt too nervous to join him. Andrew's congenial smile was so familiar. He'd played with her when they were little. He once stood up for her against some older boys who used to tug on her braids at school. She couldn't believe he would order Bandit shot, and he deserved a chance to defend himself.

"I heard something bad about you," she said. "I heard you had one of the stable boys shoot Bandit."

Andrew's face tightened, and his mouth turned into a hard line. "That's right, I did."

She flinched and looked away as the last hope in his innocence died away, but her gumption quickly came back. "How could you?" she demanded. "Bandit was a good and loyal dog. Eager to please . . ." Her voice trailed off because it hurt too much to think of him.

"Sam needs to know there are consequences for bad behavior."

"Does Papa know?"

Andrew nodded. "He said it was harsh but fair. He doesn't want the family name tarnished, and cheating can do that. He wants the problem nipped in the bud, and so do I."

"It was badly done," Jedidiah said. "I'd have stopped it if I'd known. That's not how a man should handle things."

"I'm Sam's father, and you've got no say in how I raise him."

Jedidiah wasn't used to having anyone contradict him. He stood, anger darkening his face. "That may be, but this is still my company, and I've got say here. Look around you, boy!

Everything you see here, I built. That factory. That warehouse." He banged his fist on the desk, making the pencils in the cup rattle. "I bought this very desk with money I earned from the sweat off my brow, and I don't like to see a man who would shoot an innocent dog sitting at *my* desk. I trained Clyde to take over the company, but now he's got highfalutin ideas about Congress. I wish Marianne was a man. She'd be a worthy person to sit at that desk."

Andrew stood. "Now, Grandpa," he said in a placating tone that only ratcheted Jedidiah's anger hotter.

"Or little Tommy, for that matter! I don't care if the boy was born on the wrong side of the blanket. You let me down. That's not how a man acts." Jedidiah was shouting now, his face mottled with rage.

Bandit was gone, and there was no undoing it, but they were still a family, and she hoped Jedidiah didn't say something he would regret.

She laid a hand on her grandfather's arm and tried to speak calmly. "We've said our piece. There's no point in belaboring the matter."

Andrew looked grateful for her intervention. Jedidiah was so angry he might make good on his threat to throw Andrew out of the company.

Her grandfather's eyes narrowed, but he was starting to calm down. "It's all right for a man to have a little wildness inside," he said. "That's how the Lord made us." He stood before Andrew and held up a clenched hand. "You see that fist? I've been fighting since I came out of the womb. I fight and claw and conquer because that's how a man survives in this world, but don't you ever turn that fist on a woman or a child or a helpless animal. *Never again*. Do you hear me, boy?"

"Yes, sir." Andrew met Jedidiah's eyes with his chin held high, but there was a hint of fear in his face. Jedidiah could fire Andrew, and there'd be nothing Andrew or Clyde could do.

"Then we'll be on our way. Come along, Marianne."

She obeyed, but Jedidiah still twitched with anger as he stormed out of the office. She glanced back to send a parting look of sympathy to Andrew.

Instead of contrition, she saw rage on her brother's face.

Seventeen

Luke climbed the stairs of the Department of the Treasury, one of the grander buildings in the government, with a row of white granite columns stretching across the front. From the outside it looked like the epitome of strength and stability. Inside it was a rabbit warren of small offices and a maze of hallways.

Luke headed toward the bureau for counterfeit detection, where his future brother-in-law worked. Caroline, his dazzling sister who held Washington high society in the palm of her hand, was getting married next month to one of the most buttoned-down men on earth. Nathaniel Trask loved rules so much that he probably slept with a copy of the Constitution tucked beneath his pillow, but Caroline was madly in love, so Luke had been trying to get along with him.

Today he was determined to be polite to Nathaniel no matter the cost, which would be a challenge since he already had a raging headache. Luke had no idea what he was being dosed with this week, but his symptoms had started abruptly yesterday, and they were severe. Everyone dining at his table had the same throbbing headache right behind their eyes, and Luke could only hope that Dr. Wiley would have mercy on them and stop the test early.

The good news was that Nathaniel was the Secret Service's leading expert on counterfeit, and Luke had a document he was almost certain had been faked. If so, the document would sink Clyde Magruder's chances for reelection. All Luke needed was for Nathaniel to validate his suspicions about this laboratory report so he could unleash the damaging scandal against the Magruders.

He walked through the maze of hallways until he reached Nathaniel's office. He'd made an appointment because Nathaniel's entire life was so rigidly structured that drop-in visits were discouraged. It was already three minutes after their appointment time, so Luke knocked on the door and proceeded inside, expecting to be scolded for being late.

He found his sister sprawled on Nathaniel's lap, her arms looped around his neck. At Luke's entrance, Caroline giggled and sprang to her feet, but Luke was most fascinated by Nathaniel's reaction at being caught. He straightened his tie, adjusted his cuff links, and immediately assumed the mask of a sober Secret Service agent despite the flush creeping up his neck. Luke quietly rejoiced at the evidence that Nathaniel actually had a beating pulse beneath that plain black jacket.

Caroline was completely unperturbed. "I heard you had an appointment and couldn't resist being here. You've found counterfeit?"

Luke set a folder on Nathaniel's desk. "I found a document I believe is a forgery. I need my hunch authenticated."

Nathaniel flipped open the file, his brows lowering in concentration as he inspected the laboratory report. Luke dropped into a chair opposite the desk and held his breath, watching Nathaniel closely.

"Where did you get this?" Nathaniel asked, his eyes still traveling over the lines on the report.

"Clyde Magruder commissioned some laboratory studies on chemical preservatives. The tests were done at the orders of the Committee on Manufactures, and what a surprise . . . they found that all those chemicals are perfectly safe. I don't believe it. It's got to be a fraud."

Nathaniel laid the pages on his desk and used a jeweler's loupe to scrutinize the document. Luke knew in his bones the report had to be a fake. The experiment measured bacterial proliferation in beef juices after the meat was preserved with boric acid. It claimed boric acid was an effective agent in reducing spoilage. It was deemed safe for human consumption after being tested on laboratory mice, which showed no negative effects from consuming the tainted beef juices. Luke could only wonder how the chemists asked the mice if they suffered from throbbing pains behind their eyes like the ones he had right now.

Caroline perched on the arm of Nathaniel's chair, pretending to study the report, but actually she was simply tracing her fingers along the back of her fiancé's neck. It annoyed Luke. He ought to be happy for Caroline, but it was hard.

"A little decorum, please," he said when he couldn't stand it anymore.

Caroline quirked a surprised brow at him. She lowered her hand back to her lap but refused to budge from the arm of Nathaniel's chair.

Why was he being so prissy? Luke clenched his fists and averted his eyes from Caroline as jealousy flared inside. He was happy for Caroline. Truly. And if his situation with Marianne weren't so precarious, this probably wouldn't bother him so much, but the fake document on Nathaniel's desk was going to ruin her father. Marianne believed everything Clyde said and would probably hold this against Luke. Even if their families didn't already hate each other, this document was going to do the trick.

Nathaniel straightened and looked him in the eye. "It's real."

"No, it's not." The words instinctively burst from Luke. He

had four months of consuming high doses of chemical preservatives to prove those things were dangerous.

Nathaniel held the six pages of the report aloft. "These pages check out. The letterhead from the University of Virginia Department of Chemistry is real. The cover letter has a watermark, which is almost impossible to manufacture."

"It could have been stolen."

"True," Nathaniel agreed. "But other things indicate this is a legitimate report. The numbers in the charts are not tampered with. The handwritten signatures are executed in a free-flowing manner and are likely authentic. What makes you think it's a fake?"

"Because it was submitted by Clyde Magruder, and he'll lie on a stack of Bibles if it means he can keep dumping chemicals into the food supply. That report is a fake."

"But the document is real."

He shook his head and whirled away in frustration, pacing in the tiny space.

"Luke, if Nathaniel says the document is real, it's real," Caroline said.

"Whose side are you on?" he demanded.

"Yours, darling, which is why I don't want you to go to war if this is the only arrow in your quiver."

His frustration intensified, and it felt like the walls of the room were closing in on him. "How can you stand to work in this miserable office? I feel buried alive in here."

Nathaniel's voice was annoyingly calm. "It's got a desk, electricity, and a functioning fan. I'm perfectly happy."

Luke snatched the report off the desk. "I'm taking this somewhere else for a second opinion," he groused as he left the office. Nathaniel was the leading counterfeit expert in Washington, but Luke would still try to find someone better.

His mood didn't improve once he got outside, but at least he could breathe again. His headache pounded, the lab report he'd pinned all his hopes on might not work, and he was irrationally jealous of his sister's happiness. He was poisonous company today, but then, he'd always had a foul, selfish streak deep inside. He usually managed to keep it buried, but every now and then it clawed its way back out. Was he really going to spend the rest of his life watching other men become captains of industry, steer the nation from the halls of Congress, while he pathetically translated old novels written by someone else? He was supposed to be a man, not an angry ball of frustrated ambition.

Sometimes the restless demon inside was hard to tame. He wanted to strike out for the horizon or put on a uniform and fight someone. He wanted to test his strength until he literally could not keep swinging anymore. Temptation clawed at him, but his aching head and the rules of the Poison Squad precluded getting into a boxing ring. Anything that put unnecessary stress on his already abused body was disallowed by Dr. Wiley.

So, like a dutiful boy, he would head back to the boardinghouse for lunch, tuck a napkin under his chin, and eat whatever he was served without complaint.

Caroline's rapid footsteps clicked on the sidewalk as she raced to catch up with him. "What's put you in such a snit?"

"Just one of those days."

He didn't need to say anything else. He and Caroline shared a crib until they were a year old. They grew up side by side. No one knew him as well as she did, and he didn't have to pretend with her. Around others he would crack a joke or pretend lazy indifference, but not Caroline.

"We all have those days, but try not to have them around Nathaniel," she said. "He doesn't know you very well yet."

It was Luke's fault that Caroline had to play peacemaker. Luke's fault he'd been locked up in Cuba for over a year and caused his family untold misery. He needed to tamp down this low, mean part of himself and do better.

"I'll be on good behavior," he forced himself to say.

"And you will come with me to meet with the minister tomorrow?"

Gray would be giving Caroline away at her wedding, but Luke had agreed to do the readings, which was why he should talk to the minister about the selections. It was going to be the wedding of the year, with five hundred guests, including the president and three Supreme Court justices. Caroline never did anything halfway. She'd also invited plenty of people from the McKinley administration, for it was during her service in the McKinley White House that Caroline met Nathaniel. Caroline had sent an invitation to the former first lady, though it was doubtful Mrs. McKinley would attend. Caroline and Mrs. McKinley had an epic falling-out last year, and the wound still smarted for Caroline.

"I'll be there. Are you sure the groom is going to be up for all the hoopla? He never struck me as the sort to kick up his heels and dance until dawn."

"But he knows that I am, and he is happy to play along. Rather perfect, isn't he?" Caroline flashed him a blinding smile. She and Nathaniel were opposites in every way, and yet he'd never seen her happier.

He folded her hand atop his forearm as they walked the four blocks back to the boardinghouse. "If I told you I wanted to marry someone who didn't seem like a good match, but I swore she was the perfect woman for me, would you accept her?"

"Of course."

She said it too casually. Too easily, as though she hadn't really understood his question.

"Think carefully. What if she was a blue-nosed prude? A raging harridan with no fashion sense? Could you accept her?"

Caroline still seemed serenely nonchalant. "If you loved her, of course I would."

"What if she was a Magruder?"

The light in her eyes faded. "Oh, Luke . . ."

He smiled a little sadly. "Yes. That's what I'm up against."

"Are you still trying to topple her father and grind her entire family into dust?"

"Some things never change." Which meant a happy ending for him and Marianne probably wasn't in the cards, but he couldn't help wishing for it anyway.

Caroline gave him a quick hug. "Gray may pitch a fit, but I'll stand beside you no matter what. If you choose Marianne Magruder, she will have my full support."

"Swear it."

She blanched. "What?"

"Swear it. Caroline, this may be more difficult than it seems. I'm not sure what I'm up against if she and I throw caution to the winds. I have this hankering to run away to San Francisco or sail into the sunset. With her."

"Luke, I swear I will support you and whoever you choose to marry."

A little tension faded from his spine. "Thanks for that."

They had arrived at the boardinghouse, and he bid her farewell. He had completely lost his appetite but managed to choke down lunch. Everyone at the table seemed to feel as miserable as he did, and there was an odd sort of comfort in that.

By dinner he felt worse, and by nightfall he and everyone on the Poison Squad knew something was severely wrong.

Eighteen

Marianne couldn't stay in Baltimore and attend Andrew's birthday party as though nothing had happened. Until yesterday, everyone in the family thought the sun rose and set on Andrew Magruder, but not now. Her parents had a huge argument over what happened with Bandit. Vera sided with Andrew, while Clyde and her grandfather had been disgusted. Marianne simply wanted to escape the turmoil. When Clyde gave her permission to return to Washington and miss Andrew's party, it triggered another round of tears and tantrums, but she left on the evening train without regret.

The whole affair made her heartsick. After returning to Washington, she went straight to her room and felt beneath her mattress where she hid the photograph of Luke holding Bandit. How wretched Bandit had been while struggling in the icy water. She and Luke both risked so much to rescue him, but she would do it again in a heartbeat.

She gazed at Luke's image as he beamed with pride. He was the only person who would understand her grief right now. Her heart was splitting wide open, and she needed him for comfort. It was after ten o'clock at night, but if Luke knew how heartsick she was, he'd want her to come to him.

She returned the photograph to its hiding place, then set off for his boardinghouse, where she was surprised to see the building lit up like a Christmas tree. Maybe she shouldn't have been. When twelve young men shared a house, surely there was a fair amount of carousing in the evening, even if it was a weeknight.

But she didn't hear carousing when she stood on the porch. She knocked, and the door flung open only seconds later. A man in his shirtsleeves with a serious expression opened the door. She vaguely remembered him as one of the competitive brothers who boasted about his superiority in all things the day she came to photograph the men.

"I'm Marianne Magruder. I came to see Luke Delacroix."

The man opened the door. "He's here. Come inside. You can help with nursing duties."

The front parlor looked and smelled terrible. A number of men lay on the sofas, and a few sprawled on the floor. Luke spotted her from where he was slumped in a stuffed chair in the corner.

He squinted at her. "Marianne? Is that you?"

"It's me." She crossed the room and knelt beside him, appalled at the pallor of his skin. "You've looked better."

His smile was slow in coming, but he covered her hand with his and squeezed. "I can't hear very well. And I'm dizzy. My head feels like it's going to explode."

Alarm raced through her, but she tried not to let it show as she pressed a hand to his forehead. "You don't seem feverish."

"But I've been puking all night. So have the other guys. That's why we need to stay down here near the washroom."

"Have you called a doctor?"

Luke shrugged. "Nah, it's just the poison they feed us. We'll live."

"Are you sure?" For pity's sake, the whole point of the test was to use chemicals in doses far beyond rationality.

A man sprawled on the sofa lifted a cloth that had been shielding his eyes. She remembered calling him Princeton because of the snazzy coat he wore. He didn't look snazzy tonight. "I think they're feeding us Rough on Rats," he said. "I call it Rough on All of Humanity."

There was some snickering, but it was half-hearted. The man who had opened the door introduced himself as Big Rollins. He claimed not to be suffering from the food, but his brother was among the test subjects getting the chemicals, and Little Rollins didn't even bother to wave at her from his position on the floor.

She turned back to Luke. "I'm sending for a doctor. What about the man running the experiment? At the very least, he should see exactly what you all are suffering."

"Good point," Big Rollins said. "We planned on waiting until morning, but he should probably see them now."

Luke nodded. "Fine, but I don't want Marianne being out this late. Send St. Louis to get him."

A tall, gangly man sprang to his feet. "I'll run the entire way," he vowed.

After he left, Marianne grabbed a footstool and sat beside Luke. "Is there anything I can get for you?"

"A new head?"

Her heart turned over. Even miserable, he didn't lose his sense of humor. He told her that all the men had been feeling poorly for a few days, but something changed this morning. The headaches got so bad it was hard to focus on anything. They were dizzy and listless. Luke and two others had ringing in their ears that wouldn't stop.

"Do you know what chemical was used?"

Luke gave a single shake of his head, as though any greater movement would cause too much pain. "What brings you here tonight?" he asked. "I thought you were supposed to be in Baltimore all week."

Energy drained from her at the memory of Bandit. She closed her eyes and rested her forehead on the arm of the chair.

"Marianne? What's wrong?" Luke's hand was gentle as he stroked the back of her head. "Tell me. Don't be miserable alone."

She lay there for a few moments, savoring the gentle touch of his fingers stroking her hair and wishing it could continue forever. It wasn't fair to seek comfort from him when he was so sick, but she needed this simple touch.

She took a deep breath and sat up. "My brother killed Sam's dog. Bandit. The one you saved from the ice."

Luke's face morphed from astonishment to anger, and then to heartbreaking sympathy for her. "Oh, Marianne, I'm so sorry. I know what that dog meant to you."

"It's still hard to believe, but he admitted it."

Luke leaned forward to give her a hug but immediately listed to the side. She rushed to help him back into the chair, stunned to see this normally vibrant man laid so low.

It seemed to take forever for the doctor to arrive, but at eleven o'clock, heavy treads were heard outside, and a man Luke said was Dr. Wiley entered. He was tall and broad, with widely spaced eyes and a grim manner as he entered the parlor, huffing and out of breath. The doctor seemed alarmed as he surveyed the men sprawled all over the furniture like wet rags.

"What's going on?" he asked.

"You've poisoned us," Princeton said. "I can't even think straight."

"You could never think straight," Little Rollins said. "I'm sicker than he is. He's too dizzy to walk down the stairs, but I can't even walk across the room without bumping into the walls."

"All right, let's get you on your feet," Dr. Wiley said, helping Princeton stand. "I'm going to examine each of you individually in the dining room. Then I'll decide what is to be done."

It didn't take long. Dr. Wiley only examined two men before heading back into the main room, his face resolved.

"Line up, everyone. Syrup of ipecac for the lot of you."

There were groans all around, as the syrup was used to induce vomiting, but Dr. Wiley announced the test on salicylic acid was officially over. All men would be given a reprieve for the next week as the poison was cleared from their systems, but he wanted their stomachs completely purged immediately.

"I've been heaving my guts all night," Princeton said.

"When was the last time you heaved?" the doctor asked.

"Twenty minutes ago."

"Then you've still got more inside. Come on men, snap to it." Dr. Wiley held a dark brown bottle and a spoon. Despite his militant tone, Marianne spotted the worry in his eyes. What happened here tonight had badly rattled him.

It rattled her too. He'd mentioned salicylic acid, which was one of the preservatives Andrew used in their cans of creamed chipped beef. She'd never heard any complaints about their chipped beef, but they surely used it differently than what these men had consumed.

Luke sent her an exhausted, miserable smile. "Time for me to take more bad medicine."

She squeezed his hand. "Maybe you'll feel better soon."

He shambled toward the doctor and waited his turn. Each time they were together, she marveled anew at his endless good nature. He hadn't complained, hadn't resisted. He simply saddled up and got the job done.

Over the next hour Marianne helped bring fresh water and clean linens, and tried to put a positive face on things, but it was a long night. The good news was that by fully purging their stomachs, at least the men would be able to sleep without dashing for the facilities all night long.

At midnight Dr. Wiley was closing up his medical bag when she pulled him aside to press him for details about the salicylic acid. He initially refused to divulge anything, but the moment she said that her father was Clyde Magruder, there was a shift in his attitude.

"The Magruders are one of the biggest offenders when it comes to petrifying their food with chemicals."

Her first instinct was to leap to her family's defense, but it was more important to gather information. "I'd like to know exactly how much preservative caused these men to get so sick tonight. Since you will be discontinuing the experiment, there's no harm in telling me, is there?"

He took her back to the kitchen to show her the notebook he kept locked in a cabinet. The men had been eating food preserved with salicylic acid all week, but that morning he tripled the dosage.

"Good heavens, why?"

"Because I can't test these men for the next twenty or thirty years. Using an elevated dose is an attempt to judge what long-term exposure might do to them." He wrote some equations on a slip of paper and gave them to her. "That's the ratio of chemical the men received today. I would give my eyeteeth to know the ratio used at Magruder Food."

She raised her chin. "Dr. Wiley, I truly don't want your eyeteeth."

"Do you want to do what's right?"

She folded her arms across her chest. "What are you suggesting?"

"I want the recipes your family uses. They've never revealed them, so it's impossible to know what they are releasing into the American food supply." He glanced down the hallway at the men sprawled in the parlor. "All of them are showing neurological confusion and mobility difficulties. I want to know how much salicylic acid is used in Magruder products."

She held up the slip of paper. "We don't use this much."

"Prove it."

Her father always refused to release their recipes. Could Dr.

Wiley and the Delacroixs be right? She'd always blithely accepted what Clyde and Andrew said about preservatives, but it was hard to dismiss what she'd seen tonight.

Her mouth went dry as she pondered Dr. Wiley's challenge. All the family recipes and canning procedures were in the company archive in Baltimore.

Dr. Wiley kept pressing. "Over the past few months, the Magruder company worked with the government to commission five studies regarding chemical preservatives," he said. "They released two but have refused to disclose the others, and that's worrisome. Why didn't they release the other studies?"

Down the hall, Luke leaned forward, rubbing his temples. Even from a distance she could hear him moan as he repositioned himself on the chair. The only reason Luke signed up for this ghastly experiment was because of what happened when he partnered with her father to sell coffee in Philadelphia. Luke and all the other men sprawled in misery were willing to sacrifice for a higher cause. Was she?

"I can probably get the information you're looking for," she said.

A gleam of appreciation lit Dr. Wiley's tired face. "It would be much appreciated."

The thought of returning to Baltimore in search of those recipes was dreadful. She couldn't even bear to think about Andrew, let alone politely ask him for the recipes. She was going to have to use another way to get that information, and it wasn't going to be easy.

At two o'clock in the morning, St. Louis declared that he needed to get some sleep because he had to be up at five to train for the Olympics. He dragged himself upstairs, but Big Rollins, the only other healthy man still awake, said he would stay.

As would Marianne. Her parents were still in Baltimore, and if the men took a turn for the worse, Big Rollins would need help. Most of the sick men had dropped off into a restless sleep, but Marianne sat with Luke on the long window bench. With his back propped against the sidewall and his legs stretched out, he looked as tired as a wrung-out dishrag. His skin was pasty white and still had a sheen of perspiration, but his eyes were alive.

Indeed, they hadn't torn their eyes off each other for hours. She sat on the other end of the window bench with Luke's feet cradled in her lap, wishing the sun would never rise. They had been talking for hours—softly, so as not to disturb the others who were too dizzy to climb the stairs, but it still felt like they were the only people in the world. She told him about Delia's grandiose decorating tastes and her mother's painful insecurities in Washington. He spoke of his twin sister Caroline and the adventures they'd had over the years.

When he talked about Caroline's coming wedding, he seemed terribly glum. "I feel her starting to pull away already," he said. "Ever since we were infants, Caroline and I have been a team. Two peas in a pod. Now she's moving to another pod."

Marianne never felt a sense of loss when Andrew married, but they weren't very close. Despite occasional moments of kindness, Andrew never treated her like a full member of the family, and he resented every scrap of attention their father spared her.

"I'm jealous," she said.

Luke's brows rose in surprise. "Why?"

"Don't you know how rare that is? To have someone's unquestioning loyalty no matter what? To feel like you can belong, even if you disappoint?"

"You don't have that?"

Luke's question was so softly whispered that she could barely hear it, but it slammed into her like a fist. No, she'd never had that. Aunt Stella was a glaring example of what could happen to a Magruder who displeased the family. The loyalty Luke described sounded wonderful.

"What's wrong with the man Caroline will marry?" she asked, sensing this was at the root of Luke's sullen mood.

She must have guessed correctly, because his eyes lit with embarrassed amusement, but he didn't have any difficulty answering her question. "He's a rule-follower. Stuffy."

"The horror."

He laughed, all the tension draining from his body. "Oh, Marianne, I think I love you."

The words hung in the air. Based on Luke's expression, he hadn't meant to say them. They had slipped out in a moment of inattention and exhaustion from a long night.

"Actually, I don't *think* it, I know it," Luke clarified.

"I love you too," she said. There was no point in denying it. It would probably go nowhere because they both had families to consider and nothing would be easy, but she'd never felt such a sense of belonging with anyone before. What an irony that the undiluted love and affection she'd craved all her life should finally come from a Delacroix.

On the opposite side of the window seat, Luke simply gazed at her in tired, happy exhaustion. Over the next few hours, they drifted in and out of sleep. Sometimes they talked, sometimes they checked on the others.

The first hint of dawn finally arrived, but Marianne remained with Luke on the window seat, knowing they only had a few more minutes together. The steps of the cook and Nurse Hollister sounded on the front porch as the morning began.

"You survived the night," she said with a tired smile.

Luke winced as he rose from the window seat, holding firm to the side of the wall. "Still dizzy, but my head doesn't ache as much."

Some of the others also suffered lingering effects, but most were able to climb the stairs. Luke remained with a hand braced on the wall.

"I was supposed to drive Caroline to meet with the minister this morning," he said. "I don't think I can go. The thought of driving over cobblestones is enough to start my head aching again. Our home doesn't have a telephone, but maybe I can get Big Rollins to deliver a message."

"I'll go," she said. It would give her a chance to meet Luke's sister and possibly take the first tentative steps toward some sort of détente between their families.

The town house where the Delacroixs lived was a shock. Marianne double-checked the address Luke had written on a slip of paper, because the modest three-story home simply wasn't what she expected. The Delacroixs were old money. She expected to see something like Versailles with gold trim or a castle like the Vanderbilts' home.

Instead she stood before a brick town house that looked like it had been there since before the revolution. It had the simple colonial lines of strength and solidity, but nothing ornate or lavish.

She took a steadying breath, mounted the staircase, and knocked on the front door.

A feminine voice called out from inside, "I'll be right there, Luke!" The patter of feet sounded just before the door yanked open. Caroline's face fell. "Oh, my apologies. Who are you?"

"I'm Marianne Magruder. We met briefly at the gala."

Caroline masked her surprise with a gracious smile. "How silly of me," she said and held the door open wide. "Come inside. I've been dying to get better acquainted with you. Luke is supposed to meet me for some wedding preparations."

Old floorboards creaked as Marianne stepped inside. She liked the scent of lemon wax in the front hall. "Luke asked me to tell you he can't be here today. He had a difficult night. All the men on the Poison Squad did."

Caroline caught her breath, then a door in the hallway jerked open and Gray Delacroix stood there, his face grim. "What happened?" he demanded.

Marianne took a step back. The foyer suddenly felt too small, given the way Gray towered over her in suspicious disapproval. She clutched her reticule, terribly aware of the slip of paper with the chemical equations of exactly what had caused Luke's illness. This was possibly the last topic she wished to discuss with these two people, but they were rightfully concerned about Luke.

"Some of the men had a bad reaction to the food. A doctor has seen them, and all are on the mend. It may take a few days for them to get over the dizziness and a bit of a headache."

"A bit of a headache?" Gray snapped. "Explain."

"I'm not a medical doctor. He's got a headache. I don't know how to be any more plain than that."

Gray strode to the front door and yanked a jacket off a hook. "I'm going over there."

"I think you'll find him sleeping," Marianne said.

Indecision caused Gray to pause, but Caroline was better at disguising her feelings. "Don't be difficult, Gray. Let's invite Marianne inside for a cup of tea. I'll send the minister a note to reschedule. We should get to know each other."

Gray's expression softened a fraction. "I'm not sure that's a good idea," he said to Marianne. "Your grandfather just filed another lawsuit against me."

Lawsuits were Jedidiah's preferred method of communication. He was crafty and tough but not skilled with words and preferred to let his lawyers do his public fighting. This latest court action was over an outrageous stunt Luke and Gray had engineered last year that slandered how the Magruders made applesauce.

"I know," she replied. "Why don't you just say you're sorry?"

"Because I'm not."

"Why do you hate my grandfather so much?" Marianne asked. "Because he came from humble stock? Because his accent isn't refined like yours?"

"Because he takes shortcuts," Gray said. "Look, this conversation isn't going to be helpful. I'm sure you are a very fine—"

"Gray," Caroline interrupted. "Do you remember what I relayed to you about Luke's newest fascination?"

Gray's face hardened as he turned his attention to his sister. "It's just the lure of forbidden fruit."

They were talking about her. Marianne could feel it in her bones.

Before she could say anything else, though, Caroline took her arm and escorted her down a skinny hallway toward a kitchen at the back of the house. It was a homey room, with copper pans and bundles of dried herbs hanging from a rack above a worktable. Caroline offered Marianne a seat at an old kitchen table, then floated around the kitchen, preparing a kettle and setting out teacups.

"Tell me about yourself," she said brightly. "I tried to seek you out at the gala, but you disappeared so quickly."

Because she and Luke had stolen away behind the service tent, where she had the most breathless two hours of her life.

Marianne opted for a safer topic. "I work as a photographer for the Department of the Interior."

Caroline asked all sorts of questions about Marianne's opinions on art and techniques for getting a good photograph. The effortless way she kept asking questions made the conversation easy, and Marianne soon relaxed. Caroline was about to brew a second pot of tea when Marianne noticed the time.

"Oh dear, I've missed the one o'clock streetcar back into town." That meant she would need to loiter in Alexandria until the three o'clock streetcar.

"Not to worry," Caroline assured her. "Gray can arrange for a carriage to take you home."

"No, I'll be fine," Marianne rushed to say. She didn't have enough money on her for a private carriage all the way home. "I can window-shop until the three o'clock streetcar."

"Nonsense," Gray said, appearing in the kitchen doorway. "Come. We're the ones who delayed you, so let us make it right."

It would be rude to refuse, so she followed him down the hall and out the front door. There was a public stable at the end of the street, and it looked like Gray intended to accompany her there and pay her fare. The sun was nearly blinding, and she scrambled for something to say.

There was no need, as Gray got straight to the point as they walked along the cobblestone street, his voice surprisingly kind.

"My brother is a wounded soul. What he's doing to himself with that poison study is proof of that, and it isn't the first time he's risked his life over some heroic quest. He never felt good enough in our father's eyes, and it's made him reckless and rebellious. If he spots danger, he is drawn to it like a lodestone. You need to understand this about him."

Gray paused, letting the sentence sink in. Once again, he was talking about her without saying so, but what Gray didn't realize was that she and Luke were already half in love with each other before they realized the problem of their last names.

"I hear everything you are saying," she said calmly.

They arrived at the stables, and Gray paid the fee for the carriage, then turned to shake her hand.

"You seem like an admirable woman," he said. "In other circumstances we would have been friends, but be very careful with Luke. He likes teetering on the razor's edge of trouble, and one of these days he might push it too far. You won't want to be with him when that happens."

The warning stayed with her all the way back to the city.

Nineteen

By evening Luke was feeling better. Everyone on the Poison Squad was given a reprieve from chemically treated food for the rest of the week. The last vestige of his headache was a painful reminder of what polluted food could do to a man, and it strengthened his resolve to push for government regulation of these chemicals.

That resolve made his feelings for Marianne even more difficult. He would forever remember their intimacy as she nursed him through the night. If he was a painter, he would try to capture the way moonlight lit the side of her face as she sat opposite him on the window seat, sharing her heart and soul with him. He loved her, and she loved him. They would find a way to make this work.

He glanced down the street, searching through the pedestrians and carriages in search of her. She'd promised to visit him this evening, and he felt like a lovestruck swain as he awaited her return. He couldn't stop thinking about her. The way she always knew the perfect thing to say. Her courage. The way she seemed so buoyant.

The way he might be able to use her to get an upper hand over Clyde Magruder.

Guilt gnawed at him. Using Marianne in such a capacity threatened everything they had together, but he had warned her about his low, shifty side. She just hadn't experienced it yet. Maybe she didn't believe it existed, but it did.

A streetcar came to a stop at the end of the block, and he grinned as Marianne emerged from it. She quickened her steps when she spotted him, skipping a little in delight. He held both his arms wide, and she gave up trying to be mannerly. She hiked up her skirts and ran the last few yards until his arms closed around her and they kissed each other, heedless of passersby on the street.

She eventually pulled away. "How are you feeling?"

"Better, now that you're here. What did Caroline say?"

"She invited me to tea and couldn't have been nicer. Your brother was scary."

He stilled. If Gray had said a single hostile thing to Marianne, Luke would have his head.

She must have noticed, for she laughed and touched the side of his face. "By *scary* I mean he was thoughtful and considerate and had a raft of good reasons why we shouldn't see each other anymore. Like I said: scary."

He clasped her hand and began walking down the street with her. "When do your parents get back in town?"

"Not until Sunday."

That meant they could have four sun-kissed summer days without fear of intrusion from her family. He could take her sailing on the Potomac. They could explore the city and take photographs together. Lay on a blanket and watch the stars rotate all night long.

She cut his daydreams short. "I need to return to Baltimore." He frowned, and she rushed to explain that Dr. Wiley wanted the recipes for Magruder's canned meals. "If getting those recipes will help, or if it means men like you won't have to subject yourself to this sort of treatment, how can I refuse?"

Luke was stunned. He hadn't even asked for her help, and already she was offering it. The base part of him immediately started scheming up ways to take advantage of her access to the Magruder archives. He could probably get in and out without her ever knowing. Even if she caught him red-handed, he knew in his bones she wouldn't turn him in. He could get away with it. . . .

But he was trying to be a better man. He wanted to defeat Clyde Magruder and win the princess too.

He leaned forward to kiss her forehead. "You're far too good for me."

She tugged his chin down and pressed a kiss to his lips. "Maybe. I love you anyway."

He smiled and withdrew a step. "Do the recipes contain the preservatives?"

Marianne didn't know, but there was only one way to find out. He thought carefully for how to take advantage of the situation.

"Bring plenty of film with you," he advised her. "Photograph everything you can find. Then we can turn the pictures over to Dr. Wiley and see once and for all if those recipes are safe."

Marianne set off for Baltimore on Friday morning, feeling anxious throughout the entire train ride. Maybe she shouldn't feel so wretchedly, horribly guilty. All she would do was pass on a few recipes so Dr. Wiley could assess the safety of the preservatives used in their food. Andrew and her father always claimed the miniscule amounts of chemical additives they used were safe, but that was what they thought about coffee they'd sold in Philadelphia. If the amount of salicylic acid they used as a meat preservative in their creamed chipped beef was safe, they should have no qualms in letting Dr. Wiley analyze it.

Once in Baltimore, she hired a private carriage to take her

straight to the Magruder factory. With luck, she would be able to take photographs of the recipes and catch the four o'clock train back to Washington.

It was the day of Andrew's big party, and knowing her sister-in-law, Marianne doubted Delia had let Andrew go to the office today. She still was cautious as she approached the office building. The blinds in Andrew's office were open, and a peek inside revealed the room was empty.

Good. Had Andrew been in the office, she would have been forced to swallow her disgust over Bandit and beg his permission to look through the company archives. Now all she had to do was get the office secretary to unlock the door to the archive.

Mrs. Carlyle was a matronly woman who had been Clyde's secretary and now worked for Andrew. Vera had once told Marianne that if any woman was going to be waiting hand and foot on her husband eight hours a day, she had better have a face like a bulldog. That fit Mrs. Carlyle to a T. It wouldn't surprise Marianne if Delia encouraged Andrew to keep Mrs. Carlyle on for the same reason.

Mrs. Carlyle looked surprised as Marianne entered the small foyer area. "I would have thought you'd be at the birthday festivities," the old secretary said.

"Who would have guessed that a thirtieth birthday party could cause such a ruckus," Marianne said with a laugh. "The party won't start until five o'clock, but everything is chaos at home. I thought I'd take the opportunity to look through the family archives. Can you unlock the door?"

Mrs. Carlyle didn't hesitate as she reached for an enormous ring of keys and led the way to a locked door at the rear of the building. To call this room an archive was a bit of a stretch. It was a windowless room filled with filing cabinets and old advertising posters. Marianne pulled the lever on the switch plate, and a bare lightbulb illuminated the room. Dust prickled her nose, and the musty odor surrounded her as she stepped inside.

"Is there something I can help you find?" Mrs. Carlyle asked. "I probably know the contents of this cave better than anyone."

Marianne shook her head. "I'll be fine," she said. "I don't want to keep you from your work."

Mrs. Carlyle nodded and left, but the door remained open. Marianne counted out the space of a dozen heartbeats, then closed the door. She intended to take plenty of photographs, and that was best done in private.

Magruder's Creamed Chipped Beef had been their best-selling product for decades. It was an adaptation of an old family recipe from when Grandma Magruder cooked it up by the vat in her home kitchen and sold it in mason jars to workingmen in the neighborhood. They didn't start adding chemical preservatives until decades later after mass production began.

Marianne started in the first filing drawer, but it contained nothing but old billing records. Other drawers held machinery repair manuals and personnel files.

Then she found an entire drawer of files about the Delacroix family.

Delacroix? Her eyes widened. This wasn't what she came for, but it was impossible to resist temptation. She yanked out the first file and opened it.

It contained the bill of sale for *The Sparrow*, the ship Jedidiah bought to irk the Delacroixs, whose ships had been seized during the Civil War. Magruder family legend celebrated how the man born in a cabin with a dirt floor became so rich that he bought and burned the Delacroix ship simply to prove how far he had climbed. As a child, the story made Marianne proud. Now that she held the bill of sale for the long-ago ship, she wasn't sure. It had been a petty act of spite, not the action of a wise or kind man.

She turned to the next page in the file, and her heart plummeted.

Jedidiah had filed an insurance claim on the ship. *The Sparrow* had been fully insured through Lloyd's of London, a company so far away that they probably never learned the details of how that ship caught fire. She ought to have known her thrifty grandfather would figure out a way to be fully compensated. This crime took place almost forty years ago, long past any legal consequences, but her respect for old Jedidiah had been dealt a blow.

She shook her head. It didn't matter. She came here to get the recipe for Creamed Chipped Beef and any other products using salicylic acid as a preservative.

The third cabinet held the recipes. A whole drawer contained canning and preservation procedures for their fruit pie fillings. These were no simple recipes. They required ingredients by the barrel and complex steps for feeding the ingredients into machinery and tank-sized vats. The recipe for apple compote required four hundred pounds of diced apples, thirty pounds of butter, and sixty pounds of brown sugar. Then came a list of unfamiliar terms. Three pounds of powdered fruit pectin, a cup of erythorbic acid, and two cups of sodium bisulfite.

She prepared her camera. This recipe made an immense amount of apple compote, and a few cups of chemical enhancers were probably harmless, but only Dr. Wiley would know for sure. She took a photograph of the recipe and returned it to the file.

An entire filing cabinet was devoted to their canned meat products, and she pulled the files for Deviled Ham, Corned Beef Hash, Chicken Spread, and Creamed Chipped Beef.

The recipe for Creamed Chipped Beef was much lengthier than the apple compote. Three hundred pounds of thinly sliced cured beef, forty gallons of condensed milk, eight gallons of soybean oil, and six pounds of cornstarch. Then came the list of chemicals. Calcium chloride, sodium metabisulfite, maltodextrin, and salicylic acid. Was four cups of salicylic acid a lot for a recipe this size? She couldn't begin to guess. She laid the recipe flat on a table to take a photograph.

In ten minutes she'd made photographs of all the meat recipes. Pangs of guilt plagued her the entire time, but Dr. Wiley was a good man. He wasn't going to steal these recipes. All he would do was determine if they were safe.

Throughout it all, she thought about *The Sparrow*. The incident had happened before she was born, and maybe her grandfather had become a different man. It wasn't for her to judge. This archive brimmed with proof of her family's industry and success. She should be proud of her family. She *was* proud of her family.

After she'd photographed the recipes she came for, curiosity drove her to the last filing cabinet. Her father had commissioned numerous studies into the safety of their preservatives over the years, and she'd bet her bottom dollar they were stored in this last cabinet. According to Dr. Wiley, her father's congressional committee sponsored five additional studies just this year. Only two of the five studies had been released to the public. Where were the other three?

It didn't take her long to find them. The new studies were in a file clearly labeled the *Congressional Committee on Manufactures*. Copies of all five studies were here. The results of the experiments were filled with chemical equations and terminology she didn't understand. She didn't know how to interpret them, but Dr. Wiley would.

She photographed the entire file of test results. As soon as she developed the film, she would turn the studies over to Dr. Wiley, who would know what to do with them.

On Saturday morning Marianne went to the Gunderson Photography Studio and paid to have use of the darkroom for the entire morning. It took hours to develop all the film she had taken in Baltimore, but by noon she had it processed and the photographs enlarged. The problem was that she had no idea where Dr. Wiley could be found.

Luke would know. From the studio she went to the boardinghouse to turn the pictures over to him, but he wasn't there.

"He's visiting his family," Princeton said when he answered the door. "Dr. Wiley is giving us all a week off the test, and Luke said he had business back home."

Marianne thanked him and headed for the streetcar stop. The photographs felt like an albatross around her neck, and she wanted them out of her hands today. The quicker she could turn them over to Luke, the quicker she could shake this feeling of disloyalty.

Except when she stood on the stoop outside his town house and knocked, there was no answer. She knocked again and still had no response, but the sound of laughter carried on the breeze from behind the house. She skirted around the side of the house to a backyard surrounded by a brick wall.

The wall was too high to see over, but Luke's voice could clearly be heard on the other side, engaged in some sort of good-natured argument with several others. She ran her fingers across the mortar of the old brick wall, quickly finding a crevice that provided a toehold. Slinging her satchel securely across her body, she reached for the top of the wall and hoisted herself up, the grit rough beneath her palms.

She peeked over the rim and saw a group of people lounging on a blanket on the grassy lawn, a picnic spread out before them. Luke had his back to her.

"Hello?" she asked.

Five people swiveled toward her in surprise, and Luke leapt to his feet.

"There's the prettiest sight I've seen all day," he said as he crossed toward her as if this happened all the time.

"I don't want to disturb you," she said to the others still sitting on the lawn. "I simply came to give Luke something." That something being a photographic stack of reports that should have been submitted to the government instead of being buried in her family's archive.

"Come join us," Luke said. "My family is trying to evict me, and I could use someone on my side." Her eyes widened in surprise, but he was laughing, as were the others, so the threat couldn't be too serious. "Come to the front, and I'll let you in."

She scurried through the overgrown grass on the side of the house and met him at the front door. Before she could say anything, he swept her into his arms to steal a lingering kiss. Her tension from the past twenty-four hours drained away in the comfort of his embrace.

"Let's go join the others," he said after he finally released her.

He led her down the center hallway and out to the back garden, where he introduced her to Nathaniel Trask, his future brother-in-law, who didn't look too stuffy, since he wore an open-collared shirt and rolled-up sleeves. She had already met Gray and Caroline, but Gray's wife was the only one not sitting on the grass. Annabelle wore a loose white gown and sat on a bench beneath a pear tree, gently fanning herself.

"We're *not* evicting Luke," Annabelle said. "We just don't know if we're going to turn his bedroom into a nursery, or if it will be in the addition we're planning to build onto the back of the house."

A glance at Annabelle's waistline explained why she was sitting on the bench instead of sprawling on the picnic blanket like the others.

"I'm sorry for intruding," Marianne said. "I merely came to deliver some photographs to Luke."

"Photographs?" Caroline said. "Show us! Luke has been bragging about your wonderfully artistic pictures."

Her fingers curled around the satchel. Photographs of old recipes and scientific studies were surely the least artistic pictures she'd ever taken.

"They're just dull, government pictures," Luke said, neatly saving her from an explanation. "Let's not change the topic of how I am to be banished from the family home to make way for the coming infant."

Gray rolled back on the grass and covered his eyes. "Such melodrama!" he moaned. "Miss Magruder, please join us. Perhaps you can reel Luke back from the cliff of despair he is determined to enjoy."

"Only if you call me Marianne," she said, sinking to her knees on one of the blankets.

Caroline filled a plate with some sliced pears and a wedge of cheese. Everyone ate with their hands instead of silverware. How refreshing this was! Picnics in the Magruder household involved tables set beneath a tent with maids serving meals and a musician playing an instrument from a tactful distance.

Here the only music was a couple of sparrows chirping overhead.

The next hour was perfectly delightful, but throughout it all, the cache of photographs tugged at her conscience. She needed to pass them over to Luke in private. Her fingers curled around the rim of the case that was hidden inside her satchel.

Luke must have noticed, for he sprang to his feet. "Let me show you the harbor at the end of the street. I spent half my childhood escaping my chores there."

His hand was warm as he helped her rise. She said farewell to the others and followed Luke down the hallway of the house. He slipped inside a book-lined study and turned to her.

"Here's what I found," she said, turning the case over to him.

"What did you get?"

"Everything, including all five studies commissioned by the Committee on Manufactures. Recipes too. Dr. Wiley swore he wouldn't use the recipes for anything other than assessing their safety."

Luke flipped through the recipes quickly but slowed as he reached the scientific studies, letting out a low whistle. "I've been looking for these," he said. "The committee released two studies, but the other three seemed to disappear." He held up a few of the photographs. "Voilà. You've found them."

She shifted uneasily. "I can't make any sense of them. Will Dr. Wiley be able to figure them out?"

"You can bet on it," he said confidently.

"What happens then?"

Luke paused, studying her with a scrutiny that made her uncomfortable. "Those studies were commissioned by the government. The people have a right to know what they found. Don't you agree?"

Of course she agreed, she just didn't know why they had been buried in her father's archive and what would happen if news of them became public. When she said as much to Luke, he was ready with an answer.

"If there is anything dangerous in those studies, that's all the more reason for the results to be made known to the public." He secured them in a locked cabinet, then turned to her, his expression light and cheerful once again. "Let's go to the harbor," he said. "I adore my family, but I don't want to court my favorite girl in front of them."

As always, his smile melted her heart. She felt better now that the photographs were out of her possession, and she eagerly followed where he led.

Luke held Marianne close to his side as he led her toward the port of Alexandria a few blocks down the street. Wooden boardwalks lined the harbor, sea gulls wheeled in the breeze, and the briny tang of salt filled the air.

"Your family seems so friendly," Marianne said. "They seem easy. Natural."

He glanced down at her. "Yours isn't?"

"My family is friendly. They just aren't easy."

They had arrived at the harbor, their footsteps making dull thuds on the old wooden boardwalk. Marianne drifted to the fence overlooking the choppy water, looking pensive as she stared into the distance.

"Can I tell you a secret?" she asked.

"You can tell me anything." He gently turned her shoulders to face him. She glanced around the harbor as if she feared being overheard. A crew of longshoremen were off-loading a ship, but they were a hundred yards away. Marianne still lowered her voice to a whisper.

"My mother . . . Vera Magruder, I mean . . . isn't really my mother. My father had an affair with an opera—"

"Shh," Luke said, laying a finger on her lips. He knew what

she was going to say. Dickie Shuster had told him everything months ago, and Luke wished he could smooth the anxiety from her face. "I know all about it," he said gently.

"How could you possibly know?"

She looked mortified as he told her about a journalist in Washington who made it his business to know all manner of unseemly gossip.

"Dickie Shuster?" she repeated when Luke mentioned his name. "I think I met him. He was an odd little man. Strange clothes."

"That's him," Luke confirmed.

Marianne groaned and plopped down onto a nearby barrel. "This will kill my mother if it ever gets out. How can I stop him?"

Luke hunkered down beside her and took her hand. "Dickie has known forever," he said. "He tends to sit on information and will only use it if he thinks he can milk it for something big. In this case, I don't think he will. Dickie likes your father and would rather keep him as an ally."

"How do you know this?"

"Because I keep my ear to the ground. Dickie and I are a lot alike that way. This city is full of powerful congressmen, but there are people behind the scenes who can move the chess pieces without sitting in elected office. Dickie is one of those people."

"You are too."

He kissed the back of her hand, then flashed her a little wink. "That would be bragging." Emotions whirled inside as he struggled to define them. "I feel like I'm at a turning point in my life. I was drawn to you the moment we met on the ice. You're smart and pretty enough to tempt a monk, and I'm no monk. Marianne, I can't walk away from you again. I want to marry you someday. If you don't want that too, tell me now."

She gazed back at him, hope mingled with fear in her face. "I can't."

He swept her into his arms, knowing he should be daunted by the challenges ahead of them but only caring about the here and now. They loved each other and would find a way forward, no matter what.

Twenty-One

The next month was the most exhilarating of Marianne's life, mostly because of her clandestine meetings with Luke. She no longer felt guilty about meeting him. The icy time last February when her father put his foot down felt so long ago. Besides, respect for her family's position regarding the Delacroixs had plummeted ever since she saw those files. The Delacroixs didn't file false insurance claims, look the other way when a dog was killed, or hide inconvenient scientific studies.

Her life was busier than ever because the McMillan Plan was gathering steam. The proposed park in the middle of the city meant each building slated for demolition needed to be photographed inside and out. The reclaimed space would be filled with acres of open lawn where tourists could exhaust themselves walking hither and yon, more than two miles of parkland in all.

Luke passionately endorsed the McMillan Plan, but Marianne mourned the loss of the buildings and the arboretum. Luke accompanied her every day as she created photographic memories of the buildings that would be torn down. Although they got along like a house on fire, they argued incessantly about the coming National Mall.

"We will finally be able to appreciate the grandeur of the city," Luke enthused. "We can't do that with *this* standing in the way."

He gestured to the Redwood Tree House, a charmingly ridiculous exhibit that had once been on display at the 1893 World's Fair in Chicago. It was an actual redwood tree that had been imported from California. After the World's Fair, it had been moved to a permanent home outside the Department of Agriculture. It had a twenty-six-foot circumference, large enough to have been hollowed out to accommodate a staircase inside that led to a viewing platform at the top.

Her task today was to photograph it. The rough texture of the bark made for an interesting image, especially since she included Luke in the picture. She regularly asked him to be in her photographs, but at least today she had a good excuse. How could one appreciate the size of a redwood unless a person stood next to it for scale?

"Stand there and quit making fun of me," she said as she unscrewed the cap of her viewfinder.

"Are you going to get weepy over this old redwood?" Luke teased.

"I'm getting weepy over everything that's going to be torn down to make way for your fancy park."

He held still while she took the photograph, then dove straight back into his arguments. "Sometimes you have to clear away the old to make way for the new and improved. Come on, let's climb this thing."

It was musty inside the tree trunk as they climbed to the viewing platform at the top. With the summer breeze on her face and the fully leafed trees in the arboretum below, it almost felt like they were at the top of a primeval world. Luke braced his arms on the railing as he gazed toward the Washington Monument, one of the few structures tall enough to be seen over the thickly wooded trees. Even the spires of the Smithsonian castle could barely be seen because the ugly blot of the Washington Gas Works obscured most of the view. The Baltimore and Potomac Railroad Station also sat in the middle of the proposed National Mall.

"Someday we will be able to see for two full miles," he said. "The mall will be like a smooth carpet of grass stretching from monument to monument."

She shook her head and pointed to the Gothic splendor of the B&P Railroad Station. "That is the most beautiful building in the entire city, and it's only thirty years old. You want us to tear it down?"

"We *must* tear it down. Marianne, just imagine! On one end of the park we'll have the Capitol, where our nation's laws are being created as we speak. At the other end will be memorials to our greatest heroes. This mall will be a hymn to the nation, built of granite and grass. This is the *only* place in the entire country for such a park. Go build your piddly railroad station somewhere else," he said with a wink.

When he spoke so passionately, she could almost see his vision. It would take decades and cost a fortune, but it would be appreciated by generations of people long into the future. Someday soon all this would be swept away. Even the grand old redwood tree in which they stood would be torn down, and people would forget it had ever been here.

"It's still sad to see it all go," she said.

"Change is always a little sad, but exciting too, don't you think?" Before she could answer, he reached for her camera. "Let me take your picture. At this exact moment you are the prettiest girl I've ever seen, and I want to remember you this way forever."

"Because I'll be old and grizzled someday?"

"You certainly shall, but not today," he said, looking down through the viewfinder. She instinctively knew how to stand against the railing and tilt her chin for the best angle.

"You're wasting film," she said as Luke proceeded to take a second and then a third photograph of her. She didn't need to ask why he was doing this. They both knew these stolen afternoons couldn't last forever, and someday these photographs might be all they had left to remember this time.

"I'll pay for the film," he said, not even lifting his gaze from the viewfinder as he took another photograph.

"Taking pictures is cheap and easy. It's developing them that is the challenge."

His fingers stopped moving. "Truer words were never spoken." His words were calm, but she sensed the tension just beneath the surface.

This was a difficult subject, and she probed gently. "Will you help me in the darkroom?"

"Must I?" He cocked a brow at her, probably trying to charm her, which usually worked. But not today.

Luke's claustrophobia was getting worse. It began the day they visited the prison together, when the experience awakened bad memories and old fears. Last week when he helped her in the darkroom, he'd abruptly left after only two minutes, claiming he needed a drink of water. Yesterday he'd accompanied her to photograph the interior of the B&P Railroad Station. Spare parts were stored in a windowless room crammed to the rafters with supplies. The moment she and Luke entered, he unknotted his tie and tugged at his collar. His complexion was pasty and covered with perspiration.

"Are you all right?" she had asked.

"Not really," he admitted. "Go ahead. I'm not leaving. But be quick about it, please."

Her work took only a few minutes, and the moment she was finished, Luke stumbled outside, drawing in huge gulps of air even though the atmosphere in the repair shop had been fine.

His symptoms were getting so bad that she wondered if he would be able to join her in the darkroom at all. "I'll have six rolls of film to develop on Friday," she said. "I could use help hanging the wet images."

"The part that's done with the window shades drawn?"

"The very same."

His mouth tightened. "I'll be there," he said as grimly as though he were facing an execution.

"Good," she said, but a little laughter had gone out of their day.

Marianne's photography assignment on Thursday took her to Fort Myer, a US Army post directly across the Potomac River. She'd been asked to photograph the row of homes informally known as General's Row, where some of the nation's top military leaders lived. It was a lovely, tree-shaded street with spacious red brick homes set well back from the road. It was a typical assignment except for the person selected to accompany her.

Colonel Henry Phelps.

Usually a job like this would be assigned to a low-level clerk, not a colonel, and Marianne sensed her father's hand in this. Clyde had been pulling strings to throw her and Colonel Phelps together for months, and he probably not only arranged the assignment sending her to Fort Myer, but hand-selected her escort too. Colonel Phelps was in his mid-thirties, had light brown hair with a fine mustache, and ramrod-straight posture. Many women would find him appealing.

"This is some of the finest military housing anywhere in the country," Colonel Phelps said as they walked up a flagstone path leading to the first house on her list. The Victorian home featured a wraparound front porch with white railings.

"Have you ever lived in such a place?" she asked while setting up her tripod.

"Heavens, no. I grew up in a third-story tenement in Pittsburgh, where my father worked in a steel mill. I've never actually lived in a proper house. I went straight from the tenement into the army, so it's been a barracks life for me." His eyes took on a wistful look as he gazed at the stately homes on General's Row. "Maybe someday I'll be on this street."

She took her first photograph, then cranked the roll of film. "Don't you have to be a general first?"

"That's the plan," he pointed out with a good-natured smile.

He continued talking about his family while she took pictures. He had a brother who was a steelworker and an uncle who worked as a machinist for the railroad. Both his sisters married millworkers. Colonel Phelps was clearly the pride of the family, the one who had already cracked through the barriers of class to make his mark in the world. He carried her satchel as they moved to the far side of the home for another set of photographs.

"Tell me about your own family," he said courteously as she began her next round of pictures. "I believe I read that your father has a sister, but I don't know more than that."

She turned to him in surprise. No one ever spoke about Aunt Stella, and she was surprised he even knew of her existence.

"How did you hear about Aunt Stella?"

"I've been reading whatever I can find about your family," he said. "Your grandfather is a fascinating man and widely lauded in the press. I saw mention of a daughter long ago, but then nothing. Did she pass away?"

Marianne thought carefully before answering, for this wasn't the time or place to air old family scandals. "Aunt Stella left home after she got married."

After she was banished from the family. The man Stella loved was a member of the Lenape Indian tribe. He had worked as a builder in downtown Baltimore, and Jedidiah said he would disinherit Stella if she continued to carry on with an Indian.

"Where did she go after getting married?" Colonel Phelps asked.

She pretended great concentration as she fastened the camera to the tripod, all the while trying to figure out how to tactfully answer the question.

"I'm afraid I don't know," she finally said. After Stella left Baltimore with her husband, it was as if they vanished from the face of the earth. To Marianne's shame, she didn't even know the husband's name. He'd always been called merely "the Indian that Stella married."

An awkward silence stretched as Marianne began taking pictures. After it became clear she intended to add nothing more about her mysteriously missing aunt, Colonel Phelps picked up the conversation.

"Family is very important," he said. "In a way, you and I have much in common. Your grandfather came from humble roots but made something of himself, and now his progeny have all benefitted from that. I feel a similar obligation."

"My goodness, such a long-term thinker," she teased.

"It's no laughing matter," he said. "Hard work, accomplishment, reputation . . . all of these things are vital if a man is to claw his way out of poverty."

"You're right, of course." She kept her tone light, but why did he have to be so serious? She had always worked hard and protected her reputation, but she still found time for fun and laughter along the way.

"Your father invited me to dinner on Sunday evening."

"He did?"

Colonel Phelps nodded. "He said that your brother and his family would be in town, and I asked for the chance to meet them."

It seemed like Clyde wasn't the only one keen to see an alliance between herself and Colonel Phelps. This morning almost felt as though she was being interviewed for a position as a prospective general's wife. A position she didn't want, but how was she to slow this momentum?

"Andrew and his family are coming to hear a speech my father is giving on Monday," she said. "We are all very proud."

"As you should be. There's nothing more important on this earth than family."

On that she was in complete agreement with Colonel Phelps. Too bad the rest of her family never felt that way about Aunt Stella.

Luke wasn't going to allow the darkroom to defeat him. His stint in a Cuban jail had already cost him fifteen months of freedom; he wasn't going to let it rob him of a normal life now that he was out. That meant he had to be able to walk into an enclosed space without a crippling attack of panic. These spells needed to be conquered, because they were getting worse.

Marianne was already setting out the trays of solution when he joined her in the darkroom.

"You don't have to be here," she said. "I shouldn't have pressured you the other day. Six rolls of film aren't too much for me to handle."

"I need to be here." He took down jugs of chemicals from the shelf and set each beside the correct tray. Having something to concentrate on would help divert his mind from the crawling sensation skittering across his muscles that urged him to escape and run.

Besides, he wanted to see how his photographs of Marianne in the tree house came out. She'd been so beautiful, with dappled sunlight in the background and the woodsy scene carrying a timeless aura.

When it came time to darken the room, Marianne clicked on the tungsten lamp before crossing to the windows. Knowing she was about to draw the window shade made his restless need to climb the walls even worse. Maybe standing by the door would bring relief. Marianne might not even notice this humiliating weakness starting to strangle him once again.

She placed a hand on the heavy drape. "Ready?" she asked. Her face was full of compassion. She knew *exactly* what he was feeling.

"Ready."

She lowered one drape, then the other. He forced his lungs to pull in a breath of air.

"Are you all right?" she asked. There was just enough amber light to see the pity on her face.

He could lie and say everything was fine, but his heart was beating so fast he was becoming dizzy. This wasn't imaginary discomfort, it was real. His skin prickled, his vision blurred. He couldn't get ill. Tomorrow was Caroline's wedding. There would be time to deal with this humiliating weakness another day.

"I'm sorry, Marianne, but I've got to get out of here," he said. With the last of his dignity, he summoned a smile. "I want a copy of the picture I took of you in the trees. I'll wait for you outside."

Relief hit within seconds of escaping the darkroom. His lungs filled naturally. The crawling sensations eased. His body felt better, but his humiliation was complete. No man wanted the woman he loved to see him like that.

He paced the sidewalk outside while pondering how to put a good face on this for Marianne. This stretch of sidewalk was in a rough part of the city, but he could breathe out here and savor the sunlight on his face.

After an hour, Marianne emerged, weighed down with a satchel slung over her shoulder and a crate in her arms. He rushed forward to help with the crate.

"Sorry about that in there," he said. The excuses he'd toyed with to explain his behavior all seemed foolish now, so he simply told the truth. "Enclosed spaces are still tough for me."

She headed toward a bench farther down the sidewalk. "That's okay."

He joined her on the bench, setting her crate of supplies on the walkway. A peek inside showed several rolls of undeveloped film and boxes of celluloid paper.

"It looks like you didn't get your work finished," he said.

"Only about halfway. Six rolls of film were too ambitious to tackle in an hour."

And she'd been counting on his help to get it done. If he hadn't bolted out of there like a weakling, they could have finished the job. "I'm sorry for letting you down," he said. "As mortifying as this is, I'm glad I don't have to pretend with you."

She squeezed his hand. "It's no bother, Luke. I know today didn't go so well, but I need to get the rest of the film developed. I've reserved some time tomorrow morning, if you'd like to try again."

He shook his head. "Tomorrow is Caroline's wedding. She will hang, draw, and quarter me if I'm late."

"How silly of me!" Marianne said. "I knew it was coming, but I'd forgotten it was tomorrow. Tell me about it." She looked properly enthused. There must be something about weddings that spoke to the female soul.

He began to describe it to her. Five hundred guests were expected, including all manner of politicians and industrialists. The reception would probably echo through the ages. "President Roosevelt was called to Boston, so he won't be attending, but every other high-ranking official and officer in the city will be there."

"Including Colonel Phelps," Marianne said, a hint of unease in her voice.

The name was familiar. Colonel Phelps was one of those officers who'd vaulted to prominence during the Spanish-American War, and he was a trusted advisor to the president.

"Why do you bring him up?" Luke asked carefully.

"My father is very keen on Colonel Phelps," she replied, watching a pigeon wrestle with a crust of pretzel. "He's been invited to our house for dinner on Sunday."

Clyde Magruder didn't do anything lightly. If Colonel Phelps was invited to dinner, Clyde had a reason. Luke cut straight to the chase. "Colonel Phelps seems like the kind of man your father would like for a son-in-law."

Marianne looked almost relieved that he had said it, rather than owning it herself. "There's no doubt that is what he'd like."

"And you?" Luke held his breath. He and Marianne hadn't made any vows to each other, and she was free to court a more suitable man if she wished.

She snorted. "You have no competition from Colonel Phelps. He's so stiff and formal, I think he's got laundry starch running through his veins."

Unpleasant thoughts took shape in Luke's mind. Maybe she wasn't taken with Colonel Phelps, but her status-hungry parents were going to pressure her to reconsider. Marianne continued talking, recounting a handful of encounters she'd had with the colonel over the past few months. Jealousy flared. It didn't matter that Marianne didn't care for Colonel Phelps. Luke didn't like the prospect of anyone else courting her.

"Why didn't you tell me about him before?" he asked.

"Because he is *nothing* to me, but I felt dishonest letting it continue without telling you. He's invited to our home on Sunday for dinner. Andrew and Delia will be here to watch my father's speech on the House floor. Papa thought it would be a good chance for Colonel Phelps to meet the rest of the family."

Luke's jaw tightened. "And what do you think?"

"I think I'm sorry I told you," she said. "I don't want to add to your burdens. You've already got so much on your shoulders with the Poison Squad and the *Don Quixote* translation. And now your sister's wedding. Everyone is supposed to be deliriously happy at a wedding, but I know tomorrow won't be a day of undiluted joy for you."

His heart turned over. How easily she could read him, and

even this low, selfish part of him didn't seem to repulse her. "I'm such a lousy rat for feeling that way."

"Tell me what I can do to make these next few days easier for you."

The open-ended offer triggered an avalanche of wild dreams. Run away to California with him, go dancing under the moonlight, drink wine straight from the bottle. He lowered his request into the realm of something a little scandalous but not too difficult.

"Meet me at the arboretum tomorrow night. Ten o'clock. The wedding festivities will be over, and we can steal a few hours together. Can you get away?"

"I can," she agreed with a reassuring smile.

"Thanks."

It was such a puny word for his boundless gratitude. He needed her company more than she could know, for Caroline's wedding was going to be tough. He was hanging on by a thread, but knowing Marianne would be waiting for him at the end of the day was a talisman that would make it worthwhile.

Twenty-Two

Luke wolfed down breakfast at the boardinghouse, grateful he was in the control group this week. He had personally appealed to Dr. Wiley to be spared chemical concoctions in the days before Caroline's wedding. The doctor refused to confirm Luke would be in the control group, but the old bachelor had a huge sentimental streak he kept deeply hidden, and Luke was certain his request had been honored.

He headed to the Delacroix town house, where a team of seamstresses, a florist, and a hairdresser had already arrived to help Caroline prepare. Gray would be giving the bride away, and Luke still ached at the thought that after tonight, someone else would forever be first in Caroline's affections.

Gray's wife was in the front hall, taking an inventory of a huge mound of wedding gifts piled on the hall table.

"Good heavens, you look lovely," he said to Annabelle, who was already dressed for the wedding in a breathtaking gown of canary yellow silk. It was a soft, floating gown that easily accommodated her expanding waistline.

"Caroline's doing," Annabelle replied with a wink. "We visited three different dressmakers before she was satisfied with a design for it."

As a farmer's daughter from Kansas, it had taken Annabelle a while to adjust to the elegant fashions of Washington's high society. Annabelle normally preferred to dress simply, but there was nothing normal about today. This was going to be the wedding of the year, and Luke's formal suit was waiting for him upstairs.

"I'd better get dressed as well. I take it Caroline is still upstairs?"

Annabelle nodded. "She's with the hairdresser. The train of her gown will get crumpled in the carriage, so the wedding dress has already been delivered to the church. We leave in an hour so she'll have plenty of time to get dressed." She glanced at the clock with an expression of baffled amusement. "I never realized it took so many hours to get properly dressed."

He leaned in to kiss her cheek and forced himself to sound cheerful. "Hang in there. You're doing a great job."

Today was already harder than expected. He was thrilled for Caroline. Of course he was. And he was a master at faking good cheer even when he didn't feel it.

Ten minutes later Luke was inserting a white carnation into the lapel of his black cutaway coat. He was in full formal attire, with a high starched collar and a lavender silk cravat secured with a tiny diamond stud.

Time to face Caroline. He flipped open the lid of a slim velvet box, gazing down at the gift he'd had custom-made. It had galled him to commission it, but Caroline deserved to know that he was fully prepared to accept Nathaniel into their family. Would she understand the symbolism of the brooch he designed for her? He didn't want it getting lost among the dozens of gifts already mounded in the hall below, and he wanted to be there when she opened it.

He crossed the hall to her bedroom, where the hair stylist was putting the finishing touches on an artistic coiffure. Most of Caroline's hair was artfully coiled atop her head, but plenty cascaded down her back in loose spiraling waves.

He met Caroline's laughing gaze in the mirror. "Can I steal two minutes?" he asked as the hairstylist left the room.

"You can have as many as you want," she said. "Or at least as many as you need before ten o'clock. That's when the carriage arrives to take me to the church."

"Dad always called us two peas in a pod," he said as he retrieved the slim box from his pocket.

Actually, *everyone* called them two peas in a pod. As twins, they had shared the same womb and arrived into this world within six minutes of each other. They shared a crib for their first year and a school bench when learning to read. They had an uncanny bond of camaraderie as they grew older, but it was time to say good-bye to their exclusive friendship and widen it to include others.

"A wedding gift," he said casually as he set the box on Caroline's dressing table.

"Can I open it now?"

"Please do."

She lifted the lid and gasped at the brooch. He needn't have feared she would miss the symbolism, as her eyes misted in understanding.

The brooch was five perfectly cut diamonds nestled in a green enameled hull. Five peas in a pod. Over the past year, the bond he and Caroline shared had finally widened to include their sober older brother. When Gray married last year, Annabelle became a part of their family too. And now Nathaniel made five. They were five peas in a pod. No more Luke and Caroline, the intrepid duo who'd set Washington society on fire. It was time for them to loosen the bond and permit sunlight between them.

Caroline rushed to him, surrounding him with her lemony perfume as she embraced him, careful to protect the sculptural masterpiece of her hair.

"Thank you, Luke. You can't imagine how much this means

to me. Nathaniel has no family. He's been alone most of his life. I know you aren't natural friends, but—"

"Shh," he interrupted. "In a few hours, Nathaniel will be one of us. Never doubt it."

A knock sounded at the door. "The carriage is here," Gray said from the opposite side. "It's early, but perhaps we should leave now. Rumor has it there will be quite a crush at the church. Something about a big wedding with all of Washington society invited."

Luke offered his arm. "Shall we go?"

Luke sat in the front row of the church next to Annabelle as Gray prepared to walk Caroline down the aisle. He spent these last few minutes scanning the guests in the pews. No Magruder would be invited to Caroline's wedding, but Luke was on the lookout for Colonel Phelps, Clyde's hand-picked suitor for Marianne's hand. Luke had met the colonel a few times over the years and had never heard anything but praise for the army's youngest colonel. That didn't mean Luke had to like him.

At ten minutes to eleven, the church was almost full. He was used to pomp and ceremony, and it was on full display this morning, with the church bedecked in white orchids and the guests wearing satins, silks, and uniforms.

But not everyone was lavishly dressed. Caroline and Nathaniel had lived at the White House during the final year of the McKinley administration, where they formed tight friendships with their fellow staff, and those people were here in force to celebrate Caroline's wedding. For once, instead of cooking, cleaning, or gardening, the White House servants would be treated as honored guests at the most festive party in town.

His gaze strayed to a cluster of men in uniform. There were

probably half a dozen officers here, but Luke instinctively focused on his rival. Colonel Phelps wore his blue dress uniform with epaulets at the shoulders and a chest full of medals and ribbons. The colonel caught Luke's gaze and sent him a polite nod.

Luke turned around. He wasn't going to let that man spoil his enjoyment of Caroline's wedding, but he didn't feel the need to extend the hand of friendship either.

Nathaniel stepped into place at the front of the church, dressed in tails, a starched white collar, and an indigo satin vest. Nathaniel usually dressed like a puritan, but there was nothing fusty about him today. He looked flushed with good health and happiness.

Then Nathaniel's eyes widened in surprise, and quiet whispers stirred through the crowd. Luke turned to see what had caused the commotion, and it wasn't hard to see. Ida McKinley, the former first lady of the United States, was walking down the aisle with the aid of a cane on one side and her middle-aged sister on the other. Caroline had been Ida's personal secretary and almost like a daughter to the infamously difficult first lady. Their falling out last year was a wound that still ached for Caroline.

Nathaniel beamed at Mrs. McKinley's unexpected arrival and stepped forward to escort her into the pew behind Luke. A few minutes later, the organ began playing Mendelssohn's classic wedding march, filling the church with its joyful and majestic chords. Pride filled Luke's chest, and he turned to see the church doors at the end of the aisle open, revealing Gray and Caroline.

She looked as radiant as a queen. The bodice of the gown had a high collar and long sleeves made of ivory satin but shot through with gold embroidery. She beamed as Gray walked her down the aisle. Luke flashed her a wink, and she winked back.

Then she saw Mrs. McKinley, and her composure cracked.

Once Caroline was alongside the older woman, she dropped Gray's arm and leaned over to embrace the former first lady.

"Thank you for coming," she whispered. "A thousand times, thank you!"

"I wouldn't miss it for the world," Ida McKinley said. "Although it looks like you're driving your brother into the poorhouse with that gown."

Caroline beamed. "You would be disappointed in me if I didn't."

Luke laughed but still had to reach for a handkerchief. His embarrassing tendency for getting weepy-eyed was coming on strong, and it looked like Caroline's wedding was going to be his Waterloo.

The wedding reception was held in a clubhouse on the outskirts of town. It was a good thing the weather was fine, allowing them to open the French doors so the crowd could spill out onto the flagstone patio. Flowers adorned the tables, music filled the air, and uniformed waiters circulated with a selection of delicacies.

Luke ate nothing. His stomach growled during the champagne toasts, during which he casually held aloft a flute of wine to toast the bride—it would have looked awkward if he hadn't—but he was still a member of the Poison Squad and needed to abstain from eating or drinking anything other than plain water.

He met Gray's eyes across the dance floor. His older brother raised a toast to him and drained the glass. This was a change of pace! Luke was supposed to be the hard-living, reckless one. Now, when he should have been popping corks and kicking up his heels at Caroline's wedding, he obeyed the rules and didn't let a morsel pass his lips while Gray picked up the slack.

It was stuffy inside the clubhouse, so he made his way outside into the warm evening. Then a tiny old woman with a surprisingly strong grip pulled him aside to castigate him for supporting Caroline's work on the McMillan Commission.

"Tell your sister I cannot countenance the removal of the arboretum outside the Department of Agriculture," she said in an iron-hard voice. "Those trees are a treasure to the city, a green oasis amidst the concrete rubble."

"Ma'am, they will be replaced by miles of open parkland. The view will be—"

"Who cares about a view?" she barked. "It's shade trees this city needs."

Others joined the conversation. Political chatter was commonplace whenever more than a dozen people in Washington gathered, and soon the talk drifted to the upcoming budget, the restructuring of the War Department, and even the arrival of two bald eagles at the zoo. Maybe it wasn't the thing to discuss politics at a wedding, but Luke loved it. *He loved it.* What a blessing that after years of struggling to find a meaningful purpose in this world, he'd found it right here in his hometown.

Then Caroline and Nathaniel came outside, and attention shifted to them as a photographer set up his tripod to take a special photograph Caroline requested. During her time at the White House, she shared a dormitory with nine other women who worked in the building. Two cooks, two telephone operators, three maids, a seamstress, and a laundress. Today they were all respectably dressed, but their work-roughened hands gave them away.

One of the older women seemed reluctant to join the others for the photograph. "We're not the sort for a posed photograph," she said.

"Nonsense!" Caroline exclaimed. "You nine ladies are the only sisters I ever had."

The older woman beamed in reply and fell into place. Soon the women left, and Nathaniel posed with a group of Secret Service officers for their photograph with the bride. Jokes flew as the former White House colleagues reunited for the first time in almost a year.

A group of army officers, including Colonel Phelps, stood only a few feet away. Old instincts kicked in, and Luke immediately started eavesdropping. Often people felt compelled to jabber when they were anxious, but Luke had always found one could learn far more by simply listening. He held the glass of flat champagne in his hand, pretending to enjoy the view but privately scrutinizing Colonel Phelps.

The officers were speculating about additional army encampments moving out west, and if there was any room for promotion by accepting postings that far out of the limelight.

"If a rebellion in the Indian territories happens, it will come quickly," Colonel Phelps said. "Things may appear calm at the moment, but the promotions will go to the men out in the field, not the staff officers in Washington."

Personally, Luke would like nothing better than to have Colonel Phelps transferred out west. Perhaps Hawaii.

Soon the conversation shifted to the quality of the crab salad and the bacon-wrapped filet mignon. Luke's stomach growled, but he had fended off worse hunger pains than this, and he was curious to hear Colonel Phelps's opinion of Caroline's gourmet selections. If Colonel Phelps aspired to an alliance with the Magruder family, he would have to become a fan of potted ham and chicken spread.

Sadly, Colonel Phelps said nothing disparaging about the food. He comported himself like a perfect gentleman for the entire ten minutes Luke eavesdropped.

Until the colonel slipped and made a derogatory comment about Nathaniel. "I don't personally know the man, but a Delacroix marrying a civil servant is a bit of a step down, isn't it?"

Luke didn't wait to hear the reply. He pushed away from the wall and approached the group of officers. "That 'civil servant' is my brother-in-law," he said coolly.

Colonel Phelps blanched and took a step back. "My apologies," he said. "I had no idea any family members were in the vicinity."

"Obviously." Luke's gaze flicked to Colonel Phelps's collection of medals and the epaulets on his shoulders. "Nathaniel Trask doesn't have medals or a fancy title to prove his heroism. He has worked quietly behind the scenes for years, but he's the reason the paycheck you draw each month isn't rendered worthless by an ocean of counterfeit. He is the kind of man that keeps the heartbeat of America strong, and I am proud to call him my brother."

He hadn't bothered to lower his voice, and several people were surreptitiously watching him. He didn't care. He wasn't going to stand aside and let Caroline's husband be insulted at his own wedding.

"My apologies," Colonel Phelps said. "I've heard nothing but fine things about Agent Trask."

Luke nodded his head in concession. "Myself as well."

He turned away, rubbing his chest and wondering at the strange ache he felt. He was lonely. Marianne should be here. He was proud of her and didn't want to sneak behind her parents' backs any longer. He was ready to venture into the world with the woman he loved beside him, but he feared Marianne might never be able to cross that bridge.

Marianne waited for Luke on a bench in the arboretum. The moon was bright enough that she could show him the pictures she developed that morning. The ones they'd taken of each other in the treetops were dazzling, probably because they looked so happy.

"For you," she said as she handed him the box of photographs. "Two for you, and two for me. They aren't fully dry, so be careful for the next couple of days, because they can still smudge."

Luke was somber as he gazed at the photograph she'd taken of him standing in the trees. "You need to be careful with these pictures for longer than that," he said. "Your father would implode if he caught you with this."

She didn't want to dwell on her father. Their time together was too fleeting to waste it on worries. "Tell me about the wedding. Tell me everything."

He started pacing before the koi pond in the center of the arboretum. "Caroline was beautiful, and the music almost made me weep. The weather held, and the setting was perfect. The food smelled and looked good, but I can't vouch for how it tasted. All I know is that I was mostly miserable because I kept missing you and wanted you there. I'm tired of running around behind people's backs. I want us to be together. I love you, and that's never going to change. Please say you feel the same."

The hint of uncertainty in his eyes cut straight to her heart, and she stood to clasp his face between her hands and look straight into his eyes. "You adorable man. I fell half in love with you when we were on the ice, and then all the way when you found out my last name was Magruder and you still treated me like I was a princess. I know we have stumbling blocks ahead of us. I'll clear them away. No more waiting."

Instead of looking delighted, he looked even more worried. "Your parents might disown you, like they did your Aunt Stella. I can't bear being the cause of that."

"*You* won't be the cause of it. They will."

He grabbed her hand and pressed a kiss to her palm. "I love you so much," he murmured. "I need to know what you are willing to risk for us to be together."

"Everything," she said without hesitation.

"Would you be willing to skip a fancy wedding? Walk away from your family's fortune and burn the bridges behind you?"

"Fetch me the match," she replied, and he smiled but sobered quickly.

He squeezed her hands. "Your father hates me. He's already destroyed my office, and it will get worse once he knows our intentions are serious. Are you truly willing to walk away? Follow in your Aunt Stella's footsteps?"

She swallowed hard. She didn't even know what happened to Aunt Stella, so how could she answer? All she knew was that she loved Luke, and if her family couldn't accept him, she would follow wherever he led.

"You once painted a dream of San Francisco," she said. "A place where we could have a garret apartment and live like vagabond artists."

It was hard to keep speaking when he kept kissing her, but she loved every moment of it.

"We'll try to do everything right," Luke whispered as he traced kisses along her jaw. "We'll be patient. I'll behave myself. I'll offer a truce with your family and turn the other cheek. Whatever it takes, we will find a way."

He shed his coat and laid it on the grass for her. They watched the moon and the stars rotate overhead. Tomorrow their world might topple over in chaos, but for tonight, they held hands and dreamed of the world to come.

Twenty-Three

Luke was still floating on air the following morning as he headed to church. The pieces of his life were falling into place. The moment he reached the pew, he was going to fall to his knees, give thanks for the miracle of meeting Marianne, and pray for wisdom in navigating the tricky road ahead. It wasn't going to be easy, but they loved each other and were ready to move forward.

It was a perfect July morning, and a few parishioners mingled outside, which was typical.

What wasn't typical was the horse-drawn police wagon parked outside the church. Two uniformed officers loitered near the wagon, and another sat on the driver's bench. It was one of those covered paddy wagons with bolted doors in the back and a small window covered by bars. No one else was paying the police any mind, so Luke crossed the street and headed toward the church.

An officer intercepted him. "Are you Luke Delacroix?"

"Yes." How did they know his name? He swallowed hard, all his senses going on alert.

"We have a warrant for your arrest. You have been charged with spying on Congress and need to come with us."

The bottom dropped out of his stomach. He'd done a lot of sketchy spying over the years, but never on Congress.

"That's nonsense," he replied. "I haven't spied on anyone." Not in Washington, anyway.

The officer thrust a form in his face, suddenly making this feel very real. And terrifying. Luke reached for the warrant, but the officer held it back. "Read it from here," he ordered.

It was hard to read with his head so dizzy, but his name was typed on the top line. The charge was spying on a member of Congress, but it didn't say who or when. Clyde Magruder was probably behind this. It meant hiring a lawyer, and Luke's bank account was already drained from Caroline's wedding present. He could get a loan from Gray, but this was a disaster.

He beat back the momentary panic and managed a nonchalant tone. "It's Sunday," he pointed out. "I can't be arraigned today. Why are you even bothering with an arrest? Give me the warrant, and I'll show up in court tomorrow to settle this."

"We have orders to take you into custody now," the officer said. "A cell is waiting for you at the District of Columbia Jail."

A different officer yanked Luke's right hand behind his back, and the cold metal of handcuffs clamped around his wrist. The third officer unlocked the heavy latch on the back of the wagon.

"You don't have to do this," Luke rushed to say. "I'll ride on the front bench. You don't have to lock me up."

But they were already driving him toward the rear of the wagon. Luke looked helplessly at the aghast parishioners standing outside the church. He recognized Mrs. Lancaster, a woman who sometimes cleaned at the boardinghouse.

"Tell Princeton to get my brother," he shouted to her.

She nodded and said something in reply, but he couldn't hear as the two officers lifted and shoved him into the back of the wagon. It was dark. Stifling. The doors slammed, and then the bolt slid into place.

He was trapped.

A suffocating blanket of panic enveloped him, making it hard to breathe or think. Instinct took over, and he dropped to the floor to slam the flat of his foot against the door, over and over. It didn't do any good, and within a minute the wagon was rolling down the street.

He was on his way back to jail, the same one where he'd humiliated himself with Marianne all those months ago. He couldn't go back. He wouldn't, but it was time to calm down and get ahold of his senses.

Behind his back, the handcuffs were loose. He was still thin and hadn't been able to put on any real weight on Poison Squad rations. It hurt, but he folded his thumb tight against his palm and pulled his hand against the metal cuff. Then pulled harder. The skin tugged and pain seared, but he didn't let up until he yanked his hand free.

He darted to the bars covering the narrow window on the back of the wagon. Instinct drove him to jerk on the bars even though he knew it was pointless. He couldn't let himself be locked up in the DC Jail. The smell. The clanging noises. It was too much like the other place.

Don't panic. Whatever else, he must not panic. His family had money. Soon he would have a lawyer. He had rights.

And clutching at the window bars was a stupid way of alerting anyone watching that he'd escaped from his handcuffs. He let go and dropped onto a hard bench bolted to the side of the wagon. The ride seemed endless as the wheels rolled over bumpy cobblestones. Twenty minutes? Thirty? It felt like forever, but soon a marshy smell indicated they were nearing the Anacostia River and getting closer to the jail.

The panic returned, causing sweat to pour, his heart to pound. There was no way he was going to walk into a jail cell. Never again.

The jail was built on an old army base surrounded by an

open field, but if he could make it to the trees, he could get away. He at least had to try.

The wagon rolled to a stop, then shifted as the driver got off the front bench. Casual voices from the policemen mingled with the jangling of keys. They didn't suspect anything. Luke stood but kept his hands behind his back as the door was unlocked. One of the officers reached up to help him down, but the others were already heading toward the jail.

Luke elbowed the officer in the face and shoved him to the ground, then leapt free and made a dash for the trees. The handcuffs still dangled from his left wrist, but he was free and running for his life.

Shouts came from behind. They were giving chase. Yelling. Ordering him to stop. A stitch in his side felt like a knife in the ribs, but he sprinted through the pain.

He made it to the woods! His feet ripped through the undergrowth, twigs and limbs scratching his face as he stumbled forward. A root nearly sent him sprawling, but he regained his balance and kept running. The men were getting closer.

A huge weight slammed into him from behind, and he hit the ground, dirt and grass filling his mouth.

"Idiot," a man growled in his ear.

He couldn't breathe. A thousand pounds was sitting on his back. His arms were wrenched behind him and another set of handcuffs snapped into place. This time when they lifted him, they weren't so gentle.

Luke spit out a mouthful of grass and dirt. "I'm not going back to jail. I didn't do it."

"Sure, sure," the officer said, driving him forward.

It was hard to keep his balance with his hands manacled behind his back, and the cops had no mercy, shoving him harshly forward until he fell on his face and couldn't even break his fall. Rough hands hauled him upright, but he hit the dirt three more times on his way to the jail.

Then the grim, granite-stoned building loomed straight ahead. Running had been stupid, but panic had gotten the better of him. He still had to think of a way to get out of this. For once he hadn't done anything wrong. He was completely innocent. He hadn't spied on Congress.

But Marianne had.

The documents she photographed had been commissioned by her father's congressional committee, but Luke had been the one to hand them over to Dr. Wiley. Clyde was going to find a way to pin this on him, and it was going to be hard to wiggle off the hook.

"We've got a runner," the cop said as he dragged Luke in the door and shoved him toward a counter.

The clerk at the desk didn't even bother to look up. "Put him in solitary, then."

This couldn't be happening. Not again. But the clang of the locks sounded hideously familiar, and then Luke was propelled down a dank brick corridor. The edges of his vision began to blur, and prisoners behind bars laughed and jeered as he passed. Then through another set of locked doors to a cell with no bars, only walls.

"You'll be in here for a while," the guard said, nudging Luke inside.

The four walls were concrete block, and the only furniture was a board chained to the wall. He closed his eyes as fear engulfed him. Then came the closing of the door and the clanging of the lock.

He couldn't breathe. It took all his effort to will his lungs to function.

Perspiration rolled down his face, but he'd survived this before. Prison was nothing new to him. When he was in Cuba, he had biblical passages engraved on his soul. He stumbled toward the cot and sat, bowing his head in prayer. He knew all the passages of comfort, and he said them over and over.

It wasn't working. Wasn't God supposed to answer?

But there was no answer. Only taunting laughter echoing down the hallways, the smell, and the suffocating sense of doom.

Gray arrived two hours later. The warden wasn't taking any chances with Luke, and he was clamped into leg-irons and handcuffs before being led to a small meeting room. It had a wooden table, two chairs, and painted concrete block walls.

Gray was pacing in the confined space when the warden led Luke into the room. At least the guard had fastened his handcuffs in the front so he could offer Gray one of his hands to shake.

Gray squeezed his hand but maintained a grim silence until the warden left the room and closed the door. Luke flinched at the sound of the lock clicking into place.

"Spying on Congress?" Gray asked, his voice dripping with angry disbelief.

Luke lowered himself into a chair. "I didn't do it. I'm completely innocent."

"Then what convinced a judge to sign a warrant for your arrest?"

"I'm *mostly* innocent," Luke amended.

Gray's face turned to stone as he took the seat on the opposite side of the table. "Explain yourself."

"I can't provide any more details than that."

Gray stood and kicked his chair, sending it skittering across the room and banging into a wall. "Don't pull that with me," he demanded. "How did this happen?"

In the past two hours, Luke had plenty of time to piece it together. Marianne had taken photographs of studies paid for by the Committee on Manufactures. That was almost a month ago. Marianne knew he intended to pass them along to Dr. Wiley, but Luke also pounced on the chance to write an anonymous article about them for *Modern Century*. Clyde knew Luke wrote for *Modern Century* and assumed he had stolen the documents. Anyone would.

Luke hadn't spied on Congress. It was Marianne who ferreted out the studies and turned them over. Luke was merely the journalist who sounded the alarm, but he couldn't clear himself without condemning Marianne, and that would never happen. He didn't think Clyde would expose Marianne to the justice system, but Clyde might not have a choice. Now that the police and a judge were involved, if the finger of blame pointed at someone else, Clyde might have lost his ability to walk it back.

Even if Clyde could spare Marianne, he would never forgive his daughter for playing a role in this. She would be cut out of the family just like poor, doomed Aunt Stella. That meant there was a limit on how much Luke could disclose.

He focused on the peeling paint in the corner of the room while figuring out how to parse his words. "I think it has something to do with an article I wrote for *Modern Century*," he admitted. "Clyde serves on a congressional committee that ordered five studies on chemical additives. They released two that show the chemicals in a good light and buried the others. The article I wrote appeared last week."

"How did you get your hands on the studies?" Gray demanded.

"I can't tell you." He turned in his chair so he didn't have to see the anger in Gray's face.

"I'll hire a lawyer for you tomorrow, but he won't be any help unless you tell us what's going on. How did you get those buried studies?"

"Gray, please stop asking." Acid churned in Luke's stomach at the thought of being confined here overnight. Maybe even longer. He'd naively hoped Gray might show up with a bag of money to post bail and get him out of here.

"You *owe* me," Gray said, his voice cutting. "You put us all through the wringer last year, and I have no desire to repeat the process."

"That makes two of us."

"Then tell me who gave you the information. That's your best chance for getting out of here."

This room was too small for yelling. It made the walls feel like they were closing in, and it started getting hot. Luke dropped his head into his hands, unable to meet Gray's eyes and unable to expose Marianne. It would ruin her. Even if she could endure the fear and humiliation of being locked up, she would lose her family. The Magruders were not a forgiving lot.

"I can't tell you who gave me the studies, but Clyde knows I work for *Modern Century.* He knows the studies found their way to me, even though the article was anonymous. I think he is to blame for this."

"Then he'll be made to answer for it," Gray said in a quietly lethal voice.

Twenty-Four

The dining room in the Washington town house was small, but Marianne managed to fit place settings for seven adults around the dining table that featured their best china, an assortment of goblets for each person, and a trio of silver candelabras, all for Sunday night's dinner with Colonel Phelps. Marianne never had much interest in entertaining, but her mother and sister-in-law vied for dominance as they planned the five-course meal. Delia showed off her calligraphy skills by penning lovely place cards, while Vera perfected the floral arrangements.

"The evening will start with the lobster bisque," Delia said. "After that will come a nice baked brie pastry. Marianne, do you know if Colonel Phelps likes brie?"

"I have no idea," she said while setting a butter knife alongside each bread plate.

"You need to learn the colonel's preferences," Delia said. "The key to a man's heart is in fulfilling his culinary desires."

The only man's heart Marianne was interested in was Luke Delacroix's, and since he'd spent the last five months eating controlled meals with the Poison Squad, he wasn't too fussy. Everything about tonight's meal seemed a little too elegant for her taste, and she envied Sam, who would be eating in the kitchen because tonight's affair was for grown-ups only. These days, Sam preferred the company of the servants anyway. He was still cowed and sullen around Andrew because of what happened to Bandit, and Marianne suspected the damage from that spiteful act would haunt the boy for years.

The table was starting to look overstuffed with three glasses at each place, along with three different forks, two types of knives, and a bread plate. Then Delia stepped forward to add more, and Vera nearly exploded.

"Delia, I've already told you there is no room on the table for the individual saltcellars."

Delia paid no mind as she set another tiny bowl beside a place setting. "But they're so precious!" she defended. "All the best families use saltcellars instead of a shared saltshaker."

Delia had brought the saltcellars all the way from Baltimore specifically for this dinner. Each miniature bowl was made of amethyst crystal cut to look like a thistle, and had a tiny silver spoon with a matching amethyst at the finial. Marianne couldn't decide if they were charming or tacky.

Vera clearly thought they were tacky. "Once we have the floral arrangements on the table, there will be no room for saltcellars."

Delia lifted her chin and began removing the crystal bowls. "What a shame this table is going to look very common for Colonel Phelps."

Marianne continued setting out the butter knives and said nothing. She wished people would stop making such a production over Colonel Phelps, but what could she do?

By seven o'clock all the guests had gathered in the parlor for an aperitif. Andrew and Delia could both be counted on to comport themselves with ease, but old Jedidiah was always a question mark. Her grandfather had the intelligence to carry on a conversation with anyone, but some people were put off by his back-country accent and coarse sense of humor. The first thing her grandfather said to their guest of honor was to apologize for the way Marianne and Delia looked "so darn pooped."

"The womenfolk spent all afternoon out in the backyard, skinning the coons I caught for supper," he said in a teasing voice as he shook Colonel Phelps's hand.

Delia froze in mortification, but Colonel Phelps took it in stride and knew exactly the right thing to say.

"I'd have come earlier if they needed any help," he said with an engaging smile. "I did my fair share of hunting and skinning when I was out west with the cavalry."

Jedidiah nodded in approval and launched into a discussion of army rations during the recent war. Marianne stood a few feet away, trying to see the army's youngest colonel with new eyes. If she wasn't already so dazzled by Luke, could she have been attracted to him? He had an easy manner with Jedidiah. After twenty minutes, Colonel Phelps had established a better rapport with the crusty old man than Delia had managed after twelve years of marriage.

At last it was time to proceed into dinner, and Colonel Phelps offered his arm to escort Marianne into the dining room. He murmured all the right compliments for her mother's fine presentation and the elegance of the setting, but all Marianne could see were the amethyst saltcellars that had mysteriously reappeared beside each place setting.

Vera noticed too. She went white around the lips while trying to graciously accept Colonel Phelps's compliments.

Why did Delia have to do that? This evening was already stressful enough for Vera without petty attempts to see who could outshine the other.

At least the presentation of the soup course and brie pastries went well. The main course of quail with truffles was next. Vera was explaining the process of making the truffles for the elegant dish when a disturbance sounded in the hall.

It sounded like two men were arguing. A man's voice she

didn't recognize was angry and insistent, but his words were too muffled to understand. Their butler was just as adamant.

"Congressman Magruder is not at home to visitors," the butler insisted.

Her gaze flew to her father, who looked annoyed as he set his linen napkin beside his plate. A frazzled maid hurried to her father's side. "There's a man at the front door. He's very angry and pushed his way inside."

"Who is it?" Clyde demanded.

The maid held up her hands. "I've never seen him before."

Clyde rose just as the double doors to the dining room burst open. Good heavens! It was Gray Delacroix, his shirtsleeves rolled up and hair disheveled. The butler was right behind him, dragging on Mr. Delacroix's arm to pull him back, but Gray shook him off and pointed an angry finger at her father.

"You've gone too far this time," he snapped at Clyde. "I want you to drop the charges against my brother. He's a journalist, not a spy."

Marianne's mouth dropped open. Had Luke gotten into trouble? Whatever happened must have been serious to send Gray into a temper like this.

Her father struggled to maintain a calm demeanor. "That's for a court of law to decide."

"So you admit that you're behind this?" Gray demanded.

"I'm not admitting anything. Your brother has a bad habit of landing in jail, so it ought to be familiar territory for him."

Marianne gasped and stood. "Luke is in jail? What happened?"

Clyde shot her a glare, and she dropped back into her seat. A glance around the table showed that nobody else noticed her slip of the tongue in using Luke's Christian name. All the others were gaping at Gray, who stepped farther into the already overstuffed dining room to look directly at Jedidiah.

"Did you know anything about this? I always thought you had more sense than anyone else in this vulgar family."

Jedidiah folded his arms across his chest and locked gazes with Gray. "I don't know what you're talking about, boy-o, but you've interrupted a fine meal and aren't invited. Get out."

Colonel Phelps stood. "You have been asked to leave," he said. "I suggest that you do so."

"Wait!" Marianne burst out, jumping back to her feet to stand beside Colonel Phelps. She couldn't let Gray leave until she understood what was going on. "Don't go yet. Please, tell us what's happening."

Colonel Phelps looked between her and Gray in indecision but made no further move to throw Gray out.

"My brother published an article critical of your father," Gray said, struggling to speak in a rational tone. "Clyde ordered Luke arrested for it, and even now he's sitting in the District of Columbia Jail. Are you telling me you don't know anything about this?" he asked her.

Every eye in the dining room turned to stare at her. Her mouth went dry, and her heart thudded so hard that everyone could probably hear it. Jedidiah shifted in his chair to see her better, disbelief beginning to show on his aging face.

Fear paralyzed her as the implications sank in. This was about her photographs of the scientific reports. She'd given them to Luke, and he'd been jailed for it. Heat flooded her body, and a wave of dizziness came over her. It would kill her parents if she confessed to it. Jedidiah would hate her forever.

Ten feet away, Gray's penetrating gaze demanded answers. A stronger woman would confess what she knew, but cowardice won out.

"I don't know anything about this," she whispered.

"But your father does." Gray swiveled his attention to Clyde. "Surely you didn't expect me to take this lying down. Not when you've thrown my brother in jail."

"That's exactly where he should be for spying on Congress," Clyde said.

"It could have been anyone," Gray said contemptuously. "Plenty of people knew about those studies, and any one of them could have sounded the alarm. One of the scientists who didn't like seeing his research buried could have done it. A lab assistant from the study. Someone from your own company." He paused. "Or your own family."

Gray didn't look at her, but that comment was aimed at her. He knew, or at least suspected. She held her breath, but Clyde didn't catch the inference.

"Who else has a history of publishing articles in *Modern Century* but your brother?" Clyde scoffed. "He's the guilty party, and he's exactly where he deserves to be."

Gray's eyes gleamed in carefully restrained anger. "People have been locking up journalists ever since the printing press was invented. You don't have to like what he wrote, but fight it out in the court of public opinion. Throw open your books and let the public see, if you have nothing to hide. But if you fight dirty, I'll fight back. I'll hire an army of lawyers to unleash a storm of litigation unlike anything you've ever seen. You think I've stoked up negative press in the past? Just wait. This is a First Amendment issue, which means every journalist in the country will be on my side, and they will rip your reputation from sea to shining sea. I will fight for my brother with everything I have. If you want a war, you'll get one."

Gray turned on his heel and left the dining room but yelled a parting shot over his shoulder. "From sea to shining sea, Magruder!"

Andrew's temper unleashed the moment Gray was gone. "The gall of that man!"

The strength in Marianne's legs drained, and she dropped back into her chair. Andrew and her grandfather both gave free vent to their outrage, but Clyde tried to pass off the intrusion as a run-of-the-mill commotion.

"The life of a congressman," he said in a lighthearted tone, even though his knuckles were white as he gripped the armrest of his chair. "Come, we mustn't let this kerfuffle spoil our fine dinner. The quail is getting cold."

An awkward silence descended as people picked up silverware to begin eating. Delia filled the void, chattering about the origin of her amethyst saltcellars. Colonel Phelps gamely followed her lead, commenting on the fine cut of the leaded glass.

It was impossible for Marianne to participate in the conversation. Guilt warred with shame. Luke had shown her the article he wrote for *Modern Century*, and she approved of it. How could she not? She had seen exactly what those chemicals did to men in the poison study, and Luke's article blamed the congressional committee for stifling the studies, not her father. The world needed *more* such research, and it was wrong to hide those studies.

It was her fault Luke was in jail, and she didn't even have the mettle to stand by him and admit what she'd done. Luke was probably climbing the walls of his jail cell while she dined on quail.

At the far end of the table, Vera scrutinized her, and Marianne forced herself to take a tiny bite of quail. It tasted like ashes and landed in her stomach like a lead weight. She set down her fork.

"Marianne, everything is all right, isn't it?" her mother asked. A hint of iron underlay Vera's words. It was a command as much as a question.

"Yes, I'm fine," she confirmed.

But Luke wasn't fine. He was living out his worst nightmare, and it was all her fault.

It was nine o'clock before Colonel Phelps took his leave. Vera retreated to bed, complaining of a migraine brought on by the stress, but Marianne helped the maids clear and tidy the dining room. It would settle her restless nerves, but nothing could ease the indecision that battled in her mind.

One thing Gray said haunted her. *I will fight for my brother with everything I have*, he'd vowed. He said it with strength, confidence, and conviction.

And when Marianne had the opportunity to be equally brave, she'd cowardly denied all knowledge of what had happened. Shame weighed heavily as she gathered the linen cloth from the table to carry outside for a good shaking. As she passed the closed door of Clyde's study, she overheard him talking with Andrew and Jedidiah inside and cocked her ear to listen. Andrew was adamant that they had every right to press charges against whoever revealed the contents of those studies, but Jedidiah worried it would only direct more attention toward something they wanted hidden.

"Grandpa, stop panicking about things that haven't happened yet," Andrew said.

His condescending tone didn't go over well with Jedidiah. "I may be old, but I know how the world works, boy."

"I have the matter well in hand," Clyde said, his voice silky with confidence.

It made her afraid. Luke couldn't even tolerate being in a darkroom for an hour to develop film, but he'd been trapped in a jail cell all day. Given the confidence in her father's tone, it sounded like Luke's stint in jail could grow into weeks or months. Years.

She drew a calming breath and headed to the small, brick-lined garden behind the town house to shake out the tablecloth. Humid night air surrounded her as the chirp of crickets sounded in the distance.

She hadn't comported herself with honor tonight, but she could still try to get Luke out. Jedidiah was right. In making a federal case out of this, the Magruders would draw attention to everything they wanted hidden. Perhaps she could make her father see reason without destroying herself in the process.

She stepped back inside the town house and draped the tablecloth over the railing to be folded later, then knocked on the door of her father's study.

"Come in," Clyde said.

A wall of cigar smoke enveloped her the moment she entered.

"Yes, Marianne, what is it you need?" Clyde asked. She was clearly interrupting their meeting, and he probably thought she was here for nothing more consequential than asking what he wanted for breakfast in the morning. She wished that was the case.

"I think Grandpa is right about this," she said, not even bothering to disguise the fact that she'd been eavesdropping. "Why can't we ignore the article in *Modern Century* and hope it doesn't cause any waves?"

"I don't ignore it when spies rummage through my business affairs."

"Your affairs, or Congress's? I gather Mr. Delacroix was charged with spying on Congress, not you or Magruder Food."

"Why do you care?" Andrew challenged.

"He saved Bandit. He can't be all bad."

"A dog?" Andrew scoffed. "Let me be sure I understand your position, Marianne. You would rather be loyal to a Delacroix and a dog over your own family. Your *family*. Have I got that right?"

Bandit was dead because of Andrew, and now he had the gall to look at her as though she were the contemptible one. She met his eyes squarely. "One man risked his life to save a stranger's dog, and another shot that same dog in an angry fit. Who is the more worthy man?"

Splotches of anger appeared on Andrew's face, but before he could say anything, Jedidiah intervened.

"Be careful, girl," Jedidiah said. "You're walking a fine line and need to think carefully before saying more."

He was right. She could confess everything right now, but it wouldn't unlock the prison doors for Luke. She swallowed back her anger as she looked at Andrew.

"As always, you are a model of wisdom and compassion," she said, not bothering to mask the disdain in her voice.

Frustration and shame roiled inside her as she headed upstairs. She couldn't help Luke if Clyde ordered her to Baltimore or if they cut her out of the family completely. They did it to Aunt Stella, and they could do it to her. They angered, frustrated, and exasperated her . . . but she loved them and always would.

And tomorrow she would start working to get Luke out.

Marianne was cautious as she joined the others at the breakfast table on Monday morning. Vera had yet to appear, pleading a headache, but the others had gathered, chattering about Clyde's big speech before Congress this afternoon as though the catastrophe of last night hadn't happened.

"I'll be talking about tax law for hoofed livestock," Clyde said. "Those are valuable animals, but they can die in their pens while waiting for the tax man to sign off on miserable paperwork. No hoofed livestock should be at the mercy of a neglectful government."

Sam's fist tightened around his spoon as he sent a worried glance toward Clyde. "Does the government shoot and kill hoofed livestock?"

Marianne's heart squeezed. Ever since her brother shot Bandit, Sam had grown increasingly fearful of all manner of things. He worried about Vera's pet parakeet coming to harm, or if rosebushes felt pain when their blooms were cut. It was all Andrew's fault, and her brother never expressed a hint of remorse for his cruel treatment of Bandit.

Clyde evaded Sam's question with the ease of a natural politician. "You needn't fear for the livestock, Sam. My plan will assure every animal is properly accounted for. Livestock are valuable creatures."

The tension around Sam's mouth eased. "I think so too."

The fact that Sam was still traumatized by what happened to Bandit seared, and Marianne shot a glare at Andrew. "You should be so proud."

The subtle insult was understood by everyone at the table except Sam, but Andrew didn't bat an eyelash. "I am, Marianne. I am," he said smoothly.

No normal family would tolerate what happened to Bandit. Their family was blessed with wealth and privilege. They had everything anyone could ever need, and yet still people had to walk on eggshells, fearing the next outburst, scandal, or unforgiving punishment. Who was to blame for all this?

She looked at Andrew, then at Clyde, the leader of their family. She stood and addressed her father. "Why do you tolerate this? Why do you look the other way?"

She truly wanted to know. This wasn't how a loving family should operate, but Clyde was the only one with the authority to put his foot down and demand change.

A pause lengthened in the room, disturbed only by a few birds chirping outside the window. Her heart pounded, and she prayed that Clyde would see reason even as she quaked in fear of his reaction.

"Sit down, Marianne." He spoke calmly, but the order was unmistakable.

She sat, a complete and total coward. This family was off-kilter, and she was too fainthearted to correct it. Could she live with this the rest of her life? She loved Sam and her parents too much to imagine leaving. Even though they sometimes made her frustrated and angry, she would be unmoored without them, so she'd sat down like a coward.

"My speech is scheduled for one o'clock," Clyde continued.

"I suggest everyone arrive early so we can have lunch in the congressional dining room beforehand."

Marianne intended to see Luke this morning, not spend the day at the Capitol. She chose her words carefully.

"I need to pick up my list of assignments from my supervisor," she said. "It's what I always do on Monday morning."

"But not today, surely," Clyde said. "Your mother wants everyone to ride in the carriage as a group to the Capitol."

It was time to gather the threads of her shattered courage and fight for something. Luke had to be her priority this morning, not submitting to the niceties of her maladjusted family.

"I'll still have plenty of time to make my way to the Capitol for your speech after I see my supervisor."

"You're not riding with us?" Delia asked pointedly.

"I have a job," she replied as she rose, eager to leave the table. "I need to pick up my list of assignments for the week, and I'll meet everyone to watch Father's speech at one o'clock."

She did indeed pick up her assignments, but by eleven o'clock she was headed to the jail to see Luke. Would they let her see him? She'd never visited an incarcerated person before, and maybe there were restrictions or procedures.

It wasn't going to be easy. She learned that the moment she walked through the main doors and asked to visit a prisoner. She was directed down a maze of poorly lit and twisting hallways where visitors were instructed to ask permission. She took her place at the end of the line and waited, glancing nervously at the clock ticking on the wall and hoping she'd have enough time to visit Luke and still see her father's speech.

At last it was her turn, and she approached a thickly muscled officer manning the counter. "Your relation to the prisoner?" he asked.

"A friend."

"No friends can visit," he said brusquely. "Family or legal counsel only. Next."

He turned his attention to the next man in line. It was a blow, but there was no point in arguing with a man who didn't have authority to change the rules, especially since she had other allies in this building. Superintendent Castor had been a decent man when he met with her in February. He'd been disappointed in the Department of the Interior's lack of action from the pictures she'd taken. Perhaps she could persuade him to let her take more today.

The superintendent's secretary gave her the bad news. "He's in meetings all morning, but he has an opening at three o'clock if you can come back."

Marianne had no choice but to agree.

Troubles with the streetcar delayed Marianne's trip back to the Capitol, and it was five minutes after one o'clock when she finally arrived. An usher opened the door to let her slip inside the gallery overlooking the House floor, and her mother shot her an incendiary look, for her father was already speaking. At least Sam sent her a cheerful wave before going back to hanging on the railing to watch Clyde in the chamber below.

Marianne crept toward an empty seat, wincing at the squeak it made as she sat. She ignored the poisonous look Delia sent her and scanned the House floor. What a disappointment! Only a dozen congressmen were in their seats, and her father spoke to a mostly empty chamber. Still, she straightened in pride as she watched. Clyde urged a revised system of taxation for livestock that would benefit small ranchers throughout the country. It was a well-reasoned proposal. The fact that Magruder Food would benefit if this legislation passed shouldn't be held against him.

What a shame there weren't more people to hear it. Her gaze traveled to a cluster of spectators in the front row of the gallery. Given how they were jotting notes on pads of paper, she suspected they were journalists, and one was looking directly at her.

Dickie Shuster. His yellow jacket was so loud, she was surprised it was permitted in these dignified chambers. He sent her a smile and a nod, and she returned it. Barely. Luke had warned that Dickie had long known the scandal about her birth, and it was disconcerting to see him here.

Her father's speech came to an end, and time was allotted for questions from the floor. Marianne scanned the few congressmen in the chamber, hoping one of them would raise their hand as her father patiently waited to field questions. He'd been preparing responses to possible challenges for weeks, but no one seemed to be paying any attention. After a few moments, the man sitting in the speaker's chair broke the silence.

"Seeing no questions, the House shall now move for the presentation of a bill to provide pensioner burial stipends, sponsored by the gentleman from Rhode Island. Thank you, Congressman Magruder."

Clyde gathered his notes and left the podium. That was it?

Clyde returned to his seat while another man rose and began his presentation, but it all seemed rather anticlimactic. Apparently the only congressmen gathered in the chamber below were ones who had speeches lined up to deliver to the nearly empty room.

She leaned over to Vera. "Can we go now?"

"Shh!" Vera said angrily. Marianne's tardiness still annoyed her mother, but it was hard to sit here and listen to pension benefits when she had a three o'clock meeting with the jail's superintendent. A glance at the others indicated they all intended to sit quietly and listen to the rest of the presentations this afternoon. How could she escape?

Her gaze landed on Dickie Shuster, who gave her another smile and then a pointed look toward the exit door. He wanted to speak with her.

It was all the excuse she needed. "I'm going to speak with Mr. Shuster," she whispered to Vera, then left without waiting for permission. The chair let out a painful squeak as she rose and angled her way down the aisle toward the exit door. An usher held it open for her. Dickie came right behind.

"What a surprise to see you here today," Dickie said with an artificially bright smile.

"Really? I thought it only natural to come for my father's speech."

"Of course, of course." Dickie's voice echoed down the marble corridor. How ironic that there were more people in the halls than in the chamber. "Actually, I'm glad for the opportunity to see you again. Tell me, do you have any insight into the recent article that appeared in *Modern Century*? I can't imagine it went over very well in your family."

How much did he know? "Why do you think I'd know anything about it?"

"You have an affiliation with the Poison Squad," he said. "I saw the photographs you took of the young men. Delightful photographs, by the way. You are to be congratulated."

"Thank you, but I don't have anything to say about what was written in *Modern Century*."

The article was an embarrassment for the Magruders. She'd always blindly accepted what her father said about the safety of chemical preservatives, but now she'd seen proof that at least some of them were dangerous. According to Dr. Wiley, the levels of salicylic acid used in Magruder's Creamed Chipped Beef were unacceptably high. It wasn't bad enough to cause immediate illness, but it was impossible to know the effects of long-term exposure. Luke had done the right thing in sounding the alarm about it.

She hurried down the corridor and quickly got lost in the confusing maze of hallways, but Dickie followed closely behind. Soon she was in the hall of statues, a cavernous room lined with life-sized sculptures of American heroes. Tourists crowded the room to gawk at the statues, but Dickie kept pelting her with questions, coming uncomfortably close to her association with Luke.

She gave up trying to evade him and spoke frankly. "I once met a man who said you were not to be trusted. He warned that you were cunning, clever, and underhanded."

Dickie's look was part amusement, part pleasure. "*Moi*?" he asked innocently. "I am a harmless guppy."

"A guppy with fangs, claws, and a poison pen."

"I rather like that analogy. Who said it?"

She shook her head. "I'm not telling."

"It sounds like something Luke Delacroix might say. He's in jail, in case you are interested. Did you know that?"

She folded her arms across her chest and stared at him, praying her expression revealed nothing. "Once again, I can't imagine why you think this is relevant to me."

"The war between the Delacroixs and your father is heating up again," Dickie said. "Given that the article appeared in *Modern Century*, it surely came from Luke. The more interesting question is how he got his hands on those studies."

Her breath froze as Dickie scrutinized her. She was under no obligation to speak with this man and turned to walk away. Dickie followed, pelting her with more questions as she headed toward the nearest usher.

"This man is bothering me," she said to the burly usher. "Can you detain him while I leave the building?"

"Of course, ma'am."

Dickie looked incensed, but Marianne ignored him as she hurried toward the great rotunda and out the front door of the Capitol.

She made it to the jail in time for her three o'clock appointment, but the news was not good.

"I'd welcome more photographs," Superintendent Castor

said. "The problem is that I'll need to get authorization from the city administrator. That will take at least a week. At least, that was how long it took when I applied for permission to take photos last February. Can you wait?"

She'd wait until the stars fell from the sky, but hopefully Luke would be out of jail well before the week was out. Still, it was best to be cautious.

"I can wait," she said.

A guard led Luke down the narrow hallway to the meeting room where he'd be allowed thirty minutes with his attorney. The leg-irons made it hard to walk, but his escape attempt meant he had to wear them every time he was outside his cell. They were painful and humiliating, clanking with every step and hobbling him like a criminal, but nothing was as bad as the crawling sense of panic that had been with him since the moment of his confinement.

The meeting room wasn't much larger than his cell. It was intended for two people, but Gray would be there as well, so they'd be crammed together like sardines in a tin. His mouth went dry and his skin broke into a sweat at the prospect.

"Give me a minute," Luke said to the guard just outside the meeting room. He used his sleeve to blot the sweat from his face and neck, then forced himself to breathe normally. He didn't want Gray seeing what a pathetic wreck he'd become after less than twenty-four hours of confinement.

He also needed to keep his head screwed on straight to come up with a way out of this fiasco without implicating Marianne, and Gray wasn't going to make it easy.

"Thanks," he said to the guard. "I'm ready now."

The guard nodded and opened the door. "Thirty minutes," he said as Luke stepped inside the matchbox of a room. Mr. Alphonse, a criminal defense attorney with a huge walrus mustache, stood and shook his hand. Gray was on the far side of the table and there wasn't enough room to maneuver around Mr. Alphonse for a proper greeting, so they simply nodded to each other.

"What's going on?" Luke asked as soon as they were all seated.

"Bad news," his attorney said. "I asked the judge of the DC District Court to intervene in the case, citing your desire to protect a source under the First Amendment protections afforded for the freedom of the press. He declined to intervene." Mr. Alphonse put on a pair of spectacles to read from a letter. "'It is my opinion that the House of Representatives is acting within its rights to detain those in contempt of its authority.'" He took off his glasses. "That means that unless you want to plead guilty, this case is going to trial. The judge is going to side with Congress, and unless you give up your source, you are likely to be found guilty."

It felt like the walls were closing in on him. It was like he was back in Cuba, locked in, trapped, helpless. He couldn't last in here forever, but he couldn't throw Marianne to the wolves either.

Gray leaned across the table. "Luke, you can be out of jail by the end of the day. Just tell Congress what they want to know."

Nausea welled up inside him, and he prayed he wouldn't be sick. It would be the ultimate humiliation. He shifted in his chair and turned away so Gray wouldn't see how badly this hurt.

"Don't worry about me," he said. "I'll be fine."

Mr. Alphonse's voice was calm and professional. "As your attorney, anything you tell me will be held in complete confidence. If you give me the name of your source, I can appeal to that person or his attorney for a means to mitigate the damage. It's your best shot of getting out of here."

Revealing Marianne's name to his attorney would be the first crack in the dam. It might seem harmless at first, but it could lead to events he couldn't control.

"Is it her?" Gray asked, watching him carefully.

Luke met his brother's eyes. "What makes you think it might be her?" He was glad Gray didn't bring up Marianne's name. Mr. Alphonse had promised him confidentiality, but Luke didn't quite trust him.

"Just a feeling I have," Gray said. "If it's her, the law might go easy on her. She has connections."

Luke's heart pounded. "Those connections might throw her out into the cold."

"It was the risk she agreed to take."

"I won't." All hope for a quick release from prison evaporated, and he looked at Mr. Alphonse as a crushing sense of resignation took root. "I'm not saying anything. Please prepare for a trial."

Luke sat in the cafeteria, a plate of unappetizing hash on the table before him. On either side, men wolfed down the meal, but Luke had no appetite. The irony! He was at last off the Poison Squad, but anxiety made it hard to eat. He'd been here a week and was already losing weight.

He lifted his eyes to scrutinize all four corners of the ceiling. It was a tall space, probably around fifteen feet high. There were narrow windows near the tops of the walls for light, but they didn't open. If he was to escape through those windows, he'd have to bust them out, and there was no guarantee what he'd find on the other side. Barbed wire? Armed guards? Dogs? These cafeteria windows would be a last resort, because he'd seen better means of escape elsewhere.

"If you ain't eating that, I am," the man on the bench next to him said.

Luke clutched his plate. "It's mine," he said brusquely. He'd get the hash down eventually, but the heaving in his stomach needed to subside first. At least the cafeteria had more space than the cell they locked him in at night, but the smell and the metallic clanging noises were the same as in Cuba.

He lifted his spoon to his mouth, his nose twitching at the

scent of bleach still on his hands. His work assignment was in the laundry, generally considered the least desirable job in the entire jail due to the hot dryers and harsh chemicals. Others were assigned to kitchen duty or cleaning the common areas, but most of the men worked in the sewing shop, feeding huge spools of canvas fabric into industrial-sized machines to cut tents, sailcloth, or anything else the US military wanted made with cheap convict labor. The sewing jobs let the men sit down, which made them desirable, but Luke wouldn't trade his job in the laundry for any of them.

The laundry had the best means of escape.

The next time he made a run for it, he would do it wisely. It might take a while to learn the prison schedules and the best means of escape. He had to be patient, since he'd likely only have one shot at it.

And frankly, he wouldn't even try until after he was convicted, which was almost a certainty. Unless he turned in Marianne, there was no way he could wiggle off this hook, and that meant he'd probably be sentenced to serve at least five years. He started hyperventilating at the thought, and then the shakes got him.

The man next to him pounded him on the back. "What's wrong with you?"

Luke slid the plate of hash to him. He wasn't going to be able to eat it, and the other guy was a mountain of a man who gladly started wolfing it down.

Luke couldn't take this for five years. He couldn't. He rested his forehead in his hands, filling his nose with the stink of bleach and despair.

"Fifteen minutes," a guard shouted, signaling their break for dinner was halfway over. Luke would have another hour of work in the laundry before he'd be returned to his cell.

"Now that's a sight for sore eyes," the guy next to him said through his mouthful of hash.

Luke looked up, and his heart nearly stopped. Marianne! It couldn't be, *but it was!* A guard escorted her into the cafeteria as she carried her camera looped around her neck. She scanned the crowd, and he lifted his chin.

Her gaze locked with his. He wanted to vault off the bench and run to her, but he stayed stock-still and drank in the sight of her.

She glanced away and quickly took a picture of the steel rolling cart that carried pitchers of water. Somehow she had finagled her way inside the prison to see him. He could tell by the way she'd been searching the faces of the prisoners from the moment she entered the room. She was here for him, and he loved her for it.

She casually strolled toward the first long table of prisoners. "Tell me," she called out to the group in a loud voice, "if I was to take pictures documenting what it is like to live in this jail, where should I go?"

It was a strange question, but one of the men sitting at the front table stood to answer. "Take a picture of my face," he said, pointing to the lines fanning from his eyes. "You see those lines? They've got Sergeant Holtzman's name on them."

"Take a picture of the latrines," another man said. "You've never seen anything so disgusting as those pits."

Luke instinctively knew what she was asking and waited for the ruckus to calm down.

"Take a picture of the laundry," he called out.

She met his gaze and moved a few steps closer to him. "The laundry? And where is the laundry?"

"It's on the west side of the building," he said. "The inside would make for a good picture . . . but you'd be better off taking pictures from the outside."

She cocked her head to listen closely. "And why is that?"

"Interesting vents," he said without hesitation. "Never let it be said that the District of Columbia Jail lacks for modern amenities. Those vents funnel heat outside the building. Moisture too. It's probably best to photograph them in the early mornings, before lunch."

She nodded. "I understand." She gazed at him, and he wallowed in the sensation. Just being in the same room with her was a balm to his soul.

The guard escorting her began to get impatient. "Look, lady, are you going to take pictures in here or not?"

The trance was broken, and she stepped away. "Yes!" she said, quickly preparing her camera for another shot. She moved to the end of the table and beckoned the prisoners to face her.

Luke turned away. This wasn't how he wanted to be remembered. It was mortifying enough to be stuck in here without it being immortalized on film.

"Thank you," Marianne said, and he could only assume that meant she'd completed her picture, but he still didn't turn around. As much as his spirit rejoiced at seeing her, it hurt too. He was beaten down, humbled, and miserable, but Marianne's arrival sent a jolt of adrenaline into him that could sustain him for weeks.

He finally turned to admire her. She met his gaze, radiating confidence and compassion. He loved her, and somehow they would find a way through this.

The following morning Marianne approached the west side of the prison with a combination of dread and exhilaration. She suspected Luke planned to communicate with her through the vents he'd mentioned.

Which was why a huge chunk of her quivered in trepidation. To the bottom of her soul, she feared his imprisonment was her doing, and their meeting today would probably confirm it.

The granite bricks of the jail had never looked so gloomy as she approached. She glanced around the prison yard, but there didn't seem to be any guards patrolling the premises. She didn't even know if what she was doing was legal. Was it illegal to wander off the path and communicate with a prisoner through a laundry vent? At least the camera she clutched would be a convenient excuse should anyone question why she'd strayed from the path.

There was no shrubbery to hide behind as she approached a set of three vents sticking out from the side of the jail. The lawn was lumpy and uneven as she picked her way across it, but soon she was on the scrabbly limestone pebbles that abutted the jail.

Damp heat and the rumble of machinery came from the low metal vents. One was about the size of a pie plate, but another much larger opening was a square fan flush with the bricks. She squatted down to peek through it. The blades of the fan spun so quickly it was almost as though they disappeared, letting her see the huge rotary drums and aluminum tubing inside the laundry room.

Near the back of the cinder block room, she spotted Luke wearing a striped prison uniform as he unloaded a mass of wet sheets from one of the rotary drums into a basket. Were there other men nearby? She couldn't see any, but she dared not call out to him.

She gave two quick claps of her hands, and he immediately looked up, spotting her through the vent. He held a finger to his lips to convey silence, then casually spoke to someone else in the room. A moment later, a man dressed in the same prison uniform left the laundry, and Luke darted to the vent.

"Hello, beautiful," he said through the opening. "Wait there while I open the other vent."

He disappeared, but she heard scraping from the pie plate vent a few feet away. She went to stand before it, and Luke's hand came through the opening. She fell to her knees and grabbed it, pressing kisses to his palm.

"Watch out, I smell like bleach," he cautioned. "We've got

about five minutes before Stillman gets back from his toilet break."

That didn't leave her much time to pry the truth out of him. She withdrew her hand and squatted low so she could see his face through the vent. She drank in the sight, amazed at how happy he looked to see her.

"How did you figure this out?" she asked.

He snorted. "I spotted the possibilities the first hour I was assigned here. I've got nothing better to do than plan various means of escape."

"But you won't, will you? Luke . . . it will go worse for you if you run."

"I don't know," he said. "It depends on how things go."

A lump of dread settled in her stomach. "This is my fault, isn't it?"

"Never," he said fiercely.

"I know what the charges are. I know it's because of those studies and—"

He reached through the opening and laid a finger on her lips. "Shh," he soothed. "It's not your fault. It's not your fault."

But his finger trembled, and she sensed his anxiety from that single bit of contact. She pulled his hand away from her mouth so she could see him again.

"Why didn't you tell them it was me?"

His smile nearly broke her heart. "It would have killed a piece of me to do that," he said in a ragged breath.

"I want you to. If they bring charges against me, I'll be okay. I'm not afraid of enclosed spaces. I'll be okay."

"So will I." But for once he didn't sound like his usual brash self. His tone was pale and thin, and he sounded exhausted.

"What can I do to make this easier?"

"Come back tomorrow. I'm here every day."

He should be out planning how to reinvent the city for the new century. He should be dancing at weddings, teasing members of the Poison Squad, stirring up the world with one fiery article after another. He didn't belong locked in a jail, doing laundry.

"I guess this was one way to get you off the Poison Squad."

Sorrow made his eyes glint. "I feel like I'm letting the other guys down."

"Don't," she rushed to say, wishing she hadn't brought it up. He was so endlessly generous with his time and his body. Now he was suffering in jail because of her.

He glanced over his shoulder. "Stillman is coming back," he said and quickly set the ventilation tube back in place. She shifted over to the window fan but pressed against the side of the wall so no one inside could see her.

"I'll be back tomorrow," she promised.

Twenty-Seven

She met Luke at the laundry vents for the next four days. They were only able to steal a few minutes while his fellow inmate took his break, so there wasn't much time to waste arguing, but she broached the subject of Luke's defense at every meeting.

"You don't even have to use my name," she said. "Just tell them that someone with connections on the inside gave you the pictures."

He squeezed her hand through the vent opening. "Never, never, never," he vowed, his voice warm with affection, and each word felt like a caress.

The prospect of being exposed terrified her, but she wished he would do it. They couldn't keep meeting like this forever. Their secret meetings would eventually be discovered, and the punishment would fall entirely on Luke. This situation had to come to an end sooner or later, but he would never turn her in.

The only way to help Luke was for her to confess, and she would have to start by telling her parents. Would they let her continue living with them, or would she be banished from the house? At least when Aunt Stella was cut out of the family, she left with a husband. Marianne would be all alone.

She pondered the dilemma as she brewed a cup of ginger

tea for her mother on Saturday afternoon. Vera's headache was brutal today, and she lay upstairs with the blinds drawn and the windows closed despite the heat of the July afternoon.

Marianne put a few daisies into a bud vase because Vera liked that sort of touch on a tea tray. She was about to carry the tray upstairs when the swinging door to the kitchen banged open. Andrew stomped inside, followed quickly by Delia.

"You missed the rose competition at the Smithsonian," Andrew said, his expression sour.

Marianne bit her lip. Delia had brought a potted rosebush all the way from Baltimore to enter the competition. Her sister-in-law was supremely proud of her hybrid roses and had prepared a speech for the judges as part of the contest. Marianne hadn't been about to miss her morning with Luke to watch Delia preen in a flower contest.

"I'm sorry," she said. "I'm afraid I had to work today. How did the competition go?"

"Work," Andrew scoffed. "You don't have to work, you *want* to work. You flit all over town to take silly pictures and can't be bothered to support your own family. You were late to Dad's speech, and now you've disrespected Delia by ignoring her efforts in the rose competition."

Marianne sent a conciliatory nod to her sister-in-law. "I'm sorry I missed the contest. I had commitments today, and I hope you don't take it as a sign of disrespect that I couldn't be there."

"You ought to try a lot harder," Andrew said. "You're only a part of this family because Dad insisted on it. You're here on sufferance."

Marianne whirled on Andrew. "How dare you!" She scrambled for other words, but her mind went blank at the horrible comment that touched every one of her deepest insecurities.

"Your mother was an opera singer," Andrew said. "Dad paid her a thousand dollars to disappear, and she gladly took it. You were welcomed into this family even though your mother was little better than a tramp who—"

"Shut up," she said. "My mother is upstairs. I've been looking after her while she has a migraine. I hope you enjoyed yourself at Delia's garden party."

"*Your mother* took a thousand dollars to go away," Andrew retorted. "If I'd been there, I could have dickered her down to a few hundred."

She threw the bud vase at him, but he ducked as it smashed against the wall, spattering him with petals and water. He flicked a few droplets from his cuff and smirked.

"Very classy," he taunted. "Blood will out, won't it, Marianne?"

Mortification rushed through her. She was becoming exactly what she feared—someone who threw things and yelled and raged.

The noise brought her father storming into the kitchen. "What's going on in here?" Clyde demanded, his face a thundercloud as he surveyed the broken vase and water trickling down the wall. Jedidiah followed, making the kitchen uncomfortably crowded.

Anger crackled in the air as Andrew lifted his chin and rushed for the moral high ground. "Your daughter couldn't be bothered to attend Delia's rose competition," Andrew said. "Delia has been tending that rosebush for months, but Marianne decided to flit around town playing photographer."

Clyde turned a stern glance on her. "Marianne, you know that I am proud of your work, but family is important. If your duties at the Department of the Interior interfere with that, perhaps it is time to resign. You don't need the money."

Andrew preened at Clyde's words, and she couldn't let it go unchallenged. Andrew's loyalty to their family company came at a huge cost: three people in Philadelphia who drank tainted coffee.

"Is family the most important thing?" she challenged her father, then turned her attention to Andrew. "What about treating people with dignity, even if they don't share the same blood?"

"Marianne, blood is the only reason we tolerate you," Andrew said.

"Quiet, boy," Jedidiah smoldered. "You've always run a little hot for my taste, and Marianne is as fine as they come."

"At least I have my priorities in order," Andrew said. "I always put this family first. She doesn't. She waltzes all over town for her own fun, taking pictures. Anyone could take those pictures. Sam could take those pictures. I've grown our company and made us plenty of money in the past two years."

"Is money all that matters to you?" she asked. "Even if it means sacrificing our integrity? Putting other people's lives at risk, even though they aren't blood? Do we owe *them* loyalty?"

Clyde swiveled a look at her. "What are you driving at?"

It was time to confess. It was going to be the hardest thing she'd ever done, and so many people were going to be hurt, but it was the right thing to do. This might be the last minute on this earth when she would still have the love and affection of her father.

She drew a heavy breath and looked at Clyde. "Thank you for taking me in when I was a baby," she said, her voice starting to shake. "Thank you for supporting little Tommy too, even though I know it hasn't been easy on you or Mama. Your loyalty to me and Tommy means the world to me."

Clyde stiffened. "But?"

"But I found out some bad things about Magruder Food." Her voice almost failed her, and she swallowed to try again. "I was the one who revealed those studies to the *Modern Century*."

Clyde's face went white, and he stared at her in shock, but Andrew exploded.

"You did what?" Andrew roared.

"You shouldn't have buried those studies," she said, lashing out at Andrew because it was easier to blame him rather than her father or grandfather. "You know the chemicals we use can be dangerous, but you're using them anyway."

He pushed her shoulder, shoving her back a few feet, and she retreated. Anything to get away from the rage smoldering on his face. "So you betrayed us," he spat.

Marianne looked to her grandfather for help.

"That she did," Jedidiah said, his aging voice rough with fury as he glared at her. "A greater case of disloyalty I've never heard. If you had complaints about the way Andrew ran the company, you should have brought them to me, girl."

She withered beneath her grandfather's smoldering words. As always, the truth hurt the most.

"Get out of here and go to your room," Clyde said, refusing to look at her.

"Papa, I'm sorry—"

"Go to your room," he said again, his voice coldly furious.

She obeyed. She owed him that much. Her body trembled so badly that it was hard to climb the stairs, but she got to the top, where she saw the closed door to Vera's bedroom.

Mama hadn't gotten her tea. Vera still didn't know what had happened downstairs. A piece of her wanted to run to Vera and fling herself on the bed and cry in her mother's arms.

It would be selfish. Vera would soon learn what she'd done, and she would side with Clyde.

Marianne kept walking to her own bedroom, stepping inside and closing the door.

Twenty minutes later the bedroom door banged open and Clyde strode in. "You didn't give those studies to *Modern Century*, you gave them to Luke Delacroix," he said in a deadly calm voice.

She swallowed hard. "Why do you think that?"

Instead of answering, Clyde strode to the wardrobe and flung the doors open. He grabbed the two boxes in which she stored personal photographs, and dumped them on the bed. There were over a hundred pictures of Mama, Sam when he was a baby, and other family pictures. Clyde riffled through them, but he wasn't going to find any photographs of Luke. She wouldn't keep them in such an obvious place.

He grabbed a dresser drawer and dumped the contents on the floor, throwing the drawer to the side, where it banged against the wall. She flinched when he used his feet to kick through her clothes, but he didn't find anything. He yanked up her mattress, but there was nothing there.

Then he saw the large envelope taped to the underside of her bureau drawer and froze. Her mouth went dry when he reached for it, opening the flap and lifting out a dozen enlarged photographs. Luke holding Bandit fresh out of the ice. Luke gazing at her with all the love in the world as they stood in the treetops.

Clyde tossed the photographs on the bed, his lip curled in disgust. "How long have you been carrying on with him?"

She couldn't answer.

"How long?" he roared. He grabbed her face and forced her to look at him, his fingers digging into her cheeks.

She still couldn't talk. Her tongue seemed fused to the roof of her mouth, and it was so hot she might faint. Anything she said could cause Clyde to banish her forever. She'd lose everything. Had it been worth it?

She glanced at the picture on her bed, the one of Luke sopping wet and holding Bandit, an exhausted, happy smile on his face.

"That was the day it started," she whispered. "And it never stopped."

He let go of her face. Her jaw hurt where he'd clenched it, but that was nothing compared to the pain in her soul.

"You aren't to leave this room," he said, his quiet voice throbbing in intensity. "Your meals will be delivered here. You aren't to have any contact with the rest of the family. We will inform you what we decide."

She waited until his footsteps retreated down the stairs before staggering to collapse on the mattress. She couldn't help Luke anymore. All she could do now was pray.

Twenty-Eight

Sweltering heat from the laundry dragged on Luke's energy. The rotary drums of the drying machines emitted constant waves of warm air, and the vent didn't do a good job siphoning off the heat. It had been hot in Cuba, but it was a natural heat. There was nothing natural about the man-made heat pouring out of the laundry. It was over a hundred degrees in here, and the air barely moved. His hands were inflamed by the bleach and sweat that cracked his skin and made them sting.

To make it worse, Marianne hadn't visited him today. So far, she'd always come in the mornings, but it was almost dinnertime and she still hadn't appeared at the dryer vent. He'd left the laundry for thirty minutes at lunch and had asked Stillman if there'd been any sign of a visitor while he'd been gone.

"No sign of that girl, if that's what you're asking," his fellow inmate said with a wink. At first Luke tried to hide Marianne's visits, but Stillman quickly caught on. Luke had slipped him a few sticks of candy Gray brought him, and that was more than enough to keep Stillman quiet about Marianne's visits.

Luke lifted another armful of wet sheets into the drying drum, trying to use only his forearms to spare the cracked skin on his hands. He closed the door on the drum and pulled the metal lever to start the machine into motion.

A guard entered the laundry room. "Delacroix! You've got a visitor in the meeting room. Hands out for the cuffs."

Luke swiped an arm across the sweat on his face. He hated meeting Gray looking like this. His prison uniform was soaked with wash water and perspiration, but maybe the unexpected visit signaled something good. His lawyer planned to file an emergency appeal to a higher court, and maybe there was already some movement on that front.

The guard locked the handcuffs and leg-irons onto him, then led him out of the room. Luke followed, but the leg-irons made it impossible to move more than a few inches with each step. Damp strands of hair were plastered to his face, and he felt as limp as a wet rag as the guard opened the door of the meeting room. Luke shuffled forward.

Clyde Magruder stood inside. Luke immediately went on the alert. A hint of a sneer tugged at Clyde's mouth when he saw the handcuffs and leg-irons.

"Charming," Clyde said.

Luke recovered quickly. "It's always a pleasure to see you, Clyde."

Clyde glanced at the guard still standing in the doorway. "Close the door and leave us," he ordered.

"Yes, sir," the guard said.

Luke tried not to cringe as the locking mechanism slid into place, trapping him in this enclosed environment with his bitterest enemy.

Clyde kicked a chair a few inches and ordered him to sit.

Luke refused. "You can order the guards around, but not me."

"Suit yourself." Clyde sat, folded his arms across his chest, and glared. "It has come to my attention that you have been carrying on with my daughter." He tossed a stack of photographs on the table, damning proof of the relationship.

A crushing weight settled on Luke's chest. This was why Marianne hadn't come today. She was in trouble and probably suffering at this very moment because of him. He wouldn't volunteer any information, but he had to stop aggravating Clyde. This needed to be handled as carefully as a time bomb. Clyde held all the cards, and Luke could only gather information.

He pulled out the chair and sat opposite Clyde, setting his hands on the table, letting Clyde see the cuffs and his completely defenseless position.

"I know she was the source for that incendiary article you wrote," Clyde said.

At this point Luke would normally start taunting Clyde about the article, but not today. If he aggravated Clyde, Marianne would be the one to pay. All he did was raise a brow, an invitation for Clyde to keep talking. He braced himself to endure a round of insults or slurs against his family, but when Clyde finally spoke, he said the last thing Luke had been expecting.

"I am prepared to drop all the charges against you, provided you leave the city and never see my daughter again."

Luke drew a quick breath of air but tried not to get his hopes up. It was probably just a cruel taunt, like a cat playing with a mouse.

"I don't believe it," he finally managed to say. "Why would you open the prison door when you've got the opportunity to twist the knife even deeper?"

Clyde's eyes narrowed. "As much as I would love to twist that knife, it would cost too much. My objective is to expunge you from my daughter's life. I can't do that if she harbors misplaced guilt over you."

Luke wouldn't trust Clyde to make him a ham sandwich. "You don't have the power to drop the charges. The complaint against me was filed by the chairman of the Committee on Manufactures. That's Roland Dern. Get him in here to make the promise, and I'll consider it."

"Absolutely not," Clyde said. "You have already endangered my daughter's reputation by involving her in this scandal."

Luke leaned back in his chair. "Did I? Or am I languishing in jail because I'm protecting her? I will never do anything to hurt Marianne, and that should say something about my regard for her."

"Take your regard and get out of town with it. My daughter is on the verge of becoming engaged to Colonel Henry Phelps, a man of valor whose good name will honor and protect her."

It was a slap in the face, but Luke tried not to show how badly this hurt. The worst thing was that it was true. Colonel Phelps *did* have a sterling reputation. He was a decent, battle-tested man with no demons inside. Marianne probably would be better off with Colonel Phelps, and it sickened him.

But he would never take a payoff to turn his back on her. Marianne was the one pure thing in his life. She made him want to be a better man. She inspired him to reach higher, try harder, and seek out the better angels of his nature. He would protect Marianne, no matter what the cost to himself.

He stood, the leg-irons making a loud clank in the barren room. "No deal."

The guard led him back to the laundry, where the heat and confinement threatened to suffocate him.

Marianne didn't have much experience with boredom, and the hours stretched painfully in her bedroom prison. It had been two days, and Clyde made good on his threat to send all her meals upstairs and had forbidden her from mingling with the rest of the family.

Her bedroom door had no lock, but the force of Clyde's anger was more effective than any dead bolt. She stayed in her room, but the isolation terrified her. Some people might be able to be alone, but she wasn't one of them. She already knew what

Andrew and Delia thought of her, but what did Vera think? Surely her mother had been told, but Vera made no attempt to see her, and that snub spoke with the power of a trumpet blast.

It had been two days. It was hard to guess how long Clyde intended to enforce this banishment, because she'd never seen him this angry before. She sat on her bed and stared at the four walls, counting the ways she could have lived the past six months differently. She could have been more honest with her parents about Luke or been more forthcoming about negotiating a truce with the Delacroixs. It probably wouldn't have worked, but she owed her parents more than she'd given them.

But was it *all* her fault? If she could design a perfect family, no one would ever fear being kicked out or shunned. Over the last few months she'd learned terrible things about her family, but none of it could stop her from loving them. She had been planted in this family, put down her roots with them, and clung to them as naturally as a vine clung to a trellis. She didn't want to be ripped out and torn away. No matter how badly they treated her, she still wanted to belong.

A gentle tapping on her bedroom door made her sit bolt upright. It wasn't time for dinner yet, so perhaps Vera was coming to see her at last.

"Yes?" she asked, racing to the door and tugging it open, but it was only Bridget, the downstairs maid. Marianne tried not to let her disappointment show.

"This came for you in the mail today," Bridget said, holding a package. It had been opened because Clyde was inspecting everything going in or out of her room to prevent communication with Luke.

Marianne took the package without looking inside. "Thank you," she said. "How is everyone downstairs? Has my mother's migraine lifted?"

"Oh yes, ma'am. She's been right as rain for more than a day now. She went out shopping for a new tea set this morning."

"Good." Although it wasn't good at all. If Vera was feeling better, she could have come to comfort Marianne. Or yell at her. Or intervene for her. Instead, Vera chose to ignore her, which was the most painful of all.

"What about Andrew and Delia? Are they still here, or have they gone back to Baltimore?"

Bridget glanced down the hall in unease. "I'm sorry, ma'am. I'm really not supposed to be speaking to you."

Marianne nodded and watched the maid go. It wouldn't be fair to risk someone's job just because she was lonely and afraid. She closed the door and pulled the wrapping away from the package, and her heart nearly stopped.

Don Quixote!

She'd ordered a copy from the bookseller months ago, and now it was here. The front of the book was beautifully embossed with gold foil, showing the silhouette of a gangly man holding a lance, staring at a windmill in the distance. The top of the book had the title *Don Quixote* in a lavish font, and at the bottom was the author, Miguel de Cervantes. Marianne opened the front cover, where Luke's name was listed as the translator in much smaller font. Whoever was screening her mail obviously hadn't inspected the book carefully, or it would have been thrown into the fire.

He'd done it! Luke got this book across the finish line even though the process terrified him. She hugged the heavy tome to her chest, so proud of Luke but desperately wishing he could be here to share this moment.

Well! At least now she would have something to fill these long, dreary hours. She hopped onto her bed, cradling the book and savoring its weight and all that it represented. This was a monumental accomplishment, a labor of love that proved Luke Delacroix was no feckless dabbler. He was a man of immense talent and dedication, even if he hid it beneath a layer of breezy charm.

She gazed at his name on the title page, then turned it over to read a brief dedication.

Amazing women have inspired men
from the dawn of literary history.
Cleopatra, Helen, Guinevere, Juliet, and Dulcinea.
To these legendary heroines, I add my own,
and her name is Marianne.

She couldn't even breathe. Oh, Luke, what a wonderful, magnificent dreamer. Thank heavens her parents hadn't seen this, or she would have been banished to Siberia!

She shot off the bed, energy prickling through her veins and making it impossible to be still. For the past two days she had let herself be boxed up in this room. No more. She had to be worthy of that dedication. She had to be worthy of Luke and her own God-given intelligence to make a difference in the world.

Luke was locked up in jail because of her. She had to do something to help, but what? She couldn't storm the jail to break him out or make a legal argument in a court of law. She wasn't a person of influence who could call on connections.

She paced. It was time to stop counting the ways she couldn't help and think about how she *could*. She'd give anything for even a fraction of Luke's connections. He was a prince of the city and had a thousand friends. She was a newcomer and had no one.

That meant she had to be clever about this. She needed to rouse an army of Luke's allies and supporters, and she instinctively knew who they were.

The Poison Squad.

If those bombastic, hyper-competitive men knew Luke had been locked up for publishing a story about noxious chemicals, they would climb over each other to be first in line to help.

All she had to do was figure out a way to get to them without alerting her father.

She waited until four o'clock in the morning to make her escape because no one in this household was an early riser.

Men on the Poison Squad were. Luke told her that St. Louis got up at five o'clock every morning to train for the Olympics before breakfast, and the Rollins brothers rose early to study. Marianne expected at least a couple of the men to be awake to greet her.

Guilt ate at her as she snuck out of her bedroom. The house was dark, and she crept in stocking feet down the hall. Even the sound of her heart pumping blood in her ears felt loud as she tiptoed downstairs, clutching a pair of shoes to her chest. She waited until she was outside to tug them on.

Twenty minutes later she was on the sidewalk outside the Poison Squad's boardinghouse. A light illuminated one of the upstairs rooms, and she scurried up the steps, knocking with vigor to get that unknown person's attention.

It was St. Louis, already dressed for an early morning sprint through the deserted city streets. "Aren't you the photographer lady?" he asked.

She stepped inside the house. "I am. The last time I was here was the infamous night of the mass poisoning. You ran to fetch Dr. Wiley."

"I remember," he said. "You were holed up with Delacroix over there on that window seat all night. Say, where is he these days? He disappeared on us."

"That's what I'm here about."

St. Louis's eyes widened in disbelief when she told him about Luke's arrest and why he'd been taken into custody. He rounded up the Rollins brothers and Princeton, the only other men awake at that hour. All were aghast at what had happened to Luke.

"Was he the one writing articles for *Modern Century* all along?" St. Louis asked.

She nodded.

Princeton's normally gregarious demeanor was unexpectedly grim. "Are you telling us that Congress knew those chemicals could make people sick and buried the test results?"

"It was only a single committee that knew," she said. And one of the men on that committee was her own father, which made it hard to hold up her head, but that was the reason she was here.

"How can we help?" Princeton asked, and Marianne smiled, knowing she'd come to the right place.

Luke listened in amazement as Gray recounted what had been going on in the outside world over the past week. Gray and Mr. Alphonse told him the good news as they sat in the tiny meeting room.

"The Poison Squad are the most popular men in town," Gray said. "They're giving daily interviews to the newspapers, and Dr. Wiley isn't reining them in anymore. There's an annoying Italian who is always touting the extent of his suffering and hamming it up for the press. He announced he would be signing autographs at the base of the Washington Monument tonight."

Luke grinned. "Nicolo will do anything for attention, especially if it involves attention from the ladies. Keep talking."

This was too good to be true. The Poison Squad was trying to gin up as much attention for his case as possible, and they were doing a bang-up job of it. The Associated Press and Reuters had picked up the stories and wired them to newspapers all over the nation. Even some of the foreign newspapers were carrying the story of the brave young men putting their lives on the line for science, but Luke didn't care about the foreign press. All he cared about was putting enough pressure on Congress to get him released from jail.

"All the stories are being spun in your favor," his lawyer said. "Journalists don't like people being thrown in jail for reporting the truth, and the pressure is on Congress to explain why they have been suppressing those studies."

"What are they saying?" Luke asked.

"Congressman Dern is doing all the talking," Gray said. "He's claiming the studies weren't suppressed, they were merely being withheld pending a complete analysis of all the data, and frankly, he's got a valid point. He's incensed about the article you wrote and isn't backing down."

"Then we dial up pressure in the press," Luke said, but Mr. Alphonse shook his head.

"The only fight that matters is the one in court, not the press. Congressman Dern has a better hand of cards than we do if this case goes to court, and he's bracing for a long battle."

The familiar prickling sensation forced Luke to stand and start pacing in the tight confines of the meeting room. There was barely any space to move, but the thought of remaining locked up indefinitely made it impossible to sit still.

"Can I get out on bail until the trial?"

"We've already tried and failed," Gray said. "Your only shot of getting out of here is revealing how you got your hands on those studies. If you give us the name—"

"That's never going to happen," he interrupted.

"I repeat: If you give us the name, we can have you out of here within twenty-four hours."

"And you'll have my soul in tatters." Luke dropped back into the chair. For the past few minutes his spirit had been soaring, and he'd stupidly begun to hope that the power of the pen might break open his prison door, but it wouldn't happen. He braced his forehead in his hands, staring at the cracked paint of the table.

He didn't want to be here. He was dying in here, his soul shriveling up, but the thought of doing anything that would hurt Marianne had the power to stop his breath. He sagged as the words came pouring out.

"I won't ever turn my back on her. She is my brightest star, my inspiration for wanting to be a better man. I'll stay loyal to her no matter what the cost."

Gray turned to Mr. Alphonse, his voice heavy with reluctant admiration. "I'm afraid he's not going to budge. It's time to prepare for trial."

Marianne's banishment to her bedroom was lifted when Colonel Phelps asked to escort her to a ribbon-cutting ceremony at the Smithsonian's National Zoological Park. It was a daytime event, and it would have been perfectly acceptable for Colonel Phelps to escort Marianne on his own, but he worried about public perception and asked Vera to accompany them.

"Are you feeling all right, Mama?" Marianne asked as she walked beside Vera toward the zoo. It was a warm summer's day, and Vera had insisted on wearing her tightest corset because Mrs. Roosevelt would be cutting the ribbon for a new exhibit and Vera wanted to look her best.

"I'm fine," Vera said in a shallow breath. She could be on the verge of fainting, but she'd never admit it in front of Colonel Phelps, who was walking on her other side. Vera still wasn't quite at ease with Marianne's exalted suitor.

Several hundred people had arrived to see the dedication of the new bird enclosure featuring a pair of bald eagles. The newly arrived eagles promised to be the most popular animals at the zoo, and Mrs. Roosevelt wanted to do the honors.

"Let's find a spot in the shade," Marianne said, nudging Vera toward the cluster of people already gathered in a tree-shaded spot beside the bird house.

"There's plenty of room next to the podium," Vera insisted. There was no dissuading her. Marianne reluctantly found a spot near the podium where Vera could show off her wasp-waisted gown and impressive summer bonnet.

Mrs. Roosevelt soon arrived, smiling and nodding to the assembled guests. High-society socialites eager to rub shoulders with the first lady stood alongside sweaty tourists and sticky-fingered children. Journalists began scribbling in their pads, and a few newspaper photographers took pictures as the director of the zoo introduced the first lady.

"Thank you for that generous welcome," the first lady said after stepping up to the podium. Edith Roosevelt was an effortlessly graceful woman. Despite her gaunt face and plain features, there was something immensely kind in her intelligent face. Marianne and Colonel Phelps eagerly clapped along with the rest of the tourists, while Vera gently patted the palm of her gloved hands. Vera always thought showing too much enthusiasm was tacky.

Eventually two zookeepers emerged from behind a screen, each carrying a bald eagle perched on their arm. Both eagles immediately lifted off to settle on high branches near the top of the caged-in area.

"Absolutely magnificent," Colonel Phelps said. "Let me see if I can persuade the gamekeeper to give us a private showing."

"Oh, yes, please!" Marianne enthused.

Colonel Phelps set off, but Vera preferred to mingle with the crowd around Mrs. Roosevelt. Before they could get any closer to the first lady, Marianne spotted a grim-faced man heading straight toward them. She would recognize that bushy red mustache anywhere. It was Congressman Dern, the chairman of her father's committee. He gave her a brusque nod.

Vera smiled politely. "Roland, how delightful to see you."

"I'm afraid my visit is no cause for delight," the congressman replied. "I'm looking for your husband. It's a matter of some urgency. The maid at your house said he could be found here."

Vera shook her head. "We dropped him off at his accountant's office on our way."

Congressman Dern shifted in discomfort. He looked annoyed, embarrassed, and hot in the pounding sun. He met Vera's eyes. "The matter concerns both of you as well," he said. "Is there somewhere we can go to speak privately?"

A terrible sense of foreboding descended as Marianne and Vera accompanied Congressman Dern down the path toward the duck pond. The crowds were thinner here, as most people were admiring the bald eagles.

"What's going on?" Marianne asked. "Is my father all right?"

"That remains to be seen," Congressman Dern replied. "I was given advance warning of an item that will be printed in the *Washington Evening Star*." He met Vera's eyes, the first hint of sympathy breaking through his annoyance. "I am sorry to report the item is about your husband and an opera singer."

Marianne gasped, her eyes darting to Vera, but her mother absorbed the dreadful words with admirable sangfroid. "What opera singer?" she said with a lifted chin.

"An opera singer your husband was acquainted with twenty-six years ago."

It became difficult to breathe. Oh, good heavens, she mustn't faint. Mama needed her now more than ever.

Marianne swallowed hard and took a fortifying breath. "Twenty-six years ago?" she said stiffly, anger beginning to replace fear. "That makes it old news."

Congressman Dern tilted his head to look at her. "It sounds as if you are familiar with the substance of this story."

Vera cut her off before she could reply. "That story is nonsense. Do you hear me? Nonsense!"

A few bystanders turned to look at them curiously, and Colonel Phelps must have heard Vera's outburst. He crossed the park toward them with concern on his face. "What's going on here?"

Vera was shaking now, her face white and tears beginning

to threaten. "This man is circulating torrid gossip, and I won't stand here and listen to it."

"Madam, it was not I who spread the gossip," the congressman said. "I merely thought it fair to warn you and your husband."

"Warn them about what?" Colonel Phelps asked as he drew alongside them.

Vera's bottom lip began to wobble as she realized Colonel Phelps was on the verge of learning this horrible story. Marianne's only duty right now was to protect Vera. She was prepared to unleash a storm if either of these men uttered another word to upset her mother.

She put a protective arm around Vera's trembling shoulders. "Gentlemen, I am escorting my mother home now. She's not well."

"Allow me to assist," Colonel Phelps said. "I shall summon—"

"Please don't bother. I shall see Mother home." She sent him a warning glare for good measure. Colonel Phelps looked taken aback at her blunt demeanor, but she didn't care. Vera's reputation was about to become target practice for the vicious gossips of Washington society.

Guilt ate at Marianne like acid. It was because of her that this was happening. Vera never wanted to raise an illegitimate baby, but she did it to please Clyde. Now this ugly story had been dredged up from the past, and it was Vera who would suffer the most. Marianne and Clyde had the resilience to deal with it, but Vera didn't.

With most people still at the bald eagle exhibit, it was easy to summon a cabbie to drive them home. A few journalists loitered at the edge of the park, writing up their observations of the ribbon-cutting. She scanned their faces quickly, grateful that Dickie Shuster was not among them. If she'd seen that backstabbing man, it would be hard to restrain herself from physically assaulting him.

Once in the carriage, Vera sat stiffy on the bench opposite her, staring bleakly into space. It was a six-mile ride home, and Marianne prayed they could get there before Vera became physically ill.

"Mama, I'm so sorry," she said.

"Don't speak."

The two words cut, but Marianne obeyed without question. This was her mother's worst nightmare. Vera didn't deserve this.

The moment the carriage drew alongside their town house, Marianne raced for the front door, not even waiting to help Vera alight. She ran to the back of the house and found the downstairs maid.

"Go get my father," she urged. "Tell him it's an emergency. He's needed home at once."

Marianne wrung out another cold compress to lay across Vera's forehead. The curtains had been drawn, and Vera lay like a wounded dove atop her bed. Marianne smoothed the edges of the compress, then dabbed a tissue to catch a droplet of water that threatened to roll into Vera's hair.

"Shall I rub your feet?" Marianne asked. When Vera was distraught, these little gestures meant so much to them both.

The barest movement of Vera's chin indicated a yes. Marianne slipped the stockings from Vera's feet, then began the slow, methodical rubbing of first one foot, then the other.

All the while she planned to burn Dickie Shuster in effigy. Luke had warned her about the shifty reporter, but she couldn't imagine anyone would be so vicious as to resurrect a decades-old rumor merely to gin up a little unseemly publicity.

The slamming of the front door and heavy footsteps on the staircase indicated Clyde was home. Instead of being relieved, Vera's face crumpled, and tears threatened once again.

Clyde flung open the bedroom door and stepped inside. He must have been informed about the nature of the brewing scandal, for he sank to his knees beside Vera and grabbed her hand.

"Darling, I'm sorry," he said. His necktie was askew and his hair disheveled. Marianne couldn't recall ever seeing Clyde quite so distraught as he poured his heart out to Vera. "This is all my fault, but I'll figure out a way to protect you. I swear it."

Tears leaked from Vera's eyes, but she didn't pull away. "It's all going to come out," she wailed. "An opera singer. An *opera* singer! The humiliation is too great. I can't bear it."

"Shh, darling," Clyde soothed, looking on the verge of tears himself. "The blame is all mine. I will shoulder it and protect you. We all will."

Vera drew a ragged breath. "Marianne said that horrible little man from the newspaper is responsible. We must do something. A lawsuit. Demand a retraction. Something!"

Clyde whipped around to stare at Marianne. His expression was a curious mix of surprise and calculation. Then it cleared. "Go to your room," he said. "I'll join you when I can."

She was relieved to go. Watching this painful exchange between her parents was uniquely horrible, and she was glad to flee from it.

She hid the copy of *Don Quixote* under her bed. The only thing that could make this day any worse was if her father learned of Luke's role in the book and spotted the dedication.

From across the hall, the sound of Vera's wailing made her flinch. Then came the crash of glass shattering against the bedroom wall. It was probably part of the tea set, because two or three additional smashes followed in short order. Throughout it all, Clyde's low voice could be heard consoling, pleading, and apologizing. It took around twenty minutes for the firestorm to pass, and all the while Marianne tried to predict what this would mean for her family.

People would stare at her when she left the house. They

would whisper and speculate. She had nothing to be ashamed of, but knowing she was at the root of her mother's public humiliation still hurt. This was also going to damage Clyde's chances for reelection, but the very worst thing would be if reporters started scrounging around Clyde's private life and learned of Tommy. It was one thing to have cheated on a spouse twenty-six years ago, but Tommy was only two years old, and exposing that affair would ruin Clyde's political career forever.

A quiet tap on her door sounded, and she let Clyde in. He closed the door but didn't turn to face her. He just leaned his forehead against the door, his shoulders sagging and exhausted.

"It wasn't Dickie Shuster," he said quietly.

"What? How do you know that?"

He still didn't turn to face her. An uncomfortable silence lengthened in the room as Clyde clenched and unclenched his fists. She'd never seen him this devastated. He slowly rotated, then made his way to her bed, moving like a sleepwalker. He sat but hung his head low, staring at the floor. He looked ready to weep.

"It was Andrew," he said.

Her own brother? Strength drained out of her knees, and she dropped to the floor where she stood, unable even to make it to the chair.

"I don't believe it," she finally said. "I can't." While she could easily imagine Andrew doing something to hurt her, he wouldn't do this to Vera. Never.

"Believe it," Clyde said. "Think! Dickie Shuster works for *The Washington Post*, not the *Evening Star*. He doesn't have anything to do with this."

"Then what makes you think it was Andrew?" she whispered.

"I paid the clerk at the front desk of the *Evening Star* a hundred dollars to tell me the source. Andrew did it last week. The same day you confessed to turning those stories over to Luke. He did it to hurt *you*, not Vera."

Another wave of grief settled on her, weighing her down. She doubted she could get up off this floor if her life depended on it. The betrayal was so absolute, so cutting and deep. Did Andrew hate her this much?

"Does Mama know?"

Clyde's head shot up. "No! And you're not to tell her. It would kill her. Andrew has always been her favorite."

That wasn't a surprise, but it hurt that Clyde didn't even realize what he'd just said.

"What should we do?"

His eyes narrowed. "This is my mess. I'll clean it up. Just do whatever Vera asks of you. All right?"

"I promise."

"I need you to swear to it, Marianne." For once her father looked completely shattered and dependent on her. "Knowing it was Andrew could push her over the edge. She can't handle this right now."

It didn't seem right to withhold information to protect Andrew, but everything Clyde said was true. "I swear it."

Clyde nodded. "Thank you. It's almost five o'clock, and the *Evening Star* will be released by six. I'll find a copy, and the two of us can review it together. Dealing with Roland Dern will be a nightmare, but I'll handle that tomorrow."

Marianne nodded. She suspected that after tomorrow they would all carry a scar that would never fully heal.

Thirty

Vera canceled her round of afternoon calls the following day, but there was no hiding from the scandal. Marianne was in the kitchen with Vera to review the grocery list when the downstairs maid brought a tray carrying three calling cards. Two were from senators' wives and one was from the wife of the postmaster general.

"I must play this like the role of a lifetime," Vera said grimly, then snapped her fingers. "Quick! Help me tighten this corset a few more inches. These women may outrank me, but my figure shall put them all in the shade."

The flash of fighting spirit was a relief to see. Marianne quickly adjusted Vera's corset and ran upstairs to fetch powder for her mother's nose.

"You look lovely," she whispered as Vera set off to face the women.

"Polish the tea set while the water boils," Marianne instructed Bridget, the downstairs maid. "I'll run to the bakery and buy whatever I can find to serve." They hadn't been expecting this and had no gourmet delicacies that would show Vera in a positive light.

Marianne had a stitch in her side from running as she arrived at the bakery. "Please box up every tea cake you have, and two loaves of white bread." There was enough cucumber and watercress at home to make tea sandwiches, and it would have to do.

By the time Marianne returned home, two more congressmen's wives had arrived to call. "How is it going?" she asked Bridget as she set the box of pastries on the kitchen counter.

"Your mum is holding her own," Bridget whispered. They quickly cut the crusts from the bread to make triangular tea sandwiches while the maid talked. "People are polite, but they keep asking after your pa. We all know what they're dying to know, but your mum is handling it like a queen."

The front bell rang again, but the smock of Bridget's uniform was drenched in spilled tea. Marianne's poplin gown was still presentable. The bell was pulled again.

"I'll get it." Maybe it wasn't quite the thing for the daughter of the household to answer the front door, but there was nobody else.

Unfortunately, it was Congressman Dern's wife waiting impatiently on their doorstep. Marianne showed her into the parlor and brought another chair for Mrs. Dern. All conversation stopped while Marianne was in the room, but it resumed the moment she left. Marianne pressed her ear to the door to eavesdrop.

The postmaster general's wife spoke with an oily voice. "What a lovely young woman your . . . ahem, what a lovely young woman your *daughter* is."

Vera's voice was tight. "Indeed she is."

The postmaster's wife continued in her delightedly somber tone. "My dear, we are all thinking of you in this challenging time."

Marianne didn't care what people thought of her. She just wished this day could be over for Vera.

The doorbell rang again. Instead of another caller, it was only a message boy holding a small card addressed to Vera.

"Thank you," she said, tucking it into her pocket to deliver later.

It was a trying afternoon, but by three o'clock it was over. Vera was shaking after the women left. Marianne sat with her in the parlor, the remnants of the hastily assembled tea strewn around the room like battlefield casualties.

"Dreadful women," Vera said. "After they saw you, all they could do was ask questions. 'How old is your daughter? Twenty-six? How interesting! What lovely coloring she has.' That horrible Mrs. Sharpe wanted to know if you can *sing*. We all knew what she was driving at, but I had to sit here and smile and offer her more tea cakes. The witch. I would have liked to rub that tea cake in her fussy, overly tight pin curls. Everyone knows pin curls went out of style last decade."

Marianne said nothing, just let Vera unfurl the list of petty insults she'd been dealt. While some of the women were there to gawk, Congressman Dern's wife seemed kind and only wanted to support Vera, but nothing was sitting well with her mother today.

"This came for you while the ladies were visiting." Marianne set the thick envelope on the table.

Vera perked up and opened the note, the corners of her mouth turning down as she read. "It's from Colonel Phelps," she said stiffly. "He sends his regrets that he won't be able to join us for dinner on Sunday."

Marianne remained frozen, her chin high. "Did he say why?"

"He didn't. But I think we all know."

It was another kick in the teeth. Colonel Phelps was an ambitious man on the rise and couldn't accept the illegitimate daughter of an opera singer as his spouse.

The paper crackled as Vera wiggled the letter back into the envelope. "He may change his mind once this all blows over."

"I doubt it." Marianne spoke without heat or anger, just resignation. She loved Luke too much even to consider Colonel Phelps, but his rejection still hurt.

Vera dropped the note, curled over, and started weeping.

Marianne rushed to embrace her. "Mama, it will be all right!" she soothed. "Don't worry, I didn't care for Colonel Phelps. All I care about is you. Please don't cry."

"Oh, Marianne," Vera sobbed. "You are the best, even though you're not my own. You know I love you, right?"

"Of course, Mama."

Vera wiped her tears, taking some ragged breaths and gradually composing herself. "Now, darling," she said, "please don't take this amiss, but I think things would be easier if you left town for a little spell." At Marianne's gasp, Vera rushed to explain. "Only for a little while, darling! You could go live with Andrew and Delia and have a nice visit in Baltimore. I think it would be easier for everyone."

Marianne looked away so Vera couldn't see the hurt on her face. Going to Baltimore was impossible. Not only would she rather strangle Andrew than look at him, she couldn't bear to be that far away from Luke. She couldn't even see him, but the Poison Squad was doing their best to rally support to his cause.

"I know you've been feeling cooped up here," Vera continued. "If you were in Baltimore, Andrew would be able to keep an eye on you."

"I'll talk to Papa about it," she said noncommittally.

Perhaps there was a way to capitalize on this latest catastrophe that could benefit Luke, but it would come at a terrible cost.

Marianne intended to intercept her father the moment he arrived home so she could warn him of Vera's plan to ship her off to Baltimore and into Andrew's smothering protectorate. She wouldn't go to Baltimore. At least, not without some significant concessions.

To her surprise, old Jedidiah had come from Baltimore and

was with Clyde as they arrived home at the end of the day. She greeted them both at the front door.

"Hello, Grandpa," she said cautiously. This was the first time she'd spoken to him since confessing what she'd done, and he gave her a stiff nod but no smile. It was enough. At least he had come to support Clyde in the face of this latest blow.

"How's your mother?" Clyde asked without ceremony.

"She's upstairs, getting dressed for dinner," she replied. "Eight women called for a visit this afternoon, and she survived it with only a few dings to her dignity. She's also hoping to send me to Baltimore, and I'd like to speak with you privately before you agree to anything."

Marianne had spent all afternoon planning how to take advantage of the rapidly shifting family dynamics. Maybe she was aiming too high, but timidity wasn't going to get her anywhere. She wouldn't meekly go to Baltimore without winning a huge favor in return.

"Has she figured out it was Andrew?" Jedidiah asked.

She shook her head. "We didn't discuss it."

"I never trusted that boy," her grandfather said to Clyde. "Too ambitious. He was handed everything on a silver platter and didn't develop the muscle to fight on his own. It's made him sneaky and mean."

"Quiet," her father urged. "Vera might overhear."

Jedidiah snorted. "She needs to find out about the boy sooner or later."

"Later," her father urged. "There's only so much she can handle right now."

Dinner was a tense affair, and Clyde briefly reported that Congressman Dern had asked him to remain on the committee to assist with the pending tariff resolution, but recommended he consider searching for another committee appointment by the end of summer. It was a humiliation, but at least Clyde was allowed to save face in the short term.

After dinner, Vera returned to her room upstairs, and Clyde retreated with Jedidiah to the study. Marianne rose to join them.

"If I am to go to Baltimore, we have some issues to discuss."

Her father's mouth turned down, but he gestured her inside. Would having Jedidiah here help or hurt her case? Her grandfather mistrusted Andrew but had always warmly approved of her, so that was good, but he was also the hard, unforgiving man who had turned his back on Aunt Stella.

"Yes, Marianne, what is it?" Clyde asked once the door was closed behind the three of them. Jedidiah sat and began filling his pipe, but Clyde remained standing, as did she.

She saw no point in softening her words. "Mama wants me to leave the city because I am an embarrassment to her."

The blunt statement had the desired effect. Clyde winced and sent her an apologetic look, but his words offered no comfort.

"Then please do so," he said in a pleading voice. "You know your mother and I both love you, but it would be easier on her if you go. Just for a short while. This is entirely my fault, and I'm sorry."

On a night like this, when her father was being attacked from all sides, she ought to be supportive and relent. She couldn't. Not when Luke's freedom was on the line. Now was the time to fight.

"Yes, it's your fault," she agreed. "And yet you want me to go live with Andrew. *Andrew*, of all people. I'll go to Baltimore, but only in return for a favor."

Clyde tensed, and even Jedidiah looked up from his pipe, waiting expectantly.

"I want you to get Luke Delacroix out of jail. I want all the charges dropped, and I want—"

"Forget it," Clyde interrupted.

"But *I* was the one who gave those studies to Luke. *I* was the one who spied. We all know that."

"I'm not going to put you in jail, Marianne."

"Thank you, because I'd rather not go to jail. But Luke doesn't belong there, and I want him out."

"And if I get him out, you'll go to Baltimore?"

"I will."

"Not good enough. I want the two of you separated permanently. Forever."

A weight landed in her stomach. She'd always known that choosing Luke would mean her family would cast her out. They'd done it to Aunt Stella, and they would do it to her. If she fled to Luke, her father would continue his quest to ruin the entire Delacroix family.

It would be better to engineer a cease-fire. Luke's freedom was worth it, and she could ensure her father lived up to his word.

"I promise I will leave and never contact him again," she said, her heart splitting as she spoke, but she had to stay strong while forging this deal.

A calculating gleam lit Clyde's gaze. "You won't return his messages or let him see you either?"

"I have no control over what Luke does. His own family can't control him, so how can I? But I can promise to leave Washington and never contact him again. Papa, we have each other over a barrel. If Luke somehow lands back in jail, our deal is off. I'll come back to Washington and get the warden to marry us in a prison ceremony. I'll share his jail cell if I have to."

"You wouldn't," Clyde said.

"I would," she vowed. "And I have contacts in Washington who will be watching to ensure you live up to your end of the bargain. If Luke gets arrested for *littering*, you'd better see that he gets out of jail before nightfall."

Her father's eyes narrowed as he parsed her words. He clenched and unclenched his fists, a crafty look on his face as he considered the implications. The only sound that could be heard was the ticking clock from his desk.

"We have a deal," he finally said, and Marianne didn't know if she should laugh or cry.

Things moved quickly after that. Over the next few days her father called on Congressman Dern and various attorneys to undo the legal quagmire he initiated when he set the wheels in motion to accuse Luke of spying.

Clyde's preoccupation gave Marianne the freedom to solve the longest mystery of her life.

What happened to Aunt Stella?

The only person to have contact with Stella after she was banished was Esther Magruder, Jedidiah's wife and Stella's mother. They carried on a secret correspondence for years, and Marianne remembered glimpsing those letters, always written in Stella's distinctive purple ink. There had been a short-lived scandal after Esther died when it was discovered the old woman had hired an attorney to create a bequest for her daughter. Esther foresaw Jedidiah's opposition and set funds aside to posthumously battle her husband in court in order to pay her daughter that bequest. She lost. Stella was never even notified of her mother's attempt to remember her in her will.

Marianne snuck into her father's office in search of clues as to where Stella had gone. Letters? Her grandmother's will? Perhaps Clyde had Stella's address secreted somewhere in case he wished to contact her about important family matters.

After an hour of searching, Marianne finally struck gold. Clyde kept a file of legal papers documenting Esther's failed attempt to leave her daughter a bequest. One of the papers contained Stella's last known address in Carson City, Nevada.

Marianne retreated to her room with the prized address and pulled out her copy of *Don Quixote*. Was she as foolish as Don Quixote, seeing the world through rose-tinted glasses and fighting for impossible causes? Just because Aunt Stella wrote with purple ink and dared to elope with the man of her dreams didn't mean she was some sort of heroine, but Marianne still liked to hope she was. She hoped Stella found happiness with her dashing husband in the wilds of Nevada, where they built a perfect kingdom of their own.

Near the end of the week, her father came to her room.

"I have a deal with Congressman Dern," he said in a clipped voice. "Lawyers are preparing an agreement. Delacroix will be released tomorrow afternoon. I have notified Andrew to expect you on the eleven o'clock train to Baltimore tomorrow morning."

Relief trickled through her along with a wallop of dread. This was suddenly all very real. She had known it was coming, but it was still hard.

"I shall be ready."

Both her parents accompanied her to the train station the following morning. It was the Baltimore and Potomac Station, the wonderful gothic building she had once explored with Luke. This would probably be the last time she ever saw it, for it was due to be torn down soon. It made the lump in her throat grow even larger.

Vera noticed. "Don't cry, darling," she crooned. "You won't have to stay away too long, and think how much fun you'll have in Baltimore."

Marianne nodded. How typical for Vera to completely misread the situation, but she had no desire to clarify things. The train was drawing near, billowing clouds of steam as the engines slowed. The breaks squealed, and heat poured from the locomotive. Clyde looked so stern, even though he had won almost everything. She was leaving Washington and had agreed not to contact Luke. Wasn't that enough for him?

She met his eyes. Her imperfect, stern, but loving father. They had both disappointed each other, but on this one thing, she couldn't let him break his vow.

"Please keep your word about Luke," she said, knowing that even mentioning his name was a risk, but it had to be said. "I know you don't approve, but I love him, and I'm doing this on his behalf. Please don't let me down. I don't think I can bear it if you do."

Clyde gave the tiniest nod of his head. "I will keep my word. I expect you to do the same."

She nodded. Vera gave her a farewell hug, but Clyde still seemed angry and offered only a handshake.

Two hours later, the train pulled into the Baltimore depot. Andrew awaited her on the platform, and he was alone.

Good. She would deliver on every promise made to her parents, but nothing extra. She had come to Baltimore exactly like she promised, but now she was free.

"How was the ride?" Andrew asked as she stepped onto the platform. All around her passengers were disembarking, porters unloaded trunks, and people hugged loved ones.

This was not going to be a loving reunion.

"Fine," she replied. "Papa knows it was you who squealed to the press about my real mother."

Andrew blanched. "No, he doesn't."

"He paid a hundred dollars to learn the source of the story, and what a disappointing surprise it was. He and Jedidiah both want your head on a platter."

Andrew looked sick. He reeled a little and grabbed a light pole for balance. "Does Mama know?"

"Not yet. She'll probably figure it out once Grandfather replaces you in the company, which is surely coming."

The breath left Andrew in a rush. "He can't do that. I've given everything to this company. I'm next in line."

"Jedidiah can step back in."

That triggered another round of protestations from Andrew. He hadn't even bothered to apologize to her. All he worried about was scrambling to secure his own position in the company. She let him ramble as she set off for the ticket window, opening her reticule to retrieve her money clip.

Andrew followed. "Maybe Dad will side with me," he said. "Grandpa is getting old and senile. He can't even use an adding machine."

It was an effort to keep her voice steady, but she managed it. "Grandpa doesn't need to take over the company. Papa is probably going to lose his next election, thanks to you, which means he'll be able to take back the reins. Congratulations. You're about to find out what it's like to venture out into the world on your own. As am I. I came to Baltimore exactly as promised. Now I am going to buy a ticket to Nevada. Goodbye, Andrew."

An hour later she was on her way to find Aunt Stella and learn what it felt like to no longer be a Magruder.

Thirty-One

Luke's spirits were glum as he met with Mr. Alphonse for the latest update on his legal situation. It was just the two of them this morning, and the meeting was easier without Gray there. Luke didn't have to pretend that his spirits were holding up with Mr. Alphonse.

"A court date has been set for November," Mr. Alphonse said. "This is good because it will let us prepare—"

"Good?" Luke cried out in disbelief. "I can't last in here until November." He held up his hands, cracked and blistered from the bleach in the laundry, but he couldn't be reassigned elsewhere in case Marianne came back. It was obvious Clyde was keeping her on a short leash, but he still hoped.

"November is only four months away," Mr. Alphonse said. "And we need as much time as possible to prepare for a constitutional challenge. I am gathering briefs from interested parties who want to weigh in on freedom of the press, and those will be our most powerful weapon. Your motive in publishing the story was honorable, but it was against the law unless we can mount a constitutional challenge."

Mr. Alphonse continued outlining his position, but it was all horrible. They were going to have to fall on the mercy of the court with nothing but a single sentence from the Bill of Rights to shield him. If they failed, he was looking at five to seven years of imprisonment. Could Marianne wait that long? Could he? He'd never been tested like this and didn't know if he'd survive it. This had been harder than he expected.

A rattle at the door surprised him. The bolt slid free, and Superintendent Castor stepped inside.

"On your feet, Mr. Delacroix. Officer Galloway is going to unlock those shackles you're wearing."

Luke stood and held out his hands, not even bothering to ask why. It would feel good to have the irons off his wrists and be capable of walking more than a few inches at a time.

His lawyer was more curious. "What's all this, then?"

"Change of plans," the superintendent said. "The word just came down. It's all over. Congress is backing down, and you are free to go."

Luke blinked. If this had happened in Cuba, he'd suspect it was a cruel jest, but Superintendent Castor had always been a decent man who wouldn't taunt like that.

Luke still couldn't quite hope. "Are you sure?"

Castor gave his lawyer a slip of paper, and Mr. Alphonse read quickly.

"You're a free man," his lawyer finally pronounced in amazement, but Luke still stared, unable to process this abrupt turnabout.

He could leave? Walk out the door and be a free man again? He swiveled to gape at Superintendent Castor, praying this wasn't a dream.

"All I ask is that you leave out the back door," Mr. Castor said. "Reporters are gathering on the front step, and it's a bit of a mess out there. Your brother is waiting for you out back."

Luke blinked faster. Tears threatened because Gray was here and this wasn't a joke and in a few minutes this hideous nightmare might all be over. "Whatever you want," he choked out.

He wouldn't even return to his cell. There was nothing there he wanted. He just needed to get out of this windowless dungeon and into the clean air.

The moment his leg-irons were off, he followed Superintendent Castor down the hallway. The sensation of striding freely without the oppressive shackles was a marvel. His heart pounded so hard it was probably echoing off these concrete blocks, but he was smiling too wide to pay attention.

Mr. Alphonse held the door for him, and it was bright outside. It took his eyes a few seconds to adjust, but then Gray was striding toward him, laughing and tugging him into a mighty bear hug.

"Welcome back," Gray said.

Princeton was there. So were Nicolo and St. Louis and the Rollins brothers. They surrounded him and clapped him on the back, hooting and congratulating him.

Caroline and Nathaniel were there too, and Luke gave his brother-in-law a back-pounding hug. "When are you going to quit getting arrested?" Nathaniel teased.

Luke managed a laugh but stared into the cloudless blue sky, thanking God for his liberation. *Thank you. A thousand times, thank you, God!* He was grateful not only for his freedom, but the blessing of good friends and family.

There was only one thing that would make this morning utterly perfect.

He looked at Gray. "Marianne?"

Gray's face dimmed a little. "I haven't seen her. She's been lying low."

Luke nodded. He'd known ever since Clyde's nasty visit two weeks earlier that their meetings had been discovered and Marianne was probably paying a penalty for it. He'd go searching for her as soon as he bathed and changed into a fresh set of clothes.

But something about Gray's expression warned him there was more bad news coming.

"She's been caught up in a scandal involving her father," Gray said. "Something about an opera singer."

Luke closed his eyes. Marianne was going to hate this, and he needed to provide whatever comfort he could. "I'd better go find her. She was always terrified of that getting out."

"She knew?"

"She knew," he affirmed. "Have any other salacious stories about Clyde come out? Perhaps involving a boy named Tommy?"

"Not that I've heard."

That was a relief.

Strange. Six months ago Luke would have gloated had Clyde's dirty laundry received a public airing. Now he understood that he couldn't hurt Clyde without the people in his orbit getting sucked into the downfall as well. He loved Marianne more than he hated Clyde, and that meant he'd do anything to protect her from the consequences of her father's misbehavior. It meant that instead of nurturing his resentment, Luke had to learn to become a positive force where the Magruders were involved.

Maybe sending Marianne into his life was God's way of compelling Luke to reexamine his own cocksure arrogance in looking at the world. Stranger things had happened, and he was up to the challenge.

It felt strange, traveling across the country with a numb spirit but curious eyes. Marianne was heartsick over leaving Luke behind, but her artist's eye hungrily devoured the changing landscape speeding past the train window as she headed west. By the end of her first day, she was in the rolling green hills of Appalachia. They soon gave way to fields of corn in Ohio and Indiana. Then the land changed to the boundless flatlands of Kansas and Nebraska.

Was she running away from something or toward something? The fate of Aunt Stella had always been a mystery. Seeking her out gave Marianne's lost soul a sense of direction. Could a woman be expelled from a family and still be happy? Had Stella's Lenape husband made her happy? Was she even still alive?

The train stopped every few hours at railway depots in small, dusty towns. Passengers got on and off, but Marianne always went in search of a newspaper. Places like Mapleton, Utah, didn't have a lot of news to report other than their failing iron ore mines, but thanks to the Associated Press, national news from all over the country was telegraphed even to small towns like these.

Three days after setting off on her journey, she saw the story she had been looking for. On the second page of the *Mapleton Register* was a story reporting the activities of the Poison Squad. The most important passage was in the second paragraph:

> Luke Delacroix, an inaugural member of the Poison Squad, was briefly imprisoned in the DC Jail for premature exposure of laboratory studies commissioned by Congress on the safety of chemical preservatives. Mr. Delacroix was released on Tuesday when Congress withdrew charges in reaction to negative publicity surrounding his arrest.

A crushing weight lifted off her chest. *Luke was free.* Her father had kept his word.

She gazed out past the feedstore and the post office to the fields beyond. *Thank you Lord! Please let him be happy now.*

Beneath this huge western sky it felt easier to be closer to God. Maybe it was because she'd been stripped away from her family, friends, and every familiar guidepost in her life. Without those crutches, perhaps it was only natural to look *up*. She was putting her faith in God to find Aunt Stella and perhaps a direction for her future.

She boarded the train and continued traveling west, but she saw the world through new and hopeful eyes. Her sacrifice had worked. Luke was free, and in an odd way, she was too. She was without family or encumbrances. She could make her own way in the world. She had a camera, a sound head on her shoulders, and the desire to do something good. If there were any other requirements for success, she hadn't heard of them.

Five days after leaving Washington, the train arrived in Carson City, Nevada, a small, prosperous town of fewer than five thousand people. It bordered the Sierra Nevada mountain range and had an arid desert quality mixed with hints of green mountain scrub and pine trees.

Marianne was a mass of jumbled nerves as she disembarked at the train station. The only thing she knew about her aunt was that as of six years ago, she lived at 5 Dover Street. The coming meeting had her tense with anxiety. What happened to a woman who sacrificed everything for love? Marianne was about to find out.

The air in Carson City felt fresh and crisp. The sky was the bluest thing she'd ever seen, but this landscape was so alien. Was Stella even still here?

Marianne headed straight for the train station ticket window. "What time does the train leave?" she asked.

"They've got a two-hour break to water and refuel," the clerk replied. "They leave at one o'clock sharp."

"Thank you."

The man gave her directions to Dover Street, and she paid extra to store her heavy portmanteau in a storage room at the depot. It was too heavy to lug the half mile to Dover Street, and she wouldn't be staying if Aunt Stella was no longer here.

Dover Street was lined with small but respectable homes. Number 5 was an immaculately kept single-story house painted white with purple shutters. It had a low-slung hip roof and a wide front porch. There was a man on the roof, nailing shingles into place.

Was this the man Stella married? With his straight dark hair and bronzed skin, he looked like he could be an Indian.

He also looked angry. He was shouting down to a woman who stood in the front yard with a bowl of something in her arms.

"I'm not coming down for lousy egg salad," the man said. "I can tell just by looking at it that you made it wrong again."

"I didn't make it wrong," the woman hollered up, one hand on her hip and spine stiffening in anger. "I made it exactly like I did last time, and—"

"And it was wrong last time!" the man interrupted.

"Maybe if you weren't so persnickety, you could appreciate

healthy food." The shrewish woman had the same shade of chestnut hair as Clyde, with a few threads of silver and lines fanning from the corners of her eyes.

"You tossed out the yolks," the man growled. "What's the point of egg salad if you toss out all the yolks? I may as well eat shoe leather."

"Oh, the unspeakable horror," the woman bellowed in a tone so loud it echoed off the neighboring houses. "The torture of enduring poorly prepared egg salad! I can hear the angels weeping for your agony."

The woman continued shouting insults, but the man had gone back to hammering and probably couldn't hear her over the racket.

Marianne recoiled in dismay. She could turn around and get back on the train to keep heading west. It would spare her having to speak to these people who were so petty as to argue on a public street over egg salad.

But was it possible this wasn't even her aunt? Maybe these horrible people had bought the house from Stella, and her daring aunt was living happily with her husband somewhere else. She couldn't leave without asking.

"Excuse me, ma'am," she asked, interrupting the woman's tirade. "Are you by chance Stella Magruder?"

The older woman gasped. The man on the roof dropped his hammer, and it skittered down the shingles to plop harmlessly into the shrubs.

"I used to answer to that name," the woman said. "I'm Stella Greenleaf now."

"Oh." The last hope that Stella was blissfully sheltered within the loving arms of her forbidden lover in a high-desert paradise evaporated. Marianne wished she could run away and pretend this meeting had never happened, but she was here now and had to see this through. "I'm Marianne Magruder. Clyde Magruder is my father."

The older woman pressed a hand to her chest. "My goodness," she finally stammered.

The news seemed to have rendered Stella speechless, but not so her husband. Mr. Greenleaf was standing on the roof, both hands braced on his hips. "Who threw you out?" he called down. "Clyde or old Jed?"

"No one," she answered. "I figured out it was time to leave all on my own."

"Hang on. I'm coming down." Mr. Greenleaf was remarkably nimble as he reached the edge of the roof, lowered himself to plant a foot on the porch railing, then sprang to the ground. He wiped a grubby hand on his trousers before offering it to her, his eyes dancing with laughter.

"I'm Joseph Greenleaf," he said. "This is my wife. You're welcome to join us for lunch if you can stomach lousy egg salad."

Stella threw a dish towel in his face, but he caught it, and both of them started laughing.

Maybe this wouldn't be so bad.

Perhaps she'd been naïve, but Marianne had assumed she would be automatically welcomed into Aunt Stella's home. That wasn't the case.

"You have the whiff of a girl who is running away," Stella said as she brought Marianne a sandwich in the compact kitchen near the back of the house.

"I'm a photographer," Marianne defended. "I'm taking pictures out west."

Joseph scrutinized her, chewing his disagreeable egg salad sandwich while his dark, relentless gaze made her shift in her chair. He finished his sandwich, drained a glass of milk, then slammed it down. "Tell us what really drove you all the way across the country, and we'll be glad to support you however we can. But I don't want any trouble from the Magruders, and I don't want to open my home to a woman with secrets."

She told them everything, including the scandal of her illegitimate birth and the ill-fated romance with a man her parents disapproved of that led to his imprisonment.

"I agreed to leave Washington in exchange for his freedom, and my father took the deal."

"And you intend to honor your word?" Joseph demanded, his voice and face stern. "No running off to your young man now that he's out of jail?"

She would honor her word to the letter. "I vowed not to initiate contact with him, and I won't. I'm more than two thousand miles away." If Luke managed to contact *her*, however, all bets were off. "All I ever wanted was a normal family. I don't think that's too much to ask for."

"That's it?" Joseph demanded. "You ran away to the desert hoping that it would magically give you a normal family?"

"It's a lot more complicated than that," she said, glancing uneasily at her aunt. Why was Stella letting her husband interrogate a virtual stranger like this?

"Maybe you're hoping for the wrong things," Joseph said. "Maybe you should start looking for a stronger faith, or victory over temptation, or the strength to extend a bit of grace to someone even if they don't deserve it at all. How about demonstrating a bit of godly obedience?"

Resentment built inside her. She just saw this man practically shout himself hoarse over his wife's egg salad, and he had the gall to challenge her character?

"I don't know what I'm looking for!" she burst out. "I'm not a perfect person, and I'm lugging around an avalanche of guilt over what I've done. If I knew how to fix it, I wouldn't be here."

Joseph and Stella retreated outside to discuss what was to be done with her. This wasn't the sympathetic welcome she'd expected. Hadn't they once been young and insanely in love?

Hadn't they risked everything to elope? More than anyone, they ought to be understanding of her plight.

"All right, you can stay," Joseph said when he and Stella finally returned to the kitchen. "Sometimes it's good to escape into the wilderness for a while to sort things out. You can stay for forty days, a good solid biblical number that will be time enough to get your priorities straight. You are to send a telegram to your parents, assuring them you are safe and being looked after. We're not rich like the Magruders, so I'll be putting you to work. Stella and I both work at the silver mine west of town, and there will be a job for you there. I'm a pastor, so you'll be going to church on Sundays, and you can help me finish building the bell tower on Saturdays."

Joseph leaned forward to pierce her with a hard, disconcerting look. His voice was firm as he continued. "And at the end of each day, in the quiet of night while the world sleeps but your soul awakens and searches, I want you to think about why you felt compelled to run here and what role God, Jesus, and the Holy Spirit ought to have guiding your choices in the future."

She rocked back in her chair. Well! She'd never had a preacher size her up so bluntly before, and she didn't like it.

But that didn't make him wrong, and she reluctantly agreed to Joseph's conditions.

Luke couldn't find Marianne, and it was driving him crazy. She had quit her job at the Department of the Interior, and three consecutive days spying on the Magruder town house revealed nothing.

That meant he had to pay a call on Dickie Shuster, the man who had his fingers on the pulse of everything that went on in Washington. It took him an entire day to track down the wily reporter at the horse races, where Dickie sat in the stands with a pair of binoculars—presumably to watch the horses but actually to observe people. Luke intended to rip Dickie's head off his shoulders for leaking that claptrap about Marianne's parentage, except Dickie didn't do it.

"Her brother spilled the beans," Dickie said. "Rumor claims old man Magruder always liked Marianne better than Andrew, and the young princeling thought he could throw a little mud on his sister without his parents ever figuring out who squealed. I only know about it because I have a weekly lunch with the reporter who let the cat out of the bag."

"Does Clyde know?"

Dickie nodded. "He knows, and Vera finally figured it out too, but she's blaming Andrew's wife for it. Vera and Delia have always despised each other. According to the servants in the house, Vera and Delia had a huge shouting match. Vera accused Delia of forcing Andrew to expose Clyde's affair because Delia was jealous of Marianne—something about how Marianne is naturally charming while Delia had to buy approval with a fortune in cosmetics and artificial hair extensions. All nonsense, if you ask me, but Vera refuses to see reason where Andrew is concerned. Anything he does wrong will always be blamed on Delia."

Luke mulled over the appalling tale. In exposing Marianne, Andrew had taken a hatchet to his parents as well. But was Luke any better? He had systematically gotten men booted out of Congress, heedless of the collateral damage, in order to advance his private objective.

"Why don't you ask what you really want to know?" Dickie prompted.

"And what's that?"

Dickie didn't even bother to hide his gloat. "Let's see if I can remember. I recently read a charming bit of commentary. It suggested that in the last thousand years, a handful of women have achieved immortality in the world's collective imagination. Guinevere. Juliet. Dulcinea. And dare I add . . . Marianne?"

Luke fidgeted in embarrassment. Maybe he'd gone a little overboard in that public declaration, but he wouldn't take back a word of it. "Do you know where she is?"

"I have no idea," Dickie said, raising his binoculars to stare at something in the crowd. "Good heavens, have you ever seen a frumpier ensemble than that beige coatdress Congressman Dern's wife is wearing? She's far too young to be dressing like a matron in a convent, but I guess some women have conservative tastes."

Congressman Dern was the chairman of Clyde's only congressional appointment. That Dickie chose to mention his wife could not have been a coincidence.

"And why do you suspect Mrs. Dern is dressing like a grim Mother Superior?"

"Probably because she doesn't like being associated with scandal." Dickie turned the binoculars toward other sections of the bleachers. "Neither does her husband. I heard Mrs. Dern paid a call on Mrs. Magruder for tea. That was quite a reversal in the social pecking order. My hunch is that she is putting on a public show of support for the embattled Mrs. Magruder, but she isn't happy about it. And Marianne, the catalyst of the entire scandal, is nowhere to be seen. I'd guess she was sent back to Baltimore."

Luke doubted it. Ever since the incident with Bandit, Marianne despised her brother. That made him worry something else had happened to her, and he'd already squandered the past three days looking for her. He wouldn't waste any more.

He needed to go confront the lion in his den.

Luke waited across the street from the Magruder town house until Clyde returned well after dark. He watched Clyde pay the cabbie, then head up the stairs into his house.

Clyde wasn't going to welcome this visit, and Luke prayed for wisdom and patience as he mounted the steps. The first floor was fully illuminated, and masculine voices came from inside. Luke adjusted his collar, dragged his fingers through his hair, and braced himself before knocking on the door.

Footsteps sounded, and Clyde soon opened the door. His eyes narrowed. "What do you want?" Hostility crackled in his voice.

Luke held up his hands, palms forward in a placating gesture. "I've come to inquire after Marianne. I'm worried about her."

"You can't see her," Clyde said. "Go home." He tried to slam the door, but Luke stuck his foot out to block it.

"I don't want to cause trouble. I just need to be sure she's all right."

"Of course she's all right. I know how to take care of my own daughter." Clyde came out onto the porch, driving Luke back a few steps on the narrow landing. "I would never let my daughter be lured into a distasteful alliance with a scoundrel who only wants to use her to score a point against me."

Luke straightened, refusing to let Clyde push him back any farther. "I love Marianne. I would never do anything to hurt her."

"You've already hurt her," Clyde shouted. He grabbed Luke by the lapels of his jacket and slammed him against a pillar, but Luke wasn't going to retaliate. He needed to keep a cool head to learn what had happened to Marianne. He shrugged out of Clyde's grasp and moved a few feet away.

Old Jedidiah Magruder soon came plodding onto the porch as well, his face a mask of distrust. "Throw him out," the old man growled.

"I'm not here to cause trouble," Luke said, his hands again raised in supplication. "I just need to know where Marianne is."

"She's somewhere you can't hurt her," Jedidiah said. "Take your fancy airs and your blue blood and get out." The old man's voice was caustic and his face hard, but Luke had a smidgeon of respect for the man who clawed his way out of poverty and into a house like this. Maybe he could be reasoned with.

"I can't just leave," he said. "I love her and need to know she's safe. Her disappearing like this isn't natural. Something is wrong."

"Something has been wrong since the moment you got a decent girl to spy on her own family," Jedidiah spat.

"Yeah, about that," Clyde said, his voice low with menace, closing the space between them.

Luke itched to defend himself and fight, but he couldn't. Not against Marianne's father. He retreated to the far end of the porch until his back was to the railing and there was no room left.

Clyde punched him in the jaw. Luke's head snapped to the side, and he grabbed for the wall. The salty tang of blood leaked into his mouth, but he swallowed it back. He waited until his vision steadied before straightening to face Clyde again.

"I'm turning the other cheek, Clyde. Go ahead and take another swing if you want."

Clyde's eyes narrowed in anger. "Don't flaunt that holier-than-thou drivel at me. You colluded with my daughter to spy on her own family. What does your fancy Bible have to say about *that*?"

Luke sagged a little but managed to keep looking Clyde in the face. "It says I should never have let the situation get this bad. I won't abandon Marianne. I have connections all over the city and in half the states as well. I'll call down the moon if I have to, but I will find her."

"Be careful," Clyde said, his voice lethally calm. "You've just managed to worm your way out of a spying charge, but don't think I can't bring the hammer down on you again. I'll honor my word to Marianne, but if you so much as touch a blade of grass belonging to me, I'll have you thrown in jail until you're old and gray."

Clyde and Jedidiah retreated into the house without a backward glance. Luke flinched at the slam of the door, and a sick feeling took root in his gut.

Something Clyde had just said put the situation into terrible clarity. He'd vowed to honor his word to Marianne. Honor his word about what? A promise like that would not have been made lightly. It came at a cost to someone, and Luke suspected his sudden release from jail had a lot more behind it than pressure from the Poison Squad.

Marianne had struck a deal with Clyde. He closed his eyes

in anguish as the pieces fell into place. They'd sent Marianne away, and it was all his fault.

He carefully navigated down the porch steps, pain in his head throbbing with each step.

No matter what it took, he was going to find Marianne.

Luke moved back into the boardinghouse even though he wasn't a member of the Poison Squad anymore. He couldn't live with Gray or, even worse, with Caroline and her husband at their new home on Twelfth Street. It was hard to be around happy people when his own heart had been stomped flat. At least Gray and Annabelle behaved themselves with decorum, but Caroline made no effort to mask her enthusiastic physical appreciation of her husband, showering affection on Nathaniel, laughing with him, tugging on a lock of his hair and begging for a kiss. It was nauseating. Luke was fully aware of how irrational he was being but didn't care.

Misery loved company, so he made himself at home in the Poison Squad's parlor. He slept at the boardinghouse in the evenings, but during the days he prowled around town, looking for a clue as to what happened to Marianne.

He doubted she'd gone to her brother. Marianne resented Andrew ever since he shot Bandit, and it only took Luke a few minutes to confirm she wasn't there. He asked Princeton to place a telephone call to Andrew's house, and the servant who answered the phone claimed Marianne wasn't staying there. The same thing happened when Princeton called her parents' house in Baltimore.

Late one night, Luke lounged in the window seat where he and Marianne spent that miserable night together when he was so sick. He gazed at the postcard she'd sent him of San Francisco during the few months when they'd been separated. She'd written only three words on the back of the card: *The Promised Land*.

Was she waiting for him in San Francisco? It was where they'd dreamed they might someday escape to live in a garret apartment and listen to the foghorns in the morning. San Francisco was a dream, a golden mirage, but he didn't think she would go there without him. Marianne had felt like a redheaded stepchild all her life. If her parents ordered her out of the family home, he had a hunch she would go in search of her long-lost Aunt Stella, a woman who shared Marianne's rebellious streak. If he could find Aunt Stella, he suspected Marianne would be nearby.

Finding Stella would be a challenging task, which was why Luke turned to Nathaniel for help. Instead of offering useful advice, his new brother-in-law was appalled.

"Are you insane?" Nathaniel asked, halfway rising from the desk chair in his cramped Treasury office. "You don't know Stella's last name, or her age, or even what state she lives in. You don't even know if she's alive, and yet you want me to find her?"

Luke didn't let Nathaniel's ire fluster him. "Caroline said you were a good detective."

"I am, but I'm not a magician. Why don't you go apologize to Clyde Magruder and try to patch things up? Maybe he'll relent."

Nathaniel was intelligent, but he was also a newcomer to the family, or he'd understand how ridiculous that suggestion sounded. Luke cut straight to the chase. "There has to be a record of this woman somewhere. Marriage certificates? School records? What about the census? Could we find her through the census?"

Nathaniel leaned back in his swivel chair and looked at him as though he were a simpleton. "You could try all those places and probably come up empty, or you can choose the path of least resistance."

Luke sat up straight. "And that is?"

"Servants know everything," Nathaniel said simply. "Start there."

Luke was embarrassed not to have thought of it himself. Some of the servants in Clyde's Baltimore mansion had been employed by the Magruder family for decades. The house would be empty, since Clyde, his wife, and his father were all currently in Washington.

The next morning Luke set off for Baltimore, and by lunchtime he was walking up the front path to the Magruders' imposing three-story mansion set far back from the street. He straightened his tie, adjusted his collar, and knocked on the front door. Clyde would like nothing better than to make good on his threat to throw Luke into jail for eternity if he violated so much as a blade of grass, but timidity would get him nowhere.

"My name is Luke Delacroix, reporter for *Modern Century*," he introduced himself to the cheerful maid who answered the door. "I'm doing some research on Magruder family history. Might I speak with the longest-serving member of the household staff?"

It was shockingly easy to gain access to the house. Within five minutes he'd been shown into the kitchen and introduced to Mrs. Nellie Rumsfeld, the housekeeper, who was eager to discuss her thirty years of service to the Magruder family. She insisted on preparing a pot of tea for Luke and filled his ears with all manner of insight into the family before he was able to steer her in the direction of Stella Magruder.

"I always liked Miss Stella," Nellie said as she poured Luke a third cup of tea, her palsied hands shaking and sloshing a little over the rim. "That girl was as tough as nails, but I liked her. It was a shame she had to run off to get married. Stella and her mother corresponded for years behind old Jedidiah's back. The man she married was a carpenter and a minister. Stella said he was like Johnny Appleseed, except instead of planting trees, he planted churches. Whenever a letter came from her, Mrs. Magruder told me to hide it from Jedidiah and put it straight into her hands."

"And where were those letters from?" he asked, holding his breath and praying the housekeeper had a good memory.

She did. Luke straightened his spine, excitement beginning to surge as he pocketed the last-known location of Stella and Joseph Greenleaf.

He was on his way to Amarillo, Texas.

Marianne soon adjusted to life with Stella and Joseph, though it took a while to become accustomed to their relentless bickering. She awoke her first morning in Nevada to hear them arguing about who forgot to bring in the laundry the night before. They argued about how long the drought would last, who did more chores, and the right way to boil water. In time, Marianne realized they enjoyed jousting with each other. It wasn't the sort of humor she appreciated, but that didn't make it wrong. Stella and Joseph were both tough, demanding, and forthright people, but they were also honest. They set high standards and demanded Marianne meet them, working days at the silver mine and weekends at the church.

A week passed, then a month.

On Sunday mornings Joseph led a congregation of ninety people in worship. The church was a plain building of well-hewn planks, clear glass windows, and a simple altar. All of it had been built by Joseph's own two hands. The bell tower was still under construction but would soon feature a set of stairs, a belfry, and a spire.

And then Stella and Joseph would move on to plant a new church somewhere else. That sort of itinerant life seemed exhausting to Marianne, but it suited Stella and Joseph. As soon as a church was established, they pulled up stakes and moved on.

Joseph's style of leadership was plain and straightforward. He preached that problems, no matter how complex, could be boiled down to the fallen nature of man, and the best way to solve them was by turning to simple wisdom in the Gospels. How would Jesus handle betrayal, secrets, and avarice? The virtues of love, humility, charity, and forgiveness might not solve the problem, but they could serve as a balm in an imperfect world.

Maybe it was the distance from Washington, but Marianne's complicated family histrionics no longer seemed quite so unique. Backstabbing, secrets, and lies dated all the way back to biblical times, and the same book provided plenty of guideposts for how she could have handled things better.

She still longed for a perfect family, but it didn't hurt so much anymore. She was both fallen and forgiven. Her mission now was to learn how to navigate the world in a way that extended forgiveness to other fallen people in her life.

On her fourth Sunday, while helping set up the refreshment table for fellowship after church, Marianne had the oddest experience. Like always, she helped lug the table outside, cover it with a cloth, then placed a rock on each corner to secure the tablecloth from the relentless winds coming off the mountain. Parishioners brought fruit and cookies, simple food that would take the edge off hunger so everyone could relax and socialize following the service. There were no gourmet foods or amethyst saltcellars here, only humble fare where fellowship was more important than impressing others.

Marianne stepped back a few paces to watch an elderly couple approach the table and set a can of peaches alongside the stack of tin plates. A couple of children picked dandelions to fill a cup for table decoration. Marianne considered rushing for her camera to immortalize this perfect moment in the country churchyard.

Then she thought better of it. Sometimes it was better to live in the present. A breeze caressed her cheek, almost as though it approved of her decision. She leaned into it, accepting it, even as the tablecloth lifted and rippled in the wind, tossing over a plate of cookies. One of the women laughed and found a few more rocks to anchor the cloth.

A sense of well-being descended. This *was* how life was supposed to be. Not perfect, but lovely all the same. It was a peaceable kingdom, a community of believers, and they had welcomed her with open arms. Luke had once spoken of the comfort that sometimes came out of nowhere, and he credited it to the Holy Spirit of God reaching out to encourage the awakening inside. Was that what this was? The scales were falling from her eyes, and she was seeing the world as it really was, not as she wished it could be.

Perhaps she was finally growing up. Paradise on earth didn't exist, but God still blessed them with the tools they needed to be happy, even in a sometimes imperfect, fallen world.

The sun hadn't yet risen above the horizon, and Marianne was still bleary-eyed as she and Joseph walked alongside the wagon loaded with rough-sawn lumber. She helped Joseph with carpentry work every Saturday. He'd already taught her how to use a hand plane to smooth the boards to make risers on the bell tower stairs, and perhaps they could finish them today.

Joseph unharnessed the horse while Marianne unloaded the boards, stacking them outside the front of the church. It was probably still too dark inside the church to start work, but she'd get the supplies ready.

It was the blue hour. The sun hadn't risen above the horizon yet, and the faint, shadowless light gave the desert an unearthly beauty. She'd always loved the blue hour, and her heart ached with the memory of when she and Luke took pictures during that magical in-between time at the navy shipyard. Her forty days with Joseph and Stella were drawing to a close, and she'd still heard nothing from Luke. If he didn't contact her soon, she'd have to press on to San Francisco and hope he'd find her there.

She was carrying a box of tools into the church, heading down the center aisle toward the half-finished doorway that led to the church tower, when she stopped. A grubby man lay on one of the pews, his filthy boots hanging over the end. A battered hat covered his face, muffling a snore. Her gasp echoed in the still-dark church, but the vagrant didn't stir.

She raced outside and straight to Uncle Joseph, who was still tending the horse. "There's a hobo sleeping in the church!"

Joseph didn't seem alarmed. "That's why I never put a lock on the door of any church I build. A church should be open to wandering souls."

Marianne's heart still pounded from the unexpected fright. For a worldly man, Joseph could be terribly naïve. "He could have robbed you blind last night."

Joseph gave her a condescending look as he finished tying the horse to the hitching post, then calmly headed inside. She followed at a cautious distance, clutching the toolbox to her chest. She had a hammer to defend herself, if need be.

"Good morning, son," Joseph boomed in a hearty voice as he strode down the aisle without fear.

The vagrant roused, peeling up from the hard pew and rubbing the small of his back with a groan. His dark head turned, and he flashed them a devilish smile.

"Luke!"

She could hardly believe it. He looked like a tramp, with his disheveled hair and clothes. He could use a shave, but oh, that smile was the same, and an explosion of joy blossomed inside her.

"You came for me," she said, her voice weak with relief.

"Of course I came," Luke said, standing to hold his arms wide.

She dropped the toolbox and raced into them. He held her close, and it felt like coming home. This was where she belonged. No words were necessary as she clung to him and he gently rocked her from side to side.

She pulled back for a kiss, but to her surprise, Luke disentangled himself and walked down the aisle to greet her uncle. "Are you Joseph Greenleaf?"

"I am."

Luke's grin was hearty. "I went to the church you built in Amarillo. What a place! They welcomed me with open arms but said you'd long gone and pointed me to your next church in Santa Fe."

Joseph's smile turned skeptical. "Were those folks decent to you? Some of them got a little squirrelly after I left."

"No fear of that," Luke said. "They couldn't have been nicer and had only fine things to say about you and your wife. They gave me your current location here in Carson City, but I was curious about what else you've built, so I stopped to see your churches in Grand Junction and Flagstaff on my way here. Well done, sir!"

Joseph laughed and returned Luke's handshake with vigor. The two men seemed like instant best friends as they swapped stories about the crazy people at the Santa Fe congregation. Joseph wanted to know if the Flagstaff roof was holding up and if Mrs. Mulroney made Luke one of her famous rhubarb pies. How easily they laughed and traded quips. Luke showered Joseph with praise for the craftsmanship he saw in each church and the fine people he met along the way.

Marianne fidgeted. "I'm beginning to feel a little left out."

Luke's rich, irreverent laugh rumbled. "We can't have *that*!" he said, drawing her into his arms and kissing her deeply. He bent her over his arm, and his hands were everywhere.

She hoped Luke wouldn't drop her as she tore her mouth away to risk a glance at Joseph. "My uncle is very strict," she cautioned.

Joseph rolled his eyes. "You two go out in the east field. I've got no interest in watching you spooning with your Romeo, and he's proven himself a decent man. Plus, I'll be able to keep my eye on you the whole time."

Luke grabbed her hand. "Let's go."

They ran down the aisle and outside to the yarrow field. The sun was rising, birdsong sounded in the distance, and Luke's embrace had never been more passionate.

"I can't believe you found me," she said breathlessly between his frantic kisses.

"I'd have searched to the ends of the earth."

His lips trailed up the side of her jaw and behind her ear, and she squeezed him tight, still amazed that he was here and cared enough to come for her. She hadn't broken her word to her father. Luke sought her out, not the other way around.

"Why did you run away?" he asked.

There were a million reasons, but the main one was that she couldn't bear knowing he might languish in prison for months or years because of her.

"I cut a deal with my father," she said, still clasped in his arms. "I promised I would leave Washington and not contact you. I figured a good spy like you would find me eventually."

"You know who else is a good spy?"

She shook her head.

He didn't take his eyes off her, gazing down with love and affection blazing in his warm face. "Your uncle. He's been watching us from the top of that half-finished bell tower since we got out here."

She didn't care. She was proud of Luke and wanted no more secrets, no more hiding or waiting. She tightened her arms around his back and squeezed. "There are no more barriers between us."

"Good. I fully intend to marry you. If you'll have me, that is."

Was there any doubt? Luke was the beginning, middle, and end of all her girlhood dreams. "Uncle Joseph could marry us. Then we can get on a train and be in San Francisco in a few hours. It will be like we both imagined."

"We could," he said, but there was a note of hesitation in his voice.

She pulled back a few inches. His smile was gone as he cupped the side of her face.

"I take it back," he said, his expression serious. "We can't run away, Marianne. We need to go back to Washington and ask your father's permission to marry."

"What?" she screeched. A squirrel startled, scrambling for cover as her shout echoed off the mountainside. "He'll never agree. Never!"

The idea of Luke walking up to her father, hat in hand, and obediently asking for her hand in marriage was absurd.

As if he sensed her confusion, he rubbed his hands up and down her arms, squeezing gently. "Despite my long and colorful history of breaking the rules, I'm trying to be a better man. A better Christian. And one of the few direct commands ordained by God is to honor your mother and your father. It's right there as the fifth commandment. There's no other way to read that one. I wish there was."

She drifted a few steps away to plop down on a boulder. "In that case, we'll never get married. It will never happen."

Luke hunkered down beside her and reached for her hand. "We have to at least ask," he said passionately. "The commandment doesn't order us to mindlessly obey your parents, it orders us to *honor* them. Which means no running away to San

Francisco or getting married behind their backs. We will give them the respect they are owed." He swallowed hard, as if bracing for the battle ahead. "That means I'm going to approach Clyde in a civil manner and humbly ask permission to join his family. He may call down fire and brimstone on my head. The last time we saw each other, he punched me in the face and threw me off his property, but I'll do my best to forge a truce."

Her gaze trailed into the distance, seeing nothing but problems ahead. She had already consigned herself to walking away from her family and living like Aunt Stella with a new family created from scratch. After all, it would be Clyde, not she, who made it impossible to remain in the family.

But she was the one who bought the ticket out west. She was the one who ran away rather than confront the challenging tangle of family drama at home. The fact that she doubted they could have made much progress was no excuse for not giving her parents the opportunity. Even now, she was certain Luke was heading straight toward a buzz saw in asking Clyde's permission, but Luke was right.

As was Uncle Joseph, who preached that a life guided by the Christian virtues of love, humility, charity, and forgiveness would be more successful than her intemperate actions of the past. They needed to make this final overture to her parents, even though Marianne feared it was going to be hopeless.

Thirty-Five

It was going to take four days to travel by train to Washington, and Luke spent most of that time sweating bullets. Despite the confident air he tried to project, he was terrified of showing up at the Magruder household on bended knee, but he was going to do it. Marianne would carry a lifelong scar if she turned her back on her parents, and that meant Luke had to reconcile with them.

The long train ride gave them plenty of time to discuss what had happened over the past month. As anticipated, the reviews for *Don Quixote* were savage. Up until the date of publication, Luke had harbored a tiny hope it would be hailed as a masterpiece, but reality came crashing in with the first review.

He showed it to Marianne the morning after they'd settled in to their private compartment on the train heading back east. He watched as her eyes traveled over the review that called his translation an abuse of the English language that layered emotion on with a smothering trowel of overblown sentiment.

She scowled as she read, finally dropping the magazine onto her lap. "This is nonsense. Whoever wrote this was probably a fusty college professor who doesn't have warm blood in his veins. I *loved* your translation! You should submit a rebuttal to the magazine. Defend yourself. Fight for the quality of what you produced."

She continued ranting, but he no longer cared what highbrow professors thought of him. Uptight college academics had a right to their opinions, and people who liked a more passionate style were equally entitled to their view. They were both right, and the novel was selling amazingly well among ordinary people despite the reviews. Besides, he had bigger battles on the horizon.

Like winning Clyde's consent to their marriage.

He clenched his hands and folded his arms, instinctively bracing himself for the coming implosion.

Marianne noticed and misinterpreted his actions. "Who cares what that reviewer thinks? If I ever meet him in a dark alley, he'd better fear for his life."

He choked back a laugh, wishing his only challenge was battling the slings and arrows of lousy book reviews. Marianne was the real prize, and the only battle he cared about winning.

Luke held Marianne's hand as they walked toward the Magruder town house. A chilly gust of wind sent a spray of autumn leaves scuttling down the street, and he sank a little deeper into his coat. He'd faced a lot of challenges over the past few years, but making peace with Clyde Magruder was going to be the hardest.

He released Marianne's hand when they came in view of the town house. He wouldn't further antagonize Clyde by flaunting his affection for his daughter.

"It's a Saturday, so both my parents should be home," Marianne said for the fourth time. She'd been babbling ever since disembarking at the streetcar stop. It was her nerves talking. Marianne babbled when she got anxious, while he got silent.

Frankly, they were both terrified.

They rounded the street corner and saw a wagon loaded with boxes right outside the Magruder household. A pair of laborers lugged a trunk between them, and Clyde stood on the front stoop, directing another man carrying a rolled-up carpet.

"What on earth is going on?" Marianne asked. "Oh heavens, I hope Mama hasn't finally thrown him out. She threatens all the time, and that's an awful lot of trunks. Look! Some of Mama's hatboxes are stacked on the porch. Maybe she's the one leaving?"

Luke's unease grew. Arriving in the middle of a marital dispute would be the worst possible time to make his appeal for Marianne's hand in marriage.

Clyde hadn't noticed them yet. He was too busy securing the strap around a trunk on the front porch. Then Vera emerged, bringing Clyde a mug of something hot. Clyde nodded his thanks as he took the mug from his wife and drank. Vera placed a hand on Clyde's shoulder, then returned inside.

"Okay, they're not fighting," Marianne said. "That's good. I think I'd have to run back to Carson City if they were fighting, because my father can be—"

"Marianne," Luke interrupted. "It's all right. We need to take the bull by the horns."

"Okay, you're right. Of course, you're entirely right. I'm just a little nervous and sometimes I babble . . ."

She jabbered the entire block until Clyde spotted them. He dropped the hatbox on the pavement, his face full of venom.

"Have you been with *him?*" he roared, gaping at Marianne in disbelief.

Marianne shook her head. "I went to Aunt Stella's, just as I said in my telegram. Luke found me there, and we've come back home."

"Together?" Clyde turned and hurled his mug against the side of the house, and coffee dribbled down the bricks. His face was white with anger as he vaulted down the stairs toward them.

Luke held up both hands in appeal. "We had separate sleeping compartments. I didn't lay a finger on her."

Clyde's streak of curse words singed the air, but Marianne was staring at the wagon overflowing with trunks and household belongings.

"Papa, what's going on? Are you moving somewhere?"

"Back to Baltimore," Clyde said bitterly. "Congratulations, Luke. You got what you wanted. I've withdrawn my name from the November elections and will be returning to private life."

Marianne's face fell, and it looked like she'd been shot. "Oh, Papa, I'm so sorry."

She rushed to embrace him. Clyde stiffened. He didn't shove her away, but he didn't return her embrace either. Clyde glared at Luke over the top of Marianne's head, his face accusatory.

Luke swallowed hard. The cascade of scandals Clyde had endured would have been hard for any politician to overcome. They hadn't been Luke's doing, but Clyde's acrimony was going to be directed at him anyway.

Clyde pushed Marianne aside and closed the distance between them. "What were you doing with my daughter?" he demanded, giving Luke a firm shove and pushing him off the sidewalk.

Luke retreated a few steps. "I didn't touch your daughter—"

"Hogwash. You spent days in close confinement with her, traveling back from wherever my sister ran off to. Don't tell me you didn't touch her."

The two men loading the wagon gaped at them. Luke kept retreating. "Let's head inside," he suggested. "This conversation shouldn't happen on a public street."

"Please, Papa," Marianne said.

Clyde flung the hatbox on the porch at one of the laborers and stormed inside without a backward glance. Luke offered his arm to Marianne, and she took it. Her hand was shaking.

His was too. It felt like their whole world was riding on the next five minutes.

It was cool and dim inside the house, but Clyde stood right behind the front door. He slammed it the moment they crossed the threshold, startling them both.

"Well?" Clyde demanded. "Explain yourself."

This was it. Additional workers packed boxes in the parlor, but Clyde ignored them and was waiting for an answer.

Luke drew a deep breath and met Clyde's gaze without faltering. "Sir, I love your daughter with everything I have. I can offer her a solid home and support both her body and spirit. I would like your permission to marry her."

"Get out of my house."

Luke ignored the order and continued speaking. "I will care for and honor Marianne forever. I will do my best to befriend her family. I am prepared to walk away from old offenses. I want a reconciliation between our families. This is Marianne's deepest wish, and that makes it mine as well."

The words didn't make a crack in Clyde's wall of ice. "I'm cutting her off, so you won't ever get a dime from me. I'll resurrect the charges against you and see you imprisoned. I'll ruin that rabble-rousing magazine you work for."

Luke kept his voice calm. "None of it will make a dent in my regard for Marianne, and no matter what you do to ruin me, I won't retaliate. I will defend myself and my family as best I can, but from my point of view, the war between you and me is over. I love Marianne too much to strike at her father."

"Clyde."

The single word was softly spoken from the balcony above, and they all looked up. Vera Magruder stood on the balcony and had heard the entire conversation.

"We have discussed this," Vera said tightly. Her face was stiff, and it was impossible to judge her mood, but her words were a quiet order directed at her husband.

A pause stretched as Clyde stared up at his wife, some form of unspoken communication flying between them. At last he turned to Luke, his face still hard.

"My wife thinks you proved yourself by staying in jail instead of betraying Marianne. She thinks Marianne can depend on you, but I don't. I think you're only in this to score another point by winning my daughter away from me."

"Give him a chance to speak," Vera ordered from the top of the staircase, and she turned her attention to Luke. "Continue."

Hope took root as he spoke directly to Vera. "Marianne can depend on me to stand by her side, even when times are difficult. I will work to rein in the animosity within my family. I want to look forward, never back."

He turned his attention to Clyde, searching for the words to undo three generations of hostility, but those magic words didn't exist. He reached into his heart and simply told the truth. "The past can't be changed, but I am willing to walk away from it. Trying to settle old scores with new malice is a losing proposition for all of us. I love Marianne. I won't keep battling your family, even if a marriage between me and Marianne never happens. It's over. You've won."

Clyde's eyes narrowed, his face turning speculative. Marianne was shaking in her boots beside him, and Luke felt just as helpless, but the ball was now in Clyde's court.

Clyde broke his challenging stare to glance up at his wife on the balcony, then to Marianne, then to Luke.

"I haven't always been the best or most honorable of husbands," he finally said. "But I want better for my daughter. I am selfish enough to demand more in a son-in-law than I have delivered in my past."

Luke's heart pounded hard, and it was a struggle to control his breathing. Was Clyde about to bend? The pitiless look on his face was as cold as always, but there was no mistaking his words.

Clyde looked at Marianne. "Is he the one you want?"

She nodded.

"Why?" Clyde demanded.

Everyone in the room, including the laborers, turned to listen to her. She swallowed hard and began.

"He's made me want to be a better person," she whispered. "A better Christian, a better daughter. He's the one who insisted we come back to ask your permission when all I wanted was to run away to San Francisco. Papa, when I'm with Luke, I have the courage to do anything, even when it isn't easy. I think the family and the future I can build with him will be hard and challenging and full of joy. I couldn't ask for more."

Luke's heart felt like it would burst. If Clyde wasn't standing five feet away he'd scoop Marianne off her feet and whirl her in circles.

Clyde still wasn't looking at him. His mouth was downturned as he watched Marianne carefully. "This isn't going to be easy," he warned. "Your grandfather will snarl and fight. Andrew and Delia will be even worse. But you have my blessing."

He extended his hand to Luke. The relief crashing through Luke made it hard even to return the handshake. Clyde's face was full of skepticism and annoyance, but also a hint of respect.

They could build on that.

Thirty-Six

Four Years Later

"We survived," Marianne said to Luke in happy exhaustion as the train arrived back in Washington, DC. Visiting her family in Baltimore was always a challenge, but their four-day sojourn had gone well.

The goal had been to take a new set of family photographs, now that Tommy was openly recognized by her parents. Bringing Tommy into the family had been the last straw for Andrew and Delia, who moved to Atlanta. Marianne missed Sam terribly, but the move was probably best for everyone concerned. Andrew had never truly been forgiven for his role in exposing Marianne's illegitimacy. All hope of Clyde ever returning to Congress was lost when news of Tommy's birth became public, but Vera came through the firestorm with flying colors. She welcomed Tommy into her home for regular visits, even though it hadn't been easy.

Respect, humility, and forgiveness were the bywords she and Luke had lived by in dealing with her family, and at last it was beginning to bear fruit. Luke would never be bosom buddies with Clyde, but things had gotten easier since Marianne and Luke's daughter was born five months ago. Clyde doted on his first granddaughter, and little Rosie was a perfect topic for Clyde and Luke to chat about during these family reunions. They were now able to be cordial with one another, and it was enough.

Rosie currently slumbered in her basket on the floor of the train compartment. Marianne glanced out the window at the station platform, eager to find a carriage and get home, but her gaze snagged on a familiar figure among the bystanders.

"I wonder why Gray is here," she said.

Luke ducked to peer through the window. "I have no idea," he replied, a hint of concern in his voice. Gray wasn't the sentimental sort who took off work to meet a train, so it was a little worrisome. Luke draped the slumbering Rosie over his shoulder, leaving the baby basket and their luggage for the porter to unload.

Marianne's concern eased as Gray smiled in greeting when they reached the platform. "Back in one piece, I see," he said, shaking Luke's hand.

"To my horror, little Tommy now looks up to me like a big brother," Luke said. "The prospect is terrifying. I'm not sure I'm up to the responsibility."

Gray never tired of teasing Luke for his reluctant evolution into a responsible uncle and father. Gray and his wife now had three children under the age of four, and Caroline had a son the same age as Rosie. Caroline and Luke still seemed to be going through all the major stages of life in tandem. They got married in the same year, and their first children were born within a day of each other.

Gray led them to a waiting carriage and held the door for them. "Caroline is throwing an impromptu party, and I was ordered to bring the two of you straight to her house. I hope you aren't too tired. A nanny has been hired to look after all the children, and Caroline will have my head if you don't come."

"What a shock, Caroline is throwing a party," Luke teased. "What's the occasion this time?"

Gray clapped him on the shoulder. "It's a surprise. But don't worry, you'll like this one."

"Do we need to go home and change?" Marianne asked. One never knew what to expect with Caroline. She threw charity galas and formal parties all the time but was equally comfortable hosting a summer picnic on the grass.

"Come as you are," Gray said. "People are already gathering, and we shouldn't be late."

Luke wasn't happy about the diversion. "The elm trees were planted on the National Mall while I was gone," he said. "Four hundred American elms lining the park from the Capitol to the Washington Monument. I wanted to see them."

"I've seen them," Gray said. "They look like twigs."

"Ah, but use your imagination," Luke urged. "Twenty years from now they will provide a glorious avenue of shade for the masses." He had taken over Caroline's spot on the McMillan Commission after the babies were born. Caroline wanted a year off to indulge her long-awaited motherhood, and Luke had promised to keep her seat warm until she was ready to return.

Progress on the National Mall was fully underway as old buildings were torn down and scaffolding erected to build new ones. Gray, being Gray, thought it a waste of taxpayer funds, but Luke had always loved to dream big. Marianne enjoyed listening to the two men trade arguments over the mall. When Gray and Luke got warmed up on a topic, they could go at it for hours. They were completely different in their outlooks on life, but that was what made their friendship so unique. Their differences were celebrated, not scorned, and it was a joy to be a part of such an accepting family.

The top of the carriage had been folded back. It was a perfect June evening, and the fresh air felt good after being cooped up in the train. Fifteen minutes later they rounded the bend onto Caroline's street, where a handful of men had already gathered on her front lawn.

"Hey, that's Princeton!" Luke said, standing in the carriage to wave to his old comrade from the Poison Squad. Luke didn't even wait for the wheels to stop rolling before he hopped down and gave Princeton a back-pounding hug.

Gray's eyes twinkled in amusement as he helped Marianne and the baby out of the carriage. There were dozens of men here, but Marianne only recognized a few. She spotted St. Louis and Dr. Wiley standing among a cluster of politicians on the front porch.

"A reunion of the Poison Squad?" she asked Gray.

He nodded. "Among other things. Caroline rounded up as many as she could find on short notice. There's a big announcement to be made."

It looked like he wanted to say more, but he was dragged away by Annabelle to help set up tables in the backyard.

Marianne hoisted Rosie over her shoulder and navigated through the crush of people to the upstairs bedroom where a nanny watched over the children in various stages of demolishing their supper. She surrendered the still-slumbering Rosie to the nanny, then headed back downstairs, scanning the odd assortment of people gathered for the party. Politicians, journalists, scientists, and government clerks crowded the main floor of the house.

Caroline spotted her across the crowded parlor and rushed to close the distance between them. "Thank heavens you could make it!" she gushed. "Luke is with you?"

"He's surrounded by a gaggle of men outside. Shall I bring him in?"

Caroline nodded. "Dr. Wiley is ready to make the announcement. Can you help me get everyone out to the backyard? It's the only place big enough to hold everyone."

It took some doing to pull Luke away from the Poison Squad men, as St. Louis was boasting about his bronze medal in the 1904 Olympics. A few bottles of champagne had already been opened, and when rumor spread that there was more in the backyard, the crowd began funneling through the house to the back. Soon everyone was gathered beneath the linden trees on the grassy lawn. Dr. Wiley stood on a chair on the far side of the yard to make his grand announcement. Marianne slipped her hand into Luke's. He seemed as bewildered as she was about the cause for this spontaneous gathering.

Dr. Wiley tapped on a glass to settle the crowd, then began speaking. "Thank you all for gathering on such short notice, for tonight marks the culmination of all our plans, and it has been a long and unexpectedly difficult journey. I remember Luke Delacroix once telling me that people who expect quick or easy solutions aren't dreaming big enough. Luke? Where are you?"

"Here, sir!" Luke bellowed with a good-natured wave, and Dr. Wiley raised his glass in a toast.

"The sentiment is certainly true, as everyone gathered in this yard can attest. The fight for a pure food and drug supply has been ongoing for thirty years. Our first bill was defeated in 1880, and over the last twenty-six years we have had more than one hundred bills shot down in Congress. My friends, I am proud to say that as of three hours ago, the bill for the Pure Food and Drug Act has been passed by Congress. Today, we have won."

The cheering started before Dr. Wiley had even stopped speaking. Luke dragged Marianne into an embrace and smothered her with a kiss while everyone in the yard applauded. She managed to disentangle herself from Luke long enough to hear the rest of Dr. Wiley's speech. President Roosevelt promised to sign the bill by the end of the week, and a new agency would be created to oversee its implementation.

Dr. Wiley began pointing out members of the crowd who'd helped fight the battles over the years. He pointed out the plant explorers who searched the world to bring back seeds resistant to spoilage. He thanked the congressmen who shepherded bills through committees, the chemists and clerks who processed data, and the countless anonymous people whose daily endeavors worked to create this monumental accomplishment.

"It took the unique talents of thousands of people to arrive at this point," Dr. Wiley said. "Each of us has a purpose in this world, for God does nothing in vain. I hope that the generation who came before us is proud of how we delivered on the foundation they built for us, but our work is not finished. We need to carry on and raise up a new generation who will be ready to shoulder the challenges in the next century."

Dr. Wiley continued speaking, but Luke abruptly left Marianne's side and made his way to the edge of the yard. She angled through the crowd to reach him where he faced away from the others, his hand braced against the fence and his head low.

"Are you okay?" she asked, for he was quietly beating back tears.

He sniffled and laughed. "You know I can sometimes be a watering pot at times like these. It's been a long road to get here."

Gray saw what was happening and joined them. "You should be very proud," he said.

"You too," Luke said, and it was true. Luke and Gray had both endured huge sacrifices to call attention to this issue. None of it had been easy. It took the collective strength of journalists, politicians, scientists, and rabble-rousers. The men of the Poison Squad helped not only with the sacrifice of their bodies, but by helping draw attention to the cause. It took the quiet labor of people like Annabelle, working in laboratories to compile data. It had been a long slog full of disappointments, setbacks, and compromises. After decades of slowly chipping away at resistance, they had finally arrived at the finish line. It was the struggle that made evenings like this all the sweeter.

Marianne clasped Luke's hand. His grief over what had happened in Philadelphia was now over. It was proof that tragedies could sometimes give rise to positive change. Now that this quest was finished, Luke would probably go looking for a new mountain to climb tomorrow, but for tonight it was time to celebrate.

Once, long ago, Marianne had dreamed of a perfect family where nothing bad ever happened and life unfolded in rose-tinted harmony. That mistaken belief caused her to be hurt time and again as she dwelled on unrealistic expectations and dissatisfactions with her life. Now she understood that she should have been counting her blessings each day, for struggle and setbacks were a normal part of any relationship in this fallen world. And that was okay. Her life was filled with a wild and diverse mix of people who alternately frustrated and inspired her. Some good, and some bad, but all of them a part of this wonderful, imperfect world where each day brought new challenges and joy.

Historical Note

The Pure Food and Drug Act was signed into law by Theodore Roosevelt on June 30, 1906. As the act was making its way through Congress, it was simply known as "the Wiley Act," named after Dr. Harvey Wiley, the chief chemist at the Department of Agriculture most responsible for calling attention to the problems of adulterated food.

Dr. Wiley launched the hygienic table trials in 1902. The group of daring young men was soon branded "the Poison Squad" by newspapers covering the story. The men were required to be physically fit, of high moral character, and known for sobriety and reliability. They also had to sign a waiver of liability for any health consequences they incurred during the experiment. Surprisingly, Dr. Wiley never had difficulty recruiting subjects. As news of the study was printed in national newspapers, people from all over the country sent letters offering to volunteer.

There was high turnover among members of the Poison Squad, who rarely served more than a few months. The volunteers suffered from various ailments, including headaches, nausea, and clouded thinking. Over the years, Dr. Wiley gleaned insight into the effectiveness or toxicity of various preservatives, many of which were either considered safe for use or outlawed. Although early canned and processed foods were often tainted with shocking chemicals and fillers, the work of the Poison Squad helped determine nontoxic dosages that made the food supply safer in the coming years.

The Poison Squad was officially disbanded in 1907 when Dr. Wiley was appointed to be the first head of the US Food and Drug Administration. In 1912 he became head of the testing labs at *Good Housekeeping*, the women's magazine already becoming famous for their Good Housekeeping Seal of Approval, which conducted scientific tests on food and drugs for safety and efficacy. He died on June 30, 1930, the twenty-fourth anniversary of the passage of the Pure Food and Drug Act. He is buried in Arlington National Cemetery.

The inaugural members of the Poison Squad.
Dr. Wiley is the older man in the back row.

Questions for Discussion

1) Throughout the novel, Marianne mourns that she doesn't have the sort of family she wants. She repeatedly refers to "the way things ought to be." Is she wrong to think this way? Is there value in striving to achieve "the way things ought to be"? At what point does it become destructive?

2) Do you predict the Magruders and the Delacroixs will ever get along? Luke suggests that he plans to always look forward and never back in handling their conflicts. Is this possible? In bad situations, might it be the only solution?

3) In real life, the Poison Squad was flooded by men wanting to volunteer for service. Why do you think that was? Can you think of other dangerous or unpleasant tasks in contemporary life in which people are excited to participate?

4) Luke interprets the commandment to honor thy father and mother to mean that Marianne's parents are

owed respect rather than blind obedience. How do you interpret that commandment? Did Marianne break this commandment when she continued to meet Luke even though her father had forbidden it?

5) While working with Marianne in the darkroom, Luke observed that the problem with amusement is that once it is over, the sense of satisfaction evaporates, and that it was in doing hard things that he found the most sustenance. What does he mean by this?

6) Why do you think Luke was so sensitive about his *Don Quixote* translation?

7) After a loud fight between Andrew and his son, Marianne reflects: *She just wished she came from a normal family where harsh punishments and raging tantrums were not standard fare. Maybe someday she would have such a family, but she was learning that constantly seeking appeasement carried its own set of problems.* What did she mean by that?

8) Luke tells Marianne that he is elated by the chance to test himself on the Poison Squad. He tells her that five days out of the week, he sat at a desk and did paperwork, but his soul craved more. There was a wildness inside that needed a mission to both challenge and frighten him. How common do you think this sentiment is? Do you believe it is more common among men than in women?

9) Marianne is treated dreadfully by many people in her family, and yet she still loves them and fears being banished. Why is this?

10) As she was growing up, Aunt Stella's fate was a great mystery to Marianne that she alternately admired and

feared. Are there any legends in your family that hold a similar fascination for you?

11) Andrew is never seriously punished for the spiteful things he did to his family. How common is this in real life? What is the best way for a Christian to handle such things?

Elizabeth Camden is best known for her historical novels set in Gilded Age America, featuring clever heroines and richly layered story lines. Before she was a writer, she was an academic librarian at some of the largest and smallest libraries in America, but her favorite is the continually growing library in her own home. Her novels have won the RITA and Christy Awards and have appeared on the CBA bestsellers list. She lives in Orlando, Florida, with her husband, who graciously tolerates her intimidating stockpile of books. Learn more about Elizabeth at www.elizabethcamden.com.

Sign Up for Elizabeth's Newsletter

Keep up to date with Elizabeth's news on book releases and events by signing up for her email list at elizabethcamden.com.

More from Elizabeth Camden

Gray Delacroix has dedicated his life to building a successful global spice empire, but it has come at a cost. Tasked with gaining access to the private Delacroix plant collection, Smithsonian botanist Annabelle Larkin unwittingly steps into a web of dangerous political intrigue and will be forced to choose between her heart and her loyalty to her country.

The Spice King
Hope and Glory #1

You May Also Like . . .

Telegraph operator Lucy Drake is a master of Morse code, but the presence of Sir Colin Beckwith at a rival news agency puts her livelihood at risk. When Colin's reputation is jeopardized, Lucy agrees to help in exchange for his assistance in recovering her family's stolen fortune. However, the web of treachery they're diving into is more dangerous than they know.

A Dangerous Legacy by Elizabeth Camden
elizabethcamden.com

When Sylvie Townsend's Polish ward, Rose, goes missing at the World's Fair, her life unravels. Brushed off by the authorities, Sylvie turns to her boarder and Rose's violin instructor, Kristof Bartok, for help searching the immigrant communities. When the unexpected happens, will Sylvie be able to accept the change that comes her way?

Shadows of the White City by Jocelyn Green
The Windy City Saga #2
jocelyngreen.com

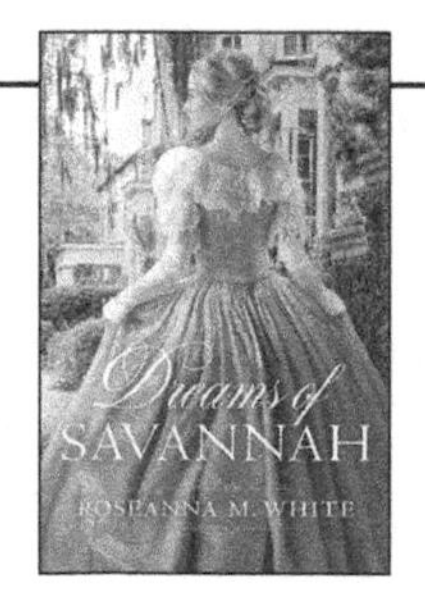

After receiving word that her sweetheart has been lost during a raid on a Yankee vessel, Cordelia Owens clings to hope. But Phineas Dunn finds nothing redemptive in the horrors of war, and when he returns, sure that he is not the hero Cordelia sees, they both must decide where the dreams of a new America will take them, and if they will go there together.

Dreams of Savannah by Roseanna M. White
roseannamwhite.com

BETHANY HOUSE

More from Bethany House

Gabriella Goodhue had put her past as a thief behind her, until a woman in her boardinghouse is unjustly accused and she is caught gathering evidence by Nicholas Quinn, a fellow street urchin against whom she holds a grudge. Nicholas refuses to lose her twice and insists they join forces—but their feelings are tested when danger follows their every step.

To Steal a Heart by Jen Turano
The Bleecker Street Inquiry Agency
jenturano.com

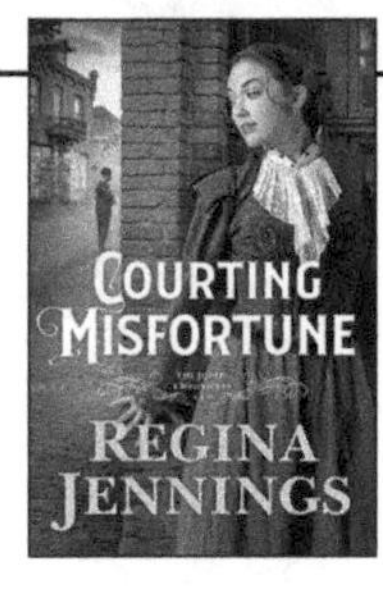

Assigned to find the kidnapped daughter of a mob boss, Pinkerton operative Calista York is sent to a rowdy mining town in Missouri. But she faces the obstacle of missionary Matthew Cook. He's as determined to stop a local baby raffle as he is the reckless Miss York whose bad judgement consistently seems to be putting her in harm's way.

Courting Misfortune by Regina Jennings
The Joplin Chronicles #1
reginajennings.com

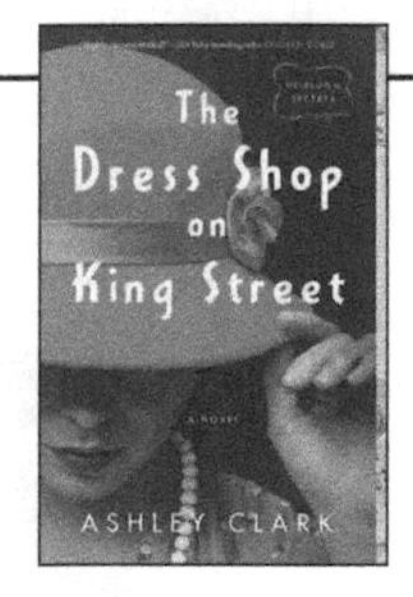

In 1946, Millie Middleton left home to keep her heritage hidden, carrying the dream of owning a dress store. Decades later, when Harper Dupree's future in fashion falls apart, she visits her mentor Millie. As the revelation of a family secret leads them to Charleston and a rare opportunity, can they overcome doubts and failures for a chance at their dreams?

The Dress Shop on King Street by Ashley Clark
Heirloom Secrets
ashleyclarkbooks.com

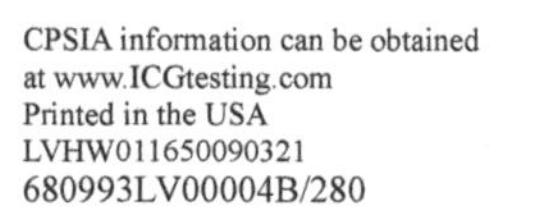

CPSIA information can be obtained
at www.ICGtesting.com
Printed in the USA
LVHW011650090321
680993LV00004B/280